CONCLAVE

Greg Tobin

TOR®

A TOM DOHERTY ASSOCIATES BOOK
NEW YORK

This is a work of fiction. All the characters and events portrayed in this book are either products of the author's imagination or are used fictitiously.

CONCLAVE

Copyright © 2001 by Greg Tobin

The Apostolic Constitution, *Universi Dominici Gregis*, copyright © 1996 by the Libreria Editrice Vaticana, reprinted with permission.

A Tor Book
Published by Tom Doherty Associates, LLC
175 Fifth Avenue
New York, NY 10010

www.tor.com

Tor® is a registered trademark of Tom Doherty Associates, LLC.

ISBN 0-812-57921-6
EAN 978-0812-57921-5
Library of Congress Catalog Card Number: 200101 8783

First edition: May 2001
First mass market edition: April 2002

Printed in the United States of America

0 9 8 7 6 5 4 3 2

To my wife, Maureen, for her steadfastness
To my sisters, Jeanne, Mimi, Peggy, and Anne,
for their tolerance

Ut unum sint. That all may be one.
—Pope John Paul II, 1996

It is impossible to be just to the Catholic Church.
—G. K. Chesterton, *The Catholic Church and Conversion*, 1926

And thus were the paths of those on earth made straight.
—*Wisdom*, 9:18

PRELUDE

Ad Altare Dei

Rome, September 9, 2001

The ancient city of emperors and apostles seemed unusually cool for the late summer season. After a four-day vacation trip to Ireland, where he had savored the morning fog of Lough Derg and enjoyed an evening's single-malt whisky in Dublin, Timothy John Cardinal Mulrennan, the Roman Catholic Archbishop of Newark, had come to Rome for a very rare private audience with the ailing pope. This was not his periodic *ad limina apostolorum* visit to report on the state of the diocese and to reaffirm fidelity to the Holy See, which was required of every residential bishop around the world every five years or so. *Ad limina* means "on the threshold," referring to the tombs of the two apostles, Peter and Paul. Instead, Mulrennan's was simply a meeting with a brother bishop and an ailing friend.

Within the 108-acre maze of courtyards, monumental staircases, archways, halls, chapels, museums, libraries, more chapels, offices, workshops, and secret corridors, above the indomitable Bernini columns that circumscribe St. Peter's Square, above the fragrant papal gardens with their fountains and flower beds and palms, stood the five-hundred-year-old Apostolic Palace.

Here, in his private apartments and semipublic antechambers and suite of offices, the Holy Father worked and prayed, ate and slept, and, it was well documented, prayed some more, day in and day out. The pontiff's living quarters were maintained by a clutch of nuns from the Milan-based order of the Sisters of Charity of Sts. Bartolomea Capitano and Vincenza Gerosa, also known as the Sisters of Maria Bambina—Mary the Child. A smart papal pre-

decessor had imported the good sisters, and his successors
had not dislodged them since, for as a visiting Coptic prelate had once pronounced, "They are not only kind and
friendly but they are excellent cooks."

By habit and necessity the Holy Father rarely saw anyone
after a full table of guests at supper; he most often ate
lightly, listened intently, spoke carefully in any one or more
of a dozen languages, and retired quickly to read, pray, and
meditate, then to sleep for four or five hours. This evening,
however, he craved the company of an old friend from the
Council years, now some thirty-six years past, Cardinal
Mulrennan.

Timothy Mulrennan, a tall athletic-looking man, enjoyed
a light minestrone, fresh asparagus, and veal casserole, with
a recent-vintage Bordeaux and a selection of fruit and
cheese for dessert. At a table large enough for ten, the
American cardinal sat to the aged pontiff's left, and the
personal secretary to the pope, Monsignor Carlo Franzonia,
a slight forty-year-old with olive skin and black, slicked-
back hair, sat silently but ever watchfully to the right.

The pope ate little and drank only mineral water; his food
was pre-cut on the plate because he had difficulty feeding
himself with a shaky right hand. It had long been known
that he had a progressively debilitating form of Parkinson's
disease, in addition to the stomach cancer that had been
diagnosed about nine months earlier and which—contrary
to centuries of previous papal practice—had been announced frankly to the world. These ills, along with broken
bones, mundane colds and sinus infections, and the painful,
lingering aftereffects of a now long-ago bullet wound, had
sapped the man's life in evil increments. The chemotherapy
treatments and the agony of catheters and the humiliation
of diapers had curtailed his planned trips to Saudi Arabia
and Moscow, both of which would have been papal firsts.
Only his own powerful will, and the transcendent will of
God, had preserved him through the historic Jubilee Year
to this day.

Nonetheless, he deftly interrogated Mulrennan about the
Newark archdiocese and the cardinal's pastoral responsibilities for 1.4 million Catholics—an increasingly diverse

population—who lived adjacent to the even larger, higher profile Archdiocese of New York, with its own newly appointed archbishop.

"Your flock has changed very rapidly and grown in generosity, Timothy. They are a fine example for others in the United States. We continue to be grateful for their sacrifices and their prayers."

"They responded wonderfully to our stewardship initiatives during the Holy Year, and they still remember your moving pastoral visit with great fondness, Your Holiness. It seems as if you were among us just a few days ago instead of a few years."

The pontiff smiled gravely. The borders of his face, once a wide Slavic map, had shrunken, eroded, and begun to fold in upon themselves. His skin was like the translucent paper of a gilt-edged family Bible. Here wars spiritual and temporal had raged for more than eighty hard years. . . . His right hand again trembled with, it seemed, a will and a force of its own.

"Much time has passed since then, my dear Cardinal. Little enough is left to me, to any of us on God's good earth. To do a small amount of good, to win one soul to Our Lord and Savior—have I accomplished as much today?"

He took a single sip of the wine, perhaps as punctuation to the meal, then wiped his mouth and rang a small silver bell that was itself centuries old. Almost instantly the white-jacketed steward appeared with an antique salver laden with tea and coffee, sugar and cream.

Monsignor Franzonia poured a half-cup of tea for the pope and steaming black American coffee for Mulrennan. These very cups, Tim mused, had likely been used by Pope Paul or Pope John, even the austere, distant Pius, who had been the reigning pontiff of his youth.

The secretary discreetly and reluctantly excused himself at the pope's unseen signal, leaving the two men alone.

"Let us go to my study, Your Eminence, if you do not mind."

Mulrennan, who had never gotten used to the honorific of his office spoken by this sainted man, his nominal "boss," picked up his coffee cup and trailed the stooped white-clad figure into the spacious, high-windowed study. The pontiff led him to a chair near a window and sat in another facing it.

"I feared that eighty-five thousand of your New Jersey people would catch cold on the night of our final mass in your football stadium," the pontiff remembered with a painfully hard-won and lopsided grin.

Mulrennan remembered how the gravid black heavens over Giants Stadium had poured hardest during the consecration, the highest, most sacred moment of the liturgy of the Eucharist. From behind the canopied altar, he and the other cardinals and bishops from throughout the United States had looked out over the rain-washed assembly on the field and in the tiered seats of the stadium. Upturned, adoring faces belied the lashing rain. He had felt so proud of these, his own archdiocesan faithful, so humbled by the quality and durability of their faith as manifested by their presence, their responses, their singing, their prayers and applause.

"I certainly ended up with a good case of the sniffles myself," Tim Mulrennan confessed ruefully. "My feet got soaked because I didn't wear proper footwear." He had squished back and forth across the platform in his usual black Rockport loafers instead of rain boots during the once-in-a-lifetime spiritual event in the mammoth professional football arena in northern New Jersey's Meadowlands.

"At least we are grateful that you *usually* display more common sense, dear Cardinal Mulrennan." A flash of the old political wit crossed his pale, watery eyes. "Yet we do worry about you at times—and wonder . . ."

Mulrennan tensed, leaned forward in his chair. What was this comment all about? It was unlike the pontiff to be vague or hesitant about any matter concerning his bishops, especially either favorites or uncooperative ones. Although sometimes indirect in one-on-one meetings, he was well known to be a stern but loving father with the often difficult college of bishops from around the world, most of whom he had personally chosen or approved from the lists submitted by his farflung corps of papal nuncios, the diplomatic representatives of the Vatican who resided in nearly every world capital. He expected—and received—personal obedience from each man he raised to episcopal rank.

Mulrennan, indeed, had himself served for several years in the late '80s and early '90s in the Curia, the pope's consultative and administrative cabinet, in the Congregation for Bishops, which gave him direct and frequent contact with other bishops from around the world. There was little to nothing that the Holy Father and his Curial officers did not know about their fellows—whether private or public, psychological, sexual, financial, personal, or professional.

"Tell me, Your Holiness, do you have something on your mind? Have I done anything to displease you?"

On the delicately carved table beside the pontiff's chair lay a marble rosary, which he touched tentatively. "Never have you displeased, Timothy. You have indeed been a good priest, a fine example to others—even in your weakest moments." He raised a single crooked index finger and looked directly into Mulrennan's eyes. "Yes, I know of your failings and your difficulties—some people are eager to whisper to their pope the sins and shortcomings of his priests—and I love you the more despite them, even *for* them. Believe me when I say this. What concerns me, however, dear son, is what others may do with certain . . . information." He continued gently to finger the brilliant rosary beads. "I want nothing and no man to harm you when I am gone—and for the sake of the Church I will not allow it. I wish only to strengthen your ministry in any way I can."

Tim Mulrennan struggled to understand the meaning of the Holy Father's words. The old man was at his oblique best—or worst, depending on one's point of view—in such moments. Despite the affection between the two men, it was difficult for the senior to communicate his emotions to the younger.

An ugly rattling sound overrode his labored breathing; the lengthy and somewhat slurred speech had exhausted him.

"I am unworthy, I know," Mulrennan said, "but I try to

seek God's forgiveness and guidance every day. I will continue to serve Him, and you, as long as I have the strength
to do so."

"Yes—the strength. I think you have that; you Americans have it in a special abundance that the Europeans of
today, east and west, seem to lack. Even though North
Americans suffer from an addiction to materialism and a
fascination with the culture of death . . . Most troubling to
me." The pontiff gathered himself painfully. "Each breath
is a gift from God. I have been given a—what some might
call a vision. Do you also have visions, my friend? I cannot
reveal mine to you here. It is the most private, most painful
part of sitting in the papal chair. I sometimes wonder if St.
Peter himself suffered in this way. We see a time of greater
rather than lesser difficulty lying ahead. Yet when you endure this hardship, with the love of Christ and His blessed
Mother, you shall know a holiness and a humility as few
men ever have."

"Teach me, Holy Father."

"Make forgiveness and repentance your watchwords,
Timothy. This I have learned—seek to be purified and it
shall be given to you in greater measure than you can imagine."

"Yes, Holy Father."

"When He calls, you must answer. You must say *yes* to
God."

They continued their conversation into the night, reminiscing about the pope's trip to the Holy Land during the
Great Jubilee and the spectacle of two million young people
in Rome that same year. At nearly midnight in the grand
but intimate sitting room adjacent to the starkly appointed
papal bedchamber, the pontiff looked up at Mulrennan with
world-weary eyes and said, "Timothy, stay with me for just
a while longer. I shall sleep little tonight. Less than usual.
Our body becomes increasingly frail, and yet the mind—
ah, it never rests. We have so much work to do. So much
we have not accomplished for God."

The pontiff spoke in heavily accented but impeccable
English and slipped in and out of the first-person plural. It
had never been clear to the American archbishop whether

he was truly uncomfortable with the magisterial or royal "we," as Pope John Paul I had been, or whether he consciously sprinkled an "I" and a "me" through his speech to achieve an effect of plainness and humility.

Mulrennan considered him a truly holy and faith-filled man, but not a man of careless or unconsidered speech—whether he had an audience of one or one billion. Never had there been a man so ideally suited for the age of mass communication as this priest-philosopher-politician-performer.

The pope was indeed frail, his once hale and agile body severely bent, shrunken with age and the burdens of office as he sat upon a maroon-colored leather chair in the soft yellow lamplight of the magnificent Vatican apartment. Between the vigorous specimen who had been elected in the prime of his life and this near-wraith racked with multiple diseases lay a chasm of years, more than a score, that were the most productive and controversial of any pontificate in centuries. Only five men had inhabited the Petrine office longer than he.

A cool Roman breeze shifted the heavy blue curtains of the open window behind the pontiff. Wisps of white hair danced on his pale ears. His voice was as clear and prophetic as an angel's.

"This I was granted: the gift to see the first years of this Holy Millennium. We opened wide our doors throughout the world to invite Christ Our Savior into our lives in the Great Jubilee Year. To Mary I prayed for the strength to live and to serve. She has honored my request, even though I have been almost a prisoner here—except for my travels to Jerusalem and to Egypt, which meant so much to me. . . ." He lifted a hand from the soft leather armrest. "I fear that the heart of the Church will not be as strong as it must to meet the increase of evil—both human and supernatural—in our world. I say that I have been blessed with a vision of the world to come, and it will be a dark place of war and famine and disease and unhappiness unless we lead our people—all people—to the light. This is what we are most urgently called to do by the Almighty Father. We cannot fail Him, my son."

A trembling arthritic finger pointed to the softly glowing electric lightbulb over his left shoulder. "We must bring light."

Mulrennan listened tensely, uncomfortable in witnessing the man's pain, watching the pontiff's tentative movement of hands and head, the eyes closing tightly to recapture the vision of which he spoke so sadly. A chill of recognition shook the American cardinal.

This man, this friend, this saint and prophet, is dying.

The knowledge disturbed Timothy Mulrennan profoundly, in a way he had never before experienced.

For decades many voices had pronounced the Church, or Christ Himself, dead—or worse, irrelevant. God's obituary had long since been written. Yet hundreds of millions of men and women of faith—many of them the poorest of people on earth—kept Him alive in their hearts and returned in greater and greater numbers every day to their Church, especially in Asia, Africa, and the Americas. Just as, in the days of the primitive Church, a pentecostal spirit was abroad. Perhaps the only thing that had for so long sustained this dying man was his faith, pure and simple, in the people of God.

"I have sought God's help each hour of each day to do His will. He is present always and has never withheld His grace from me. Still, I have failed Him."

Failure—there it was again. Yet only if measured by imperfect human standards.

"God knows *you* have not, Your Holiness," the cardinal said. "And I know it." His throat tightened, and he blinked back tears.

The pope peered at Mulrennan with liquid blue eyes. "I have 'infallibly' stated that I have failed, Brother. How dare you contradict your self-contradictory Vicar?" The tremulous hint of a smile tugged at his thin lips.

Mulrennan could not restrain a gentle laugh. "When I first met you at the Council—thirty-seven, no, thirty-eight years ago, is it possible?—I thought then that you sometimes flirted with sophistry. Now, Holy Father, I know that you are too intelligent for your own good. You do not speak *ex cathedra* with me, I hope. Do not torture yourself with doubt now as Montini did in his old age."

"You mock me, Timothy. 'Old age'!"

"No, I do not. I—"

"I deserve to be mocked. I deserve whatever punishment or reward Christ Jesus shall choose for me. Yet, I beg Him and His holy Mother not to abandon their children in the days ahead. Oh, I fear . . ."

The pope clutched the jeweled pectoral cross of his office and held it to his breast. He gazed at the gilt-framed reproduction of the Black Madonna that had hung in this room from the first day of his pontificate. She was never out of his thoughts for a second, in work or prayer or contemplation, or in rare moments of rest and recreation. He slumped in the ornate chair, a penitent clad in pure white, gray shadows painted upon his face. The air escaped his tortured lungs in a startling rush, and his eyelids fell like pale curtains. Mulrennan panicked, fearing the very worst. Was it possible the pope could die, right here and now—slip away from the prison of the flesh? He held his breath until the pope's eyes slowly slid open once more. The holy man spoke.

"Yet, hope always conquers fear. I know this. You do, too. Hope is the greatest gift of all."

After several minutes of prayerful silence within the papal chamber, Cardinal Mulrennan said, "May I have your blessing, Holy Father?" He knelt before the seated pope, who crisply signed the cross above his bowed head.

"In nomine Patris et Filii et Spiritus Sancti."

He felt his old friend's twitching, palsied hands upon his shoulders and heard a whispered prayer in the pope's native tongue.

"My son, all your sins are forgiven not by me but by your loving God, Our Father, to whom we pray in Christ's name and through the intercession of Our Blessed Mother."

Mulrennan looked up directly into the face of his spiritual mentor and leader and saw a radiant light that seemed to emanate from deep within the man.

"We learned this as children, did we not?" the pontiff continued. "Yet, do we believe it with the fervor of a child?

Do we practice forgiveness truly and without reservation, as He does? We must allow God to be God, my son— invite Him to dwell in our hearts."

"Holy Father—"

Now the tears came, unrestrained, obscuring the American cardinal's vision. He silently cursed his own inability to respond, to communicate his genuine feelings in the proper words. He said nothing because he simply could not summon the words.

He rose and left the chamber of the man he loved as dearly as his own brother. He never saw the pope alive again. Before he stepped out of the Apostolic Palace and into the Roman night, he inhaled the ageless scents of the Vatican and remembered. . . .

CHAPTER ONE

North Auburn, New Jersey, Christmas Eve 1949

The tall, slender boy in a black cassock and white surplice knelt on marble steps before the altar while the priest, whose back was turned to the people kneeling in the pews, bent over the host and uttered the most solemn words of the Holy Mass. The after-scent of incense filled his nostrils and nearly made him sneeze, but he did not allow himself to do so. Discipline. Tim Mulrennan slid his eyes to the left to watch his fellow acolyte, Dennis Connolly—his fourteen-year-old cousin, a freckled towhead two years his senior—grip the long-handled *sanctus* bell that would ring in just a moment when the celebrant raised the consecrated host. Always his heart soared almost painfully at this juncture during the mass.

The physical pain of twelve-year-old knees against hard stone was a part of the ritual that Tim took as a challenge—not to shift or squirm but to kneel with his back erect and hands folded. He believed that God watched and rewarded such steadfastness in an altar boy. Again, discipline. Besides, there were a lot worse things than a few minutes of discomfort, which he offered as a small sacrifice in thanksgiving for the many blessings in his life.

The world had survived a long and brutal war in Europe and the Pacific. Valiant American soldiers and sailors in the millions had returned to a country shorn of political illusions and rich in resources. It was hard for a boy from New Jersey to imagine what war really felt like. He read the newspapers and *Time*, listened to radio broadcasts, watched the newsreels in the local movie theater; he remembered President Roosevelt's talks and was still not used to President Truman's frank and funny twang. He listened in church and school to the ringing words of patriotism and faith in God and fear of communism. He believed what he was taught and held it in his soul and prayed for the strength to lead a good, moral life and to do his duty to God and country. He was a Boy Scout, First Class rank. He believed in the words of the Apostle's Creed and the Lord's Prayer and the Hail Mary, in the rosary and the mass and the stations of the cross, in Pope Pius XII and the triumphal rightness of the Holy Roman Catholic Church. He believed in the martyred saints and the priests and nuns of his parish; he believed in his father and his brother and sisters, and he prayed for his mother. . . .

The parish church was a massive limestone structure in the classic Gothic style that had been built by immigrant Italian stonecutters and masons twenty-five years earlier, a majestic high-vaulted house of worship planted amid the tree-adorned streets of a village west of the thriving industrial city of Newark.

Along with the grammar school, the church was the center of the Mulrennans' life, as it was for hundreds of local families. These Catholics, mostly of Irish and Italian descent, lived, loved, and worshiped fervently and clannishly, as their parents had in the old countries. With a healthy population of Jewish and Protestant neighbors, as well, North Auburn's total population was about thirty thousand souls. There were some Negro families who had lived there for close to a century, from before the village was incorporated, and they congregated at the Second Baptist Church on River Street. The Erie-Lackawanna line ran through the center of town and carried scores of residents to jobs in Newark and Hoboken, and to New York City–bound ferry boats and underground "tubes."

The bell tinkled. Tim lifted his eyes to the pure white host held aloft by the priest in view of the faithful. Always at this moment he felt the secret thrill of connection to the living Christ. He knew that it did not matter where he lived on God's earth, that this sacred rite was being performed in this same manner, at approximately the same time of day, from Rome to Timbuktu to Goa to Buenos Aires. He

was a part of something that was so much bigger than any
individual or town or nation: he was a member of the living
Body of Christ that had been in existence from the time of
the apostles and the earliest saints.

As the priest, Father John E. Newberry, held the chalice
that contained the wine soon to be the Blood of Christ, Tim
thought of his mother. She was in the church tonight, in
the sixth pew on the north side of the nave, with his father,
elder brother, and two sisters. Despite the requirement of
fasting, Madeline Anne Mulrennan had been sneaking beer
all evening as she and the family prepared for midnight
mass, dressing in their best new church outfits, then waiting
in the living room for their scheduled departure for mass
at eleven o'clock. She did not seem drunk, did not slur or
stumble or act wild, but by the forward tilt of her head he
knew from long experience that she was more than halfway
there. Somehow they all made it to the church in good time,
after a cold trek of three blocks over snow-covered side-
walks. Everyone anticipated a Christmas Eve snack after
mass and before a sleepless night and a magical Christmas
morning with gifts and hugs and tears, with Mom passed
out and Dad, James Mulrennan, whistling as he worked in
the kitchen, making breakfast for them, pretending that
there was nothing in the world wrong in his house. A man
could know no greater shame than a drunken wife, and a
family likewise for a drunken mother. Tim shuddered as
the bell announced the elevation of the golden chalice containing the holy blood of the Savior. He forced his mind to
concentrate on his duties as an altar server. His cousin Dennis seemed not to notice or to care that Tim's eyes brimmed
with tears.

*Oh, dear God, be with my family tonight and help us to
be kind and good to one another. Especially, please help
my mother to get better . . . to be well and not to get drunk
. . . to—* He did not know how to express what he felt in a
prayer to the Almighty Father.

After the Agnus Dei and the breast-tapping of the Mea
Culpa, the congregation marched forward to the railing be-
fore the altar where they knelt to receive Holy Communion.
Tim assisted Father Newberry by holding the golden paten

beneath the chins of the faithful as the priest placed a host
on the tongue; he walked back and forth along the cloth-
draped railing at least twenty times, there were so many
receiving tonight, on the day of Christ's birth.

The priest served Tim's parents. The boy smelled beer
on his mother's breath and hoped to God she would not
belch. He thought he saw her wobble and flutter her eyes
as she rose from the communion rail, sure signs that she
was now feeling the effects of her drinking. He silently
cursed her and himself for her condition—after all, if he
were a better son, student, ball player, altar boy maybe . . .
He silently prayed that God would cure her of this terrible,
sinful weakness for drink.

Minutes later, Father Newberry replaced the leftover hosts
in the gold-plated tabernacle behind the altar table. He swallowed the last drops of communion wine, then Tim Mulrennan poured water from the cruet over the priest's white,
tapered fingers. Father Newberry was in his forties, a quick-
moving, wiry man who had served as an army chaplain in Italy and France. His hair was a helmet of steely gray, and a
dark violet scar scored his cheekbone. He rarely smiled, and
maintained an attitude of cool competence toward the parishioners; he ably assisted the church's aging pastor, and
the ladies of the congregation were always attentive at his
masses. One day soon he would probably be named pastor
at another parish in northern New Jersey. He did not pay
much attention to altar servers such as Tim, unless there
was a slip-up during mass. He simply expected them to do
their part competently and without complaint.

Father Newberry dried his hands and returned the linen
towel to Tim's outstretched arm. Tim and Dennis resumed
their kneeling positions to await closing prayers and dismissal.

A huge, carved crucifix hung ominously above the altar.
Tim gazed up into the tortured face of Christ: pain and
death resided in the gilt-painted gashes on His face, but
also hope and the promise of salvation. The image of the
intricate wreath of thorns that made His crown, and which
were pushed into skin and skull, made Tim again feel the
bones in his knees. He felt the cold of the marble steps and

the heat of the Lord's passion. There were so many mysteries and questions that flowed through his mind. *How can I know God? How can I be worthy to serve God? Why is my mother—the way she is? What is God's will for all of us? Who was Jesus of Nazareth? I believe in His living presence among us—in the forms of body and blood in the Eucharist—yet how can this be, truly? Am I strong enough, faithful and obedient enough to please Him? What does He want of me?*

The mass ended, and Tim and Dennis followed the celebrant into the sacristy where they tore off their cassocks and took up their winter coats. "Merry Christmas, Father!" the boys called as they bolted from the sacristy, not pausing to request the priest's blessing, putting on their coats. Father Newberry waved and returned to the rectory. Tim pulled a woolen sailor's cap over his head as he walked with Dennis into the winter night. His open coat flapped in the cold wind, but he did not notice. He looked up into the black sky.

The cold white pinpoint stars hung so low that he felt he could lift his hand to touch them. The moon was a glowing white disc, casting its light on the snow-carpeted sidewalk outside the church. The church building itself, a massive stone structure, loomed like a black pyramid above the boys as they slid along the sloping, icy walk. Tim Mulrennan's heart was full of the spirit of the holiday and hopeful of better things. He felt clean and open and happy and alive. The world's troubles seemed far from this snowy street.

"I think Joan Fredericks likes me," Dennis Connolly announced soberly.

"Do you like her?" Tim asked, ever the friend-counselor.

"I guess I do. I'm not going to marry her or anything."

"Have you kissed her?"

"No, I don't want her cooties." Dennis barked like a wounded dog. "She's not even very pretty."

"She's nice. I've always liked her—since first grade."

"You want to kiss her?"

"No." The crystalline clarity of his religiosity was shattered by uncertainty. Didn't he want to kiss her? Or any girl? Girls . . . they complicated his thoughts. How could he be a priest if he liked girls, which, of course, he did? Kissing? Marriage? These were exotic concepts that secretly interested him deeply. What would his brother Kevin say? Kevin had girlfriends all the time; they liked his outgoing personality and athletic achievements. He was a ladies' man, as their father called him. Tim, on the other hand, felt awkward and embarrassed around girls, or even when they were mentioned.

"Sorry I asked." Dennis lifted a handful of snow and packed it into a ball that he threw at Tim, hitting him squarely in the back. The boys laughed and raced to the street corner. The Connolly kid peeled off to the right with a wave. "Happy Christmas, chump. Hope you get what you want."

"Same to you, chump." Tim lofted a snowball that landed near the other boy but did not hit him. He turned and walked toward home.

The cold air filled his lungs. He paused to gulp it in, ambled slowly along the white sidewalk, kicking up snow crystals with each step. He thought of school and friends and girls and church and home. He was reluctant to go home right away. He was all too familiar with the scene that awaited him. His mom would be drinking beer and rattling around in the kitchen, and the house would be thick with tension as everyone hoped she'd go to sleep so they could relax and open some Christmas gifts and play records on the new RCA phonograph. Tim's dad had bought a new Bing Crosby record, and Tim's eldest sister, Theresa, had a boxful of other records that she wanted to hear—she loved dance music.

His younger sister, Gertrude Anne, was just a baby, less than a year old, and would probably need a diaper change and feeding before being put to bed. That would fall to Theresa or Dad. Tim was hungry, having fasted before mass; he would eat a big sandwich and might sit down with a book or the *Saturday Evening Post* and read himself to sleep. He did not believe in Santa Claus anymore—he had up until three years ago, he thought sheepishly.

He crossed the lamplit street. He was a boy on the slippery cusp of young manhood, brimming with uncertainty

and hope, typical for any American youngster, yet filled
with a deep and sincere connection to an ancient faith. Was
this how the early saints felt, filled with a mysterious, ineffable *knowledge* of God's presence in the person of His
Son? The Blessed Sacrament was, to Tim and to most Catholics, no mere abstraction but a living reality—here in his
own parish church, in his own hometown, in his own life.
He stopped, looked up again into the star-scored predawn
blackness of Christmas Day 1949 in New Jersey, U.S.A.
A boy who *believed* with his entire physical and spiritual
being.

He stood perfectly still, arms hanging loosely at his side.
The cold bit into his uncovered hands and wrapped itself
around his pale neck.

*What is happiness? What is justice? Why does Mom
drink? Who are You, God?* These were questions of faith,
not doubt. Why was he blessed—or cursed—with the need
to believe, to accept the mysteries of God's unknowable
universe? He murmured a short prayer, "Glory be to the
Father, the Son, and the Holy Ghost, as it was in the beginning, is now, and ever shall be. Amen." Words of faith.
It felt so right to believe, and it hurt so bitterly to see his
mother behave the way she did. He could not shake the
hurt, even in this moment of quiet joy.

He walked on, past the town's public library building
that looked like an old brick castle, where he had spent
many hours studying and reading. He knew every bookcase
and every aisle, every sound and smell of the place, and
felt at home there, too. Now the windows were dark, and
he imagined himself inside, like a spy—spying on what, or
whom? He smiled at his own perverse imagination.

Tim crossed Orchard Place and turned up the next block,
walking in the middle of the deadly quiet street, pushing
the snow with the toes of his shoes. His steps made a soft
crunching sound. In the dull yellowish light of a streetlamp
he saw the mist of his breath. "Merry Christmas," he
breathed, and watched the words come out in cloudy fragments.

He walked once around the block before he came to the
back door of his house, paused before he entered, and

shook the snow from his shoes. He stepped inside, through a dark narrow passage cluttered with shoes and shovels, entering the warm, brightly lit kitchen. His mother and elder sister bustled about, preparing the family's midnight snack; Tim observed his mother, looking for signs of impairment. She seemed perfectly—too perfectly?—normal, and she spoke to him over her shoulder.

"Where have you been, Tim? We thought maybe you got lost."

"Just took my time getting home. I like the snow."

"Well, you'll catch your death if you don't button up your coat. Take off those wet shoes, and help your sister set the table."

Madeline Anne O'Casey Mulrennan, thin and plain, brown-haired, wearing a festively decorated apron over her church dress, gave every appearance of normality: suburban mother and faithful Catholic wife. Her oval face was neatly and subtly made up, with thin eyebrows and red lips, her hair curled and lacquered. A faux pearl necklace and matching earrings added a final elegant touch. But Tim's eyes went straight to the brown Pabst bottle that stood next to the kitchen sink—always the open beer bottle. He tried to meet his sister's gaze, but Theresa, her blond hair pulled back in a ponytail, was busy putting pickles and olives into the glass serving tray, concentrating on the task and not paying any attention to him.

"Sure, Mom." Tim kicked off his shoes and hung his coat on a metal hook by the back door. He took some plates from the cabinet and shuffled out to the dining room in his damp socks. After a few more trips the table was set and laden with sandwiches and drink for all. The baby was in bed, but the rest of the family sat down to end their Christmas Eve fast.

The experience of the mass at midnight had filled him up with an intense, glowing spirituality: a longing for the presence of Jesus Christ in His childish innocence, a want to be grown up himself and already a priest or pastor with people greeting him and looking to him for leadership, a sadness for the world of sin and conflict in which he lived, including his own home. If one believed in miracles, as

Timothy Mulrennan certainly did, why then did the situation seem to him so utterly hopeless? He prayed for his mother, that she would be cured of this evil. He knew his father prayed, too. They both begged for God's intervention in their lives. Why had God not answered their prayers? Why had He allowed this awful thing to continue, to contaminate everyone in the family? Then he mentally chastised himself for questioning God; it was not his place to do so, he thought. He did not know what God's will was for him—let alone for his mother and the others in his family. Perhaps there was some complex plan that he might never comprehend.

He was suddenly shaken by the clear, cold image of his mother's death, half wishing that it would happen, which created an inkling of the vast and deep relief that it would bring. Simultaneously he felt enveloped by a deep sadness, mingled with guilt, as if the sin were in the thought itself. . . . Quickly, he shoved the feeling deep down inside himself. It was wrong to have such thoughts, he scolded himself silently.

He watched her as they ate. She seemed gay enough, but not out of control as she had been so many times in the past. No flying forks or plates. His father also kept an eye, as did Theresa and Kevin, his older brother, who had more than once carried Madeline to the bed or couch when she passed out, before Dad came home. An hour later, free of major mishap or confrontation, the Mulrennans retired for the night with expectation of a relatively happy Christmas Day—as long as she didn't get sloshed too early in the day, before other family members and guests came over to the house . . . God willing.

Sunday, January 21, inflight to Rome

Timothy John Cardinal Mulrennan shifted his slender six-foot-four frame in the business-class seat on Continental-Alitalia flight 80 from Newark International Airport to Aeroporto Leonardo da Vinci in Fiumicino, outside Rome. This was a last-minute trip on a route he had taken many

times over the past decade. The pope was dead, and the
funeral observances would be held within a few days, with
the conclave to elect the next Successor to St. Peter required by Church law to begin no fewer than fifteen and
no more than twenty days from the pontiff's passing. Mulrennan opened his eyes. He had attempted unsuccessfully
to nap. His watch read 11:54 P.M. Eastern Standard Time.
Already it was nearly 6:00 A.M. in Rome. He had left a city
frozen by a harsh January storm, after a bleak, wet Christmas season. The responsibilities and cares of the archdiocese remained with him, always. Yet he felt keenly and
personally the loss of the late Holy Father. He rubbed his
long, now-stubbled jawline. *Father, grant me the strength
of spirit to know and do Your will.* He closed his eyes again,
seeking solitude and quiet in the unlit interior of his mind.

Later, Mulrennan sipped an iced tea sweetened with three
packets of Equal and shifted in the comfortably oversized
leather seat.

An attractive flight attendant offered him a small plate
of warm appetizers, but he declined with the wave of a
hand. He did not feel hungry. "I'll have some fruit and
cheese later, if you don't mind," he said.

"Of course—sir," the young woman replied, apparently
uncertain as to the proper form of address due a prince of
the Roman Catholic Church. Tim remembered earlier days
of crisply uniformed and carefully groomed stewardesses
who were thoroughly trained in languages and the subtleties
of international diplomacy. Another small but important
loss over the past thirty years, he thought.

He flipped off his black loafers, stretched his long legs,
and entered his thoughts in the journal he kept on a sleek
notebook computer that glowed like a silvery shield on the
tray table over his lap. He wrote a regular column for the
weekly archdiocesan newspaper, often adapting the text of
his Sunday homily or relating a personal anecdote or ex-
amining a Biblical passage—whatever came to mind. He
typed in a few words about the late pope, then sat back and
recalled the hectic events of the past few days.

The late-night telephone call from the Vatican that no-
tified him of the Holy Father's death before it was released

to the press . . . the somber meeting with his chancery staff
to implement the contingency travel plan that he had instituted when he first came back to Newark several years ago
. . . his own personal phone calls to fellow bishops and family and friends . . . the few brief moments of grieving the
incalculable loss to the Church and to humanity. His secretary would follow him to Rome within the next twenty-
four hours to assist during the preconclave duties. His
archdiocesan vicar general, chancellor, and the auxiliary
bishops knew their responsibilities at home, and he was
unconcerned about their competence. With minimal help he
was packed and ready to depart with one bag—military
efficiency. He always traveled light. Like most U.S. residential bishops, he stayed in a small apartment in the North
American College several blocks from the slow brown Ti-
ber; he spent a few weeks a year at the Vatican, attending
to his duties as a member of the Congregation for Bishops—a holdover from his previous full-time Curia assignment to the same dicastery, or department, when he was
one of the handful of Americans who had ever held such
a leadership position in the highest levels of the Vatican
bureaucracy.

He loved Rome, but he loved his true home more. That
was why he had been so pleased to be sent back to Newark
upon the death of the previous archbishop in the mid-1990s.
These had been good years—not easy, but fulfilling. Mulrennan occasionally took time to backpack above the
Delaware River or tuck himself into a soft chair to pore
over a knotty theological tome or a Dick Francis novel, the
more intricately plotted and gruesome the better. The last
time he had been to Rome was only four months ago, and
he had known—felt in his bones—that it might be the last
time during the current pontificate.

One of his telephone calls was to his sister, Gertrude
Anne Gelbman, who had just moved back to New Jersey
after decades in New York City. She answered on the second ring.

"It's Tim," he said. "Sorry to bother you at this hour, but
the Holy Father died this evening. I have to leave for Rome
on Sunday."

"Oh, Tim, I'm so sorry for you. I know you loved him—
he was a friend. What can I do?" So typical of his sister,
always ready to help another, to address her brother's or
any family member's needs. She had been divorced sixteen
years ago and devoted herself to raising two now-college-
age boys. They had been blessed with a great mom. In
recent years Gertie had begun to focus on reviving her folk-
singing career, which she had put aside to be a wife and
mother.

"Let's get together for dinner tomorrow evening," he
suggested. "Are you free?"

"As long as I don't have to eat the cafeteria-quality food
you serve in that mausoleum you call home," she said.
"We'll meet Down Neck at one of the Spanish places,
okay?"

"Let's make it for six-thirty. I will want to get in one
last workout before I leave. I doubt there'll be any recreation time scheduled during the conclave."

"Tim?" Gertie Anne queried tentatively. "I'm feeling
afraid about this. I don't know why—but with all that's
going on these days: terrorism and wars and all the problems in the Church. I feel—I mean, I hope you're going to
be all right—you and the others, and the unfortunate soul
who will be elected."

At their last meal together just before he departed for the
conclave, Tim and Gertrude Anne had sat quietly, each with
a glass of wine untouched on the small table between them.
It was a great relief for the archbishop to pause, even for
a couple of hours, before plunging into the heart-numbing
business that awaited him. She looked at her elder brother
as she had so many times in her life—with both empathy
and puzzlement. Long since, she had come to accept his
vocation to the priesthood, but this latest turn, the call from
Rome, the impending funeral and conclave, the expected
glare of international media . . . how would it affect this
man whom she had loved so much all her life? Was it all
that long ago that they were a complete if troubled family
living in the big old house on Fairlawn Avenue in North
Auburn? All the years of fighting and crying, laughing and
loving. Three girls and three boys, one of whom lay thirty

years dead beneath foreign soil, joined now by their parents, both having passed away years ago.

Tim Mulrennan, after all, was facing his sixty-fourth birthday. He looked like a fit but stressed-out man of fifty, perhaps, blessed with beautiful silver hair still streaked with dark brown. The familiar angular face that promised interest and sympathy and—yes, corny as it might sound, holiness. Gertrude Anne had never had difficulty equating Tim with the old-time saints who peopled the books and stained glass windows of their youth. At the same time, she knew all of his flaws and shortcomings and loved him the more intensely for them.

"How are you holding up?" she asked.

"Okay, I guess. I almost broke down at mass this morning in the chapel. It hit me—suddenly. He's gone. We had time to prepare, I know, but—" He twirled the wineglass gently, watching the red liquid kiss the rim. "I loved him and feared for him. He suffered greatly."

"I didn't like him that much," his sister blurted. "Sorry to say that, and I don't mean any disrespect, really, but he was living in another century. For God's sake—" She saw that she was wounding him, so she stopped. This was one of his blind spots: the deepest reverence for a man she considered one of the most reactionary popes ever, and it had been a pretty stiff lot! Still, she did not want to hurt her brother. "Tim, what can I do for you?" She touched his hand.

"Just pray for me—and for the Church."

"What's really on your mind? You can't bullshit me, you know." Gertrude Anne smiled. She wore her reddish gray hair shoulder length and her creamy pale face still bore the youthful Irish freckles that men—other than her former husband—loved.

"I cannot imagine what I would have done or what I would have been if I hadn't been a priest. There were many times when I questioned my vocation, prayed about it— even questioned God and His will and His power. But all of it was private. I've never really told anyone. I should have. There were times, a few casual conversations with

other priests . . . I should have been more open with my
questions and doubts."

"Yes, but that is past now. You are a priest, a bishop,
and cardinal. For God's sake, Tim, relax—you don't have
to satisfy the whole world or worry about what people think
of you. The people in your diocese love you. Your family
loves you." She squeezed his hand. "Chill, as the kids
would say."

He smiled, grateful for her common sense. Still, he could
not shake the cold foreboding he felt as he faced the decisions that lay ahead. He had never been in a conclave; in
fact only a handful of the current cardinals had participated
in the previous one. Several of them were now older than
eighty and ineligible to vote. It weighed heavily on his
mind and his soul.

"What about you? How is the music career going these
days?"

Performing and recording Christian music was a direction she had wanted to take but had not, after college. For
all of her adult life Gertrude Anne had sung in choirs and
ensembles and even coffee shops in Manhattan and Hoboken, had served as a part-time minister of music in various parishes. She loved sacred as well as popular music
and was blessed with a beautiful alto voice. With her steady
boyfriend of ten years she had built a studio in the detached
garage behind her house in Browerton, the town next to
North Auburn.

"Tom and I are going to incorporate as a record label
and try to attract other artists. It's a long uphill climb, but
we're willing to try. I've got several dates booked through
Easter and a Christian folk festival in North Carolina later
in the spring. I'm pretty busy. I don't know what'll happen
if I become a grandmother—not that that's an immediate
prospect."

Mulrennan sipped the wine. He had no taste for it. His
mind was a million miles distant. She understood, and did
not engage him for a while. Some of the other patrons in
the restaurant had recognized him and whispered indis-
creetly among themselves, looking sidelong in his direction.
She sat back and admired his handsome face and erect car-

riage. He might have been a professional sports coach, a corporate or university president, a neurosurgeon, she thought. He looked like a leader. But he had chosen to serve the Church instead. Why? She supposed it was simply destined to be this way. She accepted it, as had other members of their family. It had been somewhat difficult, at first, for their father, but he had become so proud, with time. Now as Tim prepared to fly to Rome to participate in the papal conclave, she saw him in a new and different light: less as a brother than as a man touched by history. Memories of their years in North Auburn, growing up, Tim's military and seminary years, the tumultuous times with their brothers and sisters, their mother's alcoholism, their father's patience and love . . . nothing unique in the grand scheme of family life, perhaps, yet so special to her.

"I couldn't help but think of Mom and Dad," Tim said. "She's been dead for nearly fifty years now. Still hard to believe . . ." The pain of life had been too much for Madeline Mulrennan to bear. She had suffered for weeks in the hospital with liver disease caused by her chronic alcoholism. But her pain had ended . . . finally. Tim and his brother and sisters lived with theirs for years. Their dad had remarried happily, and a stepbrother had been born. They had stitched their lives back together, only to have Vietnam wound their hearts once more.

"I know, Tim." Gertie Anne touched his hand.

"I pray for her soul every day. And Dad—he's up there with her—and Kevin." Tears filmed his eyes. "And now with the Holy Father."

In a coach-class seat on the same flight as Cardinal Mulrennan of Newark, the middle-aged man wearing a gray pullover sweater and khaki slacks drank a glass of water and munched on tiny, hard pretzels. It was not obvious to anyone who might pay him the slightest attention that Francis Xavier Darragh was a retired billionaire businessman who could afford to buy out the airline, let alone a seat in the first-class section of this transatlantic flight. He wore thick-lensed eyeglasses and thumbed through an inflight magazine as busy flight attendants served his fellow passengers.

Two days before, at five o'clock, Frank Darragh had knelt by his bed for morning prayer. He closed his eyes tightly, clasped his hands, shifted his knees on the hardwood floor of the bedroom, one of thirty rooms in his home in the Country Club Plaza section of Kansas City, Missouri. He prayed for world peace, for the well-being of the Church, for the success of the Evangelium Christi movement, for his wife and children and grandchildren and for his aged mother, now ninety-four, and for his own immortal soul. He considered the latter entity to be in immediate peril. He prayed aloud, unselfconsciously.

"I know that You look with favor upon the work of the Evangelium and its people, dear Lord, if not upon everything I have done to advance our just cause. I have cleansed my heart, I have emptied the storehouse of my goods to share with those in greater need, I have chosen to follow the way of Jesus, just as He invited the disciples of His own day. I seek to gain nothing for myself, everything for Holy Mother Church. I believe that evil men would destroy her, that she must be defended by every means available against these enemies. Give me the strength to do battle with evil; give me the knowledge of right and wrong and the ability to choose the right; give me Your forgiveness for my errors and sins in my zeal to serve You. Father in Heaven, lead me to righteousness. There are dark and difficult days ahead for Your faithful people. Send Your light, Your love, Your strength to us, Your servants on earth. I pray in the name of the Blessed Virgin Mary, our Mother, and her Son, Jesus Christ the Lord."

Darragh took a rosary of lapis lazuli from its felt-lined wooden case. He held it to his face: it smelled cold and holy. He began to pray the rosary, fingering the silver Celtic cross, then the first blue bead. A huge gray-and-white tabby cat walked into the bedroom and sidled against the kneeling man, pushing his twenty-pound bulk against Darragh's leg. The animal received no acknowledgment and lay down nearby as the man continued, his lips moving in prayer. "Hail Mary, full of grace, the Lord is with thee. Blessed art thou among women, and blessed is the fruit of thy womb, Jesus. Holy Mary, Mother of God . . ."

The monstrous cat lazily lifted itself and padded out of the room. Twenty minutes later, Frank Darragh finished the rosary, kissed the cross, replaced it in its case, and rose to exercise on the treadmill at the foot of the bed, eventually to shower and dress for the day ahead. He had much to do if he was to save a minimum of a billion souls, including his own.

He drove his mother to 7:30 mass at the cathedral downtown, then treated her to breakfast at her favorite coffee shop, brought her back home for her nap, and by 10:00 A.M., he was sitting in a straight-backed chair at the wide desk in his study that served as headquarters of his multimillion-dollar philanthropic enterprise, the Mary Frances McTier-Darragh Foundation, named for his saintly mother.

In 1970, following his return from combat service in Vietnam with a Purple Heart and Bronze Star, Francis X. Darragh had enrolled in Southwestern Missouri State University business courses at night, while he worked days at McDonald's and other fast-food restaurants to support a wife and three (eventually to number seven) children. He bought into the hamburger franchise, one location at a time, but he barely broke even on these investments. He had a dream: to create his own chain of barbecue take-outs.

When all the others—including his father and brothers and sisters, and his wife—had given up on him as a lost cause, seeing him only as a flaky, starry-eyed failed entrepeneur, his mother continued to believe. In fact, it was her loan of a thousand dollars, and her ceaseless prayers, that kept the doors open to the first BBQ Stop restaurant in Kansas City, some thirty years ago. He had never forgotten. Two years later he had expanded to a dozen restaurants in three states, capitalizing on an old family sauce recipe that caught on and sold in supermarkets and by mail order. Within five years he had gone national, boasting fifty Frankie's BBQ Stops with their distinctive red-jacketed servers; and five years after that, he had 187 locations in twenty states with sales of more than $600 million. *Thanks, Mom,* he often thought. *And thank you, dear Jesus.* By 1984 he owned eight hundred restaurants in the United States alone, another two hundred overseas, as well as soft-drink bottling plants in twelve states and the best-selling potato chip brand in the world.

The business press had long since labeled Frank Darragh the BBQ King and lavished tens of thousands of column inches on his restaurant-and-beverage empire that now extended into every continent on the earth. His entrepreneurial and political résumé glittered with achievements and appointments and archconservative credentials.

During the heady Reagan-Bush years in the 1980s, he had served on the president's Foreign Intelligence Advisory Board with Clare Boothe Luce, among others, and privately funded several initiatives to aid the Nicaraguan *contras* in their war against the pro-Castro, anti-American Sandinista government. He saw himself as a Cold Warrior in the battle against Godless Communism; and when victory was declared in that struggle, Darragh gave the Polish pope the ultimate credit. The political position he craved most, U.S. ambassador to the Holy See in Rome, was never offered. He consoled himself with the presidency of the Western Association of the Sovereign Military and Hospitaller Order of St. John of Jerusalem of Rhodes and Malta, more familiarly known as the Knights of Malta. For the coming funeral he would don the costume of the knights—ostrich-plumed headgear, red tunic with golden epaulets, dark blue trousers, gaudy sash, cape and riding boots, and the distinctive eight-pointed Maltese cross—and participate in the rites of the Roman Catholic society that marked the death of the man to whom they had sworn allegiance unto death, the Holy Father.

When he finally sold off his majority share in the Darragh Corporation in 1994, the company still had thriving restaurants in all fifty states and thirty foreign countries, soft-drink bottling plants worldwide, snack food manufacturing interests, cattle ranches and agribusiness holdings, and ranked among the top three fast-food corporations traded on the New York Stock Exchange. He became executive chairman at fifty-three, with little more than cere-

monial and public-relations duties attached to that title—
and the gratitude of the hands-on executive team for staying
out of their hair. He laughed to himself sometimes at the
irony: without a college degree he had become a case study
in the top business schools and lionized as a marketing
visionary. His wife now lived in Florida most of the year,
and his kids were grown and educated, their families finan-
cially secure. He was free to do his own thing on his own
terms, from his own home. His father had not lived to see
him retire with a net worth of more than $1.7 billion and
create the foundation and devote himself to giving away
scores of millions, primarily to religious-based charities,
each year. The old man had died of a stroke in 1979. That
seemed an incredibly long time ago, a different world almost—before he became so deeply involved with the Evangelium.

Archbishop Vennholme had telephoned him one day in
the summer of 1989, just before the Labor Day weekend,
as he recalled. They had known each other from Catholic
charity events, including a successful capital campaign to
restore the century-old cathedral in Kansas City, which
Darragh had chaired. He, in turn, had admired the
Canadian-born archbishop's adamant and articulate prolife
stance. That telephone call had changed his spiritual life
forever: Henry Martin Vennholme invited Darragh to attend
a world congress and retreat of the Evangelium Christi Society to be held in St. Louis that year. Since it was so
close—only across the state—and since it was a personal
invitation from such an important prelate, Frank Darragh
accepted the invitation and spent a week mingling with
clerics and lay people from around the world. He was impressed with them, and they with him. He immediately
joined the organization and began a frequent correspondence with Vennholme. The archbishop served as moderator of the society, the direct link to the Vatican on all
issues spiritual and temporal. Darragh quickly became a
trusted counselor and financial pillar of the American prov-
ince. He saw the religious equivalent of an expanding business operation—an opportunity to apply his financial and
marketing skills to the work of the Lord.

He fully retired from the BBQ Stop Corporation in 1997, retaining only the title of chairman emeritus, putting directors' meetings, sales rallies, and presentations to Wall Street analysts behind him. He would henceforth devote himself to his passion for the Catholic lay movement Evangelium Christi, which had taken root in the United States a generation earlier, to bring its conservative message of clean living, religious observance, and the authority of the magisterium to more Americans. He opened his pockets and traveled tirelessly in the name of Evangelium Christi. Having achieved beatification for the movement's founder, Fra Giovanni Prignano, he and others now worked and prayed for canonization. If the Holy Father had survived, those final official steps to sainthood probably would have been accelerated over the next few years.

In 1998 Cardinal Vennholme nominated him for the prestigious title of Gentleman of His Holiness, one of the highest papal honors a layman might achieve. A year later, the BBQ King of Kansas City, Missouri, was elected first vice president of the Western Hemisphere section of the world congress of the Evangelium, which meant a substantial increase in travel and personal contact with Vennholme and other officers in Rome. From a third-floor suite of rooms in the Hotel Columbus on the Via della Concilliazione, literally spitting distance from St. Peter's Basilica, Darragh helped oversee the activities of the ninety-thousand-member religious society and personal prelature—at the right hand of his friend and spiritual mentor, Henry Martin Cardinal Vennholme. When in Rome he usually attended the cardinal's morning mass in one of the numerous underground chapels of St. Peter's.

Frank Darragh kept himself reasonably fit; he stood five ten in his sweat socks, with his white hair trimmed in a retro flattop, steel blue eyes that his mother loved, pale Celtic complexion, slightly knock-kneed, hopelessly nearsighted. The Sisters of Mercy and Christian Brothers had ensured that he developed good posture and readable handwriting as a youth. His father had backed them up with a generous reward to any of his children of $500 if they did not smoke or drink before their twenty-first birthdays.

Frank earned the money and rarely drank more than a token beer at Thanksgiving or Easter. He had never smoked. In turn, he had offered his own kids $5,000 on the same conditions; but none of them had claimed the reward. He'd been disappointed. He had no vices or addictions other than, perhaps, his singleminded devotion to the cause of Christ . . . for which he was willing to do anything, at any time, for or *to* anyone.

He poured himself a cup of coffee and settled in to read and respond to a small mountain of correspondence that had piled up in the few days he had been away in Florida.

The far-reaching charitable foundation did not employ anyone but Darragh and his mother, not even a secretary, so Frank answered each telephone call and opened every letter. The board, consisting of several family members, a trusted local attorney, and Cardinal Vennholme, met irregularly. It was largely a one-man show, and that was how Darragh preferred it. . . .

A shaft of sunlight had streamed through the tall windows that lined one side of the spacious study-office and fell onto his desk that morning. It was bright and rather warm for January in Kansas City, and he had made a mental note to run to the gym for his workout this afternoon. He felt stale, in need of fresh air. The telephone rang insistently. He answered it.

Henry Vennholme's voice had sounded tentative, unsteady, odd, as he greeted Darragh. "It's early evening here in Rome," he said. "I am calling to tell you the pope is dead. It has not yet been announced officially."

That call had come two days ago.

Now, on flight 80, across the aisle from Darragh sat his traveling companion, Father Anthony Ciccone of St. Cecilia's Parish in Philadelphia, a fellow Evangelium adherent. Father Ciccone, a muscular young man in black clerical garb, sat with hands folded in his lap and eyes closed. Praying perhaps, Darragh thought as he regarded the faithful priest. Would that the ranks of the American Catholic clergy were full of such prayerful men. He and Ciccone were flying to the pope's funeral with heavy, grief-laden hearts. Frank Darragh knew that the cardinal-archbishop of

Newark sat about forty feet in front of him, in business class, on this red-eye to Rome. The proximity of Tim Mulrennan made him uncomfortable, but it was important to keep tabs on this man who was no friend of Evangelium Christi.

Darragh asked the flight attendant for another packet of pretzels and a cup of water, eschewing coffee, wine, hard liquor, and even the popular soda that had made him a billionaire. He smiled to himself at the irony. God had given him so many gifts . . . now he had been presented the possible opportunity to give back to the Lord and His people.

Perhaps there would be a special reward for Francis Xavier Darragh, who longed to be one of the hinges upon which the Church turned, as in days of old when men of wealth and stature and good family were made cardinals and entered the sacred service of the Vatican. Perhaps he would be the first layman in centuries to receive such an extraordinary call to service—one day to be privy to a conclave itself! Perhaps . . .

CHAPTER TWO

Saturday, January 27, 4:47 P.M.

Mulrennan glanced at his watch and realized he must get moving if he did not want to be locked out of the Apostolic Palace and the conclave residence. He strode back across the bridge, around the old castle that housed Emperor Hadrian's tomb, and along the bland Mussolini construction, the Via della Concilliazione. Reaching the busy intersection at the Via del Belvedere, he waited impatiently to cross, watching as a city policeman directed traffic: a busy stream of omnibuses, vans, official vehicles, private cars, tonsured monks, bearded friars, black-habited nuns, ubiquitous pilgrims, an occasional bishop with a purple sash, strangers, foreigners, Romans, tradesman, thieves, the idle and the curious.

At last given the go-ahead, he dashed across the wide street and made his way to Bernini's majestic twin colonnades that enclosed the piazza like embracing arms, each with four rows of 88 pillars and 284 Doric columns, topped by 162 statues of saints and Church Fathers.

His long arms swung athletically at his side. He wore no hat, neither secular nor religious, and his stiff, close-cropped silver hair resisted the wind. His skin was burnished by a rough winter back home in New Jersey. A long navy coat buttoned at the neck obscured his Roman collar. He bent forward slightly, diminishing his six-four stature, as he increased the length and quickness of his stride. Must get back in time.

There was no doubt in his mind that he would rather be far away, back in the States sitting in his private study with a cup of coffee or a glass of wine.

The American paused for a moment at the entrance to
the Piazza San Pietro, breathing in the grandeur of the scene
before him: the oval plaza with its twin fountains and tall
obelisk, the massive statues of the great apostles, Peter and
Paul, the imposing, recently refurbished edifice of the basilica, now bright beige instead of dead gray. The plaza
itself bustled with more than the usual activity for this hour.
On the periphery of the square, platforms had been erected
to hold the representatives of the international press corps.
Tourist and penitent alike moved about, some admiring the
recently refurbished architecture, others straining to catch a
glimpse of anyone who might be of importance.

The day before, nearly 250,000 people had been there to
attend the frigid outdoor funeral mass at the conclusion of
the *Novendiales* the traditional nine days of mourning for
the late pope. Without an occupant of the Throne of St.
Peter, during the so-called *Sede Vacante* or Vacant See, the
Vatican nervously shifted gears into neutral to negotiate the
delicate days until a successor was elected. The Particular
Congregation had been formed, composed of four cardinals—the camerlengo, who was the late pope's chamberlain, and three assistants chosen from among the local
cardinals—to handle relatively minor housekeeping matters
before the General Congregation, composed of the full
body of cardinals, convened. Thus, necessary rituals were
observed, official silence was maintained, the wheels of
Church governance slowed and nearly halted, as cardinals
and hierarchs and heads of state from nearly every nation
around the world arrived to pay tribute to the dead Vicar
of Christ.

A gunmetal sky had helmeted the giant basilica that day,
causing the statuary along the columned facade to shrink
to human dimensions. The assembly had been reverently
quiet as Tim Mulrennan and five other cardinals, each from
a different continent, concelebrated the primarily Latin liturgy. A prelate from central Africa, who had left behind a
nation and a region in bloody upheaval to attend his cardinalitial duties, had offered the brief homily in French.
Afterward, nine hundred priests had distributed the Eucharist among the faithful mourners. At the conclusion of the

rite, a somberly costumed contingent of the Swiss Guard
carried the casket into the chapel of the popes beneath St.
Peter's main hall, where the man from Eastern Europe who
had led the world out of the cold war and wrenched his
postconciliar Church into a new millennium, joined more
than 140 of his predecessors.

Mulrennan pushed away the mental images of the man
who had made such a powerful impact on his own life—
in Tim's estimation a true modern saint with the purest
Christ-like vision of world harmony as well as all the weak-
nesses and shortcomings of a mortal. By others throughout
the world this man had been revered as a statesman and
reviled as a defender of the male-dominated status quo.
There were few persons in the world with a neutral opinion.

Walking across the piazza now, the American passed beneath the shadow of the Egyptian obelisk, brought by Caligula to Rome in 38 C.E. and removed to St. Peter's in
1586. Moving swiftly through the milling groups of tourists, Mulrennan imagined hearing the voice of the Genoese
sailor who violated the order of Pope Sixtus V that all spec-
tators must remain silent, under pain of death, during the
raising of the eighty-five-foot-tall sandstone monument.
The backbreaking chore almost ended in disaster when the
ropes threatened to break. A lone voice pierced the absolute
silence of the plaza, shouting, "Water to the ropes!" and
thus saved the day. As a reward, the pontiff declared that
from that day forward, all palms used in the Vatican on
Palm Sunday must come from the brave sailor's hometown
of Bordighera.

Should it become necessary in the days ahead, Mulrennan wondered, would he have the courage to be that lone
voice?

He had not been on the ground two hours when he had
received the first preconclave visit, in the tradition of the
prattiche, or informal conversations among the electors,
this one from his old friend from Florence, Leandro Aurelio
Cardinal Biagi, archbishop and Church politician extraor-
dinaire, who launched into an immediate discussion of the
"front-runner," an Austrian cardinal.

Biagi looked directly into Mulrennan's eyes. "Zimmer-

man must be elected by the third or fourth ballot, or else
La Spina will pick up enough moderates to swing the momentum toward him. I do not suppose the Africans or
Asians will ever vote for La Spina unless it becomes certain
that he will be elected within a ballot or two, and then even
some of our more liberal brothers will move in his direction. Still, I believe the votes for Zimmerman are committed at least for four ballots. I am not asking you where you
stand on this issue, my friend, but I am simply outlining
the likeliest scenario as I see it developing. That is, as the
Holy Spirit is directing me." He gestured definitively with
his hands, nut brown against the bright scarlet trim of his
black cassock, and cocked his gleaming bald head.

"What do you expect me to say? You know we are prohibited from active canvassing and politicking at the conclave, Eminence." Mulrennan smiled cagily. "My vote is
likely to go to you."

"Would that I could vote for *you*, my dear Cardinal. But
at this time we need an older, frankly more conventionally
political pope. This is the historical way of the Church—
to step away from the previous pontificate, to absorb and
moderate its direction. Zimmerman will give us this, I believe. His health has been questioned by some, but I know
nothing that would preclude him from reigning for at least
six or eight years." Biagi wagged a finger in Tim's direction. "You will be a strong papabile then. Perhaps you will
be reappointed to some Curial position and live in Rome
again for a while, eh, Timofeo?" Biagi often used the
friendly, familiar Italian form when he spoke to the American.

"I have no desire to live here again; I love my life in
Newark." Tim had served in the Curia before his appointment as a residential archbishop, earning his red hat in
Rome and taking it back to the States. "Allo, you are trying
too hard." Tim, too, had a nickname for his friend. "You
must allow the Holy Spirit to inspire and direct us. We may
not know as well as He does what the Church needs, smart ·
as we are, some of us."

"You Americans can be so naive at times, *amico*. Perhaps it is best that there are no Spellmans or O'Connors

anymore. But you—all of us—must be vigilant, wary of the forces that would turn back the clock."

"Frank Darragh tried to contact all of the Americans before we left for the conclave. I did not take his call."

"Perhaps you should have, if only to tell him your mind."

"I don't know that he'd care to listen, nor that I would care to tell him. Besides, I think he is trying to influence the election improperly."

"There are many who would do so."

"Well, I'm not going to give them the satisfaction."

The conversation with Biagi still rang through Tim's mind as he reached the Portone di Bronzo, the great bronze doors that served as a ceremonial entranceway to the Vatican, where a brace of helmeted Swiss Guards stood at attention in their most somber midnight-blue-and-black uniforms. Through the doors he passed, from the square into the dark confinement of the Vatican. As the doors closed behind him, he realized that he would not step outside this walled city-state again until a new Vicar of Christ was elevated to the Throne of St. Peter.

An hour later he walked in solemn procession with his colleagues, two by two, into the Sistine Chapel and took his seat there, inhaling the majestic, if close, atmosphere of this historic chamber. Mulrennan had already decided who would receive his vote on the first ballot: his old friend and mentor Cardinal Biagi. But he still looked around the chapel, considered his options: Zimmerman of Austria, La Spina of Turin, Ibanga of Nigeria, among many others. Each man was worthy—as were at least a dozen more from every corner of the globe. Would the conclave select a hard-line Italian, thus turning back the clock as some powerful reactionary Church factions advocated? A pastoral cardinal or someone close to the bureaucrats? Would the electors even choose a moderate, conciliatory European? Zimmerman, urbane and charismatic, led that field by a wide margin. Or would they elect a man of color to lead a Church that was growing exponentially in Africa and Asia? Perhaps a South American, or the first-ever pope from below the equator?

A tall, broad-shouldered man with black hair, porcelain-

pale skin, cool blue eyes, dramatic brows, and a fleshy nose
rose from his seat at a signal from the camerlengo. He
climbed the altar steps deliberately but with grace and energy. He walked to the temporary wooden lectern that stood
before the Sistine altar, towering over it. He looked out at
his brother cardinals and Vatican officials and staff members, some of whom would serve within the coming conclave, others who would leave the restricted area for the
duration of the election process.

Like his fellow electors, he was vested in scarlet choir
dress with the simple rochet and pectoral cross suspended
from a gold-and-red chord, and the red zucchetto, or skull-
cap, of his office.

It was said of Georg Markus Cardinal Zimmerman, "He
is more Italian than the Italians, more American than the
Americans, more French than the French, and as Austrian
as anyone would care to be."

In truth, he defied simple definition, perhaps a function of
his illustrious Vatican career as apostolic diplomat without
peer: now seventy-one and at the peak of his intellectual
powers, vigorous, polished, politic, possessor of several languages including Italian, Spanish, English, and French, in
addition to his native German. From the Second Vatican Ecumenical Council, where he served as a *peritus*, an expert
adviser on theological history, through postings to Bogotá
and Mexico City, Berlin and Kiev, ultimately as the apostolic delegate to the United States for three years in the
mid-1980s, he then became Secretary of State. Cardinal
Zimmerman had presided, the previous spring, over a rare
international synod of bishops, which many observers remarked was a dress rehearsal or preconclave, suitably
impressing 284 delegates from all over the world: bishops,
archbishops, cardinals, and patriarchs. Now, on the afternoon of the opening day, he would present the exhortation, a
special sermon concerning the duties of cardinal-electors in
the coming conclave.

Oddsmakers around the world put him at near even-up
to be elected on the first day of balloting; *Time* and the
New York Times Magazine ran his face on the covers of
their current issues; broadcast organizations led their eve-

ning news reports with his biography and confident predic-
tions of his election. Even the most discreet of media
outlets, Vatican Radio and L'Osservatore Romano, put
Zimmerman at or near the top of every list of papabili.

Zimmerman was not unaware of these expectations. He
reminded himself, and his supporters, of the hoary Vatican
adage: "He who enters the conclave a pope, leaves it a
cardinal." Yet for several years he had prepared mentally
and spiritually for this moment. Who could fault him for
it? Most of his colleagues, in fact, entered this conclave
with a sense of confidence and immense relief that there
was one major candidate to focus on. And if he earned a
clear lead on the first ballot, their jobs would be made relatively easy.

But the Austrian cardinal was not free from cavil and
criticism. He wore the label *progressive* willingly, which
offended conservatives; but he was canny enough to sidestep political land mines. Rumors of illness had circulated
among the Sacred College for several weeks before the late
pontiff's death. Phlebitis, they said. There had been mild
heart attacks, three in ten years, concealed with the cooperation of the Secretariat of State and the Apostolic Palace.
Wasn't this the same problem Albino Luciani, Pope John
Paul I, had shoved under the carpet in the years leading up
to his election and thirty-three-day reign?

No one knew for certain, and most were afraid to inquire
seriously, because it was unseemly to ask too many intimate
questions about one of their own. He did look more than a
bit pale, Tim Mulrennan thought, perhaps a winter pallor,
perhaps the stress of the moment.

However, Zimmerman commanded his audience with
ease, speaking first in flawless Italian. "Our purpose, my
brothers, was ordained by the Savior who anointed Simon
Peter to be our shepherd, representing Christ Himself on
earth. This is obvious to all of us, yet we may so easily
lose sight of the obvious in our zeal to be right—that is,
not to make a mistake. We shall not make a mistake if we
trust to the Holy Spirit to guide us in our election. The
constitution *Universi Dominici Gregis* clearly sets out our
path, and we must merely follow it with open heart and

prayerful conscience. We must enter our deliberations filled with the Gospel, not politics or favor."

As Zimmerman spoke, Cardinal Mulrennan tried to focus on the words, the message of the Holy Spirit speaking through this colleague. Mulrennan had studied accounts of the eight conclaves of the twentieth century: in 1903, 1914, 1922, 1939, 1958, 1963, and two in 1978, the Year of Three Popes. Despite the shackles of secrecy that bound all conclavists, enough information had leaked to journalists and authors to fill entire books about those proceedings. Some journalists claimed that the 1978 sessions had been electronically bugged. Possible, if not probable, Tim considered. Would anyone have the nerve to try that here, with all the safeguards, promises, and rules in force? He listened closely to the tall Austrian's homily.

"While we have taken multiple sacred oaths of secrecy, for sound canonical and historical reasons, our highest sacred duty is to each other, as the legitimate senate of the Holy Church and representatives of the faithful in every corner of our Creator's earth.

"We are brothers in Christ charged to elect a peer to a position of supreme authority over us. One of the men who sit in this room will be asked by the rest to assume the responsibility that none of us want; yet each of us must be willing to say yes to our fellow cardinals, yes to our Church, and yes to our God.

"Follow your conscience and the letter of the Apostolic Constitution, which prescribes exactly our procedures. In this way, with the Holy Spirit in our hearts, we cannot fail to do God's will in this most trying and crucial hour in the history of His kingdom on earth."

Nothing Zimmerman said in the homily was a surprise to his colleagues, but he presented the dry facts of process and canonical legalisms with a mellifluous voice and expert rhetorical flourishes. As he stepped away from the lectern, the distinguished Austrian cardinal smiled widely, touching others' hands as he made his way back to his chair.

"Extra omnes!"

With that declaration Carlos Roberto Cardinal Portillo,

the camerlengo, or chamberlain, who had been nominated
by the late pontiff to serve as chief administrator during the
Sede Vacante, ushered the last of the Swiss Guards from
the sealed rooms of the Apostolic Palace. Portillo had previously led a committee of cardinals on a final sweep of
the premises—from the Pauline and Sistine chapels to the
individual apartments opposite St. Peter's where the cardinals would reside for the duration of the conclave—warning all but authorized persons to leave.

The camerlengo and his Particular Congregation of
Cardinals, the committee of three fellow princes chosen by
the Spaniard the day after the pope's death, were accompanied by the conclave architect and a phalanx of security
technicians with electronic detection devices to ensure that
the conclave areas were free of microphones and transmit-
ters; the search party understood the unspoken admonition
that in 1978 there *were* bugs that recorded and broadcast
the supersecret deliberations to interested press and Curial
listeners. Only a handful of special personnel in addition to
the architect (whose role was much reduced by the modern
housing arrangements) and security men would remain with
the 118 cardinal-electors: cooks and dieticians, physicians,
nurses for some of the infirm electors (though none here
were incapacitated), and authorized ecclesiastics (such as
confessors, secretaries, chamberlains, canon lawyers).

The word *conclave* derives from Old Latin: *con* or *cum,*
meaning "with," and *clavis,* meaning "key."

Hence, the aged Spanish cardinal slipped the big brass
lock through the rings on the giant double doors. His hands
trembled slightly as he tried to push it closed, but the old
metal would not give. With a frustrated shrug, he gestured
to his chief of security, and the young Roman stepped over
and gently placed his hands upon the cardinal's, making
certain not to touch the lock himself. Cardinal Portillo drew
in a breath and closed his eyes. As the seventy-nine-year-
old camerlengo, the most senior voting member of the Sacred College, his was the sacred duty to seal off the
conclave from the outside world.

The two men, one a wheezing elder, the other a vigorous
youth, pushed. The creaking shackle slid into place, catch-

ing hold inside the lock with a loud clank. Portillo whispered his thanks to the security officer, who stepped back among the small group of onlookers.

Among those watching from a few yards back was Timothy John Mulrennan. As Cardinal Portillo took a few hobbling steps away from the locked doors, Mulrennan noted that the Spaniard appeared older than many of the even more senior, nonvoting cardinals. Concerned about the old man's health and stamina, he stepped forward to offer his arm.

The Spanish cardinal, a Jesuit who had been ordained almost fifty years ago, looked up at Mulrennan with bright, smiling brown eyes. He gathered his strength, inspired perhaps by the majesty of the moment, and gently patted away the younger man's proffered wrist, and said softly, "*No es necesario* . . . I am fine. *Gracias.*"

"What? Turn away such a gallant act of charity?" someone said from behind Mulrennan. "Why, Carlos, that is like rejecting Our Lord Himself."

Even before turning around, Mulrennan recognized the heavily accented voice as belonging to Cardinal Biagi, the Florentine scholar-diplomat whose finely honed political and rhetorical skills were Curia legend.

"Charity? Or pity for *un cardinale vecchio*?" Portillo replied, blending English and Italian. Like many of his brethren, he shifted easily between tongues. Most spoke Latin and Italian, as well as their native language. And increasingly over the years since the Second Vatican Council, English had become the common denominator, just as it was among the secular diplomatic community.

"The only thing old about you, Carlos, is that poor excuse for a car that still carries you around Madrid."

"Car? Why, I still drive that old Ossa *motocicleta*."

Biagi, an imposing figure with his olive complexion and a thoroughly bald head, wrapped an arm around the shoulder of the camerlengo, completely dwarfing him. "When are you going to get a real automobile? A Porsche, perhaps. Yes, a good Italian sporting car is what you need."

Portillo exposed long yellow teeth as he chuckled. "In my youth, perhaps. In my youth."

"Ah, sweet youth. This is the age for the young, like Timofeo here." He winked at Mulrennan. "Not for two old war horses like ourselves."

Later, after a short, secure motor shuttle to the conclave residence, he guided Portillo through the corridors toward their temporary *cellae*, the apartments that had been drawn by lot and would serve as their homes during the papal conclave. Mulrennan, following closely, marveled at how deftly Biagi had managed to assist the old cardinal while at the same time distracting him so that Portillo did not suspect what he was doing.

They neared the door of the camerlengo's suite, and Biagi turned to Mulrennan. "Will you be in your room? I should like to speak with you before the evening ends."

"Yes," Mulrennan replied.

"Good, I'll pay a visit as soon as Carlos and I finish our talk." He slipped his arm back around Portillo's shoulder and led him toward the door.

Just before they passed inside, Portillo turned and smiled again at the much younger American prelate. Raising his mottled hand, he made the Sign of the Cross in blessing, then disappeared into the room.

As the door closed, Mulrennan was struck by how changed, yet familiar, the Spanish cardinal seemed on this day. Hunched and shrunken by his years of service to the Church, the old, white-haired cleric looked remarkably like his spiritual mentor, the Slavic cardinal elevated to the papacy at the last conclave. It was almost as if, in passing, the late pontiff had temporarily bestowed his mantle upon the frail but capable shoulders of the Archbishop of Madrid, who would safeguard it until the new man was revealed.

Mulrennan turned and walked among a number of others down the indirectly lit corridor and made his way to his own room in the Domus Sanctae Marthae, a $20 million residence for clerical visitors and Vatican empolyees that had been constructed and designated as the conclave residence several years ago—financed largely by the Knights of Columbus. The hundred-plus suites and two dozen single rooms, all with private baths, were not luxurious; however the modern building certainly provided more livable quarters than the jerry-rigged cubicles of past conclaves.

His own single room was more like a motel room than an apostolic apartment. He did not mind; in fact, he preferred the small and spare quarters. He had a narrow single bed that was perhaps half a foot too short for his lanky frame, a plainly upholstered, rather uncomfortable chair by the double-paned slit of a window, and a small writing table, on which lay a lined tablet, since he could not use his familiar laptop here during the time of voting.

His eyes welled with tears. Caught by surprise at the sudden rush of emotion, he dropped into the chair and pressed his palms firmly together. He was not praying—yet; it was a gesture he had acquired in Vietnam, a way to relieve tension. Then he knelt on the wooden prie-dieu by the desk and joined his hands in prayer.

Moments later, a clamor arose outside his door. He stepped into the narrow hallway. "What's happened?" Tim Mulrennan asked of a black priest who whisked past in the corridor like a shadow.

"Cardinal Zimmerman," the young priest answered in English. "He has taken ill." Mulrennan put the accent in east Africa—Kenya?

Tim strode quickly behind the priest toward the staircase. On the floor below a group of men were gathered outside one of the suites. Peering through the open door, Tim saw a medical team moving around inside. Cardinals Pasquale Giannantonio and Pietro La Spina huddled nearby, whispering. Within a few minutes there were forty men, cardinals and conclave staff, crowded shoulder to shoulder. The word spread swiftly among the assembled prelates: Georg Markus Zimmerman had suffered a heart attack.

In a cold, electrically charged silence, the medical attendants wheeled a large sheet-wrapped body out on a lightweight ambulance gurney. The men in the hallway moved aside, as if pushed by an unseen hand. Two physicians emerged from the room. They spoke evenly, solemnly: "The cardinal is dead. We believe it was heart failure, but an autopsy will be required. We are sorry, *Eminenzi,* that this has occurred." Then they were gone.

Mulrennan turned to walk back to his cell, and he saw

another friend of many years' standing, Jaime Edgardo De Guzman, the cardinal-archbishop from Manila. The Filipino prelate stood with his head bowed, hands folded. He looked the picture of silent mourning and loss.

"Jaime," Tim said as he approached the smaller man who wore thick, slightly tinted glasses. The dark brown eyes rose to meet his own. "I am so sorry about this. I don't know what—" Conflicting emotions of grief and confusion rose within him. "Let's talk a bit."

"May we go to somewhere quiet, my friend?" De Guzman asked.

"Sure." He led the cardinal down the hallway toward his room. He wondered what the others, including his fellow American electors, were thinking right now. The obvious, least controversial choice had been removed from the conclave. He was certain that Cardinal Vennholme would manage his grief quickly and efficiently and push La Spina's candidacy powerfully tonight and tomorrow.

Mulrennan had already begun to adapt to this small, freshly painted room that he had been assigned; it was of more than sufficient size to sleep in and spend time in private meditation. He ushered De Guzman inside and closed the door with a soft click. Both men sat.

"Would you care for some coffee, or something stronger to drink? I could call the kitchen."

De Guzman said, "No, Timothy. I am not thirsty." The line of his mouth turned slightly upward. "Except, perhaps, for an answer to our new dilemma."

"I am curious to hear your thoughts on this, Jaime."

"I have none at this time. I was not decided who I would vote for on the first balloting. But I thought Cardinal Zimmerman would have been an excellent choice for us. We need a diplomat and a pastor—a man of experience as well as intellect. It is a difficult job to fill." De Guzman spoke easily in American-style English, thanks to his experience of several years in the States studying and teaching at Catholic universities. He had been a popular instructor in contemporary theology and ecumenism. "And you?"

"The same. It may be the only such vote we cast in our lifetime, in fact it probably will be. That's a lot of pressure

to make the right choice." Mulrennan felt at ease in De
Guzman's calming presence. He could not help but smile.
"It has been much too long since we have seen each other.
And I have promised myself that I would visit your beau-
tiful country."

Mulrennan had never been to the Philippines himself but
hoped one day to see his friend Jaime in his native environment—and perhaps preach a sermon of his own in the
old Spanish-built cathedral in Manila. The closest he had
ever been to the Philippines was Vietnam. "How has it been
for you recently? Any better?"

"During the last years of the Marcos regime, as a bishop—
a lot younger than I am now—I was trying to keep the
churches functioning as the government fell apart. It was a
difficult time for Christians throughout the country. In fact,
it still is, with corruption and chaos in the cities, rebellion
throughout the islands. Democracy has not matured—yet.
In recent time there have been so many problems . . . poorly
prepared priests, intimidation of Catholics in the distant
provinces, military pressure. The poverty in Manila itself
in crushing—overwhelming. I feel inadequate to the job
sometimes."

"Jaime, if all of us had your strength and spirituality,
we'd be in and out of here in a minute, and we'd make the
perfect choice from among a group of perfect men." Mulrennan could identify with the often insoluble problems of
a fellow archbishop. "I admire your commitment."

"Like the Little Flower, St. Therese, I have made the
'decision to love,' to embrace the suffering, my own and
others'. This is not easy, Timothy, as you know. Nor does
it mean that I am any better than any of my priests and
bishops. I have chosen this path for myself, and Jesus is
with me, always, along the way. I have surrendered my will
and my life to the Master, and He comforts and sustains
me when I falter. Every day I want to give up, but He gives
me strength."

Tim Mulrennan listened carefully to De Guzman's words
and held them in his heart. They were simple words on the
surface, but De Guzman was far from a simple man. His
spirituality was like a bright cloak of many colors; it shone

almost gaudily, but the wearer was small and humble within it. Yet he was not without his worldly-wise aspect as well.

Jaime De Guzman had left his large, poor family as a teenager to enter religious life in the Dominican Order of the Philippines. He became known in clerical circles as a skilled scholar and writer at the national seminary, and as a young friar he was snatched up by the then-archbishop in Manila to write press releases and edit the local Catholic newspaper. Father De Guzman honed his skills as a reporter and interrogator of the high and the low. He soon began to move easily within government circles, and he saw the Marcoses in operation up close. Both fascinated and repelled, the young priest learned to keep confidences and to reveal no more than necessary to his own superiors, to trade information for information. The Word as currency, he thought with some amusement.

Those well-learned lessons served him well when he succeeded the Archbishop of Manila at a relatively young age. For his annual Christmas reception he made certain the guest list included both Marcos loyalists and opposition politicians. And it was just about the only place where the two could meet without violence. De Guzman, an accomplished musician, played hymns and carols on the piano and got the warring sides to sing together—for at least one day of the year!

He had shared these memories with Tim Mulrennan over the course of their several meetings, and Tim had laughed at the image of the bespectacled, black-haired former monk hanging out with Ferdinand and Imelda Marcos, arguably the world's most corrupt husband-and-wife political team apart from the Ceausescus of Romania.

"Her feet were the ugliest I've ever seen on a woman—not that I've seen that many," De Guzman told Mulrennan once. "No wonder she was obsessed with shoes! And their relatives were a horror show. . . . Now we have the democrats, Mrs. Aquino, General Ramos, and the like. They are too concerned with what others think of them to become effective despots. It's a pity because the islands are in pure chaos."

De Guzman loved to gossip, but with surprisingly little

malice or harmful effect. Tim suspected he knew a lot more than he ever let on. Just as well—there was more than enough back-stabbing in the Vatican as it was.

"Well," Mulrennan said to his friend's comment about Therese of Liseux's simple spiritual path, "perhaps we will call you the Little Flower of Manila."

Jaime Edgardo Cardinal De Guzman smiled slyly. "And perhaps we shall call you the American Beauty."

Saturday, January 27, 11:10 P.M.

Francis X. Darragh and Father Anthony Ciccone sat at a small back table of a dim, anonymous café a full kilometer from the Vatican where the conclavists were sealed within their quarters before the first day of voting. The two Evangelium Christi members from the U.S. had walked from the Hotel Columbus through the narrow side streets to this place. Ciccone wore a simple black cassock; Darragh black trousers and a dark gray turtleneck, with a black windbreaker. They had arrived before their guest and chosen a suitable secure table that allowed them the widest view of the small room and the front door. There they waited for several minutes as their sweetened espressos cooled.

"Did you see Cardinal Vennholme before the conclave?" Ciccone asked.

"Not in person, but we were able to communicate through other means."

"I thought—" Ciccone was about to comment on the prohibition against electronic communication, but Darragh held up his hand to silence the priest. There was no reason to discuss the details; he did not want to put the priest in an awkward position—any more awkward than he would be in shortly when their guest arrived.

Darragh had met Harry C. Benjamin only once before, some six months previously when he had quietly summoned the tabloid writer to a late-night meeting at the co-op apartment he owned in New York. At that time Darragh had shared a twenty-page typescript that outlined Timothy

Mulrennan's "career of misdeeds" since 1963. This document was the result of the work of several private investigators over a period of many years, and the businessman had carefully filed away those reports and created the summary, finally sharing it with Ciccone before they had departed for Rome for the conclave. From Benjamin, Frank Darragh had elicited an agreement to investigate the allegations on his own, to verify them, and to publish his findings at the appropriate time—a time to be determined by Darragh alone. Under no circumstances would the reporter ever reveal the provenance of his story. In return, the philanthropist granted worldwide rights to Benjamin and arranged to cover the freelance journalist's expenses at a rate of $10,000 U.S., payable monthly. Even more importantly, Darragh promised the reporter an inside source within the conclave and eventually under the new papacy.

"Why?" Ciccone had asked Darragh. Since Mulrennan was far down on anyone's list of papabili.

"For the sake of the Church, Cardinal Vennholme has said that certain enemies must be exposed. Mulrennan is one—he has opposed Evangelium Christi for nearly forty years and shown his contempt for the way of renewal true within the Church. Therefore he is our enemy."

"Won't all this attention benefit Mulrennan?"

"If Benjamin does his job, Mulrennan and his liberal friends will all be discredited for a long time."

"And if Benjamin doesn't come through? . . ."

"You and I will deal with him, Father. And he knows it."

Since last July, Benjamin had already received five "expense payments" of ten thousand each via wire transfer to an Edinburgh bank account. His only communication with the American had been through coded E-mail. With the pope's passing and the conclave about to commence, Darragh would deliver the sixth check drawn on a French bank face-to-face, with Ciccone as a witness, to impress upon Benjamin precisely what he was to do. It was not a meeting he had originally sought, but the reporter had forced the issue and Darragh had finally agreed. Now he would leverage it to his own advantage. The impending confrontation had gotten his blood pumping, just like in the old days when he was building his business empire. He was so close to achieving his ultimate goal.

The philanthropist straightened as the café door opened and a tall, florid-faced man entered and came sauntering toward him. Benjamin was the pinkest man Darragh had ever encountered. Darragh wondered whether such skin color could be caused by overexposure to flourescent light or perhaps from a too-heavy diet of rare lamb, or high blood pressure. Certainly the London-based New Zealander was no outdoorsman—not the wheezy, lanky, slouching creature in an oversized tattered Burberry trenchcoat who sat down on the other side of the wobbly table.

By way of greeting, Darragh withdrew a plain white envelope containing the money from his pocket and slid it across the table. The reporter stroked it with his pink fingers before squirreling it away somewhere inside his tentlike coat.

Darragh felt distinctly unclean, and he was unhappy that the priest was seeing this transaction, but he felt he had no other choice. Ciccone had to witness the transaction and be able to identify the reporter. Besides, Benjamin had made it clear in his most recent E-mail communication—obliquely, even politely—that the businessman would be wise to agree to this meeting before the conclave voting got under way.

"It is dangerous for us both for me to be seen with you."

"You have no choice—too late, mate." The exposure of long tobacco-yellowed teeth proclaimed the journalist's self-satisfaction, even as he eyed the young American priest with practiced skepticism. "You are my 'sources close to the Curia,' if you know what I mean."

"Tell me what you want," Darragh said. For this captain of American commerce, the meeting with Benjamin was inappropriate and humiliating. But, God help him, it was a risk he had chosen to take, even if it put him in a position that he did not control. He lifted off his glasses and rubbed his eyes.

"You gotta help me tie up a few loose ends, Mr. Darragh. Such as—the cardinal's brother. I put a man on him and he came up with a whole sackful of nothin'. I mean, he doesn't live with another bloke, doesn't sleep around or even have a steady." Harry Benjamin winked. "If you know what I mean. But—I'm sure you don't." His eyes slid back and forth between Darragh and Father Ciccone.

Darragh shifted in his chair, looked around the dark café. "What should I tell you?"

"Well, you put me on to the faggot—but there's no *there* there, if you know what I mean. Now, if the big man himself were—"

"He condoned, even encouraged, this young man in a life of sin. That is wrong in itself, especially for a minister of the Gospel. If there's no recent homosexual manifestation by the brother, then I am more hopeful for his soul, if not the cardinal's."

"Sure you are. Now, my people have tracked down the woman, she lives in Budapest, but I've not got her whole story yet. Can you tell me more about her?"

"I cannot. It is all in the report—their affair when he was bishop of Jackson City, all of it. You must work with the information that I have already provided, as well as the substantial financial resources."

"You're not being very much help, Mr. Darragh, if you know what I mean."

"I am not in a position to *help* you at all, at this point. I approached you, provided some basic information, a lead on a good story. A story that could make your career, such as it is. It is your job to ferret out the details and tell that story."

Benjamin sat back and squinted at the Americans who both sat stiffly across the small table. The reporter's late wife had often accused him of being too vain to wear glasses, too cheap to buy contact lenses. A sandy forelock swung over his eyebrow. "Don't play me for a fool, mister—or a ferret, as you put it. I have thus far avoided looking into *your* private life. But who's to say I won't before this is over?"

Darragh drew in a calming breath as he felt Ciccone shift tensely beside him. When he spoke, it was with condescension rather than anger: "I am paying *you*, sir." The philanthropist observed the New Zealander's complexion: it flushed from pink to scarlet. "I don't care what you think of me or write about me. You should look to the condition of your own immortal soul."

Darragh rose and dropped a wrinkled paper napkin onto the table. His espresso remained untouched.

"Tomorrow morning they begin voting in the conclave. Your story will be ready for release when you receive the signal we have agreed upon. My name will appear nowhere in any article nor on any broadcast. And should you receive no signal, then no story will be filed. Are we clear on this?"

The reporter just stared at him. From his expression it was apparent the meeting was not going as he had planned. "You don't know jack-diddly what I've got on my own— on you or some of the others. Like the high-and-mighty Cardinal Vennholme, for instance. I know he's your mate, and he's got a stake in all this."

"I know more than you think, Mr. Benjamin. I know that your threats are baseless, and I do not fear for Cardinal Vennholme in the least. I also know that you've already uncovered more than enough information to write the story. And don't think I am not sympathetic to your situation. That is why I have brought this."

Surprising both Ciccone and Benjamin, Darragh withdrew a second envelope and tossed it onto the table in front of the man. "Don't open it here. It's ten thousand in cash. And when this business is done, you'll receive an additional one hundred thousand dollars U.S.—provided you have fulfilled your commitment exactly as originally agreed. That is one hundred thousand to you, without anyone else's involvement or knowledge—whether I tell you to run the story or to bury it forever."

"Two hundred fifty U.S.," Benjamin said without emotion.

"One fifty and not a dollar more."

Harry Benjamin scowled. He had hoped for a lot more and knew the American could afford it, but he had pushed

Darragh to the outer limit. Darragh slid his chair back as if to leave.

"Just another minute, Mr. Darragh."

As Benjamin gestured, Darragh focused on the reporter's long pink hands and his dirty fingernails. Forcing himself to look away, he sat again, cradled the small cold white cup in his own clean hands.

"Tell me who is going to win," Benjamin said bluntly. He saw Ciccone blanch as if he had been slapped.

Frank Darragh said, "I have no idea. God will govern the choice of the conclave."

"And you are His campaign finance manager."

"You give me both too much and too little credit. My purpose in employing your dubious services, Mr. Benjamin, is to ensure only one thing: that the Archbishop of Newark is exposed to the world as a fraud, unworthy of the cardinal's red hat. Within the conclave, I have no influence whatever. I have no vote to cast, no voice, no presence. I trust that the Holy Ghost will lead the men who have that responsibility."

"Your man Vennholme is playing a cagey game. He has given lip service to Fallaci of Venice and a couple of others but he and his cohorts are really supporting La Spina, former Grand Inquisitor, lately the Terror of Turin. They will tolerate Zimmerman, but they don't trust him—because they don't control him. Is that not so?"

"You are misinformed, I'm afraid," Darragh said.

The tabloid reporter flashed his dingy smile. "As prefect of the Congregation for the Doctrine of the Faith, Pietro La Spina was responsible for the enforcement of dogma and the abolition of so-called heresies. As Archbishop of Turin, he has imposed a strict diocesan regime, reversing decades of moderate-to-liberal Church governance by his immediate predecessors. He was—and remains—a strong supporter of the Evangelium Christi movement, and a close personal friend of Cardinal Vennholme. It is rumored throughout this city that La Spina's election will mean Cardinal Vennholme is appointed to be Secretary of State." The reporter sat back in his chair, his eyes shifting between Darragh and the young priest, smugly pleased with his own analysis of the conclave.

"Hateful, twisted garbage put out by enemies of the Holy Church. Henry Vennholme is a holy man with God in his heart and a clear vision for the future of the Church." Frank Darragh stood again. "You will receive a final lump-sum payment of one hundred fifty thousand dollars one month after the new pope's installation. I needn't reiterate all the terms of our contract, Mr. Benjamin, especially our understanding that your sources shall *never* be disclosed. We both understand the risks we have taken. We are on the same side, as it were—not enemies."

"You and me—gotta love it." Benjamin drummed a pen on his leg. "I wonder one thing—well, a lot of things, but—why me, Mr. Darragh? I mean, why not the legitimate press? To say that you have enough connections is an absurd understatement. And your personal involvement—even as an unnamed source—would guarantee full coverage."

It was a question Anthony Ciccone had also asked when Darragh had first presented the plan. Why release the news in a disreputable supermarket tabloid rather than a respected news source such as the *New York Times* or a broadcast network like ITN in London? The answer was simple. The so-called legitimate press would not break the story on Darragh's timetable, though they would pick up the "news" from the pages of the tabloid: the story about the story, the American cardinal and his foreign whores. And that would be more than enough . . . better, in fact, for it created just the right patina of sleaze that served Frank Darragh's and Cardinal Vennholme's purpose. When the cardinals emerged from the conclave, after Vennholme did his work inside, Mulrennan's fate would be doubly and forever sealed.

"That's a good question. You figure out the answer." Darragh consulted his cheap watch. "Wait fifteen minutes before leaving."

He dropped a few thousand-lira notes on the table as Father Ciccone moved away, and both men disappeared in a whisper of black.

When Darragh returned to his hotel suite well past midnight he heard the news on the television: Cardinal Zimmerman of Austria was dead. The cause of Evangelium Christi had been advanced by the very hand of God!

CHAPTER THREE

Sunday, January 28, 12:06 A.M.

Timothy Mulrennan pushed the straight-backed chair from the desk in his room in the Domus Sanctae Marthae. Approaching the narrow window, he looked outside, but night blanketed the city beyond the Apostolic Palace and he could see nothing. *God, how I want a cigarette!* he thought, not bothering this time to castigate himself for taking the Lord's name in vain. He could understand how God could create tobacco with its attendant pleasures and terrible consequences, but why did He have to make it so damn near impossible to quit?

It had been almost eleven years since he had enjoyed his last smoke. Correct that—had *not* enjoyed the last smoke. Still, the craving was there, a devilish creature he must endlessly battle but never conquer, must forever hold at bay. Prayer was a wonderfully effective weapon in the battle, and he used it. Most days he hardly thought of smoking, and when the pull came, it quickly passed. Then there were those incredibly dark nights—especially when he traveled long distances or faced a momentous decision, such as the one that lay ahead.

Mulrennan pressed two fingers to each temple, gently massaging the skin and murmuring a prayer. The addictive urge would pass within a minute or two, he knew. It always did. This had been God's gift to him, a little miracle in his life. He truly felt that stopping the nasty, destructive habit was the purest and most difficult thing he had accomplished—with His help—in a long time.

The cigarette urge melted away. His mind swirled with thoughts and recollections: Rome in autumn, bicycle-clogged Saigon during the war, Washington ablaze in cherry blossoms and intrigue, his heady seminary days when he felt full of the Spirit, parachute-jump training in Georgia, burned-out Newark slums one long-ago summer, wet cobbled back alleys in Berlin, his mother's troubling perfume-and-beer aroma, the dark old abbey in the desert, the mysterious cadence of the Latin Mass, the beautiful woman who had possessed him, body and soul, for what seemed now the merest blink of an eye—random but unified experiences that had shaped him and brought him to this cold, small room in the heart of an ancient empire.

Whenever he needed to sort out such thoughts, he turned to his journal, and he did so now, replacing the chair at the writing desk and flipping over a page on the writing pad. He missed his laptop, damn it; he was spoiled for good. He sat silently and still, pen hovering above the pages as if in supplication, waiting for the words to come.

The pope is dead . . . the next man will soon be chosen. I rejoice when I should be sad. I rejoice because I know that there is something in this event, this process, that summons joy to my heart. Not in death, but in life. The remarkable man I knew for so long has finally journeyed home: the man who accepted the mantle of St. Peter in sacred succession to many others.

Who will it be? The men of the past century who have put on the ring of Peter and the mantle of Sorrow have been so very different each from the other—until that moment when they searched their souls to accept the vote of their peers as the will of God. Then they became forever identified as brothers in history, and in spirit.

In the beginning and in the end, the sovereign pontiff is a mere priest, a servant of the servants of God. He has made the choice early in his life to accept many mysteries and to proclaim them as the revealed doctrines of his Church. He has undertaken a sometimes arduous life of faith: a belief in the ultimate perfectibility of every living human being. He is destined to die a failure in the eyes of most men. But in

God's eyes? That is the difference, I think.

In the beginning and in the end, the priest is a man. He is born of flesh and lives in the condition of humanity, as Jesus did. He is no different, though his vocation will take him perhaps to different places than other men. The priest is ever subject to God the Father. Is it not the same for all of us?

Mulrennan looked up from the writing pad. He was thinking of his own ordination, which now seemed a millennium ago. The Cathedral of the Sacred Heart in Newark, lately designated a basilica by His Holiness, had glowed with a spirit of sanctity that spring day: May 16, 1963. He had awakened with huge fluttering butterflies in his stomach. There was no reason to be afraid, to regret, to doubt—he had dealt with all of those emotions in the last few months before ordination—yet the magnificent reality of this final step, this time-honored sacrament, hit him full force as he faced the beautiful bright day.

Yes, he had been so full of hope and faith on that day he became a priest. And the intensity and honesty of that moment when he lay prostrate on the marble floor of the sanctuary as he took his sacred vows had never really abandoned him.

I still cling to St. Paul's three greatest virtues, because I must: to believe, to hope, and to love. There are those among my fellows who have accused me of naïveté, of dangerous theological error, when I try to 'keep it simple' (as my spiritual friends in AA put it).

He halted again, recalling the harsh reaction a few years earlier to his call for dialogue among American Catholics of divergent opinions in order to discover common ground and decrease growing polarization among hierarchy, clergy, religious, and laity. He had accepted the criticism, yet pushed the project forward. A series of meetings in Trenton, Minneapolis, and Sacramento had revealed that differences were deep and wide and that it would require prayer, tolerance, and hard work to bridge those differences before they became open schisms. Issues of abortion, sexuality, celibacy, the ordination of women, the role of laypeople in the liturgy and Church governance. He had attempted to mediate the discussions, with the cooperation of local bishops. Acrimony and mistrust seethed near the surface at each meeting. A schism within the American Church, or between the United States and Rome—his worst fear—had never seemed so possible.

Timothy John Cardinal Mulrennan shuddered involuntarily. The dark thought surfaced without warning. "No!" he blurted aloud. Unable to bear the sight of such words, he scratched out the offending sentence.

"And why not, Timofeo?" a voice asked, and Mulrennan turned to see Cardinal Biagi standing in the open door.

"Eavesdropping, Allo?" Mulrennan muttered with a forced smile. He quickly wrote the last few words in his mind, then put the pen down.

"They say the last conclave was bugged. Journalists had paid sources inside. Doesn't anyone know how to keep his mouth shut anymore?"

"I have read some of the books about 1978. A hotbed of intrigue, if the writers can be believed."

"A significant 'if.' May I enter?"

"Of course." Mulrennan stood and turned his chair, gesturing for Biagi to sit in a reading chair opposite.

"And may I close the door?" the older cardinal asked, doing so without waiting for a reply.

The two men sat comfortably, facing each other. There was a long pause as Biagi appraised his American colleague. Mulrennan finally broke the silence by saying, "And how is your health, Allo?"

"Forget my health. My people live into their hundreds." Biagi gave a dismissive wave. "I am here to talk about you."

"Me?" Mulrennan was genuinely curious and well aware that anything was possible with such a man as Leandro Biagi, whose pedigree included Medicis, Borgias, princes, counts, cardinals, thieves, nuns, and more than a few courtesans.

Biagi stared into the night. "Our best candidate has been

taken from us. Was it God—or was it man's doing?"

"Certainly you don't think this was foul play?" Tim Mulrennan protested.

"I do not know what to think, my friend," Biagi said with anger in his voice; he touched his throbbing temples. "I shall be blunt. I have been polling our brothers following the congregations—which I have found boring to the extreme. I do not know how you feel. . . ."

He referred to the General Congregations or quasi-legislative meetings that had been held over the previous days in the ornate Sala Bologna of the Apostolic compound in which the cardinals finalized preparations for the conclave and conducted the business of the Vatican, as prescribed by canon law, in consultation to the camerlengo's Particular Congregation.

"I trust you understand how momentous this conclave is," Biagi continued.

"But of course," Mulrennan replied cautiously, curious as to why the master politician would say something so obvious and elementary. His probing was surprisingly unsubtle.

"How truly important, Timofeo . . . for each of us and for Holy Mother Church." He folded his brown, manicured hands. "My brethren are anxious."

Mulrennan felt the elder prelate's eyes boring in on him. His mind raced as he tried to guess the purpose of this visit. Biagi most likely wanted his support for a particular papal candidate. The savvy seventy-four-year-old archbishop was extremely popular among the cardinals and no doubt would wield enormous influence, especially with the block of nine non-Curial—that is, the ones who were not considered rigid archconservatives—fellow Italians who would hold the key to the final outcome. No doubt Biagi wished to be a *grande elettore* or "great elector," one of the few important ecclesiastical politicians in modern history who wield the power to influence the outcome of a papal election. In olden days such great electors represented the interests of European monarchs; today they were, if anything, more like campaign managers. And in this campaign, obtaining Timothy

Mulrennan's support might help bring on board some of the other North Americans.

"Your name was mentioned more than once in our discussions, Timofeo."

"My name?" Mulrennan shook his head in genuine bafflement.

Biagi smiled. "Don't be such a little boy about this. Surely you have given the idea some thought. Some consideration."

"I'm afraid I don't follow."

The Florentine assumed a mock frown, and he let out an audible sigh. "You need to be more . . . how do I say it in English?—more *astuzia,* more cunning—politically, I mean—if you are going to be our pope."

Mulrennan heard the words, but somehow they did not register in his brain.

"Yes, my son, your name is being mentioned. I took an informal poll, and I believe you are electable, if not the most likely of choices."

There was another long silence, broken by Tim Mulrennan. "I don't believe it for ten seconds, Allo. I don't think I am the best man for the job, and further, I don't want it."

"This is not a job, or at least none like any other. It is a calling of the Holy Spirit. And if you are in fact called—"

"No one is calling me. Maneuvering, perhaps. This—this is utterly preposterous."

"Modesty and lack of ambition become you greatly, Your Eminence. But you make a campaign manager's job much more difficult."

"There is no campaign," Mulrennan said. "You are playing a game of solitaire. Of course I am flattered and grateful that anyone—you especially—should consider me in such a light. But this preconclave maneuvering is absolutely meaningless."

"Listen, I am speaking with seriousness now. You would be a more than acceptable compromise candidate among the non-Italian Europeans, the North Americans, with perhaps some exceptions, and the South Americans. By that I mean a strong second choice of nearly one-half of the College. But of course, initially, two-thirds is required for election, unless we are deadlocked over several days and go to the fifty-percent-plus-one rule. For the Koreans, Japanese, Chinese, and Southeast Asians, as well as most of the Africans—together substantially more than one-fourth of the total vote—and a few of the open-minded Italians like myself, you are a more or less solid third choice. Not that we can expect all the nationalities to vote solidly alike. The Curial group, of course, is the one you're unlikely to crack, but they now comprise less than twenty-five percent."

"All very interesting, but you haven't polled the most crucial elector—me. And I rate my chances as close to nil and my desire at less than that. Why, even if I were to be seriously considered, I am far too unconventional, even moderate."

"Yes, your so-called moderate positions have won you some Curialist enemies, and no friends in the Evangelium Christi faction. But probably even more of us are potential votes, thanks to your middle-of-the-road, pastoral image." A Machiavellian smile played at Biagi's lips. "I sense that this conclave will be less influenced by conservatives than our late Holy Father would have liked."

"Why do you say that? He personally elevated well over ninety percent of the eligible electors of the College."

"It is very like what can happen on your American Supreme Court." Biagi lifted both hands and shrugged expressively. "The justice appointed for his impeccable ideological credentials may veer in the opposite political direction, or at least temper his once-vehement attitudes. The world looks astoundingly different from a sinecure on the judicial bench—or from the Sistine Chapel."

"But these men are less politicians or ideologues than men of faith," Mulrennan argued. "Their faith may waver or strengthen over time, but they are committed to bedrock values and beliefs—as am I."

"True, of course, Timofeo. But you have demonstrated the flexibility to operate on a wider stage, beyond the secretariats and prefectures where we insiders wield such considerable, albeit chimerical powers. You are a true 'hinge' of the Church, as we cardinals were once created to be.

Among electors with whom I have spoken directly, there is a universal respect for the quality of your faith and your achievements in building consensus in the States."

Mulrennan gently remonstrated his friend. "Allo, we are not going to elect an American pope. Period. One day, perhaps. But we are still close to the age of the cold war and the superpowers, and our American Church, for all its size and many strengths, is not a picture of harmony; it is mired in disunity and controversy."

"Which you have addressed most effectively in your national bishops' conference."

"Not effectively enough. I'd wager that I will receive little consideration and only one or two renegade votes—if any—from my own American colleagues in the conclave."

"I am tempted to take you up on that wager, my Lord Cardinal."

"I withdraw my bet, but only because this is all foolishness. It is sillier even to consider the notion. Pope Timofeo the First?" He chuckled with Biagi. "It's a joke, right?"

Biagi leaned forward and reached toward him, touched his arm. "Listen to me, *amico,* I am not joking. I believe that on the first few ballots each will vote his—how do you call it?—his 'favorite son,' and you will receive only token consideration. But if by the fourth or fifth ballot one of those starters does not emerge as the *one,* then you may have a chance."

"You make it sound like a horse race."

"It is God's horse race, perhaps? Just hear me out, in all seriousness, my friend," Biagi pressed, leaning in toward Mulrennan's face. "I think you can imagine that your stiffest adversary would be your fellow North American, our dearest Cardinal Vennholme."

Mulrennan felt an involuntary shudder, and for an instant he imagined himself going head-to-head with Henry Martin Cardinal Vennholme, the former papal nuncio to the United States and once his indirect superior. Vennholme, originally from Montreal and now a senior member of the Congregation for the Doctrine of the Faith (*Congregatio pro Doctrina Fidei*), founded in the thirteenth century by Pope

Innocent III as the Holy Office of the Inquisition, also was moderator of the conservative lay religious society Evangelium Christi. He and Tim Mulrennan had long been at odds over just about every aspect of the Church's role in society at large. While Mulrennan could not take seriously the notion of becoming pope, he could not deny that Vennholme's reaction to such an event was delicious to imagine.

"Vennholme has no illusions about becoming pope himself," Biagi continued. "Too much *bagagli,* too much baggage. And far too many enemies, even within that hothouse of a Curia. But he and his Curial allies and that whole Evangelium crowd will push us to accept one of our brilliant Italian politicians, and the idea will be *molto simpatico* to many. Don't fool yourself—our Santo Papa was universally respected, if not loved, but there are many who now wish the throne returned to Italy. To them, you would be another 'great experiment,' one that some may worry will not turn out as well as the last."

"I have no desire to be anyone's experiment . . . nor, for the last time, to be pope."

"Then you and I will be the ones with much to worry about, for I do not trust Vennholme. He does not realize that the Church needs a shepherd, not a chief inquisitor. God alone will judge his motives in this conclave, but I fear the very worst. And I fear what he may be doing right now to damage you and other papabili. He is focused on two Curial favorites: La Spina of Turin and Fallaci of Venice. With names like those being advanced, I pray daily that we electors will be freely and truly inspired in our deliberations by the holiest influence of the Holy Spirit."

"Allo, I am honored by your trust, truly I am," Mulrennan said softly, his voice on the edge of cracking, "but I must ask that you desist in promoting me in any way. Let Vennholme lay out his hand. He will get caught in his own machinations; we need not play his game."

"This is no game, my Timofeo." Biagi stood to his full height and looked down intensely at the seated younger cardinal. "You are not being put forward as a pawn in some ecclesiastical chess match. Don't confuse strategy with ob-

jective. I may focus on the former, but we all must trust
that the Holy Spirit alone will, in the fullness of time, reveal
the latter. And when I hear the various names being mentioned, yours rings on their lips with a far different authority—a higher one."

Mulrennan opened his mouth to speak, to object, but the
breath would not come. His thoughts wavered between disgust and fear.

"Timothy," Biagi said, using Mulrennan's full Christian
name. "Our best hope of stopping La Spina has been taken
from us. I do not wish to see plots and conspiracies where
there are none, but I cannot help feeling there is something
amiss here. It has the odor of criminality. There will be an
autopsy, of course, but not until we have begun voting.
Have the evil Borgias risen from their graves to poison the
Church once more?"

"I think you exaggerate, Allo. Zimmerman was never a
certainty as our choice. No one is until the ballots have
been cast. You will accuse me of naïveté, I know, but truly
I do not believe there has been any foul play here. How
could it be? There have been whispers of bad health—yes,
perhaps rumors planted by his opposition. That does not
signify a plot against him."

Tim Mulrennan looked at his watch. It was nearly 1:00
A.M. There was a lousy unfamiliar taste in his mouth. Zimmerman murdered? No—that was the wildest kind of speculation. But, he knew, those who saw Vatican conspiracies
in every corner of the Apostolic Palace would assume foul
play. He recalled the fevered speculations surrounding the
sudden death of Pope John Paul I; there had been volumes
of circumstantial evidence and speculation and adding two
plus two to make five. He had never bought into the notion
of murder. Was he in denial? Did such things happen in
the twenty-first century? With a wealthy temporal as well
as spiritual kingdom at stake, certainly men were capable
of high crimes—but murder of a pope-to-be within the Vatican itself? He simply could not accept such a scheme, unless it were conclusively proven. The autopsy would answer
such questions.

"Well," Biagi continued with a rueful smile, "you said

it—I did not. You Americans are isolated to a great degree from the worst of Curial machinations. I doubt that anyone—even La Spina's staunchest allies—would dare to eliminate a candidate, even one they hated, by killing him. They probably prayed that this would happen. It proves to them that God is on their side."

"Eminenza, please stop this. We must pray for Zimmerman's soul and for those of us who remain. There are one hundred seventeen men who have a very difficult duty now. I wish to God this hadn't happened . . . oh, Jesus, that we might turn back the clock twenty-four hours! But we can't, can we?"

"There is something I must ask you, Timofeo, and you must search your own soul. It matters not whether Zimmerman was taken from us by natural or foul means. As you say, we must march forward for the sake of the Holy Church. How would you respond if you were to receive several votes on the first ballot of this conclave? I dare say it is likely now. In fact, I will cast *my* vote for you."

"It will cancel out my vote for you," Mulrennan said.

Cardinal Biagi stepped closer to the American. Tim could smell the mingling scents of incense and cologne emanating from the sophisticated Italian politician. Biagi bored into him with those brown-black eyes that had seen so much—too much, perhaps—in fifty years of service in the Church of the apostles. What would those Gallilean fishers of men say if they were here? The thought made Tim Mulrennan, the devout scholar-athlete from New Jersey, want to laugh aloud. But Biagi's gaze drew him into the intrigue of the present hour.

"Listen to me, my friend. We need you to stand up to La Spina and Vennholme and the others. Do not let your piety hinder your actions. You will not be alone. I, and many others, will stand with you."

"You make it sound like a war."

"It is, of a kind. Yes—a war for the soul of the Church herself."

His mind wheeled and raced through the scenarios of the next few days, trying to encompass and understand the possibilities, none of which included the election of Tim

Mulrennan. The late pontiff's saintly image, which had inhabited his dreams and waking hours, was a shadowy presence in the room, as if standing behind Cardinal Biagi; Tim did not actually see him, but felt the power of his love for the ancient Church of Rome. In whatever might transpire within this conclave, Mulrennan prayed that he would not betray the pope's charge to God's people: to preserve and nurture the Mystical Body of Christ.

Biagi came from the school of Curial bureaucracy and Italian politics that dated to the pontificate of Pius XII, during and after the war years. Though only one pope since 1958—Paul VI—could be said to be a product of the Curia itself (John, despite his diplomatic service, and the two John Pauls were definitively not), the institution perpetuated itself in the way of bureaucracies the world over. The men bound to the Roman Curia and like institutions marched forward, ever forward, to build and protect and empower their offices and to select their successors who would ensure the survival of the system. To what end? Self-preservation, purely and simply. It was a story as old as mankind; it would continue until destroyed by cataclysm. Even good men, such as Leandro Biagi, perpetuated such a system by their challenges to it, for they fought from within, with no intention of destroying it, only making it stronger and more pliant to their will to change.

Could evil exist within the hearts of men and women who professed to follow the teachings of Jesus? Did corruption exist within the walls of the holy capital of Christendom itself? Of course, Tim would be naïve in the extreme if he believed otherwise. History gave him the answer. Yet he always wanted to believe the best of others, to believe in the power of salvation.

Biagi had to take only two steps to reach the door. He pulled it open, then hesitated there. "Think on my words, Timofeo." He raised an elegant hand to forestall a reply. "Just think on it. And pray, my Lord Cardinal. Pray for understanding. Pray for us all."

Several minutes after Cardinal Biagi had departed, Tim Mulrennan was still seated on the wooden chair, staring at the closed door. His thoughts, which lately had run riot through him, came unexpectedly slow and deliberate. A strange sensation filled his heart, a fullness he could not describe. He wanted to laugh, to cry, to be back in the familiar surroundings of daily life back home, closer to his family, back to the often dull routine and tedious headaches that awaited him there. Anywhere but here.

In a state of near-unconsciousness, Timothy Mulrennan slid to the floor. Facing the bed on his knees, he bent his head over clasped hands, the way he had done each night as a child, the way the nuns at school had taught him.

"Protect and forgive your children, dear Father, that we may elect a truly Christ-like shepherd . . . that we may open our hearts and recognize through the guidance of the Holy Spirit the one You have anointed in heaven to lead us. Amen."

His eyes welled with tears, and he dropped into the chair and pressed his palms firmly together to relieve the almost unbearable tension he now felt.

Yes, he thought ruefully, he would gladly trade this relatively commodious room for the cramped one-man tent in which he had slept just a month before at a Boy Scout winter camp-out with his old troop from Our Lady of Mercies Parish, a rare but necessary time away from the constant press of diocesan duties. He would trade it all—his cardinal's red biretta, the honor of serving in this historic conclave, the awesome responsibilities of being an archbishop—if he could return to that campground near the Delaware Water Gap in western New Jersey and somehow stop that call from finding him, stop the news that would change his life in ways he could not yet imagine, stop the years from aging and finally taking their beloved Holy Father and leader. God's will . . . what could it be? He knelt on the prie-dieu to pray.

It was impossible to turn back the clock, but he could remember—and he did remember . . . as if it were just yesterday and he was newly ordained as a priest of God.

Rome, September 19, 1963

In opening the second session of the Ecumenical Council, His Holiness Paul VI—elected in a June conclave after the passing of Pope John—addressed a lengthy homily to his vision of the council's mission.

The nearly 2,500 Council Fathers were arrayed before him in special tiers that had been built along the sides of the great hall of worship. These men, from each continent and every major urban center on the planet, were the field generals and governors who led the pontiff's spiritual legions and provided for his people in the farflung provinces of a latter-day empire.

Paul, now sixty-six years old, almost frail looking beneath the huge jeweled papal miter, with deep-set dark eyes beneath heavy brows that sometimes twitched nervously, intoned: "O dear and venerated Pope John, may gratitude and praise be rendered to you for having resolved, doubtless under divine inspiration, to convoke this Council in order to open to the Church new horizons, and to tap the fresh spring water of the doctrine and grace of Christ Our Lord and let it flow over the earth."

Montini's plaintive scholar's voice, amplified through a system of concealed public address speakers, soared through the gigantic cruciform nave of Christendom's greatest monument. Hope and faith swelled within the young man from New Jersey as he sorted the theological and practical meanings of the carefully phrased address.

"The view of the world fills us with crushing sadness because of so many other evils. Atheism is pervading part of the human race and is bringing in its wake the derangement of the intellectual, moral, and social order, the true notion of which the world is losing. While the light of the science of nature is increasing, darkness is spreading over the science of God and in consequence over man's true science. While progress is perfecting in a wondrous way every kind of instrument that man uses, his heart is declining toward emptiness, sadness, and despair."

The pope's discourse, delivered in Latin, was so
lengthy—over one hour—that before he had finished reading it into the microphone held before him, at least half of
the noncouncil crowd in the church had discreetly drifted
out. Paul explained that he meant the address to be considered the equivalent of his first encyclical letter: "Let this
present address be a prelude not only to the council but
also to our pontificate."

In the early evening, Tim Mulrennan accompanied Archbishop Thomas Boland of Newark to a cocktail affair at the
home of an elderly Roman senator with a young wife, who
had, it was whispered, displaced both an aging spouse and
a longtime mistress. The world was indeed changing. The
archbishop immediately found his level and left Tim to fend
for himself. Again the observer, Father Mulrennan watched
the clerics and nobles swirl through the room as white-
gloved waiters balanced trays of hors d'oeuvres and champagne at their shoulders.

A thrill of experience coursed through his mind and body
as he looked across this salon full of powerful prelates and
politicians.

Monsignor Henry Martin Vennholme's hazel eyes
pierced the old-style frameless spectacles and locked upon
Timothy Mulrennan. Tim acknowledged the gaze of his fellow priest and gently elbowed through the cocktail mob
toward him. He was aware of Vennholme from some Council roster or other, but had never met him; in this closed
world of theological gamesmanship the prominent players—
in Tim's mind, "the starting lineup"—were easily recognized and wisely cultivated. Vennholme, a French-
Canadian in his mid- to late thirties, young for the scarlet
piping of a monsignor, impressed Tim with a cool, firm
handshake and direct manner.

"You are one of Archbishop Boland's young men," he
said. "A fellow North American." The words were friendly,
but there was no hint of a smile on the pale square face.
Intimations of gray touched his temples. "I am Henry
Vennholme, originally from Montreal, attached to the Holy
Office at present, but prepared to be of greater service to
the Council Fathers."

Was there no man in Rome without ambition to be something greater than—or at the very least different from—what he already was? Mulrennan was not unaware of his own ambitions, but was perhaps still young enough to be turned away from such tendencies. Sometimes he wondered about himself: *What are my true motives?* Vennholme of the neatly appointed cassock with the wide magenta silk sash and the perfect, slender black patent leather shoes was, it seemed to the younger man, clearly going places. But where?

"I have read your monograph on the future role of the laity the pastoral life of the Church. Impressive," Tim said.

"Ghost-written for the most part," the monsignor said. "But it reflects exactly my commitment to revivifying the Body of Christ as the Apostle Paul and the early Church Fathers envisioned it. Not necessarily as described in the Holy Father's homily, I might add."

The younger man shifted his posture to signal attentiveness.

After college, Tim Mulrennan had served for two and a half years in the army—years that had sharpened and matured him, and confirmed his desire to enter the priesthood. During his military service in Berlin and Seoul, Tim had acquired the useful and genteel skill of absorbing either scholarship or bombast with equal attentiveness at cocktail and dinner parties. Because he was so tall he stooped his shoulders slightly and inclined his head, watching the speaker's lips, listening hard, and filtering out the surrounding chatter.

As a military attaché—that is, intelligence gatherer—assigned to the American consulate in West Berlin, then the embassy in South Korea, First Lieutenant Timothy J. Mulrennan, detached from the Seventh Signal Corps, Third Army, NATO, had sipped Manhattans and nibbled canapés with some of the most glittering and grotesque personalities in secular diplomacy—all for love of country, he jocularly claimed to his brother Kevin, a combat-savvy Marine Corps captain based in Saigon. He did not like it then, and despised it now, but accepted such "command performances" as a requirement of the job.

"I am flattered that you took time to read it," Vennholme went on, adjusting his glasses by crinkling his nose.

"The Bishops' Committee requires that a digest of all pertinent papers be prepared every few weeks. It's part of my job to read and report on these documents."

"An important job. The Council must have the best and latest documentation. Do you find it interesting?"

"It can be—is, most of the time. The archbishop is very demanding of his staff. I am furthering my education, at least."

"Education, yes. I read somewhere that you attended Yale."

"I did—for two years. My first exposure to the wide wicked world outside New Jersey." Tim Mulrennan smiled, thinking of how far he had come since high school, how much more of the world he had experienced in that time . . . all the way to the Vatican.

"It is an important responsibility for us to preserve that world, which God created and His Son redeemed." Vennholme's eyes narrowed. "Let us continue your education. You must come with me to a meeting tonight. You will be stimulated by our discussion, I think."

"What kind of meeting?" In truth, Mulrennan wanted to go home and crawl into bed to enjoy an extra hour or two of sleep before rising at 4:30 A.M., for prayer, reading the breviary, mass, and another eleven-hour day in the office.

Vennholme glanced at his watch. "If you come with me now we will be only a few minutes late. I will tell you about it on the way." His grim face had lightened and the chilly eyes had warmed at the prospect of a young convert.

"I am very curious, Monsignor, but—"

"I will see that you are home before ten o'clock. Please, Father, it will be worth your effort, I am certain."

The monsignor had a driver who awaited him in a black Lancia parked a few blocks from the senator's residence. He and Tim walked briskly through the crisp September evening to the car. Directly, Vennholme began to outline for Tim Mulrennan the history of the religious organization called Evangelium Christi.

The founder was a middle-aged Franciscan from the Abbey of San Vincenzo outside Perugia who had awakened one Good Friday morning about twenty-five years before with the stigmata.

Fra Giovanni Prignano had left his huge, impoverished family to join the cloistered religious life as a teenager, shortly before the outbreak of World War I, and had exhibited mystic tendencies from his earliest days in the isolated monastery. A fellow monk once claimed to have witnessed the young brother levitating above the trees of the forest. Giovanni never denied, nor did he affirm the story. Others reported their opinion that he was merely a quiet, mildly retarded fellow who wielded a steady hoe and often wept during prayer. Sometimes the abbot of San Vincenzo felt compelled to chastise him for his unseemly fervor when it kept him from his more important chores.

"Work and prayer. Work and prayer," the abbot chided. Giovanni Prignano listened. "Both are needed to build the Kingdom of God."

Fra Giovanni worked hard but prayed even harder, and his reputation as a holy man flourished like ragweed beyond the cloister walls. His superiors and fellow monks grew more tolerant over the years and accommodated the trickle of pilgrims that became a torrent of fame and wealth washing through the monastery. Then appeared the stigmata, and—as one reporter quipped, "All hell broke loose."

With the sacred nail wounds in his hands and feet, and the lance wound below his breast, and the thorn pricks around his head, Fra Giovanni gained the stature of a near-saint. He also received the gift of articulate speech, which he had never before possessed. Like Moses he had been a stammerer and had shied from public discourse of any kind. Now he held forth like a latter-day Savonarola—or perhaps an Italian Billy Graham, as some wags insisted—preaching to visitors from all over the globe on the simple glories of work and prayer.

"Every man and woman belongs wholly to God. Therefore it is theft to take oneself away from God. This is a violation of the First and Fifth Commandments and a mortal sin. The Father put us on the earth as a family to love and serve Him and one another through faith and love. We must help each other remain faithful, and we must look to the Church as our common home. God speaks to us, nurtures us through His Son's holy Church. Shall we not work and pray there?"

Life magazine pictured the tonsured monk on its April 14, 1952, cover.

Paolo Chierico, a Perugian bank owner, became enamored of Fra Giovanni's simple holy message and pledged a large sum to San Vincenzo to help accommodate the influx of pilgrims. One day he sat in private audience with the black-robed mystic.

"Brother, you always say, 'Work and pray, work and pray,' but is there more I can do for the glory of the Lord and my own salvation?"

Giovanni had a great dark brow that bristled aggressively across his forehead above deep-set fiery brown eyes. He inclined his head and scratched at the unruly tangle of gray hair above his ears. "There is much all of us can do, lay clergy, and religious, to affirm the teaching of our Master, Jesus Christ. We can create learning groups among the laity to study and evangelize those whose faith has wavered. All good Catholics are charged to carry the Gospel of Christ's love to their brothers. Perhaps we can help each other in this way."

The first such study cell met a few weeks later, and Signor Chierico was elected lay chairman of Evangelium Christi. Fra Giovanni was named chaplain of the group, and he promised to pray each day for the faithful laity, that they would be granted the grace, strength, and knowledge of God's will in their mission.

The organization's membership exploded throughout Italy, then across Europe. Within three years Paolo Chierico had retired from his bank and begun to direct the movement full-time from an office in the Perugia monastery; he paid for a small staff from his own pocket, but soon contributions from all over the world trickled in. In five years there were twenty Evangelium chapters in the United States and Canada, more than fifty a year later.

The Vatican sent a representative to audit the organization's activities and its finances. Word came back to Rome: in essence, these were good people doing good works of faith. A Vatican charter was issued in 1959, ten years after Evangelium Christi had been born in the minds of Fra Giovanni and Signor Chierico.

Vennholme sat beside Mulrennan in the spacious leather-upholstered rear seat of the limousine. "Fra Giovanni lives in semiretirement at San Vincenzo. Hundreds of thousands of pilgrims have visited him in the past decade, and during Holy Week the stigmata afflict him most severely and render him bedridden. In fact, his health has severely deteriorated in recent years."

"You have met him?" Tim asked, intrigued by the story.

"Many times. I became a pilgrim in 1952—I walked into the presence of a saint. He said few words to me, but I received a powerful blessing from him. I was newly ordained, very much like you. I believed that God spoke to me through this simple, holy man. Since then I have seen him at least a dozen times. I had many lengthy discussions with Signor Chierico, as well. He died just two years ago. Then I formed the first Evangelium chapter in America—at St. Thomas More Parish in St. Louis."

The black auto cruised into the Roman suburbs along narrow·dark roads. Henry Vennholme's narrative captured Tim's imagination: the tale of a modern-day mystic who had sparked a worldwide faith-renewal movement. It was uplifting. He felt somewhat less apprehensive about attending the meeting.

Yet Vennholme's zeal—a seeming obsession that was apparent within moments of meeting the man—stirred suspicion and distaste within Tim Mulrennan. He possessed a natural antipathy toward extremists—religious, political, even sports fans whose teams were unchallengeable paragons of virtue and power—but he told himself to keep an open mind and admit the possibility that he could learn something worthwhile here.

Forty people had gathered in a grim room in the parish

house abutting a church. Gas lamps cast a dim and smoky yellow glow through the room. Mulrennan and Vennholme entered as group business was discussed and resolved: finances, meeting and worship schedules, dress code for Sunday and daily masses, secretarial chores, initiation of new Evangelium members. A local priest presided, acknowledged Vennholme, and announced the evening's primary agenda item: a lecture on the role of women, lay and religious, in Church and society. He called Vennholme to the chair to address the meeting. There was no applause, but stern faces turned to see the visiting cleric.

Vennholme patted Tim on the arm and swept dramatically to the front of the room.

"My brothers and sisters in Christ," Monsignor Vennholme began, speaking in an urbane Roman dialect somewhat elevated, Tim suspected, from the daily speech of these parishioners. "I am grateful to your pastor for his invitation to address you tonight. I, in turn, have invited a young American priest to his first meeting of our Evangelium Christi society. I hope he will discover the love of Our Lord and Savior Jesus Christ in this room." A few heads turned back toward Tim.

For nearly an hour he listened to Vennholme's message on "the special value and unique virtues of Catholic women." It was an old-fashioned paean to marriage, childbearing, service, chastity, humility, and obedience.

"God has selected men to lead and women to follow. His intent, we believe, is for women to temper the excesses of men and to provide them a constant example of virtue. This is what St. Paul teaches us. Further, God intends women to bear the fruit of His creation, just as Mary bore the Son of Man and raised Him to fulfill His mission.

"This divine schema places difficult burdens upon the man. Yes, his shoulders are strong, but at times he must rest from his labors and seek comfort and peace in a home maintained lovingly by the woman. It is no less a sacred challenge for her to be strong when he is weary, and to be submissive when he requires her to be so. Men, pray for your women. And women, serve your men with prayerful hearts."

Monsignor Vennholme stated with conviction, "We here gathered are working and praying for a salvation that will come only to a precious few. The stubborn Jew and the ignorant Muhammadan have not received the full measure of grace that we have, and we should fall to our knees to thank God for His gift to us. The peoples of the earth wander in darkness and only we have the light—in Christ's Gospel—that will show the way to those who believe. 'I am the Light,' He said. Who here will doubt His word?"

A murmur of approbation rippled through the room. Tim felt as if he were overhearing a conversation not intended for his ears. After the heady, affirming, forward-looking words of Pope Paul he had experienced an inspiring surge of energy and commitment: change—challenge to the secular status quo—was a valid, indeed a necessary, aspect of the Gospel.

The Church of this latter half of the twentieth century had assumed the role of Christ's agent of change. The earthy wisdom of Pope John XXIII had been followed, perhaps appropriately, by the worldly, restless intelligence of Pope Paul VI. So-called moderates and liberals outnumbered those who were deemed conservatives and reactionaries among the Council Fathers by a solid voting majority.

Pope John had said, at the opening session the previous year: "The greatest concern of the Ecumenical Council is this: that the sacred deposit of Christian doctrine should be guarded and taught more efficaciously. That doctrine embraces the whole of man, composed as he is of body and soul. And, since he is a pilgrim on this earth, it commands him to tend always toward heaven."

Sound Catholic theology with a definite "edge" to it, making it clear to Tim Mulrennan and to most observers which way the wind was blowing. *It was time for change. Aggioruamento.* Reform. Modernization. Unity among all Christian denominations. Again, he recalled the late pope's address last October, which he had read many times since: "In calling this vast assembly of bishops, the latest and humble successor of the Prince of the Apostles who is addressing you intended to assert once again the Church's magisterium (teaching authority), which is unfailing and perdures until the end of time, in order that this magisterium, taking into account the errors, the requirements, and the opportunities of our time, might be presented in exceptional form to all men throughout the world." These words had caused him, as a young priest, to be swept up in the spirit of the council. Yet here, in this cramped dark parish house that seemed so far from the blazing nave of St. Peter's, a very different language was being spoken by Monsignor Vennholme:

"Our True Church is the holy repository of God's grace. You will not find the Holy Spirit in a grimy synagogue or an overheated Methodist meeting house. To suggest otherwise is blasphemy. We here must dedicate ourselves to preserving the purity and purpose of the revealed Gospel as preached by the apostolic Church."

Vennholme's words bored into Mulrennan's mind like the unceasing tattoo of a military drummer. The deep shadows of a dark distant age—perhaps not as distant as one had thought—fell upon the small assembly. For that moment Father Tim Mulrennan questioned whether he had really heard those words or only interpreted them incorrectly. His face burned with anger and embarrassment.

"Brethren, I predict with unshakable conviction based on my faith in God's Church that the wicked men who seek to corrupt Christ's teaching authority and change His words to suit their misguided, even socialistic view of man's needs will be stopped before they can do any real damage to us.

"Their salvation is in jeopardy, but we shall not allow them to take *us* through the gates of hell with them. Our eyes shall always and ever be fixed on heaven, our hearts on the Virgin Mother of God, our thoughts and deeds upon Christ Himself. He did not fail us through His life, death, and resurrection. We shall not fail Him in this dark hour when the enemies of faith are gathering their strength to make war upon the faithful."

Before the meeting ended, Mulrennan slipped outside to smoke a much-needed cigarette. A blue three-quarter moon shone through the interwoven branches of a stand of olive trees. He then rode in resounding, painful silence with Monsignor Henry Vennholme all the way back to the city.

CHAPTER FOUR

Sunday, January 28, 9:22 A.M.

Timothy Mulrennan followed Cardinals Vennholme and La Spina as they filed into the Sistine Chapel.

The word *chapel* fell well short of describing the breath-stealing magnificence of the oblong, boxlike monument to Man and God that is the Sistine. Japanese money may have restored the ceiling to a near-pristine state, the colors ablaze with Michelangelo's five-hundred-year-enduring talents, but it was a purely Italian room—of the peculiarly Vatican variety: sacred, silent, stuffy, almost airless.

The other, once-forgotten frescoes that illuminated the room, against which the cardinal-electors' chairs were placed, had also recently been cleaned and restored. There were works of Botticelli, Perugino, and Ghirlandaio, which had been commissioned by Pope Sixtus IV in the late fifteenth century, a generation before Michelangelo. Of course, after the restored ceiling and altar paintings were unveiled, they garnered more attention from critics and tourists; but these other less-famous frescoes, such as Perugino's *Baptism of Christ* and Ghirlandaio's *Calling of the Apostles,* subtly drew the eye with their intriguing medieval landscapes and powerfully spiritual images of Jesus, their vivid colors and masterful details. The artists were Tuscans, favored by Sixtus and very popular in their time; the value of their gifts to us—living more than five hundred years later—is incalculable.

The 117 cardinal-electors took their closely packed seats at twelve tables, each about twenty-five feet long. Wearing their red birettas and scarlet mozettas, they faced each other in two tiered rows on either side of the chapel's long central

axis. Before Paul VI had so greatly expanded membership
in the Sacred College of Cardinals to 120, each elector had
sat on a canopied throne. For this first conclave of the
twenty-first century the cardinals occupied simple wooden
chairs with red velvet seat cushions. Yet, in its essentials,
the venue and procedure for electing the Supreme Pontiff
of the Roman Catholic Church had altered little in eight
hundred years; since 1179 only cardinals have elected the
pope (with one exception, during the Great Schism). In fact,
as far back as 1059 the cardinal-bishops were designated
as the sole electors, assuming consultation with the other
cardinals. Thus, this papal election process by more-or-less
secret ballot is the oldest such method still in practice today.

After mass at nine, this first voting session of the conclave began promptly at 10:00 A.M. with a meditation by
the donnish, disheveled David Cardinal Herrington of Great
Britain, chosen for the honor by the College for his wit and
scholarship. The meditation concerned "the grave duty incumbent on you and thus the need to act with right intention
for the good of the universal Church *solum Deum prae
oculis habentes*"—having only God before your eyes.

Next the camerlengo, Cardinal Portillo, read in its en-
tirety the 1996 Apostolic Constitution *Universi Dominici
Gregis*. Few listened to the drone of legalistic, canonical
words; most were deeply engaged by their own thoughts.

For centuries prior to this conclave there were three primary methods of election. The first and most unlikely was
per acclamationem seu inspirationem, by acclamation, a
process whereby the cardinals "as it were through the inspiration of the Holy Spirit . . . spontaneously, unanimously, and aloud proclaim one individual Supreme
Pontiff." A second means of election, *per compromissum*,
by delegation, was designed to resolve a deadlocked conclave through a formal compromise. The cardinals were to
appoint a smaller group of nine to fifteen electors and
pledge to be bound by the delegation's decision. The third
and most common method of election—and the only one
retained by Pope John Paul II—was *per scrutinium*, by
scrutiny, or secret ballot, which requires a two-thirds ma-

jority of all the cardinal-electors present. Pius XII and Paul VI had required a two-thirds-plus-one-vote total, to avoid the potential embarrassment of a bare two-thirds "squeaker," as Pius himself had experienced in his election in 1939. In case of a deadlock, after a substantial period of time and at least thirty ballots, the cardinals may agree to enact the provision for election by a simple majority.

When the camerlengo was finished reading, the actual balloting began. Tim Mulrennan tensed as the electors chose by lot from among their number three *scrutatores,* or scrutineers, ballot tellers who would mix and then count the votes, and three *recognitores,* revisers or examiners, who would recount and verify the ballots. He was relieved that his name was not drawn. These six would serve for the whole day, during which four ballots would be held—two each at the morning and afternoon sessions—with new scrutineers and revisers chosen by lot each subsequent day, as necessary. In addition, three so-called *infirmarii* were selected; these were designated in the constitution as messengers who would take a locked box and ballot papers to any sick electors who might be confined to the residence. There were none, so far, in the current conclave.

While these were purely ceremonial positions, Mulrennan was pleased when Jaime Cardinal De Guzman of Manila was chosen as a scrutineer for the first day. The sixty-six-year-old Filipino prelate was a shy man, dark and slender with raven black wavy hair, known and liked for his understated yet devastating humor, and over the years he had become something of a favorite of Mulrennan's. Not that widely known outside the Philippines by other residential archbishops, he was well respected among the Curial cardinals, who appreciated his willingness to take on even the most thankless of assignments for the Holy See.

With the assistance of the scrutineers and revisers, the camerlengo distributed the ballot cards. When Cardinal De Guzman came up behind Timothy Mulrennan and slid one onto the table in front of him, he placed his hand on Mulrennan's shoulder and gave a slight squeeze, in much

the same way a father might touch his child's arm before
an important event. Mulrennan silently lifted his head to
indicate his appreciation. He treasured their brief consultation of last evening after Zimmerman's shocking demise.

Once all the cards were handed out, Mulrennan turned
his over and read the printed words: *Eligo in Summum Pontificem,* I elect as Supreme Pontiff. There was a finely un-
derscored space underneath where the elector was to write
his choice, taking care to disguise his handwriting to avoid
identification.

Mulrennan picked up his pen and, holding it above the
card, looked around the shadowy, high-vaulted chapel: no
one spoke a word, yet the American sensed great conversations in progress. Shared glances, subtle nods, fingers
drumming, eyebrows raised and lowered. He saw the various alliances forming and shifting: especially among the
Curial-establishment Italians, joined by a variety of the
most conservative electors from the Third World, North
America, and Europe who longed for a return to the preconciliar Church. But the largest contingent by far were the
dozens of electors who were predisposed to no one and who
would strive to keep their own counsel until the final vote
was taken and a new pontiff named. He recognized them
by their veil of isolation, each staring intently at his ballot
card, avoiding eye contact with anyone else.

With Zimmerman's sudden, troubling death there was no
single candidate who stood out as a sensible compromise
in the event of a deadlock. He again visually swept the
chamber.

Mulrennan felt most kinship with these lone electors, and
almost instinctively he turned away from the several pairs
of eyes—Biagi's and Vennholme's among them—that
seemed trained at him. Gripping his pen more tightly, he
lowered it to the card. A perverse impulse, despite the canonical proscription and long tradition of the conclave,
made him want to write his own name, as he had done
when elected speaker—by a single vote—of his student
senate in the seminary. It was a side of his personality, the
need to be liked and approved, that he did not much care

for and which he had struggled greatly over the years to suppress. He smiled as he imagined his fellow seminarians hearing the news that he had been elected not a mere vice president but Supreme Pontiff! Now, there was something to write home to his sisters and brother about. . . .

Shaking away the devilish impulse, he painstakingly inscribed the name of one to whom he had denied his own personal ambition, a name that sounded like a pope's: Leandro Aurelio Cardinal Biagi.

He knew the Florentine would never be chosen. He also knew that he must honor the great friendship Biagi had shown him over the years. If ever there was a man who might have been born to be pope in a different age, it was Allo Biagi.

Replacing his pen in a grooved slot in the table, Mulrennan carefully folded the ballot in two and waited for his turn to present it. As one of the relatively newer and younger cardinals, he would be among the last to make the long walk from his seat to the Sistine altar, for the ballots were cast in order of seniority.

More minutes passed as the cardinals finished indicating their choices. Then Cardinal Portillo rose. He seemed a bit unsteady, and the elector seated nearest him also rose and offered a hand. But Portillo stubbornly waved him back to his seat and started toward the altar alone. He had tottered only a few steps when his knees buckled and he halted to steady himself. This time he did not refuse assistance when the rather husky, gray-haired cardinal came up beside him and gripped his arm. Portillo glanced up at the man and smiled acceptingly, then walked forward.

Mulrennan was so intent on Portillo's movement, so concerned that he not stumble or fall, that he did not immediately notice which cardinal had aided him. It was not until the camerlengo stood at the altar and raised his ballot above the gleaming paten-covered chalice that Mulrennan focused on the other man. At first, strangely, he did not even recognize the cardinal who stood at Portillo's side and held the aged Spaniard's raised hand in his own.

"I call as my witness Christ the Lord," Portillo intoned,

"who will be my judge, that my vote is given to the one who before God I think should be elected."

Mulrennan did not hear the words, for his eyes were locked on the man at Portillo's shoulder, the man who had risen to assist not only the camerlengo but all of them assembled for this awesome task.

"Eminence? . . ." Mulrennan said half-aloud, clasping his hands in prayer at this vision—no, this ghostly *presence* of the late pope himself.

There was no mistaking that the pontiff was looking directly at and through Timothy Mulrennan, as assuredly as he seemed to be gazing into the eyes of each man in the room. He was not the old, frail corpse who had been laid beneath St. Peter's Basilica. In the American's strange vision the late pope stood with them now just as he had looked on the day of his own election a quarter century ago, youthful and vigorous, humble and confident, prepared for the dark challenges ahead during his, the sixth-longest pontificate in history.

Mulrennan's head swam with other visions of the man— the morning they had first met, the afternoon Mulrennan had been installed as a cardinal, the very last evening he had spent with this holy man. The chapel felt as if it were moving, spinning, and he closed his eyes and gripped the table to steady himself. Soon he, too, must cast his own first, fateful ballot of the conclave.

Timothy Mulrennan looked up again toward the altar of the Sistine Chapel to catch a final glimpse of the Holy Father, but that vision had passed, and Cardinal Portillo stood alone now. The camerlengo deposited his card on the golden paten and tipped it into the large jeweled chalice. Stepping back from the altar, he walked steadily, upright, and unaided to his seat.

Back in his room, Timothy Mulrennan pulled the red cassock off and tossed it onto his bed. His breathing was sharp and shallow, and he reached for his wrist to check his pulse. He had taken the comical-looking little bus from the Sistine to his apartment, yet his heart pounded as if he had run a marathon.

Forcing calm into his breathing and his thoughts, he turned to the narrow window and concentrated on the framed vista beyond. A grayish white canopy of clouds hung suspended mere feet above the rooftops, sliding slowly toward the east. A small flock of birds lifted into the air from the nearby garden, circled once around the dome of St. Peter's, and disappeared into the cloud bank. A black-winged bug landed on the windowpane, took a few cautious steps, and darted back into the air.

He tried to focus on this simple awareness of another living creature, but more troublesome thoughts intruded, battling one against the other like adversaries in a battle line. He sank into his chair.

Mulrennan mentally reviewed all that had happened during the first voting sessions of the conclave. Following the first vote, the scrutineers had shuffled and counted the paper ballots, announcing each one as it was opened and set aside. The revisers had then verified each ballot and passed a needle through the center, stringing it on a white thread. When all were accounted, and the 117 ballots were strung in a tight bundle, the tally was called out so that each cardinal could keep his own personal count on a pad. He had prepared himself to hear his own name read aloud, and when it happened he felt a tinge of excitement and fear; his name was read twice more on the first ballot.

Biagi, he told himself. Biagi and Vennholme and two of the other American cardinals, possibly. Not Vennholme. There was little chance that such a man would support a papabile with whom he disagreed on nearly every issue of doctrine and policy. An unspoken antipathy had clouded their relationship over the years, and Mulrennan had often felt that Vennholme was keeping tabs on him, watching him, shadowing his career.

Mulrennan had stiffled any reaction when the second ballot of the morning added a fourth vote to the first three. He had given it little thought over lunch, other than to tease Cardinal De Guzman, who had received three votes himself. "Perhaps we should combine our votes and throw them behind La Spina," he had joked, knowing how much the Filipino cleric disliked the man whom he and others called the Terror of Turin. "I always wanted to be a *grande elettore*."

De Guzman had not seemed amused, and Mulrennan knew he was genuinely concerned at the prospect of Pietro Cardinal La Spina's election—with good reason, perhaps, since the reactionary Italian had started with eleven votes and ended the day with twenty.

Mulrennan's vote had also increased during the afternoon balloting, first to six votes and then nine. Fallaci fell completely out of the running; it now was clear that he had been merely a stalking horse for La Spina.

Nine, just nine—may it stay there, or die. It cannot happen. It will not happen.... Three sharp raps at the door were followed by three more. His stomach flipped as he went to the door, because he knew who would be there even before he pulled the door open.

"May I enter?" Vennholme said diplomatically.

"Sure, welcome to my luxurious salon," Mulrennan wisecracked.

"Mine is not very much better." He entered and crossed to the window by the writing desk.

The older man stood with his back to the window, framed by the early evening darkness. Mulrennan felt awkward with just the two of them standing there in the room; he had not been alone like this with Henry Vennholme for a very long time. He sat on the bed, which reminded him of Vennholme's practice of keeping low, plush chairs facing his office desk so that visitors would sit lower than he.

Mulrennan was determined not to speak first, and so he remained silent, fighting the urge to ask why Vennholme had come. Each man waited for the other to make the first move. Finally Vennholme sensed Mulrennan's tactic, and he chuckled conspiratorially.

"You have learned well, my son."

"Then this is a negotiation?" Mulrennan said.

"Ah, so there *are* still gaps in your education. I thought that by now you would realize that all conversation is negotiation."

"And what, in fact, are we negotiating?"

"First, if you will indulge me for a moment, I must take you to task."

"For what?"

"Not voting for me, of course."

"I never said I'd—"

"I know, I know," Vennholme said, raising a hand. "And I know our ballots are secret. But there's no denying that I received only one vote each time, and while it wasn't mine, I know the scoundrel who cast it."

"La Spina?"

"No, not La Spina. He voted for Fallaci, mark my word. I'm talking about Giannantonio."

"But of course," Mulrennan replied. Pasquale Cardinal Giannantonio of Gubbio, a member of the Congregation for Bishops, was a more-than-minor bureaucrat with, Tim sensed, pretensions to something greater, and he had attached himself to Vennholme in hopes of advancing his own position. It had been common to see Giannantonio sitting with Vennholme at each meal and every General Congregation during the preconclave period.

"And with only one vote, there's no point in pretending it was yours."

"I'm sorry, Henry, but I felt I must—"

"Biagi," Vennholme declared with a flat smile of understanding. "You needn't say more. But after the first two ballots, I had hoped you would change your vote—not to me, mind you. I was only teasing about that. But there's no point in staying with Biagi."

"He has twenty-seven," Mulrennan pointed out. Indeed, Cardinal Biagi had started and finished the first-round balloting with the most votes. But he was not gaining ground, and everyone knew it.

"Twenty-seven is a fine number but a long way from the required seventy-eight. And from here it will not go up— only down."

"Perhaps if no one else emerges—"

"You are too intelligent to dwell on fantasy," Vennholme said brusquely, as if taking a theology student to task. "Those two dozen have thrown in with him until a clear pattern emerges. Then they will move en masse—and at

Biagi's bidding. I consider you above such tactics, so I can only assume your support of Biagi is genuine, if naive. Am I correct? You are not one of Biagi's little soldiers?"

"My vote is my own."

"Good. Then the time has come to change it."

"To La Spina?" Mulrennan said dubiously.

Vennholme chuckled, snorted really, again. "That is why you thought I was here? To plead La Spina's case? If that were my intention, I would not have stuck with you for four ballots."

Mulrennan sat erectly, looking directly at the man, trying to gauge his sincerity. With the light behind him, Vennholme's features were in shadow.

"Then whose case are you pleading?" Mulrennan asked.

"Why, yours, my foolish young man. Yours."

"Look, Henry, I'm flattered that anyone would vote for me—and that you insist on calling me a 'young man'—but I have already told you my feelings about being considered for this office."

"The fears of a parish priest. They will pass."

"I am not going to be the next pope."

"Not if you don't switch your vote from Biagi to yourself. And don't talk to me about how it 'isn't done.' The constitution does not explicitly forbid it, even if tradition does." He shifted in his chair, and Mulrennan was silent, listening. "Consider that you rose from three votes to nine—that's three hundred percent from the first to fourth ballots. And if you'd voted for yourself, you would have been in double digits."

"I don't know . . . You make it sound as if I'm running for president or something."

"President? Nothing so pedestrian. And if you don't mind my being blunt, Timofeo"—he smiled slyly, aware that he had used Cardinal Biagi's pet name for Mulrennan—"it is not up to you to say whether or not you will be pope. That is up to the Holy Spirit."

"Aided, no doubt, by men such as yourself and Cardinal Biagi."

"If we can be of service to Our Lord, then yes, I suppose so. But the truth is a deeper one, even to old politicians like us. Only one man will be chosen as the next Vicar of Christ, and his name is already written in His hand."

"And you really think that name could be mine?" Mulrennan shook his head in disbelief.

"Do I?" Vennholme drew in a breath and let it out slowly. He clasped his hands together. "No, my young friend, I do not."

"Then why . . . why all this?"

"Because I may be wrong. What—you didn't think I could admit such a thing? Well, I know my failings, better than you will ever realize." He came around the chair and sat down. "You wonder why I am pleading your case? Yes, partly because I may be wrong about who this conclave will choose. But also because if I ultimately throw my support behind another, I don't want it said that I did so in opposition to you or anyone else."

"I would never say such a thing," Mulrennan protested.

"Of course not. But I know how talk spreads among old men." Vennholme leaned forward in the chair. "I will leave you now. But when I am gone, I want you to consider what we have discussed. I know we have not always seen eye to eye, but that doesn't alter my respect for you or change my belief that you are a papabile, if perhaps not a pope. Just say the word and I will let a few key people know that you wouldn't refuse your election. That is all they are looking for."

"I thought they—we—were looking for a pope."

"Yes, we are. But one who will not cringe from the calling, should it come. Excuse the cliché, but we seek a shepherd, not a sheep."

"But," Mulrennan pressed, "you can't deny that over the years we've envisioned that flock quite differently."

"It may seem that way to those of us on the inside, caught up in the minutiae of Church politics; but from the outside our Church, among the great mass of believers and nonbelievers alike, things look quite different. We are under assault from all quarters. It used to be the communists who threatened to cut us off from our children; now it is everything from television to the smut-clogged Internet. Within Mother Church we love our little disputes and Curial intrigues. But they are the disputes of brethren—of family. We are not so very far apart, you and I, not when compared to the gulf that exists between both of us and most of the world beyond these walls."

He crossed to the door.

"Yes, I have my doubts that you will be our next Holy Father. But could I support, indeed, work for your candidacy? First I must ask you these questions. Can you see yourself on the Throne of St. Peter? And if you were seated upon that throne, would you be tolerant of an old conservative churchman like myself? Would there be room in your Church for your so-called progressive vision and my traditionalist one?" As he held the door handle, he twitched, almost imperceptibly, like cat eager to go outside after a nice snack. "The answers we profess—the doctrines of our faith—go so far to address the questions of existence, but only so far. We are agents with free will, with the power to make decisions in unity with God or contrary to His will."

"We have more in common than perhaps you realize or are willing to acknowledge, Henry. Even though I have never been enamored of the Evangelium Christi program, as you well know, I have always admired the spiritual commitment of the membership—and the leadership, such as yourself."

"That is perhaps both too much and not enough, Timothy." Vennholme pursed his lips; it was not a smile, exactly, but an expression of resignation. "We are on the same highway, but in different lanes. Yes, we can say that much, I think. Good-bye."

"Good-bye, Henry," Mulrennan said as the Canadian cardinal slipped out into the hallway. He sat back to ponder the deeper, more Machiavellian meaning of the visit, but almost immediately there came another rap on the door. "Come in," he said.

The door clicked open. "Timofeo, you are quite popular this evening, I see."

"Allo!" Mulrennan exclaimed, greatly relieved when he saw Biagi standing there, filling the doorway with his aristocratic bulk.

The Florentine needed no invitation to make himself at home. "What did that little Canadian fox want with you?" he asked Tim as he sat, planting his hands on his knees.

Mulrennan gave him a blow-by-blow account of the enigmatic exchange.

"Do not take what he says at face value. Surely you know him and his lapdog Giannantonio well enough for that. There is no doubt that Vennholme and his Evangelium comrades—and there are about a dozen of them in the conclave—wish to elect La Spina. Our Canadian brother sees himself as Secretary of State to the new pope, at the very least," Biagi said.

"And you—don't you want that position yourself, my learned, ambitious friend? After all, you have led the voting yourself." Mulrennan was feeling almost physically sick from this overdose of conclave politics.

For the first time that night since the death of their Austrian brother cardinal, Biagi allowed himself to laugh. "Not for long. And as for Secretary of State . . . do I want it? Of course I do. I do not pretend otherwise, as Cardinal Vennholme does, playing the very soul of modesty—unconvincingly, I might add."

"Whereas you are forthright, yet diplomatic. Yes, I think you would make an excellent Secretary of State. I will appoint you immediately if I am elected!"

"You speak it as if it were a joke, Timofeo. I do not think your own election is impossible. In fact, I would be more than willing to speak to some of our confreres tonight about your candidacy. What do you make of that?"

"It is not time for an American—not yet. And as for me, I still think I'm a very poor candidate. Too moderate, too much baggage, too few friends in the Curia."

"I am able to lift some of that baggage, my friend. All you need do is ask. I will be like one of your—what do you call them—redcaps, eh?" Again he smiled at his own cleverness, revealing straight white teeth. "Remember, only Italy, my own country, has more electors than the States, our eighteen to your eleven. Perhaps it *is* time for an American. You are liked by the other Americans, and you have a good reputation among the Latins and the

Europeans. At least you are not offensive to them, which is saying a lot."

Mulrennan started to speak, but the Italian cardinal motioned for him to be silent.

"Don't try to answer now. Just think about what we have discussed, and we'll speak again tomorrow." He opened the door, then looked back at Mulrennan, a curious, bloodless smile on his pale face. "And don't be so glum, my Lord Cardinal. If I did not know better, I'd fear you don't like me, Timothy." It was unusual for Biagi to use Mulrennan's full Christian name again, rather than his pet appellation.

The aristocrat stood, shrugged dramatically and stepped out, pulling the door closed behind him.

When Biagi had left him alone, Tim Mulrennan knelt at the prayer bench and clenched both fists, touching his forehead with his knuckles. His mind and spirit were cluttered with chaotic and contradictory thoughts. Zimmerman—dead. Natural causes, it had to be. Who?—how?—why would anyone murder a cardinal of the Church within the sacred confines of the Apostolic Palace on the eve of a papal election? Surely politics and conflicting interests had not infiltrated this place . . . had they? Was he too stupid or naive, as Biagi had intimated, to see what was right in front of his face? No, it simply had not happened that way. He thought of his own diocese: how he wished he were there instead of here. Even with all the problems he faced every day of his episcopacy, at least there were real people, real faces, real needs attached thereto. He felt he was of some use, that he might make some tangible difference in the lives of some of his flock. His family: his three sisters and their families in New Jersey, his younger brother who still lived alone and worked in New York City, his parents, both now dead and free from worry and pain, his aged stepmother who had tried her best as the second Mrs. Mulrennan. Images of the fun times they had shared came into his mind—long-ago times of youthful high-jinks in their shore house at Beach Haven on Long Beach Island, games and competitions and dances and school plays in North Auburn; the haunting ache of his mother's alcoholic episodes rose unbidden, as they always did. He remembered returning from school to find her passed out and snoring on the living room sofa, leaving her undisturbed, like his sisters not sure what to do, until Kevin or their father came home and carried her upstairs, eating dinner in silence and retreating to his room to do homework through a gauzy screen of tears. What went wrong? Why did she do it? He did not know then, as he subsequently learned, that she had a disease, that if she chose, she could do something about it—that Dad only enabled her drinking by not talking about it, by smoothing over the destruction and embarrassment of her drunken actions. His sisters grew up hardened to it, with thick shells of self-preservation, but he carried the wounds into his adulthood and still mourned the loss of, or lack of maternal affection. Her death, painful as it was for everyone, was a blessed relief, and he felt guilty for thinking of it in that way. He sometimes still felt angry at God about Mom . . . and pray as he might to lessen that hurt and anger, he had never fully gotten over it. At least, not yet. And his father—a saintly man who had suffered for decades with her condition, lost a son in war, lost his job of thirty-eight years to callous corporate downsizing, had known some peaceful, mainly happy years with his second wife, Rosemary. Where was the justice? The fairness? The reward for good living? It was tough to lay it all off to the next life, though that is what he believed and preached from the pulpit of the cathedral. Didn't a good man like his father deserve more than a bit of heaven on earth for all his sacrifices? He wished he could pick up a telephone and call one of his sisters, but he could not: he and the others were forbidden any outside communication whatsoever.

Tim lifted his head, opened his eyes and gazed at the crucifix on the wall, the stark image of a suffering Christ. From the nearby desk he picked up his well-worn paperback traveling Bible and opened it to a familiar passage from Isaiah:

Arise Jerusalem, and shine like the sun;
The glory of the Lord is shining on you!

CONCLAVE 95

Other nations will be covered by darkness,
But on you the light of the Lord will shine;
The brightness of His presence will be with you.
Nations will be drawn to your light,
And kings to the dawning of your new day.
Look around you and see what is happening:
Your people are gathering to come home!
Your sons will come from far away;
Your daughters will be carried like children.
You will see this and be filled with joy;
You will tremble with excitement.
The wealth of the nations will be brought to you;
From across the sea their riches will come. . . .
You will no longer be forsaken and hated,
A city deserted and desolate.
I will make you great and beautiful,
A place of joy forever and ever.
Nations and kings will care for you
As a mother nurses her child. You will know that I,
   the Lord, have saved you.
That the mighty God of Israel sets you free.

Later, Isaiah also wrote: "You will be called 'God's Holy
People,' 'The People the Lord Has Saved.' Jerusalem will
be called 'The City That God Loves,' 'The City That God
Did Not Forsake.' "
Timothy Cardinal Mulrennan, confined in a small chamber within the walls of the capital of Christendom, more
than four thousand years after those words of consolation
had been recorded in an ancient tongue by a nameless
scribe, felt less a prisoner than a man who sought God as
had so many men before him. He knew, in his gut, that the
One he sought was indeed present within him, within these
very walls, and that he need only ask and He would possess
Tim's mortal being and reveal His will to Tim's immortal
soul.
How simple it was! Exhaustion melted away like ice in
July. *I know nothing. But He knows all. Let me be quiet
and listen to Him; let me discern His presence. I need do
no more than this. Politics and intrigue be damned! God,*

keep Cardinal Zimmerman in Your care forever . . . and let his enemies not know victory if it be at the cost of a single soul lost to salvation. I offer myself completely up to You, to do with me what you will.

When he skimmed the surface details of his life, his résumé, it seemed that he had risen almost effortlessly through the ranks: a bishop of a troubled diocese at a young age, a Curial archbishop with a good measure of bureaucratic power, then residential archbishop of Newark, the job he had not even dared to dream about as a younger priest. Yet it had not been an untroubled path.

Did all priests experience the roller-coaster ups and downs of mind and spirit, as he had? Did they fight the demons of temptation, ambition, doubt, and despair, as he had? Yet God had graced him with the ability to project confidence and empathy with people—political skills, Biagi would call them—that carried him through some of the more difficult times. And wasn't it fair to say that he was damn good at what he did—administration, communication, pastoral duties, as well as "managing up"?

Mulrennan smiled at himself, despite himself. He knew enough basic human psychology—common sense and a master's degree in psychology from the University of New Mexico during the early '80s—to understand his own shortcomings and motivations. One of his friends had characterized him as "a divided personality, half contrition, half ambition." He had winced at that, but knew that there was truth in the analysis. He would not call himself tortured, by any means, because his faith, even at the lowest moments, sustained and defined him; but at this moment, as he and his fellow electors faced such a momentous choice, he privately, silently felt inadequate to the task.

Soon he stripped down to his underwear and brushed his teeth in the small bathroom adjoining his apartment. He did not even look at his watch, nor did he set his alarm clock. He would awaken at 5:00 A.M. Vatican time, as he did nearly every day of his life, wherever he might be. He lay on the narrow, too-short bed. He cursed his Celtic warrior ancestors, who used to fight naked on the hills of Hibernia, for making him so tall. Within fifteen minutes he slept deeply, blessedly free for a time of any inkling of death or politics.

CHAPTER FIVE

North Auburn, New Jersey, March 11, 1967

Fifty-nine seconds remained in the fourth quarter. The eighth-grade basketball team of Our Lady of Mercies trailed the visiting team, Blessed Sacrament School, by five points. Father Timothy Mulrennan hoarsely shouted to his boys to call a time out when they gained possession of the ball on a broken cross-court pass by their opponents.

The new OLM gymnasium, its honey-colored floorboards gleaming beneath glaring white lights, throbbed with the exuberant cheers of home-team parents and students. Mulrennan could not help but think back to another basketball game in a darker, less spacious gym in faraway Rome, a one-on-one pickup match with a foreign bishop. He would carry with him always the memory of his time at the Ecumenical Council four years before. But those heady days were finished and would probably never return, he reminded himself. Now the job facing this parish priest was far simpler: to deliver a convincing victory over visiting Blessed Sacrament and in the process humble his counterpart, the diocesan coaching legend Father Rupert Holloway.

The referee's whistle shrieked, and the boys trotted to the bench.

Mulrennan, a thirty-year-old curate three months into his parish assignment, gathered his teenaged charges. He was a thin tower encased in black with the white celluloid square of his Roman collar like a polished diamond under his Adam's apple. Holding out his clipboard, he stooped to explain a play he had sketched in bold pencil strokes only moments before.

"We have one objective: get the ball to Fusco." He jabbed a finger toward the team's biggest player, a swarthy, broad-shouldered thirteen-year-old named Danny Fusco, the son of a brewery worker in Newark and the fourth of seven Fusco kids. The small gaggle of crewcut heads swiveled to acknowledge their teammate.

"Look—when O'Neill crosses midcourt, the rest of you clear the right side. Fusco, post up here—at the foul line—to take the pass. Kevin—" Mulrennan pointed to O'Neill, the skinny towheaded guard whose million freckles and gliding speed earned him the nickname Leopard "—pass into Danny, take this pick, and roll to the basket. Danny, you take the shot immediately unless O'Neill is open for the layup. Then I want all of you to press on their inbounds pass. Press harder than you ever have—you can be sure Father Rupe's boys'll be doing the same. Force the steal. And don't foul!"

The substitute players encircled the coach and his top five sweaty, exhausted players. Twelve team members in all, Father Mulrennan called them the Apostles. He had drilled them intensely since before Christmas, and they had responded with eagerness and spirit. They had won six of their first eleven games, the first winning season for OLM for as long as anyone could remember.

"If we score on this possession we're back in the game. There's plenty of time to catch them. I hope you guys on the bench are praying hard."

The boys pummeled each other on the back.

"Let's do it!" Mulrennan exclaimed, holding forth his fist. Each boy added his fist in the middle of the tight circle. "Ready!"

"Break!" The team shout rang to the rafters, and the players hustled out to their positions.

Mulrennan paced the blue-painted sideline with his hands shoved into his trousers pockets as the referee put the ball into play. Kevin O'Neill dribbled swiftly across half court and hooked the ball to Danny Fusco, who pivoted and released a high arcing shot. The ball snapped through the net, bringing their score to forty-eight—only three points down. The gymnasium rocked with cheers.

As Blessed Sacrament took possession of the ball, the OLM boys locked onto their opponents, their arms windmilling to interfere with the pass.

Mulrennan cupped his hands around his mouth: "Don't foul!" It was doubtful anyone heard him through the din.

Forty seconds.

The visitors successfully inbounded the ball and moved it into their own court, with Mercies covering them closely all the way. Mulrennan watched the ball move from player to player, watched his boys do their jobs, just as he had taught them. They had a chance to pull this one out of the fire—a chance!

Twenty-three seconds.

O'Neill dived to intercept a pass. He slapped it away and fell to the floor. His teammates recovered the ball and raced down the court. One boy tossed up a lay in, but it rolled off the rim. Danny Fusco followed with a quick rebound and jumped high, an opposing player slapping his arm as he put the ball against the glass. The ball hugged the rim and dropped for two points: 51–50. The referee whistled a foul.

Eighteen seconds.

Pandemonium erupted as Fusco stepped to the foul line. He glanced over to his coach, who shot him a thumbs-up. The tall teenager cradled the ball, bounced it twice, then lofted the foul shot. The ball caromed off the hoop, and an opponent snatched the rebound. The home fans groaned, and the visitors' section hooted with glee. Blessed Sacrament protected the ball, brought it down court with OLM sticking to them like glue.

Eleven seconds.

O'Neill reached in and fouled his man. Blessed Sacrament faced the first of a one-and-one. The boys tensed in their positions along the lane, arms up, ready to box out for the rebound. The shot went up—missed!

Mulrennan was certain he was having a heart attack as Fusco manhandled the rebound, wrapped his body around the ball.

Nine seconds.

Fusco passed to a teammate, and OLM crisply brought

the ball up through the tight press. They had executed this ten-second drill in scrimmage dozens of times. Now it counted.

Five seconds.

Father Tim decided not to call a time-out. Let them play. Dear Jesus, Mary, and Joseph . . . O'Neill to Fusco at the high post. Fusco pivoted, looked to pass.

Three seconds.

A tidal wave of frenzy engulfed the school gymnasium Mulrennan watched with clenched fists. He was deaf to the roar, saw only his boys and the ball.

Two seconds.

There was no open man. Fusco lifted the ball above his head and lofted a beautiful jump shot from twelve feet out. The ball slammed against the rim and bounded off with a deafening clang.

The buzzer sounded like Satan's own laughter. Blessed Sacrament's bench erupted, the boys leaping onto the court. The OLM team skulked off, heads down, toward their bench.

Tim Mulrennan did not even see Father Rupe's grin of triumph, aware only of an exquisite pang of joy that shot through him, mixed with sorrow and hurt for his boys. As a coach—and a priest—he could not have asked any more of them. These were good kids, great kids, who had played with heart and guts. They were why he was here. His joy was for his vocation. He belonged. He could help.

"Boys, gather round!"

He called them into a tight circle, and they gazed sadly into his eyes.

"You did the very best you could. No one should walk out of here feeling otherwise. We have practice on Wednesday, the next game Friday night. Now, let's say a quick prayer. In the name of the Father . . ."

The opposing coach came over and gave Tim an encouraging pat on the back. "Good group, a lot of spirit," Rupe Holloway said.

"Thanks, Coach," Tim managed, swallowing the hurt and humiliation of a loss.

After the boys had dressed and gone home with their

friends and families, Mulrennan tucked the score book and clipboard under his arm, turned out the gym lights, and locked the doors. A thick curtain of snow fell before him as he stepped outside. Our Lady of Mercies was a Gothic enclave that included a grammar school, convent, church, and the rectory where Mulrennan lived with the pastor, Monsignor Robert C. Fröeschel, and two fellow curates, or assistant pastors.

He wore no hat but turned his face up and stuck out his tongue to receive the fat waferlike snowflakes. The macadam path wound between the school building and the convent, home to eight Sisters of Charity who taught the kids and served the parish with no complaint that Father Tim had ever heard. Mostly older women, they kept themselves on one side of an invisible line that had separated priests and nuns for centuries.

Tall bare trees and a few towering evergreens stood like sentinels on the well-maintained property, now serenely blanketed in white. He stepped carefully along the slick walkway toward the rear of the large stone manse that was his new home.

Beside him loomed the majestic parish church. Completed in 1931, it had been constructed by an army of Italian immigrant masons whose families formed the nucleus of this thriving suburban parish. This was very much like the church he had known and loved as a boy, in a nearby parish, where he had been baptized and confirmed, received First Communion, made his First Confession—the sanctuary where he had last gazed upon his mother's casket before it had been lowered into the ground.

He still felt a sense of awe as he walked alongside this solid, soaring structure. To the young priest the whole of this Roman Catholic temple was far more than the sum of its stone, steel, glass, and marble. And as the parish's newest priest, he felt personally responsible for its well-being.

Not long after arriving at Our Lady of Mercies in December, Mulrennan had admitted to his pastor that he was at first disappointed not to have received a diplomatic or military assignment after his service at the Ecumenical Council.

Monsignor Froeschel was an aging war horse of a priest
with forty years' experience in the parish trenches throughout Essex County—fourteen as pastor of OLM. Upon hearing Mulrennan's concern, he had brought him into the
book-lined study, placed a whiskey in front of him, and lit
a battered briar pipe.

"My boy, you have the best job a priest could hope for.
Sure, you're not gallivanting around the globe, but you've
already done that. And how many kids from this area can
claim they've done the same? Boy grows up to become a
priest, makes his dad proud. Makes me proud, too, son."

The pastor stood six foot six and weighed more than 250
pounds, and he had on a cardigan sweater over his stained
cassock, worn open at the neck. He had been an athlete in
his day—football and semipro baseball—and he had seen
army service as a chaplain in World War II. Striding to the
stone-framed fireplace, he left a trail of silvery smoke in
his wake.

Mulrennan watched this outsized man's deliberate movements. As a boy he had been aware of and in awe of Froeschel, a giant in black who spoke with the booming voice
of God. He had been secretly thrilled and scared simultaneously when he learned of his assignment to a parish so
close to home. Now, a short time into it, he was less afraid
and itchy to know what lay in store for him.

Reading his mind, the monsignor said: "Be patient, be
grateful for your vocation, serve these people. They will
give you more than is humanly possible for you to give
back. That is the great and secret joy of a good priest."

"I want to be a good priest, sir," Mulrennan blurted. He
meant it, but it sounded almost juvenile when he heard
himself say those words.

"I pray to God every day that you are—and that I am.
We cannot, should not, go it alone. We need each other—
and we need God. You start mass on time and end it a few
minutes early—except when the bishop is here—and you'll
be well remembered. And win a few more basketball games
than you lose."

The younger priest was not certain whether he saw the
monsignor wink at him with that last statement.

"When you get to be a pastor like me you'll appreciate these things. When the team doesn't win or the roof leaks or Johnny gets spanked by Sister Mary Adelaide, you'll hear about it. Catholics are world-class complainers."

When Froeschel offered to top off Mulrennan's glass of whiskey, the young priest waved it away, saying, "I have to hear confession."

Sitting down, Froeschel puffed on his pipe and toyed with his whiskey tumbler. "There's one fact that never changes—people will keep sinning, no matter what the Church says or how we define sin. Privately I sometimes question the wisdom of the Council's decisions—especially all those revisions in the liturgy. It only makes our job as priests even tougher, to have to explain all this to folks who have only known—and believed—one way for their entire lives."

"I agree that it's rough on the faithful, but I do believe that Pope John was right to call the Council—and I want to believe that the Holy Ghost—Holy Spirit, excuse me— informed all the decisions. The Church must reform—or die. I actually sensed God's presence in the sessions I attended." Tim Mulrennan pressed his fist against the top of the little table beside his chair.

Monsignor Froeschel worried his lips around the pipestem. "I'm sure you did, my boy. But those were human beings who drafted and debated such fine theological points that ultimately only serve to confuse poor Mrs. Magliaro who hasn't missed daily mass in thirty years. Or the Driscolls with their twelve kids, two full pews on Sunday, a dozen First Communions, fish sticks on Fridays, a sick grandmother living in their house. Or your own folks— good parishioners over there across town since before my time. What do we say to them when their beloved catechism is pulled out from under their feet?"

"We've got to try. Time will answer many questions and heal some wounds."

"Ah—time . . ." The pastor's leonine head tilted toward the mantel as he gazed into the fire. "You have more of that precious commodity than I. In a few years, God knows,

I'll be a decrepit wreck, and you and the others will be left
to clean up the mess."

At five o'clock this snowy winter Saturday, Father Mulrennan slipped into the confessional and took his seat at the
screened sliding window. He kissed the cross on the purple
stole and placed it around his neck. His breviary lay in his
lap, to be read in quiet moments between penitents. When
he heard his first penitent enter the confessional and kneel,
Mulrennan pushed open the window.

"Bless me, Father, for I have sinned. My last confession
was three weeks ago."

He immediately recognized the voice of Rita Kearney, a
young mother who had been a friend of his sister's and just
a year behind him in school. In fact, they had even dated
a couple of times, set up by Tim's sister when he was too
shy to ask out a girl on his own. It was very difficult to
hear the confession of someone you knew—hence the near-
anonymity of the box and the screen.

Rita's list of failings was poignantly venial and sincerely
offered up. Mulrennan settled in for his benediction and
formulated in his mind a mild penance of three Hail Marys
and one Our Father; he would recommend that she say the
rosary once a week, as well.

"There is one other, uh, sin I need to confess, Father.
It's—I have a problem—I haven't been able to talk to anybody. . . ." Her voice trailed into the faintest of whispers.

"What is it? At least I can listen."

"Father, I—"

He could hear her steeling herself before continuing.

"I am in love with a man who is not my husband."

Stunned, not knowing what to say, he remained silent,
allowing her to speak further if she wished.

"Father—" She was choking back tears, trying not to sob
as she composed herself. "I may be pregnant with the man's
baby. I'm not sure. I don't—I don't know what to do."
Finally the tears burst through.

Tim Mulrennan wanted to reach through the screen and
hold her and reassure her of God's love. He struggled for
the correct words. She was expecting a severe reprimand,
but that was not the right answer. In the darkness of the

confessional she did not know who this priest was. He felt odd, powerful, humbled in the moment.

"Listen, you have done the correct thing in confessing this sin. God forgives you. I can tell you this with certainty. Now you must forgive yourself and mend your error the best way you can."

"But how? I don't know what else to do. I love him."

"Be quiet for a moment. Let our Lord speak to your heart. He will give you the answers you need."

Mulrennan administered benediction and prayed with the woman. Finally he said, "Are you going to be all right?"

"I think so, Father. I must get home to prepare dinner."

"Do you wish to see me at a later time? If you would like to make an appointment with me—" He leaned closer to the screen, conflicted about what he had just decided to do: to reveal his identity to her. "This is Father Mulrennan, Rita. I want to help you—in complete confidence. Don't be afraid."

The woman pulled back from the confessional screen, and the tone of her voice changed from guilt to challenge.

"Tim—I mean, Father, you know me. You know my whole family. I would be so embarrassed. If my husband ever found out, he'd take the girls and leave me. I know he would. And I have another baby to think about now."

"Your husband doesn't have to know. I am bound to silence by the confessional, and even if I weren't, I would not betray your confidence. We can discuss it, decide what's best for you."

"I don't know. . . ." She blew her nose in a handkerchief. "Thank you, Father. I'll think about it."

Then she was gone. A moment later another penitent knelt in her place.

Timothy Mulrennan returned to the rectory for supper at six-thirty after having heard a dozen confessions—all forgotten but Rita Kearney's. He was preoccupied with the young woman's problem as he sat in his place at the table next to the senior assistant pastor, Father Kenneth Wasserman, who had been at Mercies for five years, a priest for nearly ten. The priest's greeting carried the cloying odor of liquor—as usual.

"Tough loss today, boy," Wasserman said as they awaited the monsignor. "But I must say, you've won more games in half a season than I did in two miserable years as coach. You're damned good. Gave that honcho Rupe Holloway a scare."

"The kids are good, and they've worked hard all season."

Ken Wasserman's hair was a prematurely gray bristle that contrasted with his black eyebrows. He had a pale face and brown eyes and carried a slight paunch beneath his cassock. He lounged back in his chair and flicked a cigarette ash into the glass tray by his salad plate.

They were joined by Father Donald Pawlikawski, a quiet older man who had served in several local parishes, and a few moments later Monsignor Froeschel sat down and led grace. At their "Amen," the housekeeper swooped into the dining room with a porcelain tureen of beef stew. Each man ladled a generous bowlful.

Father Wasserman hefted the carafe of burgundy and filled his wine goblet, then poured for the others and sat back with a self-satisfied sigh. The men shoveled in their hot stew and green salads, sopping up gravy with warm buttered biscuits. Wasserman paid closest attention to his wine, even when the pastor spoke.

"The archbishop has asked all of us to pray for him on his upcoming trip to Rome. He feels he will retire in a year or two if the Holy Father will permit. I hope it's none too soon; we need him at the helm of this diocese." Froeschel fisted a napkin and dabbed his lips. "Tough old coot that he is."

Mulrennan had served on the staff of Archbishop Thomas Boland's Study Committee during his two years in Rome during the Council. Boland had been a demanding, meticulous boss who delighted in telling his staff, "The Holy Ghost appears in the details, gentlemen. In a hundred years our legacy will be found in these records. Get it out right, or get out." As far as Mulrennan knew, he had gotten it right, which may have contributed to the archbishop's having personally approved his rookie assignment to this parish so close to home—a somewhat unusual circumstance. He liked the "old coot" while remaining appropriately afraid of the man, who retained in his person all ordinary power of the temporal and spiritual affairs of the Archdiocese of Newark.

Wasserman said, "We could do a hell of a lot worse than Boland, I suppose." He refilled his goblet and took a large swig.

Mulrennan worried that Wasserman had a drinking problem and wondered why the others either did not notice or were not concerned. He had never seen the man falling-down drunk, but whenever there was wine or hard liquor to be had, Father Ken was at the head of the line.

Father Pawlikawski, on the other hand, was shy and quiet, almost to a fault. In his early sixties, he had seen it all, from the hardest days of the depression through the Second World War, to the Vatican Council and President Kennedy's death. He had been a less-than-renowned pastor until his recent reassignment to Mercies. His ruddy, taciturn face was set off by a fluff of unruly white hair. His soft fingers were long and tapered, and his voice was a low rumble, like distant thunder. He had been born in Poland and had come to the States when he was a baby of ten months.

Father P., as most parishioners called him, watched Wasserman with tired blue eyes. The monsignor, meanwhile, finished his meal seemingly oblivious to any undercurrents among his staff. Froeschel led the group in a prayer of thanksgiving, then left for an appointment with some ailing parishioners at a local nursing home.

Pawlikawski soon drifted away, leaving Mulrennan and Wasserman and the housekeeper, who cleared the table and refilled the carafe at Wasserman's request. Mulrennan himself took another glass and lit a cigarette.

"What's the plan for tonight?" Wasserman asked archly.

"Just some reading, I guess. I may hit the sack early."

Without waiting for Mulrennan to ask, the other priest said: "I'm heading into New York. Need to get away for a night. You're welcome to come along." He swirled the burgundy in his glass. "Doesn't it get to you after a while—I mean, living here among only men—trapped, no outlet, no freedom?"

"I don't feel that way at all," Mulrennan said, his tone a bit defensive.

"You're still green. As for me, I didn't really mind for the longest time. Then one day I woke up and wanted to scream bloody murder. Didn't do it, of course." He tipped back the glass and drained it. "Really wanted to, though."

"Is that why you drink so much?" The moment he said the words, Mulrennan knew he had overstepped.

"Don't you start in on me, pal. You keep your own underdrawers clean, like a good little Vatican boy." He slapped the glass down on the table and stalked out.

A few minutes later, from his bedroom window, Mulrennan heard Ken Wasserman's Chevrolet pull out of the garage and speed into the night. He knelt beside his bed to pray: for Father P. and Father Ken, for the scared young woman in the confessional, for Monsignor Froeschel, for the archbishop, for his own family. But he felt stymied.

"Just because I am a priest . . . do I have the answer to Rita's problem?" he breathed. "Is Ken's drinking or his anger any of my business? Wouldn't I rather be somewhere else—the chancery, perhaps, where the real decisions are made? Dear God, did You make me a priest to serve You, or did I choose this course willfully and for my own ends? Father, forgive me and guide me to do Your will."

The tumult of the gymnasium rushed into his ears, and he replayed the basketball game in his mind. A bittersweet ache welled within: he had supped on satisfaction, if not victory, today. His boys had done well, and he was proud of his role as teacher and leader. This was the Holy Spirit in action. But was His intervention limited to only that circumstance? What about the real problems of real people?

Before he lay down to sleep, he again remembered his brother priest: *Bring Ken home safely tonight, dear Lord, and let him know peace. And bring Your peace, Your grace, to Your daughter Rita.*

Father Timothy Mulrennan jogged toward the closely packed crowd of two or three hundred outside Newark's Fourth Precinct police station in the humid, electric night. "Forgive me, Rita," he whispered to no one.

It was nine o'clock on July 13, 1967, and just now he
was supposed to be meeting with Rita Kearney to discuss
her marital problems and her months-long involvement
with an unnamed lover. Several times since her confession
they had talked and prayed together. She had only grown
more adamant that her marriage was over—though her husband, a local contractor, was oblivious and thought he was
the father of the baby, which was due in about three
months. She was in love with the other man, she insisted,
and was eager to have his baby, regardless of the consequences.

Mulrennan felt he was letting her down tonight. She was
in a very fragile emotional condition, and he was certain
she would care less about his emergency mission on the
streets of inner-city Newark than his role as her counselor
and confessor—and perhaps her only friend.

More urgent business had brought him into this Newark
slum area tonight. He and Father P. had been watching
televised news reports of a riot in the making down here,
just three or four miles from where they sat in the relative
comfort of the rectory. Tim, however, could not sit still.
He had called the archbishop's office. Word came down:
he was to report to the police station immediately, to be of
assistance if he could. . . . He thought suddenly of his car,
parked a few blocks from here, but he pushed that worry,
and his concern about Rita Kearney, out of his mind.

As the young priest elbowed into the crowd, he wondered about these people who jostled him from all sides as
they surged toward the precinct station. Did they really
need him as much as Rita did? Were they even aware that
this white man in a cleric's black suit was here to serve
them in the name of his bishop?

A tiny voice amplified by a small battery-powered
speaker wafted through the heavy air: a skinny young Negro with a tall brown Afro haircut wearing a torn Rutgers
University T-shirt. As Mulrennan pressed forward toward
the front of the crowd, he caught the man's exhortation to
the milling mob.

"Whitey's pigs *will* not keep our people down! We *are*

not slaves anymore! We *will* not be intimidated by his *police* or his soldiers!"

Glancing around him, Mulrennan realized his was the only white face except for the phalanx of state and city police in visored helmets positioned shoulder to shoulder in front of the station. They held rifles at present-arms and mouths firmly horizontal. As he muscled his way closer, he looked into their hooded eyes and saw fear and bafflement and anger.

From the darkness a single rock sailed over the crowd and struck a cop's helmet with an echoing crack. Turning in the direction from which it had come, Mulrennan saw a high-rise housing project that stood now like a dark brick wailing wall against the darker black sky. The project and the precinct were close neighbors.

The cops tensed, looked around nervously. Mulrennan felt a jolt of fear-fueled adrenaline. The orator continued to harangue his audience, eliciting applause and jeers that rippled through the crowd. The young priest was pinned between two big black men who glared at him, then, seeing his Roman collar, grudgingly stood aside to allow him passage.

Above, the streetlamps glowed with yellow menace. The heat and humidity and closeness of angry humanity took his breath.

"He *wants* you in the ghetto. He *wants* you uneducated. He *wants* your children undernourished so they won't grow up to threaten his stranglehold. I say to you, brothers and sisters—we *will* not take it anymore! We *will* fight back—right here, right now! Get *out* the way, whitey, we're comin' through!"

"Yeah, brother! You tell them muthas we're comin'!"

"I'm a-tellin'!" the speaker shouted. "But are they a-hearin'? Are they a-hearin' us, brothers?"

A Molotov cocktail exploded against the station wall. People screamed, and the police line bristled with cocked guns as some jumped forward and others knelt defensively. Then a second homemade bomb erupted as it hit the precinct wall next to the main door. Gumdrops of flame splattered the sidewalk.

Tim Mulrennan stepped into the five feet of no-man's-land between the mob and the beleaguered riot cops, who crisply reformed their line.

"They hear us now!" a woman shrieked.

The agitator shouted into his microphone, "Mess with me, white man's po-lice! Mess with my people's board of edu-cay-shun!"

Rocks and brick shards rained from the project windows directly across from the police station. Mulrennan bent nearly double as he was hit by several sharp missiles. Touching his scalp and feeling blood, he ran toward the station entrance.

"Stop! Hold your position!" A state police captain advanced, held up his hand, crisp and undistracted by the roil of chaos around him. "State your business, sir."

"I'm here to meet Inspector Logue," Mulrennan shouted, wincing in pain. "The archbishop sent me."

"Sir, pardon me for saying this—I don't give a good goddamn if the pope sent you. We're in a riot here, and I have my orders. You'll have to wait."

The captain sent one of his officers inside to announce Mulrennan, who looked around, fearing more rocks or flying debris. The mob taunted the cops, their shouts echoing off the face of the brick high-rise. A wave of nausea rose within the priest. He had never been so afraid in his life.

He knew that his parishioners in North Auburn, a few miles west, were scared, too. Rumors and false reports had been passed from friend to friend and house to house throughout the entire day. Doors were locked, televisions tuned in, streets deserted, baseball games canceled, as the suburbs hunkered down to await Armageddon.

Mulrennan thought again of Rita Kearney and hoped she had received his message canceling their appointment. Surely she would not be so foolish as to go out on a night like this.

"White man's justice! Black man's chains! White man's justice! Black man's chains!" The harsh words tattooed the thick night air.

Father Mulrennan waited as the state police captain barked orders at his men. The terror of uncertainty was unmistakable in their eyes. They expected a sniper attack, certain it was only a matter of time.

A few minutes later, he found himself inside the precinct, sitting in the office of Inspector Patrick Logue, a twenty-year veteran of the Newark force. He slouched at his desk, a disheveled, tieless bear who hulked behind an array of six telephones and one overflowing ashtray.

"Glad the archbishop is concerned," Logue said after Mulrennan introduced himself and explained why he had come. "Not much he can do except call for peace and pray a lot." The inspector spat out words like so much tobacco juice.

"He wants me to stay here and talk to these people and find out what they need."

"Some of them need a swift kick in the ass, if you ask me—which you didn't." Logue held up a thick slab of a hand. "I know, I know, it's not funny business. Look, there's not much I can do for you. The mayor is beside himself—after all, he's tried to expand housing programs and open up his government to minority folks. Maybe it was just too little, too late."

Mulrennan knew that things were a hell of a lot more complicated than that. It was true that the incumbent mayor had instituted some innovative programs to reclaim the sizable population of poor and disenfranchised black citizens who became the majority following the flight of whites from the city over the past decade. Yet where were the dispossessed going to go when the banks, real estate, and business interests had bought up most of the land in the Central Ward to build a new university-hospital complex over razed residences? What were they expected to do? Why were the power brokers unable to see that they were throwing gasoline on a smoldering rag heap?

Now Tim Mulrennan found himself in the innermost circle of the inferno. *How the hell did I get myself here?* he worried. When he could be—should be?—in the air-conditioned sanctum of the rectory in his suburban parish.

The archbishop, of course, he reminded himself. This was the price of being a "star" diocesan priest. He had pushed his head over the wall of the trench and faced the withering gunfire of history. He had spoken up in the archdiocesan-wide meeting after the first night of the Newark riots. He had talked about how the Church must take action and show compassion and be an example to the religious and secular community at large. The gathered clergy had murmured their approbation and applauded his Christian admonition—this young diocesan priest with such impressive diplomatic experience.

During a meeting with Archbishop Boland the following morning, Mulrennan had sat in the prelate's majestic chancery office, admiring the mullioned windows open to admit the barest hint of July breeze.

"Go among these folks for a while," Boland had told him. "Talk to them and work with them. Report back to me what is in their minds. Our inner-city pastors have their hands full right now just keeping their parishes afloat, and this office has no one to spare for the task."

Turning then to Mulrennan's immediate superior, the archbishop steepled his fingers beneath his chin and eyed him thoughtfully. His fine, closely trimmed white hair contrasted to a face weathered and worn by ecclesiastical cares.

"Bob, I know this will be a sacrifice for you," Boland added.

Monsignor Robert Froeschel, who had known the archbishop since their seminary days, acknowledged that it was, then said, "Your call, Bishop. Tim has proven himself a good priest, and he is loved by the people of Our Lady of Mercies. Just as long as he isn't away too often . . ."

So now Timothy Mulrennan found himself seated before Inspector Logue, who proved to be of no assistance whatsoever. A few minutes after their meeting began, Mulrennan was back out on the street, left to fend for himself. He walked the pavement for the rest of the night, meeting small groups of angry black youths, skirting the National Guard outposts. The kids listened sullenly when he suggested they go home, get out of the line of fire. They could not believe he was out on the street alone, but they respected him for it. Some cursed at him, but no one touched or threatened him.

For hours he heard gunshots and breaking glass, saw or

smelled smoke. Oddly, he did not feel physically threatened but overwhelmingly sad and powerless. He did not want to sleep; he simply wanted the violence to end. But there was nothing he could do to stop it.

As the first hint of daybreak turned the buildings a soft gray, Mulrennan glanced at his watch: 5:47 A.M.

He heard an engine idling; Mulrennan turned onto a deserted avenue and saw the hulking form of a truck, wheezing like a nervous cat. He approached cautiously and at last could read the letters on its side: Tast-Mor: "Taste More," misspelled decades ago by some advertising genius. To Mulrennan, the accompanying logo of a freckled, pigtailed girl eating a white-bread sandwich was as familiar as his own skin. He had grown up eating Tast-Mor breads and cakes. It wasn't until he traveled overseas that he learned that bread came in a thousand colors, textures, and tastes. The truck somehow seemed out of time and place. The familiar was now alien in a world suddenly gone mad.

Dawn had stolen the sky almost before he realized it. There were no shadows on the street, yet a pall hung over everything he could see along the dilapidated, empty city street. He walked toward the bread truck.

Inside, the driver sat frozen, white hands gripping the black steering wheel. Mulrennan knocked on the windshield, causing the man to jump as if he had been electrocuted. When he saw it was a white man, a priest, he opened the panel door.

"Morning. What's going on? Are you okay?" Mulrennan asked.

"I'm not going in there," the man said, pointing toward the center of the city. He was a flushed, skinny fifty-year-old; Tim guessed he was a veteran driver who might have driven this particular route for a decade. More importantly, he was scared sick, his blood pressure sky high.

"This is your route?"

The man nodded listlessly.

"You know these people, these stores?"

"Thought I did. Not so sure now."

"Need some help?" He touched the driver's steely arm,

was amazed at the tension he felt. "My name is Father Tim Mulrennan."

"I'm Eddie Defino—as in *vino*. That's Italian for wine."

"I know. Pleased to meet you."

They shook hands.

"I'm not going in there," Defino muttered again.

"Where?" Tim asked.

"Nig—I mean, Darktown, Father. Where my stores are. Too dangerous."

"I have an idea. Let me drive." Mulrennan could not believe he had just said that. Nor could Defino.

The driver looked through watery gray eyes at the young priest, convinced that he must be crazy.

"Look, I think we'll be safe," Mulrennan said in a re-assuring tone. "The people need bread. They'll be glad to see us. And I'm a pretty good driver." He lied; he had driven a truck only once before, in the army.

"The company wouldn't go for that. How 'bout I drive and you unload the bread? I stay in the truck."

Mulrennan quickly agreed, and a few moments later was carrying a full tray of Tast-Mor product into the grocery on the corner. The shopkeeper watched, wide-eyed, as the priest stacked fresh loaves on the counter. As Mulrennan was about the leave, the man said: "Don't forget the stale."

Mulrennan turned and removed several old loaves.

"Thanks, Father. What happened to Ed?"

"He's out in the truck. I decided to help him."

"Glad you did. My customers need their bread."

Returning to the truck, Mulrennan clambered into the cab on the passenger's side and slid the tray between the seats and into the back. Defino jerked the vehicle into gear and pulled away from the curb. As they rattled onto the somber street, Mulrennan looked on the console and saw the butt of a .38 police revolver sticking out from beneath a dirty cap.

Defino now became an optimist: "The old lady told me not to report to work today, but I said I'd be damned if the niggers were gonna take away my paycheck. I've put in twenty-four years with this goddamned company—pardon my French, Father."

Then he glanced over at the priest and noticed for the first time the flaky brown crust of blood on Mulrennan's head. "Jeezus H. Christ, Father, what happened to you? Did they attack you?"

Tentatively exploring the wound with his fingers, Mulrennan remembered he had a blaring headache. "It wasn't me personally. I stepped into the trajectory of a brick. That was last night." Of course, the kids he had encountered in the later hours had seen the cut, the blood, probably thought he was insane.

Defino winced in sympathetic rage. "They're gonna kill us all," he spat. "You should get yourself to a hospital."

"There are others in worse shape than me."

Mulrennan watched the buildings flash by on Springfield Avenue: shopfronts, dilapidated apartments, churches, a used-car dealership. In the half-light of the new day he saw history and the potential for life in each doorway and window and hand-lettered sign. Who were these people? Aliens in their own land—in his land. An elderly black lady, dressed incongruously in a calf-length green coat, crossed the street, walking slowly and purposefully toward the nearby bus stop. A man in his thirties stood outside a shop with a large roll of duct tape, covering several long cracks in the front pane.

Over the next two hours, the two men hit a dozen more stops in the heart of the Central Ward, all medium-sized neighborhood markets, each very grateful to receive a delivery. None of the other bread trucks had ventured into the riot zone.

The truck bounced along the avenue. The morning had matured; it would be a hot day. Tim Mulrennan had not slept for twenty-four hours, and he felt his beard sprouting. He must clean up and report back to the chancery in anticipation of another long day and longer night. He considered a visit to the hospital emergency room then decided to skip it: after all, if he wasn't dead by now . . .

A half hour later, as they pulled up in front of the rectory, Eddie Defino grinned sheepishly, and said, "You done a good deed, Father. I was gonna turn back, forget the whole damn thing."

"Is that gun loaded?" Mulrennan asked, pointing to the ugly .38 revolver.

"My brother-in-law gave it to me. He's a Bloomfield cop. Yeah—it's loaded. Not that I'd use it, I think. Just feel safer with it handy-like."

Mulrennan had not handled a firearm since his army days. He thought of his brother, who was due to come home on leave from Vietnam in a few months. How would Kevin Mulrennan, Marine Corps officer to the bone, have handled the past twenty-four hours? Tim smiled to himself. Kevin knew no fear; he could handle anything. He was every kid's ideal big brother. Tim missed him.

Mulrennan shook the man's hand, then climbed out and shut the door. He watched as the truck drove off, then turned and headed for the rectory. As he envisioned a shower and shave, he felt the fear melt away but knew it was a temporary respite: If the rioting continued he would have to return to the streets later in the day and face it all over again—and retrieve his car, if there was anything left of it.

As he approached the rectory door, he was startled by a figure lurking in the shadows beside the walkway. For an instant he thought it was a prowler, but then the figure stepped into the light and stammered his name.

"Rita!" he exclaimed, hearing the terror in her voice. He rushed over and reached for her arms, but she pulled back and averted her eyes. But she was unable to hide the purpling bruises on her face.

"What happened to you?" He reached for her face, then lowered his hand, not wanting to frighten her. "Did Michael do that to you?

At mention of her husband's name, her eyes went wide with fright, and Mulrennan had his answer.

"Where is he now?" he demanded, but she raised a hand in protest.

"No. Please. Don't do anything, say anything. I—I'm all right. Really I am. It looks worse than . . ." Her voice trailed off.

Taking her by the arm, he led her to a bench alongside the walkway and sat beside her.

"Tell me what happened," he said softly.

"Last night I came here, but . . ."

"I'm sorry. I left a message with one of your kids. I was in Newark."

"Father Ken told me. He spoke to me a bit, and when I went home I decided I had to tell him."

"You told Michael about the man you've been seeing?"

"About the baby—about its not being his."

"And that's when he did this," Mulrennan said, shaking his head.

"It was when I wouldn't tell him the man's name. He went crazy. Never seen him so angry."

"Has he done this before? Has he hurt you before?"

"No," she blurted too quickly, but her eyes betrayed the truth. She started to say something, but the words caught in her throat. Lowering her head, she began to sob.

Wrapping his arm around her, Mulrennan whispered soothingly, telling her that it would be all right, that things would work out. The words seemed hollow, but he couldn't think of anything else to say.

Slowly Rita calmed down. She pulled a handkerchief from her pocket and dabbed at her tears. "I . . . I'd better be going." She stood from the bench.

"You mustn't go back there," he declared.

"But I have to. The children—"

"It isn't safe, for you or them. I can give you the name of a place to take them—a family outside the parish, a house where you'll be safe."

"He'll come after me," she said, her voice tight with fear.

Standing, he took her hands in his own. "He won't know where you are. He'll have time to cool down, and you'll have time to decide what you need to do."

As Mulrennan continued to speak, Rita slowly relented, at last accepting the idea of going away. "But I have to go home first," she insisted. "I have to be there when the girls get home from school." Mulrennan started to protest, but she cut him off, saying, "It's all right, Father, really it is. Michael—he's at work. He left at seven this morning, like usual."

"He won't come back?"

"Not till five. I'll be fine till the girls get home."

"And you'll bring them right here?"

"At two-thirty. I promise."

"If you aren't here by three, I'm coming over."

"We'll be here."

"Good." Mulrennan allowed himself a smile. "I'll make the arrangements this morning, and I'll take you there myself."

"Father . . ." Rita said, lowering her eyes in shame. "Thank you, Tim." With that she turned and hurried down the street.

For a long time Mulrennan just stood there gazing after her, a chaos of thoughts charging through him. The frightened, angry people rioting on the streets, the ugly violence in what to many must seem an idyllic marriage. And what could he do about it? About any of it? Provide a little support and encouragement, perhaps. But was he able to effect any real change in any of their lives?

Shrugging with frustration, Mulrennan turned and headed into the rectory. As he started up the stairs, he almost collided with Father Kenneth Wasserman, who looked a bit distracted—or perhaps hungover—as he came sauntering down.

"Had breakfast already?" Wasserman asked, then noticed the cut on Mulrennan's head. "Whew! What happened to you?"

"This?" the young priest said, halting on the stairs and touching the wound gingerly. "It's nothing. Decided to stop a brick with my noggin."

"Better get it taken care of."

"As soon as I hit the shower."

"Good idea." Wasserman smiled mischievously and made a face as if he'd just smelled an offensive odor. "Better hurry or the pancakes'll all be gone." He started back down the stairs, but Mulrennan caught his arm.

"Last night—Rita Kearney came by?"

"I was gonna tell you about it at breakfast," Wasserman replied a bit defensively. "She said you were supposed to meet with her, so I told her about the archbishop sending you into the city."

"She said you spoke with her."

Wasserman looked confused. "You saw her?"

"Outside a few minutes ago. She—well, she had a rough time of it last night."

"What happened?"

"An argument with her husband." Mulrennan decided not to say any more, not wanting to break the confidentiality of their conversations.

"Did he do something to her? Did he hurt her?"

"Banged her up a bit, but she'll be all right. I'm taking her to a shelter this afternoon."

"That prick," Wasserman snapped, shaking his head. "I've always hated that bastard."

"Can't say I'm any too fond of him," Mulrennan agreed. "When she was here last night, did she say anything? Anything that might help me deal with the situation?"

Wasserman thought a moment and shrugged. "It was obvious she wanted to see you. We spoke a little about her daughters, but then she said she had to be getting home. I promised to let you know she'd come by."

"Thanks," he said, then turned and continued up the stairs. At the top he glanced back down and saw Father Ken still standing where Mulrennan had left him, his expression a curious mask of anger and indecision.

Less than half an hour later, Timothy Mulrennan ran into his colleague again, this time when Mulrennan emerged from the bathroom wrapped in a towel. As he crossed the hall and entered his room, he was startled to see Father Ken seated on the bed, a suitcase beside him on the floor.

"I'm leaving," the priest announced without fanfare.

"Leaving? Where are you going?" Mulrennan closed the door and took a terrycloth robe from the hook behind it. He donned the robe over the towel.

"Not where. I'm leaving the priesthood. Period." He gestured toward his neck, pointing out that he was not wearing his Roman collar but only a sport shirt and casual slacks.

"What the hell are you talking about?" Mulrennan asked as he unwrapped the towel from beneath the robe and hung it on the hook.

"I'm getting out of this hothouse once and for all. I'm

going to get married, have a family, and start living a real life. This whole thing was a mistake . . . a bad mistake." He turned away, as if unable to look Mulrennan in the eyes.

"Let's talk about it, Ken—before you do anything rash. Have you spoken with the monsignor? What did he say?"

"Only you know, my young friend. So far, at least."

"Why are you doing this?"

"I'm not here for counseling, Tim. But you have a right to know."

"Listen, Ken, this all sounds rather hasty. If something's happened, we can figure out—"

"There's nothing *we* can do. This is something I have to do alone."

"But why, Ken? What's so terrible that we can't—?"

"You can stuff your questions, Tim. I don't have to answer to Froeschel or you or anybody else. I've made my decision, and you're wasting your breath trying to convince me otherwise. Let's face it, Tim—you're a wonder at abstractions—at the big picture. But when it comes to the dirty little things of life . . . hell, it's not your fault. The Church makes us that way. So forget about me. You'll have an easier time saving the inner city from destruction. After all, you're the archbishop's anointed, a white messiah in the ghetto."

Tim Mulrennan swallowed his anger and his pride, which were choking him. He felt a sudden urge to deck the arrogant son of a bitch. Instead he forced himself to say in a calm tone, "I don't know why you don't like me, Ken. I've tried to be a friend to you. I've tried to talk to you and learn from you. I want to be a good priest, that's all. And I don't see anything wrong with that."

"Oh, nothing wrong at all, kid. God knows this broken-down old Mother Church needs some dedicated priests. If you want to know the truth, I not only like you but I'm damned jealous of you: of your certainty and high-mindedness." He stood and picked up the suitcase. Moving closer, he stared at the younger priest straight on. "But you see, I fell in love—with a girl and with life itself. Maybe I'm wrong. I'm throwing aside my vows, I know. But it feels right. I'm dropping out. It's the right thing for me. I know it in my gut."

"Who is she?" Mulrennan asked.

"This part you're not going to like so much."

When Mulrennan heard this, he took a step backward, lowered himself into a straight-backed chair, and rested an arm on his paper-strewn desk.

"It's Rita Kearney, your friend from school days. As you already know, she's expecting our child."

The words—the reality of what had just been spoken—struck Mulrennan full force. The breath went out of him, and he just stood there, staring at the other priest.

"Don't look so shocked. You would've figured it out sooner or later, anyway. I think she was planning to tell you last night. Instead I convinced her to leave that pig of a husband just as soon as we made all the arrangements. Apparently when she got home she told her husband enough to get herself beat up over it." He started toward the door. "Well, that's all finished. She'll move out so the kids'll be safe—until we can make plans. And if that bastard tries anything . . ."

"But she's a married woman," Mulrennan called after him.

"And I'm a priest." He turned back around, his face a mask of pain. "I know all that, Tim. And we'll do something about it. She'll get a divorce, and we'll marry in a civil ceremony. Then we'll begin annulment proceedings. It will take time." He held up his hand to silence Mulrennan's sputtered protest. "We're both willing to go through the process. We've talked it through. It's not pretty, and granted it won't make the parish look too good—"

"Ken, you're insane. I have been counseling her, and I know there are a lot of other issues to be worked out. Her kids, for one."

"There aren't any *issues*. This is real life . . . we just want to be together, to start a family. She married a loser who smacks her around and mentally abuses her. Is that any good for her or her kids?"

"She's young, immature."

"She's your age, if that's what you mean. And she's not

immature. Just scared—and with good reason."

As Wasserman reached for the doorknob, Mulrennan grasped his arm. "Don't do this, Ken."

"I have to—she does, too. Someday you'll understand that we have no other choice. It's either this or kill myself with drink." A strange half-smile played at his lips. "I know you think I'm a lush, Tim, but I'm not. It's just that it's been a whole lot easier to drink than to face the reality of what I was becoming—what I'd become without her."

"The monsignor . . ." Mulrennan said plaintively. "What'll he say? What'll I tell him?"

"You'll think of something. And in a couple of weeks, after I'm settled in somewhere, I'll come back and explain it all to him myself. Until then, you just concentrate on being the good priest I never was. You can do it for both of us."

He jerked open the door but paused, looked back at his younger colleague. "I have been through hell with this, Tim. Don't think I haven't. I've prayed about it—want to do the right thing. I may sound cold and callous, but—well, I know in my heart it's the right thing in the long run. Believe me."

"I do, Ken, but isn't there another way?"

Wasserman turned and strode down the hall. Tim Mulrennan just stood there in his bathrobe, his head throbbing in unrelieved pain, watching as Father Kenneth Wasserman disappeared down the stairs.

CHAPTER SIX

Monday, January 29, 9:03 A.M.

M y Lord Camerlengo!"
The sudden voice of Henry Martin Cardinal Vennholme was so forceful, so commanding, that Timothy Mulrennan was shaken from his daydream at the morning session of the conclave. Despite having slept for several hours, Mulrennan had been groggy and was having a hard time staying alert as they prepared for the first ballot of the day. But something in Vennholme's tone put him instinctively on guard.

Vennholme, attired as all were in scarlet-and-white choir dress, rose from his seat among the most senior members of the Sacred College. Slowly he turned so that he faced the majority of the assembly, his delicate hands raised, palms outward. Again he called in clearly enunciated Italian, "My Lord Camerlengo!"

Camerlengo Carlos Juan Cardinal Portillo recognized the French-Canadian prelate with a Castilian grunt.

"Thank you, My Lord," Vennholme acknowledged with a bow to the aged Spanish Jesuit. "And forgive this priest for the words he is about to speak, for they are harsh words. Know that I speak reluctantly—but of necessity—for it is my duty to address a matter most delicate. Rumors and wild stories have been circulating through the College of Electors, and they have begun to cast doubts on the moral character of one of our brothers, leading some among this body to question whether his human failures may affect his qualifications to vote, let alone to be seriously considered papabile."

The cardinals, who had expected merely another placid

day of inconclusive voting, were stunned by Vennholme's announcement. It was not only surprising but to the knowledge of all in the chapel, it was unprecedented, at least in the last several conclaves, for one cardinal to cast doubt on another. Even the feeblest and least engaged princes felt the thunderbolt of Vennholme's bold pronouncement and sat upright, attention riveted on the speaker.

As for Timothy Mulrennan, he received Vennholme's words like a blow between his shoulder blades. His fingernails dug through the plush fabric of the red cassock into his thigh muscles.

"Most Reverend Lords, we must look within our own hearts to see what role we may have played in this . . . this unfortunate scandal. I speak not of any single man's moral failings." His gaze fixed briefly on Timothy Mulrennan. "No, I refer to our own failures as the agents of rumor and innuendo. No man should be tried and judged in secret, afforded not even the opportunity to face his accusers, if in fact there be any. For who is it who is accusing our brother, Timothy John Cardinal Mulrennan?"

As Vennholme crooked a finger toward Mulrennan, he looked almost pained at having named him. He gave the American cardinal a seemingly sympathetic smile.

"Who is it that accuses our brother? I have heard whispers and stories and incredible charges. Yet no man has had the courage to stand before this assembly and lay out the evidence that would prove or disprove any charge. I tell you truly, my brother Mulrennan, it has hurt me deeply to hear those secret attacks and to know there was nothing I could do to dispel them. And I fear now that this secret conspiracy—this gossiping of mother hens, if that is all it proves to be—shall dissuade some who might otherwise consider casting their vote for you."

Mulrennan wanted to speak, to say something, but he was so stunned by Vennholme's comments, so uncertain where they were leading, that he remained silent, immobile. He tried not to reveal his shock and hurt as he listened with the others.

"I warned my words would be harsh, but they are not directed at you, my brother cardinal. I do not know if these rumors are fact or fantasy, and if they should prove to be true, I might find my tongue unleashed in your direction. But no, today my anger is directed to the rest of us—yes, myself, too, for I have remained silent as others worked to defeat you not on your merits but on your supposed vices. It is true that we must know the character of the man who would sit on the Throne of St. Peter. But if we hold any doubts, any suspicions whatsoever, we should stand up here and lay them before the entire assembly so that they may be addressed and resolved."

He turned now to his comrade, Pasquale Cardinal Giannantonio, who looked quite uncomfortable at the attention.

"Unfortunately not all men have the strength, the moral fiber, to accuse one of their fellows. They would prefer to do their work in darkness, unseen and unrecognized. And so it sadly falls upon me to do what they cannot."

Again he addressed Mulrennan directly. The fox's smile tugged at his lips, but he held it back with effort.

"Understand, my brother, that I charge you with nothing, I accuse you of nothing. But it is a disservice to the entire conclave and all that it represents for us to pretend that accusations are not being made. And so I will reluctantly play the devil's advocate, saying aloud what cowards whisper in private. I do so not because I believe the charges but out of my deep respect and love for you, so that you may answer your accusers, hidden though they may be, and so that our fellow electors will not be governed by rumor but by the clear light of truth."

Mulrennan wanted to jump up from his chair and do something, say something, but he had no idea what that would be. As these two warring sides battled within him, he saw Cardinal Biagi staring at him with an expression that urged calm restraint.

"Once again, I must remind everyone—Cardinal Mulrennan most particularly—that these charges are not mine but are what has been whispered throughout the Apostolic Palace these past few days. I am speaking—and most reluctantly so—about a series of incidents that occurred during our brother's years as a priest in the Archdiocese of Newark. It is said that during his tenure he befriended a young woman—" He drew from his pocket a slip of paper and unfolded it. "A Mrs. Rita Kenney."

"Kearney!" Mulrennan blurted, half rising from his seat. "Rita Kearney," he added in a whisper.

"Ah, then you are acquainted with her," Vennholme said encouragingly. "But of course you would be, because you went to school together, is that not so?" He did not wait for an answer. "This Rita Kearney was a wife and mother to two young girls when she and her friend, Father Timothy Mulrennan, renewed their friendly *relationship* during his first parish assignment. . . ." He said the word almost as if afraid to give it voice.

The French-Canadian cardinal continued to speak, but Mulrennan was no longer aware, except dimly, of what he was saying. Instead he was back in the Newark suburbs, hurrying down the street toward Rita Kearney's apartment the morning he last saw her.

His hair was still wet from the shower, and his Roman collar hung askew. Even one shoe had gone untied in his haste to get over to the Kearney house and stop Rita and Father Ken from making what he was convinced would be a horrible mistake.

As he approached the brick-fronted apartment building, he saw Wasserman's beat-up old Chevy pulled at an angle to the side of the road. A police car's blue-and-red lights danced across the facades of the nearest building.

Good! Mulrennan thought as he quickened his pace. Damn fool got pulled over for reckless driving—before he did something stupid.

As he drew closer, he realized that the police car was not alone. Beside it, partway on the sidewalk, stood an ambulance, its rear doors opened wide.

Mulrennan started to run now, pushing past the onlookers who were gathering in the street. Reaching the Chevy he glanced inside but saw nothing. He looked around and spied one of the policemen. As he started toward him, the front door opened and a pair of white-coated attendants pushed a wheeled stretcher out onto the sidewalk.

The breath caught in Mulrennan's throat as he approached the sheet-draped figure. The ambulance attendants

were preparing to fold the legs of the stretcher and push it
into the back of the vehicle when Mulrennan reached for
the plastic sheet. One of the men grasped his wrist to stop
him, then noticed Mulrennan's clerical collar.

"Sorry, Father." He released his grip.

Mulrennan pulled back just enough of the shroud to see
the blood-smeared features of Rita Kearney. Her eyes were
closed, and if not for the blood and bruises she would have
seemed in a restful sleep.

"A clean shot to the heart," the attendant explained as
Mulrennan let the sheet drop back over her face. "Must've
died instantly."

Mulrennan gagged and backed away from the vehicle.
He stood in shocked disbelief as they secured the stretcher
and brought out a second one, its legs popping open as they
dragged it out of the back.

"Another?"

"Afraid so." With that the two men hurried the stretcher
back into the building.

"Did you know her?" a voice asked, and Mulrennan
turned to see a policeman not much older than himself.

"She . . . she was a parishioner."

"Rita Kearney, correct?" the young man asked, checking
his notes.

"Yes. Who did this?"

The policeman jerked his thumb toward the police
cruiser. It was then that Mulrennan noticed the wide-eyed
man seated in the back, his hands cuffed behind him.

"The husband," the officer muttered with a grunt of resignation. "It's usually that way. Looks like he came home
and found her with another guy."

For a hot moment Tim panicked: *the girls?* Then he remembered that they were safely at school, and staying with
another family who had agreed to take them temporarily to
get out of the untenable situation at home—now possibly
for a much longer period of time.

A moment later the front door opened again and a second
sheet-draped body was rolled out toward the ambulance.
Timothy Mulrennan knew in his gut what he would find
under the plastic sheet, but still he had to look, to convince

himself that this had really happened. He had a harder time recognizing this victim, for the fatal bullet had struck the side of the man's face. But in the end there was no escaping that it was Father Ken Wasserman whom they were loading into the ambulance.

"Any chance you knew that one?" the policeman asked, coming up behind Mulrennan. "The lady's boyfriend?"

"No," the young priest blurted. "No!"

"Didn't figure so. That's okay; we'll identify him."

"No," Mulrennan repeated, grasping the man's arm. "I did know him. I meant that he wasn't Rita's boyfriend. He's a priest, too. From our parish. Father Kenneth Wasserman."

"How did he know the woman?"

"He was just trying to help her."

"You sure of that?" the cop asked, unconvinced, scribbling notes in his book.

Mulrennan said, "She was having troubles with her husband. Father Ken was counseling her, that's all."

"In the wrong place at the wrong time, I guess," the officer said. He took Mulrennan's name, then returned to the cruiser.

Timothy Mulrennan's lie had held up, not just that day but through the following years. It turned out that Michael Kearney had never found out for certain the identity of his wife's lover. He had his suspicions but no proof. Wasserman had been in the way that terrible day—too friendly, perhaps, to be just a friend and counselor to his faithful wife—or was he what Mulrennan said he was? In fact, during his years in prison, where he still remained, his vague, desperate suspicions had shifted from Ken Wasserman to Timothy Mulrennan to a number of other former friends and acquaintances. No one took him seriously, and in time he and his rantings were all but forgotten, even by his daughters, who were sent to the New Jersey shore to be raised by Rita's sister.

Mulrennan never told anyone the entire truth—not even Monsignor Froeschel.

*   *   *

Not even now, as Cardinal Vennholme completed his recitation of rumors and possible moral failings. "Yes, my brothers in Christ," Vennholme said in conclusion, "these words have been bitter upon my tongue. I take no pleasure in what I have felt compelled to do. But I have done so out of love and concern." He turned to Mulrennan. "And now it is my sincere hope that, with these allegations at last out in the open, you will be able to explain what really happened and put all our brother electors at ease."

The chapel grew deathly silent as Cardinal Vennholme sat down and all eyes turned to the American cardinal. He felt their weight upon him, and it felt strangely liberating. The seconds passed without any move by Mulrennan to answer the charges. The rustling of robes and papers and the clearing of throats echoed in the Sistine. Some men cast their gaze at their lace-covered laps. A few looked directly at Mulrennan, their eyes sympathetic or accusatory. Others glanced from Mulrennan to Vennholme and back again, unbelieving.

At last the camerlengo rose and waved his thin arms. "Our brother has brought some serious charges to our attention," he said in Spanish-accented Italian rather than Latin. "We recognize our brother Cardinal Mulrennan, if he cares to answer these most grave allegations. The College in conclave shall listen and shall prayerfully consider the words of these brothers before another vote is held." He steadied himself, then resumed his seat.

When Mulrennan continued to maintain his silence, Cardinal Biagi rose, looking a bit troubled as he said, "Doesn't my brother from the United States wish to address this matter and put it to rest?"

Mulrennan could see that the Italian was trembling, and so he rose and said in Biagi's native tongue, "Out of deference to you, Eminence, I shall speak, but only to say that I have nothing to say. I will not honor rumors and lies with a response."

Pasquale Cardinal Giannantonio fairly leaped out of his chair. He had a small, round head and pink face that made him look like a child, reminding some with long memories of Cardinal Spellman of New York.

"Lies? Rumors, you say? Then tell us which aspects are so. Is it not true that you and that young woman had knowledge of each other? That such carnal knowledge resulted in a child who was to be born only weeks after the unfortunate woman's death? That your betrayal of your priestly vows led her poor husband to madness and the most awful of mortal sins? That a humble parish priest who tried to intervene paid for his selfless compassion with his life? Which of these is a lie? Which merely a rumor? Perhaps you could bring that poor, misguided woman and your unfortunate brother priest before us to speak on your behalf—if your actions had not led to their demise, that is."

Giannantonio turned now to address the larger assembly.

"His Eminence Cardinal Vennholme is far too kind. I will not be so forgiving—not with the future of the Church and the papacy at stake. The truth of the matter is that Timothy Mulrennan has betrayed his sacred office, his flock, and his faith. It is with a dark heaviness in my soul and a knowledge of my own sins that I stand before you and assert this claim. Yet the Holy Spirit has prompted these revelations as just and necessary. For the very survival of Mother Church is reposited in this body; and if we cannot honestly correct our corruptions, then surely our God-given institution is under the gravest threat since the barbarian horde stood before the gates of this city a millennium and a half ago."

Mulrennan betrayed no emotion whatever in his demeanor: He stared directly at this new accuser, unblinking, though his face was white. Pasquale Giannantonio spoke again in a voice that was far deeper, far more commanding than his usual high-pitched whine.

"You may have asked yourselves, why have these charges been carried through the conclave in whispers rather than in the open light of day?" the prelate from Gubbio said. "If they are true, why were they not brought forth before the conclave or even before the passing of our late Holy Father? Obviously these transgressions did not occur in the past few days. Sadly the answer, my friends, is that while I and others have known of these sins against the Church, the proof has been acutely difficult to obtain. I confess to having taken pains to investigate these and other matters thoroughly and fairly. And in fact I spoke to the Holy Father himself only a few weeks before he died. It was he who asked me to wait until this conclave was gathered. He—burdened with office, ravaged by physical pain, staggered by the betrayal evidenced in Cardinal Mulrennan's actions—the pope himself instructed me to speak out only when I was certain that it was necessary. It remains my profoundest desire that I not be forced to do so, for I am afraid that you have heard only a small portion of the charges I have unearthed."

Cardinal Vennholme started to rise, but Giannantonio gestured for him to sit back down.

"Don't try to dissuade me," he said caustically.

"Cardinal Giannantonio," Vennholme interrupted, "I think you should be careful about—"

"I will remain silent no longer," the Italian shot back. "Perhaps you are right—I have been wrong to speak behind Cardinal Mulrennan's back, and I beg forgiveness for such petty behavior."

Vennholme was on his feet now. "I think you must consider what you are—"

"I have considered this long and hard, and I am determined—"

"*Silencio!*" a voice exploded, and all turned to see the camerlengo up on his feet, pounding on the table. He gestured for both cardinals Vennholme and Giannantonio to sit down. "There will be silence, is that clearly understood?" the Jesuit demanded in Italian, looking back and forth between the two men. "My good Cardinal Giannantonio, if you have any new charges to lay before this sacred assembly, then I would ask you to bring them to my personal attention, and we shall determine the appropriate time and forum."

"As you wish, Lord Camerlengo," Giannantonio said with a solemn nod. "I will elucidate these charges for the holy cardinals in the appropriate tribunal, but I must now ask Cardinal Mulrennan to remove his name from consideration by this body."

"You shall do no such thing!" Portillo sputtered, pounding on the table. He drew in a calming breath. "My good Cardinal Vennholme, while we understand your desire to put an end to the rumors that had come even to my attention, I think you'll agree that enough has been said on the matter for the time being." He turned to Timothy Mulrennan, and added, "That is, unless you, my son, desire to speak now to what has been alleged."

Cardinal Biagi was about to rise, to say something, anything, when he heard a voice call out, "My Lord Camerlengo! May I address the conclave before the ballot proceeds?" Spinning around, Biagi sought out the speaker and finally saw him halfway across the chapel at a table that held a number of Asian and African cardinals.

Portillo hesitated, then gestured for the scrutineers to hold back. Rising, he said, "We recognize the Reverend Lord Cardinal De Guzman of Manila. We caution, however, that this shall be the last speaker before we resume balloting." He slumped wearily in the wooden throne and held his old head in mottled hands.

As De Guzman rose from his seat, Biagi wondered what in heaven's name the man intended to say. Glancing over at Vennholme, he saw that the Canadian was paying little attention, as if nothing the quiet-spoken Filipino might say would have any effect on the inevitable outcome.

"My Lord Camerlengo, my brothers in Christ," the Archbishop of Manila began in perfectly enunciated Italian, showing a flair for languages that was second only to their former pontiff's. "May the Holy Spirit who sustains us in faith, hope, and charity animate our hearts to accept our brother Cardinal Mulrennan's mea culpa. And may the same spirit inspire him to accept God's forgiveness—and that of his brother priests."

His voice was soft and lilting but carried through the chapel as he stood at the rear of the assembly, his hands clasped at his breast. He was not intimately familiar to many of the cardinals who lived outside of Rome. They listened carefully to him.

"Who among us, this elite spiritual college, has not sinned? Let him, as Christ said, cast the first stone at our brother."

Biagi watched the Filipino cardinal's every move, every gesture as he started down the center aisle from his table at the far end of the chapel. De Guzman was among the more junior group of cardinals appointed by the late pope at a consistory only four years prior, though he had served as the primate of the Philippines for a full decade before receiving the red biretta.

"I believe in a loving, understanding Father who is slow to angerandwealthyinHisstorehouseofforgivenessforusall," De Guzman continued as he neared the front of the chapel. "Our Father calls us to forgive one another and—importantly—to forgive ourselves. It is the sin of pride that blocks us from acceptance of His ready forgiveness. Shame is the most severe manifestation of our lack of such acceptance. All I am saying to my brother Cardinal Mulrennan is this: Do not allow shame or any other misguided feelings to hold you back from voting or otherwise interfere with your participation in this conclave. Not only is it right that you stay among us, it is needed. You belong here as a witness to God's grace and power. We need both you and your vote."

Biagi watched in fascination as De Guzman reached the front of the chapel and took his place where Mulrennan had stood before the altar. His pleasant expression suddenly darkened, his soft voice taking on a power that Biagi had not heard from him before.

"I confess that I am greatly troubled by what I have heard here this day. I come from a troubled nation of islands, far away. But in this age of computers and satellite TV, we have taken our place on the world stage—and with us our brother nations in Africa, South America, and throughout the world. And I must say, we are all troubled by what is happening within our Church."

De Guzman moved away from the altar, approaching the nearest of the tables and directing his comments first to one and then another of the cardinals, as if they were in a private conversation.

"Something quite disturbing has come to my attention—do not ask me how, for I am an old 'newshound' who has learned never to reveal confidential sources." It was well known within the Curia that he had secretly contributed stories and editorials to opposition newspapers during the Marcos dictatorship. "In fact, when I tell you what I have learned, you may not need to ask from where the news has come, for you may already have heard the same yourself."

He moved to the next table as he continued.

"Here in this Apostolic Palace, we are sealed off from the world outside." He waved his arms, as if taking in the city beyond the walls of the Sistine Chapel. "No word, no communication, is supposed to come in through these walls. And the only word that goes out must be in the color of the smoke we release through that chimney." He pointed to the stovepipe that protruded through one of the windows. "Yet I believe that the seal of silence has been breached."

De Guzman had now reached Cardinal Vennholme's table, and it was not lost on Biagi—nor anyone else, for that matter—when his next words were directed at the Canadian prelate.

"Who would break such a seal, such a sacred trust? And what would be his motive? Perhaps it does not matter, provided we do not fall prey to such machinations."

He moved on, speaking to each cardinal in turn as he addressed them en masse.

"Some of you may be wondering what I am speaking about. Others already know, because as our American friends like to say in their movies, even these walls have ears. Yes, these sacred, sealed walls have ears. And through those ears, we hear that a story is already spreading on the outside—a story about events taking place here on the inside. Apparently this morning the city, no doubt the world, is awakening to reports of scandal brewing in our conclave."

He was near Timothy Mulrennan's table now, and he approached and laid a comforting hand on Mulrennan's shoulder.

"I regret having to say this, my friend, but the stories and the scandal are about you"—he turned to the others— "about this Sacred College, for it is obvious to me that such a story could only be spread by the active intervention of one or more of us here."

This time when he turned to look at Henry Vennholme, the Canadian bolted to his feet, his voice quivering as he said, "How dare you insult me with your not-so-veiled accusations. If Mulrennan is in trouble with the media, then—"

"You will be quiet!" De Guzman snapped, stunning Biagi and the others. No one had ever heard the quiet cardinal raise his voice, and it obviously surprised Vennholme, who stepped back, struck silent. "You had your day, my brother cardinal, and you may yet have more days to come. But that day is not today, for no one—not even you—can be proud of the damage being done to Mother Church from both outside these walls and within. This is a day when the world should be reflecting on the loss of their dear, sainted Holy Father and looking with hope for our signal that a new leader has been chosen. Instead, they are awakening to lurid and, may I say, inaccurate reports of affairs and scandal among our own papabile."

He again faced Mulrennan.

"I am sorry, but that is what is being said—that you were responsible for the death of your mistress in Newark. But we know better—*I* know better. And so should you," he added, pointing a finger at Vennholme.

It looked as if Vennholme was about to reply, but De Guzman turned his back on the man, walking instead to where Cardinal Portillo was seated.

"My dear Lord Camerlengo, I beseech you to break with custom and adjourn today's session without any balloting. Too much has happened—too much is happening—and in such a climate, it may not be the Lord's hand that guides our deliberations. Instead, let today be set aside for prayer and reflection. Let us gather again tomorrow morning, after we have listened to our Lord and our own hearts. Then, with His blessing, may we cast our ballots for the next Vicar of Christ."

There was an outcry of voices, some calling for adjournment, others demanding that rules be followed and the next vote begun. Most vociferous among them was Henry Vennholme, who charged across the room, slapping the camerlengo's table as he shouted his protestations and demands.

Cardinal Biagi alone leaned back and said nothing. He wanted to speak, to engage Vennholme in battle and add his voice to the chorus competing for the camerlengo's attention. But he could not. He could no longer hear the voices, which blended into an undecipherable sea of sound lapping against the painted walls of the chapel. He was not even aware when Portillo rose on unsteady legs and declared the session adjourned, to reconvene the following morning. For just now Biagi's full attention was on the man with the small voice who had commanded such attention. He tried in vain to recognize Jaime Cardinal De Guzman in that man in the red-and-white choir vesture. But it was no longer a cardinal whom he saw. . . .

Camerlengo Carlos Roberto Cardinal Portillo hobbled out of the Sistine Chapel at the head of the red-hatted pack. In a rustle of silk and lace, the cardinals, men of many nations and myriad colors, shifted across the aisles, down the wide steps, and walked silently from the Renaissance chamber. They returned to their rooms to pray and contemplate—and some, no doubt, to caucus discreetly—until the following day when voting was to resume.

A few cardinal-electors looked back and saw that Mulrennan and Vennholme remained in their places. The two North Americans did not acknowledge each other until all the rest had left.

Mulrennan sat toward the edge of his chair and rested his aching forehead in his hands, elbows planted on the desk. He prayed darkly and silently. A table away, Vennholme swiveled in his seat and looked over at his rival with unconcealed disdain. He waited for Mulrennan to raise his head. Mulrennan sensed the other man's presence and opened his eyes.

"I see now so clearly," Mulrennan said. "I have been not only a sinful man, but a blind and stupid one. I have trusted that, on the divine scale, service to my Church and my diocese would outweigh my many failings." His angular face allowed a crooked near-smile. "I was wrong, of course. You defeated me so completely, Henry, in a battle I neither sought nor anticipated, that the only path left open to me was to surrender without condition."

Vennholme shifted the steel-rimmed spectacles on his thin nose. "I take no pleasure in this, Your Eminence." Always formal, always the proper vestiture and liturgical formulas, Vennholme never surprised or disappointed either friend or foe.

"But you do." Tim Mulrennan eased back in the Sistine chair. "You have prepared for this moment for many years. Today it arrived, and I was a helpless insect in your hands, crushed like an ant. Obviously I must have offended you. May God forgive me that offense—and may He forgive you, Henry."

Vennholme's eyes were ice. "I do my duty as I see it before God and man, and that is all."

"You have done more than that. You think you are an avenging archangel sent by God to drive the fallen from Paradise."

"So naïve—I find it infuriating." Vennholme rose and walked over to Mulrennan's table, where he stood with his hands resting on the back of a chair, facing his opponent. "Whether you choose to accept it or not, the simple truth is that I have always been thinking of the Church, not of you or of myself."

"I am not so naïve as to believe you," Mulrennan said. "I have known you for more than thirty years, Henry. You have calculated your way to this moment for at least that long. I do believe, though, that in a real sense this has nothing at all to do with me. It is a mere coincidence that I am the obstacle to your ambition. Tell me—what is the true, the full nature of your ambition?"

"The authority of the Church must be reestablished," Vennholme said simply. "There must be a new Ecumenical Council under the aegis of a new pope. The losses and mistakes of the past generation will be redressed. The Evangelium Christi organization will lead the movement of renewal: the laity and the bishops shall achieve this together."

"And why did you settle on La Spina as the pontiff of choice to preside over the new Council? Why not Henry Vennholme himself?"

Vennholme expelled a bitter, barking laugh. "I am not such a fool as to hope for that. A Canadian or an American

upon the Throne of St. Peter? Only the fantasists and liberals could hope for such an absurd election. And your
candidacy—?" He shrugged his narrow shoulders.

"Stillborn. As God intended, I suppose," Mulrennan said.

"But not without its purpose." Vennholme's tone was
almost conspiratorial.

"And what purpose was that? Why did you allow others
to think you looked kindly on my election, even if only for
a short while?"

"Because you helped clear the field, leaving primarily
you and a rightful candidate."

"An Italian," Mulrennan said, completing the thought.

"Choosing a non-Italian pope last time was something of
an aberration—though it could have been much, much
worse—and I do not intend it to become a habit. Electing
an Italian will be the first step toward renewing the
traditions that have made the Church the authoritative voice
of Christ. The See of Rome ought to be governed by a
seasoned Italian pastor-diplomat, such as Pius XII was—
the last great one. It is the natural order."

Mulrennan was astonished by the cardinal's reactionary
position—and again wondered at his own naïveté and lack
of political sophistication. How long had this game been
played?

"What about St. Peter, a Jewish fisherman? More to the
point, what of the record of the past twenty years?"

"Our late, beloved shepherd was the right man at the
right time. But his larger political beliefs, his obsession
with Jews and Muslims—and his somewhat parochial concerns for his native land—are of no value to us today. He
is dead, and his time is past."

"So the Church must retreat behind its Roman walls?"

"Retreat, no. But gird herself and prepare to defeat the
new enemies."

"Always the Sphinx, speaking in oracles and riddles,
looking for enemies in every shadow. You play a very dangerous game, Henry."

"Not a game, Your Eminence: a war. Dangerous, yes,
for men like you. In fact, your kind are finished." He rose,
an elegant diminutive figure in blazing red and snowy

white, a heavy ring of office on his left hand, a ruby-studded pectoral cross hanging to his lower chest. "It might have been quite different, Timothy. I sincerely wish it had been. You may not believe this, but it has been quite difficult and painful for me. Good-bye."

Vennholme strode silently from the chapel.

As Mulrennan sat alone in near darkness in his cell that night, all the days and years of his priesthood flooded through his memory. What was Timothy Mulrennan if he was not a priest? To be a scarlet-robed prince was an outward manifestation of his exalted responsibilities; but beneath the robes of cardinal-prince was the man-priest—and he strove always to remember that.

Now his priesthood was under attack—no, was shattered. When the time came to leave this conclave, he would have already tendered his resignation as cardinal to the new Peter: Pietro La Spina. But he did not want to relinquish his priesthood. His calling, his identity, his very soul was at stake.

To the boy Tim Mulrennan, the church's tall stained-glass windows had seemed to be colorful fingers of light, perhaps the fingers of God Himself, that embraced more than just the church as a building. Sitting in the hard, dark pews with his family, young Timothy gazed up at the ceiling above the Gothic arches, so darkly distant, and at the great chandeliers that appeared suspended by golden threads. He imagined the great crash that would result if one of them fell to the floor. Would people be killed? Would a gravity-defying miracle bring the thing down without harm to anyone?

Always a little fist of fear clutched his heart when he came into the church. The holy water within the door left a cold bead on his forehead when he made the Sign of the Cross. The smell of dying flowers, candle smoke, lingering incense, ancient marble, polished wood, must-rimed air became the smell of holiness to the boy who believed that Jesus lived in the Blessed Sacrament within the gleaming golden tabernacle behind the altar. And there were many layers of sanctity between the boy and his Lord.

He believed in cherubs with bright peachy faces and

gauzy wings, in archangels with wrestlers' physiques and swords of flame, in the Sacred Heart of Jesus bound in a piercing ring of thorns, in the Virgin Mary who never lost her pale serenity amid the violent trials of earthly life and who intervened still in the lives of the neediest among the faithful, in St. Joseph the skilled and silent carpenter and holy earthly father of the boy Jesus, in the words of the Gospel and the Acts of the Apostles and the Epistles of St. Paul to the strange-sounding people called Corinthians and Ephesians and Romans, in gentle St. Francis of Assisi with the fringe of brown hair and birds and beasts on his shoulders and fingertips, in the strange ritual and power of the rosary and the mysteries recited at each decade of cool black beads, in the distant but loving Father of the Holy Trinity who created both lightning in the stormy sky and love in the hearts of men.

The boy still lived within the breast of the priest. Before he was ordained he was a *believer*, and through the rigor of education and experience his faith was tested and tempered. He believed in fewer Truths, but those more fervently and with more certainty. His faith had been refined and clarified, lost and recaptured. It was not the static, awesome, fear-laden faith of a boy anymore—nor should it be. Yet, the boy's capacity to be struck by a beautiful image—a window, a chalice, a sculpture or painting, a passage of music, a tree upon a green lawn—remained poignantly a part of his character.

Yes, he still believed, and more importantly, he wanted to believe in the holy verities of his youth.

He believed in the apostolic succession of his Church and in its mission among all people of the earth; history was the living blood that flowed through the veins of the Church; the transmission of the Word through time was unbroken and irrefutable. Yes, he believed.

But had he been good, had he been truthful, to God?

Rising from the hard, thin mattress of his bed, he sat down at the table and reached for his writing pad. Moving the single candle closer, he took pencil in hand.

*No sleep for me tonight. I prayed to the Heavenly Fa-
ther to grant me rest before returning to the conclave
in the morning. But it is not to be. I am writing only
because I do not know what else to do—and perhaps
in this way He will allow me to sift through my confused thoughts and emotions.*

*O Creator, grant me the strength to forgive my en-
emy and myself and to walk upright in the light of
Your love. Grant me the strength to walk through this
bullshit and come out the other side. How will I face
the people of my diocese? How will I return to the
conclave and face my peers again?*

*Dear Allo Biagi visited me this evening. He had
more information about what is going on outside these
walls. How did he learn these things? But should I be
surprised in this age of hidden cameras and microphones and telephones that fit in the palm of one's
hand?*

*It seems that an anonymous informer—one of Allo's
fellow Italians, no doubt—has told him that Vennholme had met secretly with a reporter before the conclave and planted stories to discredit me and to
destroy any chance I may have had at election. This
is what Cardinal De Guzman referred to at our session
this morning, for indeed the story has been spreading
all day on television and in the newspapers.*

*I told Biagi I found it hard to believe that Venn-
holme would dirty his hands by speaking to the
press—and thus leaving a trail that could lead back
to him. But Allo was insistent. As usual he did not sit
down—he is famous for his ruminative pacing. He
shook his tanned head vigorously and said something
like, "No, this has the earmarks of Henry himself,
never one to leave something so important open to
chance misunderstanding. He is a son of a whore, Timofeo—God forgive my language. And he will bring
the entire Church down with him if we do not stop
him."*

When I told him that Vennholme had taken his per-

sonal animosity to a more extreme level than I could
have imagined or foreseen, Biagi made a weak joke
about my being human—that the events of the past day
had proven that, and so I should not be surprised at
making such a mortal mistake.

I winced but had to laugh. There is no more pride
or pretense left for me. There are only hard lessons in
humility—and a bitter taste of humiliation—to be experienced.

Yet, is it so bitter? I must ask myself: Have I not
loved God and served Him with every physical and
spiritual fiber of my being? Human—yes. I have loved
and been loved. I have failed God every day of my
life, but I have not stopped trying. I have not lost faith
in His love, His power to accept my sinful nature and
transform it according to His will.

"Like six billion other human beings, I shall never
be pope," I told Biagi. "I'm in pretty good company,
I think."

"Timofeo, you know how disappointed I am about
this. But now I am more angry than ever—and I am
going to make him sorry he was ever baptized, let
alone ordained." Those were his precise words, or
nearly so.

Still, when all is said and done, there is nothing I
can do to change the past, Vennholme's actions or my
own. So I must remain wrapped in the conviction that
this situation is in accordance with God's will. I may
not like it one bit, it may be painful as hell, but I must
accept it entirely and without reservation.

When I examine my heart and consider what is best
for the Church, I realize that I never would have
gained sufficient votes for election. The Church is not
yet ready for a pontiff from the United States, perhaps
will be one day—perhaps never. To Allo, perhaps, I
was the "best man" to stop Vennholme's juggernaut.
To Vennholme, I was just the man to set the forces in
play that will lead to his ultimate triumph.

But tonight, as I sit here alone, I find myself believ-
ing that Vennholme will indeed be stopped, though not

*in the way Biagi first envisioned. Vennholme will be
burned upon the stake of his own construction.*

*But how? Even as I sit awake, wondering what can
be done, Vennholme is also awake, plotting and planning. Of that I have no doubt. Yes, Vennholme is
awake right now. In fact, he probably has not slept
for a decade, preparing for just this turn of events.*

*I suppose I should put down this paper and return
to prayer. More prayer and less talk, less of these
impotent thoughts. We must pray and pray and pray
some more.*

*Do I even believe my own pieties? All I want is two
hours of sleep, and let everything else fall where it
may. Only God knows what lies ahead for this divided
conclave.*

CHAPTER SEVEN

Vietnam, February 1969

Father Timothy John Mulrennan, major, Chaplain Corps, U.S. Army, closed his eyes against the jarring shake of the stretch DC-8 as it flew over the South China Sea en route from the Philippines to Saigon. He tried to imagine himself back home on a commuter train, feeling the gentle rock of the rails rather than the disturbing turbulence of the Southeast Asian skies.

He kept his eyes shut, aware that opening them would reveal a sea of khaki and close-cropped heads and the disturbing realization that he was a world away from his familiar New Jersey. He kept his eyes shut, careful which memories to allow in.

"Kevin . . ." he whispered, then pushed away the painful image of his older brother before it had a chance to emerge.

He would think of other things: his first time in uniform, when things were simple, black and white, not all this gray. The DC-8 dipped and bumped, throwing Father Mulrennan against the seat back. It was as if he had been pushed into a wall. . . .

The monstrous transport shuddered and groaned, and Timothy Mulrennan opened his eyes. Nothing about his surroundings had changed. His fellow soldiers looked just as hot and uncomfortable as before—and just as incredibly young. He wondered what they thought of him, an old man of thirty-two who wore a cross on his collar. He had been out of the service for nearly a decade, after serving several years as a military intelligence operative in Seoul and Berlin. Yet here he was, in uniform again for the first time in ten years, this time not to confront the world of cold diplomatic wars but the very heated battlefields of Vietnam.

Closing his eyes again, Mulrennan sensed the memories, the images, resurfacing. He tried to hold them at bay, but something in their familiarity brought a comforting solace here at twenty thousand feet over the China Sea.

The cold rain slanted down furiously as a multitude of Mulrennans gathered for the Thanksgiving Day 1968 feast at 203 Fairlawn Avenue, North Auburn, New Jersey, the home of James Francis Mulrennan, paterfamilias of the tumultuous brood.

Father Tim Mulrennan, wearing a crisp blue button-down oxford shirt and houndstooth sports jacket, sipped from a can of Ballantine's ale and tried to follow the Army-Navy game on TV, to no avail. He doffed the jacket and threw it over the back of a chair.

Tim climbed the stairs to the third floor, where his younger sisters—Gertrude Anne and Kate—shared the big bedroom that he and Kevin had once occupied. The elder brothers' dark curtains and taped-up magazine photo "sports hall of fame" had given way to blues and pinks and yellows and flowered bedcovers. Hanging on Gertie Anne's side of the room were peace signs and Fillmore East posters; gracing Kathleen's side, the victorious Nixon and Agnew smiled benignly over her bed.

An old crucifix from Ireland, which had belonged to their maternal grandmother, marked the division of territory between the girls. Gertie Anne, a sophomore music major at Rutgers, called it the Mason-Dixon Line. Kathleen, a brilliant and hardworking prelaw freshman at nearby Kean College, accepted her sister's description as long as it was clear to all that *she* was on the "right" side of the line. In a family of traditional New Jersey Democrats, Kate was the staunchly independent Goldwater conservative who had subscribed to the *National Review* since she was twelve.

Kate sat propped against a stack of pillows on her bed, eating an apple and trying to concentrate on an open volume of Edmund Burke in her lap.

Stephen, a freckled towhead of ten, sat at Gertie Anne's feet. Gertie strummed the opening bars of "Puff the Magic

Dragon," then began to sing the lyrics, encouraging her younger stepbrother to join in. He did, tentatively, stumbling over some of the words.

Stephen was a great kid, Tim Mulrennan thought: smart and good-natured, quiet and religious. He had begun training as an altar boy, and Tim planned to ask him to serve at mass in their parent's home Friday morning.

Stephen looked up and beamed at his big stepbrother. Gertie stopped singing.

"Don't let me interrupt, please," Tim said. "I love to hear you sing—both of you." He sat cross-legged on the floor next to the boy.

Kate looked up and frowned. "I wish you would make them stop. All she does is sing revolutionary folk songs—drives me crazy."

"You were crazy to begin with, Kate," Gertie Anne said. "For God's sake, you can't see that Nixon and his crowd are going to push us deeper into the war? I wouldn't be surprised if he drops an A-bomb on Hanoi."

"Worse things could happen. And have." Kate smiled smugly. "At least we have a president who will work for peace with honor—not a commie-hugging Happy Hubert."

Gertie rolled her eyes and tossed her long golden-brown curls. "You see a communist under every bed."

"Darn right—'cause they're *there*, sister. But not for long. Talk to me in twenty years. J. Edgar Hoover will have cleaned out all the domestic subversives. The Russians will be starving, begging us for foreign aid. We'll send them folk songs and flower children; I'm sure they'll love that."

Tim laughed. "You two never change. I can hardly believe you belong to the same family."

"I know." Gertie Anne agreed. "How did I get *all* the talent?" She launched into "Blowin' in the Wind," and Stephen gamely tried to sing along but soon was lost. He hugged his knees and listened seriously, as if intent on being ready the next time his sister launched into this particular song.

Kate shook her head and pulled the book up to her face.

Kathleen Frances Mulrennan had the most beautiful flaming red hair that Tim had ever seen on a human being.

Her hair and cobalt eyes and ivory skin gave her the stunning aura of an angel—almost. When she launched into one of her religious-conservative diatribes, it was Savonarola and no angel who had come back to life.

She was afraid of no one and absolutely certain in her absolutist positions. Tim wondered whether she would ever marry, whether she could find a soulmate who could match her political passions and sweeping intellect. He knew that such a thought was unfair to her—sexist, Gertie would likely say—but such was the reality of the world. He told himself to remember to goad her into a political argument at dinner; he was feeling mischievous.

On the other hand, Kate's year-older sister possessed a deep serenity and equally fast conviction that politics was based in violence, neither well-enough nor often-enough contained, and that peace was the only answer, locally as well as globally. Her music matched her own pleasant flower-child looks: soft pink skin, emerald eyes, full lips, and turned-up mick nose.

Unlike Kate's, her youthful freckles had faded. She was sincere in her beliefs but not argumentative. She held the Church at arm's length, finding spiritual sustenance in her music. Tim imagined that Gertrude Anne would age gracefully as the mother of a large brood of wild, half-dressed savages, with a gentle long-haired husband who raised vegetables and wrote poetry....

Stephen clapped in rhythm to Gertie's singing and swayed to and fro, as if at a folk concert. She smiled brightly and raised her lilting voice. Kathleen remained blithely uninterested, deep within her conservative text. She was a devout daily mass-goer, like their father.

She looked at Tim over the top of her book. "Cardinal Cooke has been making some awfully soft statements lately concerning the war."

Tim threw up his hands. "Way beyond me, Kate. He's a very spiritual guy. I respect him a lot."

"He's no Cardinal Spellman," she said.

"That he is not. I think one Spellman per century is probably enough, don't you?"

The sound of footsteps on the stairway was followed by

a loud knock at the door, then Theresa, the oldest sister, stuck her head inside. "It's almost dinnertime." She turned to Tim. "Dad wants you to help him carve the bird."

He pushed himself to his feet. "See you cats downstairs." Gertie Anne sang on. Kate smirked. Stephen watched worshipfully as the tall man in the blue shirt left the room.

Tim followed his elder sister to the dining room. There, standing beneath a blazing crystal chandelier, James Mulrennan proudly displayed a Sunbeam electric carver. His priest-son dutifully admired it. He admired his father, as well. In the bright light of the large family dining room the broad-shouldered, long-armed man lost the lines and shadows of a careworn face that had presided at more than thirty such Thanksgiving feasts.

"Army's whipping Navy," he announced. "Should have put some money on 'em this time."

He was always lamenting his lack of gambling acumen, but it was a fact that he had never bet on a sporting event in his life. James Mulrennan played it straight with his paycheck, paid his bills and taxes, managed to save for his kids' college tuition, though each had won at least partial scholarship funds and worked campus jobs to fill the financial gap. The closest he ever came to gambling was the occasional parish or school raffle ticket.

The thick sturdy hands that grappled with the lawn mower, carving knife, rosary, or bicycle wrench had never touched a poker hand or pair of dice or slot machine handle, and only at his own daughter's wedding had those hands raised a Champagne flute or touched caviar. Many times, when not hauling a heavy briefcase home from the office, those hands had clapped for Kevin and Tim at baseball games and wrestling matches, track meets and basketball tournaments, had applauded Theresa and Gertrude Anne at music recitals and Kathleen at speech contests and debates; those hands had hoisted little Stephen atop broad shoulders and held him there securely and pinched his ears and gently slapped his butt to correct him.

Father Timothy Mulrennan came around the festively decorated table and stood beside his dad. He touched the man's arm, and said, "Impressive as hell."

"That's no way for a priest to talk, Tim."

"I suppose not, but that is one sleek cutting machine, Dad. Brings out the killer in me, I guess."

A shadow passed across Jim Mulrennan's face. "I hope Kevin is okay, wherever he is on this day."

"He'll be home in January," Tim said. "His two tours are almost over—he's a short-timer."

Jim Mulrennan had never been to war, never served in the military as had his two sons. He was proud of his Marine Corps captain and his army lieutenant, no doubt, but he and his second wife, Rosemary, wanted Kevin home safely more than anything in the world. Three-and-a-half nightmare years of silent torture had not hardened them in the least: *Let it be over, let him come home, let me hold my son in my arms,* Mulrennan prayed daily.

Soon the table was laden with food and china and polished silver as the family, eleven in number including Theresa's husband and children, sat down at 4:00 P.M. to partake of the feast. James and Rosemary each sat at one end of the table; Tim took his place at his stepmother's right, opposite Stephen. Jim asked Tim to offer the blessing.

"In the Name of the Father, the Son, and the Holy Spirit. Amen. Heavenly Father, we, Thy children, thank Thee for the multitude of graces and gifts Thou hast bestowed upon our family this day. Make us worthy to receive these blessings from Thy Hand, through the intercession of the saints and the sacrifice of Thy Son, Jesus Christ. We ask a special blessing for our brother Kevin, who is absent from this table but is serving his country in Thy name. Bring him home safely to his loving family. Bless us, O Lord, and these Thy gifts, which we are about to receive from Thy bounty, through Christ, Our Lord. Amen."

The family chorused the "Amen" and the Sign of the Cross with enthusiasm, and the plates rapidly began to fill with turkey, stuffing, sweet potatoes, mashed potatoes, gravy, string beans, fresh cranberry sauce, creamed spinach, carrots, and Theresa's infamous Jell-O salad. Tim grinned as Stephen poured gravy over everything on his plate and Rosemary relieved the boy of the porcelain boat before the gravy spilled onto the pressed linen tablecloth.

Seated at a bridge table in the corner nearest the kitchen were Tim's nephews and niece: Jimmy, age nine, and Mary Clare, six, and Thomas, five. From their table erupted the occasional squall and squabble, with one or the another parent gently reprimanding them.

At the big table James could not resist a dissertation on postconciliar Church issues.

"Would you explain to me *why* the beautiful old altar at Our Lady of Mercies has to be turned around and we must look up the priest's nose during the entire mass? . . . That is, when we visit our own son's parish. I understand the change to English, even though I loved the old Latin, but this altar thing—"

"Jim," Rosemary said, "we've had this discussion a hundred times. I'm sure Father Tim is tired of it."

The elder Mulrennan put down his fork. "I guess I'm just a thick-headed old Irishman, Rose. Some of these changes don't make a bit of sense. I'm willing to kiss the pope's ring and follow him to the gates of perdition, but leave me a little bit of the Church I grew up in. Don't you agree with me, Tim boy, even a little?" He searched for sympathy in his son's eyes.

"I do, to some degree, Dad. At least I understand your point of view. For me, I prefer to see the people when I'm celebrating the mass. I should think it would strengthen their faith to see and hear the priest consecrate the Host."

"All I can think of when I see you up there at the altar is the time you locked me in my room and the fire department had to come take me out with a ladder," Theresa put in.

"Uncle Tim did that?" one of the kids at the little table exclaimed, and everyone laughed.

Rosemary refilled the adults' wine goblets. Tim picked at his plate; the food was delicious and brought back the old times when his mother was still living, when he sat at the card table with his younger siblings, when he ached to be grown up and a part of the important conversation at the bigger table.

Kate said, "I agree with Dad. Too much change, too fast,

too little reason. I can see how the missions in Africa and Asia might benefit from liturgies in the local language. But we are a mature Church here in the States. Latin has been good enough for us for two hundred years."

"You're in the minority—at least in our generation," Theresa rejoined. "You can't turn back the clock."

"I may hold a minority opinion, but I'm right," Kate said with a cocky smile. "And you know I am," she added, pointing her fork at her priest-brother.

"For Pete's sake, Katie—you don't have to be right all the time," Theresa interjected.

"It's not that I'm so right, but you're wrong so much. And I prefer Kate, not Katie, if you please."

A vehement chorus of boos and hisses greeted the remark. Tim smiled. James Mulrennan shook his gray head. The doorbell pealed, barely audible above the uproar.

"I'll see who it is," Theresa said, and went to the front door. She returned after a moment and stood in the dining room doorway, ashen.

"What is it, Theresie?" her father asked.

The men all leaped to their feet and went to her—her husband grasped her shoulders.

"It's Kevin—the men are here—they want to see you, Dad." She slackly mouthed the words.

James Mulrennan dashed from the room. Tim followed him to the front door.

Two marines stood stiffly in the small foyer. Through the open door Tim saw a cold drizzle dampening and darkening the earth. His vision blurred as he considered the still-green grass of his father's front lawn beyond the screened-in wooden porch where, for hours and days on end, he had played Monopoly and card games and pieced together jigsaw puzzles with his brother and sisters.

"Sir, this is from the Secretary of Defense." The skinny marine lieutenant passed the letter to the elder Mulrennan.

Tim stood beside his father and watched him tear open the envelope. Over his shoulder, Tim read the words "regret to inform you . . . Captain Kevin Patrick Mulrennan, United States Marine Corps . . . reported missing in action . . . No-

vember 23, 1968 . . . line of duty . . . no further information
at this time . . . Respectfully yours . . ."

James Mulrennan's bulky frame sagged. Tim thanked the
two servicemen and shook their hands. They declined his
offer of a cup of coffee and a moment later were gone. The
entire family now stood in the front hallway. Theresa's
daughter, Mary Clare, ran to her grandfather and reached
for his hand.

"Poppy, Poppy," she said. "Was that the mailman?"

The patriarch held her little hand and burst into tears. His
wife came and hugged him tightly. The letter was a crum-
pled white wreck in his fist. Tim and the others stood by
impotently, angry, baffled, and afraid.

"What happened?" Stephen blurted.

"Kevin is missing," Tim said, his own eyes blurred, a
painful lump of sorrow in his throat.

Three months later (after pulling every string from his own
previous military service and shamelessly using Church
connections wherever he could), Father Timothy Mulrennan was back in uniform, raised in rank to major and seated
on a DC-8 bound for Saigon as a member of the Chaplain
Corps of the U.S. Army. Somewhere over the South China
Sea his rememberings had drifted into sleep, and his dreams
of Bob Dylan songs and Thanksgiving dinner were scattered by the jarring bump of the plane touching down at
the airstrip at Ton Son Nhut outside the city.

Rousing himself and standing in the aisle, Mulrennan
pulled down his duffel bag from the overhead bin and
joined the other men making their way to the forward cabin
door. As he stepped out onto the landing of a rickety moving stairway, he was struck by two things: the incredible
wall of heat and the sickening, cloying smell that nearly
caused him to faint.

"This is it, Father, sunny Vee-et-nam," the young NCO
behind him said expansively. Sergeant Jim Joe Wilson had
been one of Mulrennan's seatmates throughout the interminable flight from Oakland.

Mulrennan coughed, gagging on the stench-laden air,
then started down the yellow-painted stairs.

"What in the Lord's name is that terrible stink?" he called over his shoulder to the sergeant. With one hand he held his uniform cap in place against the hot wind, with the other he balanced his heavy duffel on his shoulder. He felt as green as any raw recruit from the sticks.

"That?" Sergeant Wilson shouted to be heard above the wind-borne drone of scores of planes and helicopters. "Why, it's Ton Son Nhut *perfume*. Otherwise known to civilians as burning shit!"

"I beg your pardon?"

"Excuse me, Father, I mean burning—uh—feces."

"I know what you mean. But who is burning it? And why?"

"Our guys," Wilson explained earnestly. "We mix it with diesel fuel and burn it to prevent typhoid or typhus or whatever the hell it's supposed to prevent. Funny thing is, the Vietnamese natives used shit for years as fertilizer. Worked for them. Helped them raise food, grow beautiful flowers, and have green lawns just like in the good old U.S.A. And the air smelled clean and natural, like God intended. Then the geniuses in the U.S. Army came along and—well, just take a deep breath and tell me if you think this is an improvement."

Mulrennan did not breathe deeply. He followed the long line of arriving soldiers, sailors, airmen, and marines across the tarmac toward a low white building on the far side of a chain-link fence. The airport teemed with activity: ground personnel scurried from plane to plane in fuel trucks and service vehicles, Vietnamese civilians whisked baggage onto metal carts and passengers toward the taxi queues, aircraft engines, both jet and reciprocating, roared like wounded beasts, contributing to the din.

Two air force Phantoms took off, and Mulrennan stopped to watch. They lifted from the earth at a seventy-five-degree angle, rocketing up on two pillars of fire that belched from their afterburners.

Just inside the tall fence he noticed a pair of Air Vietnam stewardesses as they walked by, clad in *ao-dais,* sky blue silken pants, and flowing overblouses. Sergeant Wilson stared at the young women. Mulrennan bade him farewell, but the sergeant was not paying attention to the chaplain.

As Mulrennan entered the building, a young Spec-5 approached and read his uniform name tag. The kid gave a quick salute.

"Major Mulrennan?"

"Yes, I'm Father—that is, Major Mulrennan."

"I'm Specialist Fraser, sir. Colonel Hargraves, he's the chief of chaplains, he sent me over to fetch you."

Mulrennan pointed toward the in-processing sign. "Don't I need to go through there?"

"No, sir. We'll take care of all that for you. Colonel Hargraves, he wants me to take you on out to the Red Bull."

"What's the Red Bull?"

"That's the BOQ and officers' mess where you'll be staying," Specialist Fraser explained. "You got your baggage claim?"

"Right here." He held up the ticket.

"Give it to me, I'll get the rest of your gear. Slopes take forever, and we gotta shake a leg, sir."

Less than a half hour later Mulrennan was returning the salutes of the MPs stationed at the main gate as they exited Ton Son Nhut. The traffic on Phan Thann Gian, the street just outside the gate, was incredible. It reminded the priest of Ferry Street in Newark during the Portuguese festivals. The road was jammed with jeeps, civilian and military trucks of all sizes and shapes and states of repair, colorful buses, tiny yellow and blue Renault taxicabs that darted through the stream of larger vehicles like water bugs. Smaller and even more maneuverable were the smoking, popping, three-wheeled cycles. Progress seemed to be possible only by engaging in the game of chicken, driving at breakneck speed toward any narrow opening with the hope that the opposing driver would back off at the last second.

Mike Fraser, age twenty, hailed from Appleton, Wisconsin. He shouted his biography over the honking and hooting of the traffic. He drove an open four-seater, in which Mulrennan repeatedly braced himself for a collision. But Specialist Fraser skillfully navigated the roadway, calmly recounting how he had lost his virginity at seventeen after the football homecoming dance with the daughter of the town's Chevy dealer.

They turned down Tru Minh Giang, an endless, narrow lane that stabbed into the bowels of the capital city. Mulrennan saw nothing to indicate a foreign military presence in this part of town other than the other American vehicles that whizzed past. Fraser turned off the road and stopped in front of a gated brick wall. A South Vietnamese guard checked the specialist's ID, opened the gate, and waved him through.

"This is the Red Bull," Fraser explained to Mulrennan. "You ever see John Wayne in *She Wore a Yellow Ribbon*?"

The priest indicated that he had.

"Well, here we are inside an old West fort. All we're lacking is General Custer—and the Indians. That wall there keeps the army inside and the enemy—whoever that is—outside. Here at Red Bull you got your parade ground, your flagpole, BOQs, officers' club . . . everything but the sutler's store and blacksmith, right here in the middle of Saigon!"

Fraser pulled up at a low-slung prefab building that sported a flower bed with red, white, and blue blooms. "This is the O club. You'll find Colonel Hargraves inside. I'll stow your gear in your room."

"Which room is mine?" Mulrennan asked.

Fraser pointed to a row of buildings that looked like an all-American motel complex. "You're third from the end." He shifted into first gear and sped away.

A sign over the red-painted door read, Red Bull Officers' Open Mess: Clear All Weapons Before Entering. He stepped into the dimly lighted, smoky main room, allowed his eyes to adjust, scanned the scene. It was all so familiar from another time in his life; he felt for a split second that he'd always been here, that he belonged.

There were a dozen or more officers inside, including several nurses. A slender six-footer with a steely crew cut and gray mustache approached, hand outstretched.

"You must be Father Tim Mulrennan."

"Yes, sir." He grasped the man's hard hand.

"I'm Jack B. Hargraves, chief of chaplains. It's good to have you with us. Nice flight over?"

"Long flight. I don't quite know what time it is or which end is up. But I'm here."

He liked this man immediately, tried to guess to what denomination he belonged. From Hargraves's slight drawl, Mulrennan guessed he had grown up in the South—Texas, most likely.

"Have you had lunch?"

"No, sir, I haven't."

"They serve a pretty good steak sandwich here. Join me."

Forty minutes later, Colonel Hargraves pushed his empty plate aside and dabbed his mouth with a napkin. So far their conversation had been pleasant and light, each man filling in the other on their personal and professional background. Hargraves, it turned out, was indeed from Texas and most recently had served as pastor of a large Methodist congregation in Lubbock. Now Hargraves's smile hardened, his eyes fixing on Mulrennan's.

"So, let me get this straight. You volunteered for active duty because you want to find your brother, who's MIA?"

"Yes, sir. I don't honestly know how to go about it, but I hope to develop a lead, at least find out what happened to him." Tim swallowed hard, reached for his iced tea. "My folks are devastated, like a lot of people back home. If there's any way I can bring back some concrete evidence, some facts . . . I assume he's dead, but I want to know."

Hargraves reached across the table and put a hand on the younger man's forearm. "Tim, I want to help you. I can only imagine what you and your family are going through. You won't want a specific assignment, then, will you?"

"Colonel—"

"Call me Jack."

"I don't expect a free ride over here. I want to pull my weight. That's what I told my bishop and the Catholic military ordinary. But if it is possible for you to give me an assignment that would provide some flexibility, some freedom of movement, I would be grateful."

The colonel drummed his fingers on the table for a long

moment as he studied Mulrennan. "I'm going to ask you something, and I want you to be honest with me."

"Of course."

"Are you really a Catholic priest?"

"What do you mean, Jack? I wouldn't be here unless—"

"What I mean is, I don't want the Chaplain Corps used by the army or by you or by anyone else for any reason other than its mission, which is to provide spiritual comfort and succor to the young men and women who are giving their lives and limbs in this truly godforsaken conflict. For example, I would look with great disfavor upon someone— an intelligence agent, say, or a CID investigator—who would use the cross on his collar as a cover for some clandestine activity. Do you know what I'm saying, son?"

"I do, Jack. I am an ordained Roman Catholic priest on leave from my parish with the permission and blessing of my pastor and the archbishop. I'm here to search for my brother. I believe that is God's will for me and for my family. I would not be here, probably, under other circumstances. Why would you think otherwise?"

"I did a little background research on you, Father. You were in the army before, weren't you?"

"Yes, sir."

"Military Intelligence Branch?"

Tim Mulrennan hesitated for a painful second before he answered, warily: "Yes, sir, I was MIB."

"You will understand, then, why I might be a little concerned. I asked because we have been screwed before."

"When I came on active, I asked for and received a branch transfer. I no longer have any connection with Military Intelligence."

"All right, Tim, I'm going to take your word for it. I won't belabor it. I will assign you to the position of chaplain supernumerary. That means no specific assignment; you are free to travel anywhere at all in-country. You'll check in on chaplains in the field and offer them help when it is needed—and it will be. They will appreciate a hand. You'll report directly and exclusively to me, and that only often enough to satisfy me that you are still alive."

Mulrennan flashed a smile of relief. "Thank you, Colonel."

Suddenly the weight of the past seventy-two hours crashed down hard on the thirty-two-year-old priest. He was nearly blind with exhaustion from his New Jersey-to-California-to-Hawaii-to-Manila-to-Saigon odyssey.

After fourteen hours of sleep, a shave and shower, and a change of uniform, Tim Mulrennan began his search for his older brother.

USARV Headquarters bustled like Macy's at Christmas: beyond the linoleum-topped counter in the main room dozens of desks were situated end to end, with army and civilian clerks tending to paperwork and the sound of clacking typewriter keys and carriage bells competing against the roar of several window air conditioners. A number of reed-slender young Vietnamese women with golden skin floated through the maze of desks and gunmetal filing cabinets; they wore the now-familiar multihued diaphanous *ao-dais* that Major Mulrennan had first noticed upon his arrival at Ton Son Nhut.

A pretty girl with long black hair greeted the priest as he stepped to the reception counter. "Yes, Major, how may I help you?"

"I'm seeking information about Major Kevin F. Mulrennan, Marine Corps, serial number 0-275202, and his last assignment was with First Special Forces Group. He was reported missing in action in November."

She finished jotting down the information, then said, "Just a moment, sir. I will check with my supervisor."

He watched her turn toward a glassed-in cubicle, then he stepped over to the water fountain to get a drink. When he returned to the counter he met a stocky lieutenant colonel who wore a crisp short-sleeved shirt and regulation tie. The officer smiled broadly and extended a thick hand with sausage fingers.

"Tim Mulrennan! I thought you left the army long ago, and here you are back among the protectors of democracy."

"Hello, Mike. I didn't expect to see you again. It's been too many years. So you're Colonel Bernard now, huh?"

"Just Mike between us old jumpers." Lt. Col. Michael

H. Bernard, USA, had known Mulrennan since their first day at Infantry OCS at Fort Benning. Twenty-two weeks later they attended Individual Parachute Training, jump school, from which they graduated in three weeks as fully qualified paratroopers. Both men still wore their parachute wings on their uniforms, though neither had ever been assigned to an airborne division.

Bernard pointed to Tim's collar insignia, the chaplain's cross. "Is this for real? You're a sky pilot now?"

"You better believe it. I'm a Catholic priest in New Jersey."

"I'll be goddamned. . . ." Mike Bernard's wide face flushed deep red. "Christ, Tim, I'm sorry, I didn't mean—"

"Don't worry about it. I'm getting used to it all over again. *I'm* the one who's out of my element here, not you."

"So, I hear you're inquiring about someone—a relative?" He held up the slip of paper on which the Vietnamese woman had listed Kevin Mulrennan's name and serial number.

"It's my brother Kevin. He's MIA since November."

Bernard's light brown eyes clouded with sadness. "I'm about to go for lunch. You ever been to the My Kahn floating restaurant?"

"No, I've been here less than a day. Already had one good meal, though."

"Well, the My Kahn serves the finest French onion soup outside of Paris."

The two men were on their way within half a minute.

"This isn't the best place to talk, Tim. We can get a private table there and have a quiet chat." Entering the restaurant, Bernard grasped his friend's arm. "The walls here have ears."

The My Kahn was a boat moored at the end of Tu Do Street. When the maître d'hôtel started them toward one table, Mike handed him a five-hundred-piastre note and indicated another, more isolated table at the far corner nearest the river. The man pocketed the money and led them to the preferred table.

Colonel Bernard ordered for both of them: cold beer, bowls of French onion soup, and a platter of spring rolls

accompanied by a small dish of *nuk mahm* liberally seasoned with crushed peppers.

"You'd better try just a little of the *nuk mahm* to start
with," Bernard said as he dipped one of the delicate spring
rolls into the dark sauce. "It's pretty potent."

Tim Mulrennan dipped, tasted, then fisted the beer bottle
and poured half its contents down his throat. Sweat beads
dampened his forehead.

Bernard laughed. "Third-degree burns. We'll stop by
medical when we go back."

During the meal they spoke of family and sports and
politics, then they recapped their careers. They had last seen
each other in Berlin when they had served as first lieuten-
ants assigned to Military Intelligence Branch. That was before the Berlin Wall; it felt like a century ago.

"I'm not the only one to pick up new collar brass," Mulrennan said. "I see you're wearing adjutant general's insignia instead of MIB."

"Don't let the collar pin throw you." Bernard glanced
over his shoulder to make certain he could not be overheard
before he spoke again. "I take it you still have a top-secret
clearance?"

"With crypto. It hasn't been revoked. Mike, do you know
something—anything—about my brother?"

"Why didn't you write or contact me through channels?"

"To be honest, I didn't realize you were still on active.
And I wanted to keep this very quiet—my coming here to
find Kevin. It's better if it just happens. Too much planning
might scotch the whole thing. I'm just lucky, I guess, to
run into you."

"You're smarter than that, friend. This isn't a coincidence, but I'll let it go," the colonel replied. "Yes, I know
what they think happened. And I won't sugarcoat it, Tim.
It's not good."

Mulrennan pushed his hand over his fresh crew cut and
took a deep breath. "All right. Tell me what you know."

"We think he may be a payback for Operation Phoenix."

"What does that mean? I've never heard of Phoenix." He
lit a cigarette.

"I would hope not. There aren't more than fifty people

between here and the Pentagon who know about Phoenix."

The waiter brought two more beers, and Bernard paused until he left.

"It's a project that's aimed at identifying and excising the Vietcong political infrastructure. It's run by the South Vietnamese under the direction of CIA, not Military Intelligence. It's supposed to neutralize the VC's political control in the South, hamlet by hamlet, and divest their guerrillas of the support of the people."

"Talk English, please, Mike. I've been out of the double-speak business a long time."

Mike Bernard chuckled, wiped beer foam from his chin. "There's a reason for using double-speak. When you explain what this is in the Queen's English . . . it doesn't sound very nice. What they do to people—"

"If it concerns my brother, I want to know about it."

"Phoenix operatives go into a village to find out who is and who isn't VC. When we ID the enemy, we send in an execution and eliminate the VC—along with his entire family."

Mulrennan gasped. "Holy Mary! The entire family?"

"The ARVN added that touch. Theory is, it's more of a deterrent."

Mulrennan's throat constricted, making it difficult to breathe. He struggled to spit out the words: "Are you saying that Kevin was one of these Phoenix operatives?"

"Hell, no." Bernard shook his head vehemently. "I didn't mean to give that impression. Your brother, as commanding officer of a Special Forces unit, had nothing whatever to do with Operation Phoenix."

"Then what does it have to do with Kevin?"

"You've read about Special Forces, haven't you? How they send teams out into the villages, not only to help them defend against VC guerrilla attacks but also to provide assistance such as digging wells, building hospitals, that sort of thing? That's what your brother was doing. Evidently the VC felt he was making too many friends, that he was becoming too popular with the villagers. So, in retaliation for the Phoenix program your brother was targeted. He and his driver were on their way to An Co, a hamlet just north of Quang Tri, when he disappeared."

"You say Kevin disappeared. What about his driver?"

"Oh, we found the driver, and the jeep. The man was dead and the jeep undamaged. But there was no trace of your brother."

"Then you think he was captured and taken north?"

"We have a pretty good handle on who the North is keeping prisoner, and your brother's name has never turned up. I hate to be the one to tell you this, Tim, but we are reasonably certain that they took him somewhere and held a mock trial, then executed him. Afterward, they buried him in a hidden grave, so we'll probably never find his remains."

Mulrennan was quiet for a long moment, watching his cigarette burn up in the ashtray. The blue-white smoke spiraled into the air between the two men.

"That may be the case," he said at last. The pain was evident in his voice. "But until we know for sure, I must try to find him."

"How do you plan to do that?"

"I don't know yet," he admitted. "I've been given maximum flexibility in my assignment as chaplain-at-large, so to speak, and can go anywhere I'm needed."

"Let me nose around," Bernard suggested. "I'll ask a few questions. If I come up with anything you can use, I'll let you know."

"I appreciate that, Mike."

"*No problemo.* What are old jump buddies for? I won't let your chute get tangled."

For nearly two months since his arrival in-country, Mulrennan conducted his investigation into Kevin's whereabouts. He traveled to Quang Tri, where he visited the Special Forces company his brother had commanded. The problem was, Captain Mulrennan's disappearance had occurred nearly six months earlier, and because a tour of duty was only one year, there were few left in the company who remembered him.

The priest visited all the villages served by his brother's Special Forces unit, celebrated mass for the Catholic villagers and the American and ARVN soldiers. But he had come up shy of a thimbleful of anything that might direct his search.

One night while he was on a remote location with one of the A teams, they came under heavy attack by a reinforced company of North Vietnamese regulars. It was difficult, under such circumstances, to remain a nonbelligerent, but he managed to do so. Throughout the long night he provided spiritual comfort and first aid to the besieged soldiers, keeping his eye on the nearest weapon as he performed his duties.

A few weeks later, as he stepped out of the C-130 that had taken him back to Ton Son Nhut, he was surprised to see Lt. Col. Mike Bernard sitting in a jeep, waiting for him.

"Hello, Colonel, what are you doing here?"

"Some news about your brother," Bernard said, flipping a burning cigarette butt onto the gray-black tarmac.

"He's been found?"

"No. But we have a fairly solid report that he was seen alive, in Dong Hoi."

"Dong Hoi? Where's that?"

"Well, cowhand, that's the downside of it," the colonel said. "Dong Hoi is about eighty klicks on the wrong side of the DMZ."

"I see," Mulrennan breathed, though he didn't fully.

"We're doing everything we can through diplomatic channels to find out his status. The French are sometimes able to help us, and we are pursuing this lead through that avenue."

"Thank you."

Mulrennan was so lost in thought about Kevin, about his family, that he didn't see Mike Bernard drumming his fingers on the steering wheel of the jeep and studying his friend's pained expression.

"I wonder how much of the old Tim is left?" Bernard finally asked.

"Beg pardon?" Mulrennan asked, looking up.

"The Tim that I knew in Berlin, the one who moved freely through the Eastern sector—could have got his ass shot off. How much of that Tim came to Nam?"

"Spit it out, Mike. No more riddles."

"All right. What I'm saying is that, through diplomatic channels, it might take us six more months to find out what someone on the ground in Dong Hoi could find out in a matter of hours."

"I see," Mulrennan said. "And how, do you suppose, might one get to Dong Hoi?"

"I could get you there—if you are willing to take the risk. And if you are willing to do something for me in return."

"I . . . don't know," Mulrennan said.

"That's all right," the colonel said dismissively. "Like I said, it would be very risky."

"It's not that."

"What, then?"

He put his hand to the cross on his left collar. "It's a matter of who I serve now."

"That's all right. You can forget I ever said anything."

But Tim Mulrennan could not forget it, and two days later, after much prayer and soul-searching, he contacted Mike Bernard to tell him that he would do whatever was required of him, if Bernard could get him into North Vietnam.

"Her name is Ly Linh Sanh," Bernard said. "Her hut is at the south end of the village. She will have three gourds tied to a tree limb in her front yard."

"How do you know all this?"

"Here is a new radio code. Tell her she is to start using it immediately." Colonel Bernard did not answer Mulrennan's question.

"Is it possible she will know anything about my brother?"

"She's the one who provided our initial information."

"How do I get to the village—and when?"

"I'll make arrangements for Air America to take you up there. They'll drop you in at night. How long has it been since you made a parachute jump?"

"Twelve years," Mulrennan answered, remembering . . . "and it was a daytime, static jump."

"Ah, yes—well, one parachute jump is pretty much like any other, cowhand. You'll do good."

"Right," he said sarcastically.

CHAPTER EIGHT

That thou doest, do quickly. . . . Cardinal Vennholme's head jerked upright, and he looked around his small library office in the residence, a privilege of seniority and the result of a subtly negotiated preconclave arrangement. As he glanced over his right shoulder, he half expected to see the late pontiff standing beside him, for the words had been couched in the Slav's uniquely accented French. But he was alone, on his knees before the window, face turned to the cold first promise of daylight on the conclave's third day of voting.

Lowering his head, Vennholme closed his eyes and resumed his prayers for the Church, for his beloved Evangelium Christi, for his own immortal soul. He had eaten but little at supper the night before and had drunk only water and coffee since then. Sleep had been fitful, at best, and he had dressed and come to this makeshift office even before the sun had risen. For more than an hour he had tried in vain to pray, but his thoughts had pulled him in a riot of directions. He attempted to concentrate on the events of the conclave, on his purpose here, but inevitably his mind filled with memories and images of long ago . . . of a boy and a man.

The boy Henry Martin Vennholme loved God and hated communists because God created order and communists represented chaos. He had, in fact, articulated this position in an oratorical competition sponsored by the local archdiocese when he was eleven. He thought about these matters very seriously; at the home for orphaned boys where he had lived since age five, he was known by his peers as the Scholar—a nickname and status he accepted as his due. In one sense he did not care a rap what other boys thought of him. He was more concerned with the opinion of the priests and religious brothers who administered the home.

Yet within the smart, quiet, sensitive boy who would become a priest himself, a blue flame of longing burned intensely, eternally, signifying his need to be loved and accepted and, most importantly, respected by those around him.

The war in Europe rumbled toward a conclusion: victory for the Allies. In the brick-walled orphanage of Sts. Michael and Bartholomew in the heart of old Montreal, as far from the battlefront as one could possibly be, Henry, by the time he was eleven, read books and newspapers in three languages and wrote letters to Generalissimo Franco, J. Edgar Hoover, Cardinal Spellman of New York, President de Gaulle, and His Holiness Pope Pius XII about the evils of world communism. These were the generals in the army that would defeat the Antichrist Stalin's forces of darkness. Stalin and Lucifer were one and the same in the mind of young Henry Vennholme; and he made this notion the basis of his award-winning contest speech.

He felt acutely uncomfortable as he stood before the judges and the audience in the low-ceilinged, smoky basement meeting hall of a local parish church. There were forty persons in attendance, including the dozen or so competitors for the oration prize. Henry wore a black suit and black tie. He had scrubbed himself raw in the bathtub and brushed his teeth until his gums bled. He had no written text; he had memorized the words and could recite them in his sleep:

"God loves Man, whom He created in His image and likeness. The communist hates God and therefore hates Man, though he professes to speak for the 'masses.' Logic and experience demand that Christians condemn the communist's false philosophy and strive to erase this blasphemy from God's lovingly created earth."

Perspiration ringed his neck, absorbed by the stiff-starched collar of his shirt. His voice was not powerful, but his words—those of a thoughtful adult spoken from the mouth of a child—seized the hearts of his listeners. He believed in the words, put his faith in their power and God's power, not his own.

Later, he stared at the fourteen-inch painted plaster statuette of the Blessed Virgin that he had won as the top prize in the competition. A plaque with his name was attached to the base beneath her sandaled feet. He had beat out several boys from other Catholic institutions, and he felt a full belly of satisfaction in his decisive victory. He understood that he should probably be more humble in his moment of triumph, but it was difficult. He was so much better than all the others. The judges certainly thought so.

Henry had been born special. He did not know why, but he accepted this as a fact. He had never really known his parents, who had put him up for adoption—which had never come to fruition—when he was an infant. Even if they had sinned, or been unable to care for him for some other reason, they, too, must have been specially blessed by Almighty God—to have such a son! Perhaps he was destined to be a great teacher or a saint. He trusted in his destiny. It would take him away from the darkness and squalor of this place.

Within these walls he had known triumph and despair. As he bent over his books in his room, lit by a single forty-watt bulb, he willed himself far away in time and space. . . .

Vennholme found himself back in the library at the conclave, grown old, bent in prayer. Prayer came harder to him in this phase of his life; he had to work at it, rely on the training and discipline of a lifetime to stay with it. He tried to push away the crowding images, but they thrust themselves upon him, forcing him to remember:

The Secret Thing made him angry and made him ashamed. He could never tell anybody—not even his confessor—what had happened to him. God knew. God would forgive the victim and punish the evildoer. That is the way of God, and young Henry believed with his entire being in the way of God.

He questioned why it should have happened to him. He had heard whisperings and accusations among the other boys in the home. There were suspicions against one of the

brothers who taught mathematics. How could this be? It
was that particular brother who had done it to Henry, starting one Christmas Day when Henry was twelve and most
of the orphanage staff were off for the holiday. It continued
for two years, then stopped suddenly. During class time the
brother acted as if nothing were amiss, as if nothing untoward had happened between himself and Henry.

But it had happened! The Secret Thing caused Henry
deep fear and anguish and shame, and he secretly wondered
if it might be some sort of retribution for the pride he had
felt upon winning that award a year earlier. How could he
have allowed it? Couldn't he have stopped the man? The
brother was neither big nor very powerful; he had not overwhelmed Henry, rather had seduced the boy with promises
and threats.

"You must never tell anyone, or God shall punish you
for the filthy things you have done," the man had told him.
Young Henry smelled coffee and wine on the man's close
breath and cologne mingled with stale tobacco and perspiration in his clothing.

Henry Vennholme believed him at first. It ate at his soul
for weeks and months. When the actual contact ended, he
felt both relieved and saddened; he knew a part of his life
had ended, felt somehow less vulnerable, less a boy and
more nearly a grown man. He awoke some nights sweating
and retching. His roommates ignored his suffering; they had
their own problems. They came and went. Even the brother
who had violated him left after a few years. Henry stayed
until he turned seventeen. The Church authorities decided,
in their wisdom, to continue the education of this promising
orphan.

He entered university prepared to excel. He was blessed
with a good brain and the ability to delay gratification until
a task—no matter how arduous or painful—was completed.
He majored in economics and religion, attaining a dual degree in just three years. He had no time for undergraduate
social life. Occasionally he took a beer with some of his
colleagues, even smoked a pipe now and then. But he allowed no one to get close to him, not that they were clam-
oring to. In his sophomore year he took up tennis, an

individual rather than team sport. He competed whenever he could, and with a vengeance. With his wiry frame and quick hands he was good, superior in fact. In the spring and summer of each subsequent year he found release and validation on the clay tennis courts of the city.

In seminary he regained the teasing moniker of Scholar. Even among the elite corps of seminarians who did not shrink from hard academic work, who thrived on the detail and intricacy of theology and canon law, Henry Vennholme stood out. One of his classmates went further and called him Monsieur Iron Ass. He was capable of spending long hours in the high-vaulted musty library that reminded him eerily of the bygone days in the Orphanage of Sts. Michael and Bartholomew. Would he never escape the dankness and darkness of that place?

From the earlier, darker times he felt drawn to the priesthood, strongly and inevitably, and he held on to this belief in his vocation through every doubt and trial.

First in his seminary class. Ordination by the archbishop at the cathedral in Montreal. Graduate studies in theology and canon law in Rome. Tennis when he could find a worthy opponent, which was not very often. Attached to the Congregation for the Clergy, a plum appointment for a young clergyman: this dicastery dealt with issues of the clergy, seminaries, catechetics, and local church finances. More long days of hard work and long nights of painful memories and loneliness. Discovery of the Evangelium Christi philosophy. Revelation! Life and purpose!

Father Henry Martin Vennholme, the lonely, wounded boy, considered himself the most fortunate of men. Wasn't he?

For who among his old seminary colleagues could claim to have achieved anything approaching his curriculum vitae, his rise to power and influence in the Church at this century's dawning? Had not the Holy Father himself embraced the new cardinal in consistory, placed the symbolic red biretta upon his steely clean head, overtly praised the work of the Evangelium leaders, lay and religious? And who was the de facto supreme leader of the movement? Cardinal Vennholme, the Sostituto or Head of First Section for General Affairs of the Secretariat of State, one of the most powerful members of the Roman Curia.

He had come a long way from Sts. Michael and Bartholomew, yet he again found himself alone and on his knees in a strange room praying to a God who had been often absent from his life. This seemingly indifferent God heard but did not always respond to his servant. Vennholme felt the frustration of a persistent suitor who had not yet won the complete commitment of his innamorata; he had felt her breath upon his face, but she was not there when he reached for her in the middle of the night.

And what was there? A voice sometimes—often a mocking one. *Scholar,* it proclaimed, dripping with condescension. *Monsieur Iron Ass.* A leering voice that came to his room when he was alone, unprotected, a mere boy.

That thou doest, do quickly. . . .

The words came again, and Vennholme repeated them aloud, steeling himself for the violation to come.

But he was alone. There was no brother pushing him down onto his hands and knees, breathing heavily upon his back and telling him to keep his mouth shut or else he would go to hell. No Christ alone in the desert exhorting the Tempter to do quickly whatever he is going to do so that the Savior might triumph over sin and evil. No, the words came with ineffable sweetness and sadness, falling upon Vennholme with the weight of a father resigned to the failings of his son.

That thou doest . . .

"No!" Vennholme blurted, jumping up from his knees and spinning around. He shook himself to clear the horrible nausea that had settled in his chest. "Alone, I am alone," he muttered.

Feeling a wave of dizziness, the cardinal sat down at his desk and placed his head in his hands. He did not try to pray, but he whispered a simple silent request, begging for relief from the twin burdens of righteousness and remorse. God and loneliness were the twin pillars of his existence.

Vennholme did not know how long he had been sitting there when he was startled by a knock on the door. He sat upright and glanced at his watch and saw that it was 7:00

A.M., and he whispered, "Biagi," remembering that they had agreed to meet at that early hour, before the next voting session of the conclave. Rising, he strode to the door and summoned a smile as he pulled it open and greeted the Italian.

"Leandro, my friend. I trust you slept well?" He used Biagi's native tongue.

The Florentine's polite smile looked as forced as Vennholme's. "As well as could be expected," he replied, also in Italian, as he entered the room.

Vennholme closed the door and showed Biagi to one of the chairs in front of the desk. He sat down in the other rather than returning to his desk seat, signaling that he wished to speak informally.

"I'm an old man," Biagi said abruptly, "and my powers of concentration are failing. Let us dispense with niceties and focus on the subject at hand."

Vennholme did not bother to counter Biagi's claim of failing mental capacity, which he knew was not so. "Cardinal Mulrennan," he declared soberly.

"Yes, you requested this meeting to talk about my dear son Timofeo, so I shall let you begin." Biagi fixed the French Canadian with a stern eye that indicated he had little patience for the maneuverings that usually accompanied such discussions.

"Yes, I did. I am concerned about his candidacy."

"About his fitness as papabile." It was more a statement than a question.

"I have no desire to judge the man," Vennholme said, summoning as much sincerity as possible. "But I worry about perceptions, for in these times perception can be as important as reality."

"Then you don't believe he is unfit to be pontiff but merely may be perceived as such?"

"The moral authority of our Church must be inviolable. It is hard to see how that can be if the moral authority of its leader is under attack."

"By you."

Vennholme bore the sting of Biagi's sharp words without reacting. "You believe I am being too harsh on Mulrennan?

When I spoke up in the conclave, it was only to diffuse the rumors being circulated by Giannantonio and others—and to give our brother a chance to answer them."

"Please, save your theatrics for the others." Biagi leaned forward, pressing his palms against his knees. "It was a wonderful performance, but it did not fool me. Pasquale Giannantonio is a puppet; words do not come from him but through him. It was easy to recognize the true voice."

Vennholme forced himself to breathe slowly, to pause before replying. At last he said, "Yes, we will dispense with niceties. When this conclave opened, I was willing to entertain the idea, astonishing as it might be, of an American pope—even of this American as pope. Indeed, as of this morning I remain open to the notion, but the door is about to close."

"It has closed," Biagi said in a near whisper. "Be honest about it, Henry."

Vennholme released a measured sigh. "Yes, La Spina is my man, but he is a man without imagination, I am afraid. Then again, imagination is not always the most desirable trait in a pontiff. But there is no denying that in today's world, charisma counts even more than competency, and even I must admit that our handsome, vigorous Timothy Mulrennan possesses that in full measure."

"And more than a measure of competency," Biagi argued.

"In the eyes of some, perhaps. But for this old conservative, I cannot help but fear where a man such as he might lead us."

"At least he would lead rather than follow," Biagi said pointedly.

"Ah, you speak of the Evangelium."

"That's what you want, Henry, is it not? A pope who will follow the dictates of your Evangelium Christi?"

Vennholme shook his close-cropped head slowly. "You misunderstand completely. But then again, how can someone outside the movement comprehend the heart of those within?"

"Heart? You consider controlling the Throne of St. Peter to be an act of the heart?"

"I—that is, we—have no desire to control. But like the heart, we wish to abide. We seek only a Church that honors our movement, our intentions. We seek fertile ground for the seed to grow. You see, we do not believe the Evangelium Christi to be some sort of secret fraternity, some political scheme." Vennholme pressed his pale hands together, as if in prayer. "You may choose not to accept this, for you have your suspicions, and this I understand, but we believe we have been called by our Lord and that He alone has set us on our path."

"A path that denies all others," Biagi offered bluntly.

"Not at all. We do not concern ourselves with other paths, for we know we have found the one lit by the flame of the Holy Spirit. We trust in that path and in God. And if it is His intention that Timothy Mulrennan be the next Vicar of Christ, so be it."

As Biagi leaned back against the chair, Vennholme could see that the Italian was weighing his words, debating how much trust to place in them. "Do you truly believe it might be God's will that Timothy become the next pontiff?"

"I have not ruled out the notion. But first I must ask you this question, and I hope you will show me the respect of answering plainly and truthfully."

"I will answer in truth or not at all."

"What I must know is simple. Would Cardinal Mulrennan, as pope, be willing to support the growth of Evangelium Christi? To retain its status as a personal prelature? At the very least not stand in its way? If he would agree to that, then I might be willing to support him." The late Holy Father had, indeed, recognized Evangelium Christi as such a personal prelature, which meant that the organization had the right to establish seminaries and to educate the faithful, as long as it violated no canon laws.

Biagi tilted his noble head. "I cannot speak for him, of course, but I don't believe he would accept such a bargain—not to become pope, not even to avoid a scandal. And, remember, the constitution of this conclave forbids any such arrangement. As for Evangelium Christi, you know that he holds great reservations about—"

"Damn his reservations!" Vennholme surprised himself

with the outburst. He took several seconds to be silent, breathed and forced calm back into his voice. "You and I, Biagi, we are alike in many respects. We have walked the hallways of the Apostolic Palace. We have seen what goes on behind the Vatican walls. This is no place for an idealist, an innocent. This is a place where arrangements must be made, where politics must be the servant of a higher policy. And if good ends may result from an alliance between Evangelium Christi and a so-called progressive American pope, then it is for such men as you and me—"

"Leave me out of your schemes," Biagi snapped, rising from the chair. "I'm an old Vatican warhorse; I know how this game is played. Yes, I have walked these halls and the streets of Florence and around the world among our brethren, and I have walked with my American friend. And believe me, you will not get Timothy Mulrennan to play this game. Nor will you get him to climb into bed with your Evangelium Christi." Leandro Biagi shook his finger accusingly at the Canadian.

"It's not *our* bed that worries me," Vennholme said to Biagi's back as the Italian headed for the door.

Biagi turned. "I don't believe for a moment that anything happened between Timothy and that woman in Newark."

"Of course not," Vennholme agreed with a smug smile. "In fact, if you will speak with Cardinal Mulrennan, if you will convince him that an alliance might serve both our needs, then I could be induced to arrange for that unfortunate bit of scandal to disappear."

"You can do such a thing?"

"Mulrennan can do it himself. But since he chooses to maintain his silence, yes, I can show that his actions not only were without dishonor but showed true Christian spirit."

"Then you knew it was a baseless charge even when you made it?"

"When Giannantonio—"

"Yes," Biagi said with a curt wave. "When you had Giannantonio make it."

"What I know, and can show, is that your candidate was protecting the reputation of a fellow priest."

"Then it was your duty to speak up."

"That was for Cardinal Mulrennan to do."

"Perhaps in not speaking, we have seen the true measure of the man."

"Perhaps," Vennholme said. "But I fear there may be another motive at work—one far less selfless. It was for that reason that I considered it important to see how our next pope might respond to a charge of breaking his vow of chastity—even a baseless one. Believe me, it was for his own good that we allowed this matter to come to the surface, where it could be aired and ultimately dismissed."

Biagi's eyes were harsh slits. "I confess I have never liked you, my dear sir. And I like you even less today than before. And I promise you this: The next pope, be he Cardinal Mulrennan or one of the Swiss Guards, shall see you and your Evangelium in hell."

"What or who you like is of no concern to me," Vennholme declared, leaning forward in his chair. "What does concern me, what I asked you here to discuss, is not that incident in Newark. If that were all in Mulrennan's past—in his curriculum vitae—" A heavy dose of sarcasm flowed into his voice. "Well, if that were the case, then we could dispense with all this dancing around and get down to the real business of finding common ground and choosing him as our next pontiff. But no, there is more, much more, and it troubles me greatly. You seem to forget that I have known him for a very long time and watched him, from close up and from afar."

"Enough of this posturing," Biagi said impatiently. "What is it that you have on Cardinal Mulrennan?"

"I will let him tell you about it himself. But it wasn't that incident in Newark. No, it was another place, another woman entirely. And I know something of it firsthand. Ask him about Vietnam—about a woman named Ly Linh Sanh. Ask Timothy Cardinal Mulrennan about his *wife*."

Vennholme sat back and watched the color drain from the wily Italian's face. Both men were silent for a long time, and when it became obvious that Biagi was not about to reply, Vennholme continued.

"Yes, ask His Eminence about that little Vietnamese wife

of his. Then ask him if he wants to be elected our next pope—and if he's willing to support Evangelium Christi to accomplish it."

"To buy your silence, you mean."

Vennholme merely shrugged, but the gesture spoke volumes.

"Good day, Eminenza." Biagi pulled open the door. "As for your considerate offer, I can assure you that the answer will be the same no matter what dirt you have unearthed. Timothy Mulrennan will never make a political arrangement, with you or anyone else, to sit on the Throne of St. Peter. And there is nothing you or even I could do or say to change that truth."

Turning on his heel, he jerked the door shut and strode off down the hall.

By the time Pasquale Cardinal Giannantonio joined Henry Vennholme in the library, several minutes later, the Canadian cleric had fully absorbed and analyzed his conversation with Biagi and come to a decision.

"How did it go?" Giannantonio asked in a near whisper, as if afraid to unleash some primal force that could be seen building on Vennholme's features.

"We will wait no longer," Vennholme said in Italian.

"You've heard from Cardinal Mulrennan?"

Vennholme did not look up from the papers on his desk. "I don't need to. Biagi is right. Mulrennan will never be of use to us. Not as pope, at least."

"Then it is time?"

Vennholme tapped the folder in front of him. "It is time."

Giannantonio kept his eyes lowered to the floor.

"All is in place for contacting Signor Darragh?" Vennholme asked.

"Everything has been arranged, just as you directed." He looked up at Vennholme. "I assure you, no one will ever find out that the communication came from within the conclave."

"They had better not, or your career is over."

"How soon shall Signor Darragh proceed?"

"Let him do quickly what he must do. I want the story to break this very day."

"All of it?"

"I've already discussed with Darragh what we need. He'll instruct the writer to begin with Newark and that woman in Vietnam. The rest will be revealed in the coming hours."

"And me?" Giannantonio asked, eyeing the folder on the desk. "Shall I continue my denunciation at the morning session?"

Vennholme started to push forward the folder, then withdrew it. "No, brother, I think not."

"No?" Giannantonio looked genuinely surprised.

"The situation has changed, and so must our tactics."

"But why hold back, if the outside press is going to release the story anyway, can't we use that as leverage here?"

"We are not holding back." Vennholme stood and folded his hands in front of him. "On the contrary, our denunciation shall go forward. But I will be the one who makes it." Seeing Giannantonio's look of disappointment, Vennholme came around the desk and wrapped an arm around his shoulder. "You have played your role to perfection, my good friend, and you shall be rewarded in kind—by me and by our next pontiff."

Giannantonio's pained expression softened into a satisfied smile.

"Speaking of the next pope, have you sent for La Spina?"

"He is outside, Your Eminence."

Vennholme clapped him on the back. "Then by all means show him in!"

He gave Giannantonio a gentle push toward the door, and the cardinal exited the library, and a moment later the imposing, black-cassocked Archbishop of Turin stood in the doorway. Pietro Cardinal La Spina was a few inches taller and nearly one hundred pounds heavier than the slightly built Canadian, his face a swarthy, scowling mask that elicited trembling terror from his chancery staff and the parish priests of his densely populated archdiocese. He had held a number of top Curia posts during his more than twenty years as a bishop, including five years as the prefect of the Congregation for the Doctrine of the Faith, formerly the much-feared Holy Office, or Inquisition, and in each had been equally respected and loathed for his imperious micromanagement.

The Holy Father had grown closer to and fonder of La Spina during the last several years of his pontificate and had appointed the loyal cardinal to the archepiscopate of Turin to give him the pastoral experience that he lacked. Not since Pius XII had the cardinals elected a man pope without any direct administrative experience in a diocese. La Spina could not, in fact, claim the affections of his flock, but he ran an efficient, solvent archdiocese; and he was a favorite of journalists, who could count on a stern, pithy quote from the splenetic prelate on nearly any doctrinal or political issue.

"Let the enemies of the Church speak out and make themselves known to defenders of the True Faith; we should call a modern crusade against the new infidels and heretics and cleanse them from the earth, not with the weapons of man but with the Sword of Truth." This in answer to a reporter's question: "Eminence, what is the greatest challenge you face in the new year?"

Known as the Terror of Turin, or the Pope's Lion, Pietro Cardinal La Spina, pastor and Church doctor, was on everyone's short list of papabili and had emerged as the odds-on favorite choice among conservatives and Curialists. The fact that he was called Peter was not lost on the more creative journalists and die-hard antireform supporters.

"My friend Pietro!" Vennholme embraced the stocky Italian cardinal, greeting him fluently in his native language. "Come in, come in. And thank you for seeing me at such an hour. I hope our friend Pasquale Giannantonio did not disturb your sleep."

"Sleep has become a scarce commodity. I wonder if it has always been this way in conclave."

"We should ask some of our senior colleagues, though there are not many who were around for the last conclave. Do you wish for some coffee or perhaps a glass of wine?" He gestured La Spina toward a chair.

"Prayer and herbal tea usually help me sleep, and I had both in good measure during the night. But yes, perhaps a cup of coffee is in order."

La Spina's voice and manner were usually gruff, but Vennholme sensed that he was affecting a more humble, questioning tone this morning—a sure sign that something was troubling him.

As Vennholme poured some rich French roast brew from the carafe on the desk, he noticed that the visitor's hand was trembling ever so slightly—the effect of a sleepless night, perhaps, or a further indication of his worry.

But worry was an uncharacteristic trait in this old friend from the clerical wars of the past three decades. Like Vennholme, and most of the current cardinal-electors for that matter, he had been a young priest during the Vatican II era, and it had profoundly influenced his development as a theologian—primarily because he had stood for thirty-five years in firm opposition to many of the Council's actions. That opposition had tempered and sharpened him, as slowly, fitfully, he and comrades like Vennholme had steered the Church back "on course" to preconciliar positions and practices in several significant areas: liturgy, vocations, celibacy, evangelization.

In areas where he disagreed with the Holy Father and some few moderates within the Curia—areas such as ecumenism among Christian denominations, dialogue with Jewish and Muslim leaders, improved relations with such foreign communist powers as China and Cuba, recently relaxed policies regarding liberal theologians—La Spina respectfully, measuredly, but definitively, made known his views. He was no shrinking violet, certainly. And not a man to let show his worries.

He accepted the cup of hot coffee from Vennholme, pushed his thick brown finger through the delicately curved porcelain handle. The steam played up around his prominently hooked nose as he listened to the Canadian, who took the seat across from him.

"So, we are very close now to a victory—that is, your election, which shall send a message to the entire world that the Church is united in faith and marching in the correct direction once again. I predict that you will be elected on the second ballot today, if not the first."

Vennholme closely watched his companion: La Spina

was fidgeting now like a nervous, overweight girl.

"Henry, I have my own questions—I mean to say, if I were to be elected, I do not know whether I should accept. I feel—" His thick eyebrows fell, and his lidded brown eyes flicked around the room in discomfort. Modesty, doubt, self-revelation, all were very unlike the stolid symbol of reaction that the Archbishop of Turin had become. "I feel unworthy of election."

"You will accept your election! There is no doubt, no room for personal feelings in this matter, Pietro. None."

"But, my friend, it is such an awesome responsibility. I am healthy, but . . . you see, I am full of misgiving."

Vennholme was stunned at the thought that La Spina might be posturing in order to receive some sort of assurance, some praise or benediction. Such vanity had never revealed itself in the man. Vanity—or perhaps a more subtle game?

Pushing away the troubling thought, Vennholme declared, "God has given you the strength of a bull. You can handle anything, if it is His will. I believe that, and so do you. You have held some of the most responsible positions in the Church. Pietro, I believe you were born to be our pope, our shepherd, in this age of a new millennium. Certainly, compared to any of the others—"

"There are other acceptable candidates, Henry. Some are very fine men, from many parts of the world."

"The American included? Surely you don't number our friend Mulrennan among them."

"I believe he is a man of faith, if a troubled and misguided one."

"But certainly no pope," Vennholme snapped.

He forced himself to pause again and breathe slowly. He gave La Spina a compassionate smile.

"You are having these momentary qualms, Pietro, which is a very natural reaction. It is like the night before a marriage. What groom hasn't thought about running away? Perhaps we have taken too long in the balloting to get to this point. But you stand on the threshold of something so very—so exquisitely—important . . . for all of us."

Vennholme leaned back in his chair and peered at the

black-clad papabile. La Spina's reactions, even his slightly hunched posture, impressed Vennholme as so uncharacteristic of the oftentimes mulish prelate. Suddenly he was struck with an insight.

"Biagi . . ."

As the name slipped from his lips, he knew it with a certainty: Somehow Cardinal Biagi had made contact with La Spina and planted these seeds of doubt within the man. How? What could that clever politician have said to him?

"You have spoken to Biagi."

"No. Last night he asked me to meet with him. I sent him a note instead, saying I would not. I cannot imagine what he would want to speak with me about."

"Oh, I most certainly can," Vennholme spat. "You disappoint me, my friend. I did not expect that you would or even could lose heart at such a crucial time."

"It is not that at all," La Spina protested. "I have a strong faith that the conclave will choose the right man. I want that to happen. But in this moment, at this hour, I am struck with the thought deep inside that it is not I. I am not certain how to explain it without sounding weak." He said the expression in thickly accented English.

"I will hear none of it." Vennholme dismissed the notion with a backhanded wave. "Very unexpected, and disappointing, Pietro. It cannot be so. I have worked so hard. The others, the Italians, the men of faith among us who have sacrificed—even the late Holy Father himself virtually anointed you as his successor. You yourself have said it to me privately many times. Surely he had the gift of seeing these things. Surely he knew—"

"I understand that you have labored to lay the groundwork for this, my friend," La Spina replied, his voice tentative and respectful. "I had to tell you, though, what my thoughts are. Perhaps you are correct and it is nothing but a momentary spasm of fear. I do wish this conclave would finish its business, for my sake as well as the others'."

Vennholme's smile was warm, genuine. This was a strong man, a good man, despite his human frailties—a man to lead the Church in the third millennium of its life. "Let us pray together, Pietro. Kneel with me."

He glided to his knees and lifted his hand to support the bulky cardinal from Turin, who hit the floor with a reverberating thud and a wince. Arthritis had taken its toll on the peasant-born prelate, and pain was his constant companion.

Vennholme bowed his head and closed his eyes tightly in concentration; he intoned in English, "Heavenly Father, we are but Your humble servants, and You are our good and faithful shepherd who would never abandon us in our need."

Pietro Cardinal La Spina interpreted the words in Italian, silently in his mind. His face remained a dark stoic mask. He wondered how he had come to this place in his life, in the life of the Church—and knew his own unworthiness. Yet—if the work of Christ must be done . . . if there was no one else to do it properly, should he not gladly make himself available? Was this God's will for him?

"Heavenly Father," Vennholme continued, "give us, Your servants, the strength this day to accomplish the task that lies before us."

That thou doest, do quickly.

CHAPTER NINE

Vietnam, April 19, 1969

If it had not been for the opening shock, Tim Mulrennan could almost believe that the chute was not open at all, for when he looked upward the black canopy all but disappeared in the night sky. The Pilatus Porter that had dropped him had already made a 180-degree turn and was heading back to the South, to relative safety. The chopper would be back on base in twenty minutes.

Mulrennan was scheduled to be back in twenty-four hours—provided he encountered no difficulty in the North and provided the Air America—in reality, CIA—helicopter scheduled to pick him up was where it was supposed to be when it was supposed to be there.

Rapidly the dark earth rushed up to meet him as he gripped the control lines, feeling very little control over his immediate situation. His first task was to land, and he had to slip hard, to the right, to avoid a dark, dangerous thicket of trees. He hit the ground cleanly and rolled into a landing fall with no injuries other than not being able to breathe for about a minute. Fifteen minutes later he had the chute buried. He consulted his compass, then started toward the hamlet of Dong Hoi to find the hut of Ly Linh Sanh.

Five hundred yards beyond a small rice paddy, he saw the few dim lights of the village. He calculated the location of the woman's hut and walked slowly, deliberately, in that direction. He immediately found a tree, but there were only two gourds tied to the lowest limb. He paused. Had one of the gourds fallen off? Was the fact that there were gourds at all enough to justify his knocking on the front door? Mike Bernard had been very specific, and Mulrennan knew enough about the intelligence business to know that three gourds meant three gourds, not two. Could it be a warning?

Mulrennan skirted the southern end of the hamlet and looked for his three gourds. At two other huts he set the dogs to barking and caused one resident to come out with a flashlight to look around. He melted into the darkness and thanked God there was no moon on this night.

There were no gourds anywhere, so he returned to the first hut. If only Bernard had not been so damned specific about three gourds! Mulrennan moved around the tree and finally saw it: a third gourd *behind* the limb, which had been invisible from his angle of approach.

He rapped softly on the frail wooden door and a moment later was standing face to face with a breathtakingly beautiful woman, about thirty years old. She had high, well-accented cheekbones and dark almond-shaped eyes framed by lashes that seemed of the most delicate black lace. From the light of a single oil lamp he could see that her skin was smooth and golden, her movements as graceful as palm fronds in the breeze. She wore black silk pajamas that were amazingly seductive yet distinctly prim and proper.

"Please, come in, quickly," she said in English, stepping back to admit the American soldier. She walked outside and quickly scanned the area around her hut before returning inside. "No one saw you?" she asked pointedly.

"No. I was very careful."

"Good."

She motioned him to a table, then went around the hut, making sure the windows were all covered.

"I am supposed to give you this." He dropped the revised code book on the table.

With hardly a glance at him, Ly snatched up the book, walked over to the southern wall, and removed two loose boards. Behind the boards, Mulrennan saw a wireless radio. Ly put the book on top of the radio, then replaced the two boards and placed a cracked vase in front.

"You are very brave to bring the new book to me," she said as she approached the opposite side of the table. "Why did you come? Is there not a Vietnamese man you can trust?"

She sat down and placed the little oil lamp between them. As she looked up at his face, her eyes widened in surprise—in fear—and the breath caught in her throat. Mulrennan started to ask what was wrong, but she raised a finger at him and stammered, "You—you have come back."

"Me?" he said with a sheepish shrug.

"I know you. . . . But this cannot be."

Mulrennan saw the recognition in her eyes, and then it came to him with a sudden shock. "My brother," he said simply. "You know my brother, Kevin."

Ly Linh Sanh looked genuinely confused. "Kevin?" she asked, pronouncing the *v* with great difficulty.

"Captain Kevin Mulrennan." He removed a wallet-sized picture from his buttoned pocket and placed it on the table in front of her. "I'm his brother, Timothy Mulrennan. That's why I came instead of one of your countrymen. My brother has been missing these past six months, and I was told you might know something of his fate."

Placing her hand over the photograph, Ly Linh Sanh closed her eyes and for a long time just sat there, breathing heavily. Slowly her breath grew calmer, steadier, and at last she crossed herself and looked back up at him.

"I thought I see one of your ghosts. You and your brother—you look much alike."

Mulrennan had never thought there was much similarity between him and his strapping, handsome older brother, but he realized that an Asian woman might see similarities he did not.

"Then you have seen Kevin?" he asked, trying to suppress the tinge of excitement he could not help but feel.

"Yes, I see him," Ly said. "I am sorry, but he is dead."

She said the words softly, compassionately, but they struck Mulrennan like a hammer. He felt his eyes welling with tears.

"I am sorry to give you this news. He a brave man, and he accept his death bravely."

"Where . . . where is his body?"

Ly Linh Sanh shook her head, and tears ran down her cheeks. She did not answer.

"The body—" he pressed, reaching toward her, then pulling his hand back.

"I do not think you will want to see his body. It was mutilated and burned, then it was buried."

Mulrennan forced down the bile that rose in his throat. "I want to visit the spot where he is buried."

"No, you must not. It would be most dangerous for you."

"I accept the risk. Please. My search won't be over until I can at least say a prayer over his grave. You have to tell me where he is."

"If you must go, it better if I take you. But it is almost morning. Too light. Tonight, when it is dark again. Then I will take you to your brother."

"I must be at the pickup point in twenty-four hours."

"There is time," she assured him. "Your brother . . . Kevin . . . he is not far away."

Tim Mulrennan spent that day inside the hut, always close to a small hiding area Ly Linh Sanh had fashioned beneath her bed. But no one approached the building or disturbed them, and they were able to speak together on and off throughout the day. Ly was careful, however, to go about her usual business in her yard and in the village, so as not to arouse notice or suspicion among Dong Hoi's staunchly Vietcong residents.

During their conversations, Ly explained how Mulrennan's brother had been captured in the South and brought to the village, where he was subjected to interrogation and then a communist show trial. Mulrennan did not ask for any details of the interrogation, for he knew it would have been brutal. He knew, too, that his brother would not have given them any information other than name, rank, and serial number.

During the trial, she told him, the "people's prosecutors" charged that he was not an ordinary soldier but rather a murderer who sent his soldiers into the villages to kill men and women, entire families who were loyal to the People's Republic of Vietnam.

Declared guilty and sentenced to death, Kevin Mulrennan was executed by firing squad, and his body was laid out for two days to allow the citizens to vent their wrath against the American imperialist. He was spit upon, kicked, hacked, and finally burned, before the communist authorities of the hamlet buried what was left of him. By then his remains were unidentifiable as human.

Well after sunset, Ly Linh Sanh led Tim Mulrennan from the hut and along a circuitous path through the outskirts of the village. They traveled for more than a mile but ended up doubling back toward the village until they were within a quarter mile of where they'd started. There, on a gentle rise of land that overlooked the surrounding rice paddies, a single large rock marked the burial site of the American prisoner. It looked like any other rock, until Ly turned it over and showed Mulrennan the cross that had been carved on the underside.

"Did you do that?" he asked as he knelt over the grave and traced the carving with his finger.

She shook her head. "Your brother a very brave man. I would have done it, but another already make the mark. I am not the only one who hates the Vietcong."

There was something in her voice, something in the look in her eye that was apparent even in the thin starlight. Mulrennan realized that he was not the only one to have lost a loved one to this war. He wondered who it had been. Her parents? Perhaps her husband or lover. He sensed her pain and honored it in silence.

Turning the stone back into position on the grave, the carved symbol hidden against the cool earth, Timothy Mulrennan stood and bowed his head. Raising his right hand, he made the Sign of the Cross, and intoned:

"Memento etiam, Domine, famulorum qui nos praecesserunt cum signo fidei et dormiunt in somno pacis.

"Ipsis, Domine, et omnibus in Christo quiescentibus, locum refrigerii, lucis et pacis, ut indulgeas, deprecamur. Per eumdem Christum Dominum nostrum. Amen."

When they got back to Ly Linh Sanh's hut, it was 2300 hours—six hours before the helicopter was scheduled to arrive at the pickup point. While it should take him no more than two hours to make the journey, he knew that prudence dictated he get started at once.

It was when they were saying good-bye that Ly Linh

Sanh said, "You have not asked about me—about why I hate the Vietcong so."

"I know you must have your reasons."

"Five of them." She gestured toward the south. "They lie in five graves, three days journey from here . . . my parents, my sister, my husband . . ." Her voice cracked as she added, "Even my little one. They took over our village in the South, near the border. Many were killed. Others . . . were used for their pleasure."

Mulrennan saw in her expression that she was so used, saving her from her family's fate.

"Afterward I decide to come here."

"To the North?" he said incredulously.

"What better place to fight my enemy? Many have been uprooted by the war, and I was able to fit in as a seamstress." She gestured toward the foot-powered sewing machine in the corner. "I will stay here as long as I must—until I see my enemy defeated. I make that promise over the graves of my family—and to my friends in the South who help me contact your military before I come to Dong Hoi."

"You are a brave woman, Ly."

She shook her head vehemently. "I no longer a woman. They make me into something else, and I will use that to fight them, as long as I am alive."

They spoke a few minutes more, and then Timothy Mulrennan rose to leave. Ly Linh Sanh picked up the oil lamp to lead him to the door, then abruptly turned back to the table.

"You forget this," she said as she picked up the picture of Kevin Mulrennan. She held it forth.

He was about to take it, then realized he had copies at home. "Would you like to keep it?" he asked.

"For me?" she said with a touch of excitement. She looked down at the picture, then up at him again, as if comparing their features so that she would be able to remember the small differences.

"I would like you to have it," he told her. "And I know my brother would, too."

There were tears in her eyes again, and she nodded, then

slipped the picture into a pocket of her trousers.

The two headed to the door. Before Ly opened it, Mulrennan took her hand in his and felt how work hardened
yet delicate it was.

He opened the door and started out, but she stopped him,
reaching up to the cross on his collar. She touched it gently,
much as he had traced the symbol on the bottom of the
stone.

"You a priest among your people?" she asked, and he
nodded. "Pray for us, Father Mulrennan. For all of us."

He touched her hand a final time, then headed into the
darkness.

Timothy Mulrennan had gone more than a mile when he
heard the snap of a branch and pulled up short. It was
probably nothing, he told himself, for all was again silent
save for the sudden pounding of his heart. He waited a
moment, then continued, a bit slower and more cautiously.

A few minutes later he heard it again. This time he was
certain that someone or something was close behind, and
he reached instinctively for the pistol strapped to his side.
He had tried to leave it behind, but Mike Bernard had refused to let him go on the mission without a side arm.
Later, after the parachute jump, he had even considered
throwing it away, and now he was grateful he had not.

As Mulrennan raised the pistol in front of him and turned
around, he mentally reviewed all the appropriate Scripture
passages, trying to convince himself that there is no sin in
defending oneself. But could he? Would he actually be able
to pull the trigger against a fellow human being, even if it
meant saving his own life? And what if it was an innocent
person? What if it was Ly Linh Sanh?

The thought of pulling a gun on Ly Linh Sanh so startled
him that he lowered it and took a step forward, peering into
the darkness in search of whatever it was that had made
that noise. He wanted to call out Ly's name but couldn't
risk someone else connecting the two of them. At last he
whispered, "Hello?" in Vietnamese.

The reply came in the muffled retort of a gun, the searing
pain of a bullet tearing through Mulrennan's upper left arm.
He let out an involuntary cry as he was knocked back off

his feet, probably saving him from the second shot, which went whizzing just over his head.

The pain quickly transformed into a strange numbness on his left side. But he wasn't thinking about that—only about how to get out of the line of fire. He was on a path through an open field with low vegetation and a few stunted trees on both sides. He crawled off the path into the brush, listening for any sound of his attacker.

Suddenly he realized he was still holding the pistol in his right hand. He tried to remember what Bernard had told him but couldn't even recall the type of weapon or number of bullets it held. He could only pray now that it was loaded.

There was a rustling sound off to his right, then the clear sound of someone approaching. Mulrennan lay there on the ground, making himself as small as possible in the brush, struggling to keep his breath as quiet as possible. No more than twenty feet away, a dark form moved along the pathway, closing in on the spot where he had fallen. The figure took a few cautious steps, paused, took a few steps more. Mulrennan tracked it, his hands shaking more with fear than pain. When the dark figure was within ten feet, Mulrennan was able to discern the silhouette of a man and even saw a glint of light on the barrel of what appeared to be a pistol.

Saying a mental prayer of forgiveness, Mulrennan squeezed the trigger and waited for the jerking blast. Instead there was a faint rasp of metal as the safety engaged and kept the weapon from firing. It was enough of a sound to draw the man's attention, and he swung to his left and fired again. Mulrennan dove to his side just in time, groaning as he landed on his wounded left arm. Another shot went wide as the priest fumbled with the gun, jerking at the safety mechanism. Praying it was properly disengaged, he drew up the pistol and squeezed the trigger. The bullet found its mark, catching the man in his belly and dropping him to his knees.

Mulrennan thought he saw the man's pistol fly from the impact of the shot. He knew he should fire again, just to be certain, but something held him back. Gripping the pistol, he rose from the brush and approached the pathway.

As he drew closer, he saw that the man wore the uniform of a Vietcong and looked no older than a boy. He writhed on the ground, gripping his stomach and gurgling blood.

Holstering his pistol, Mulrennan walked up to the young man and knelt at his side. He started to reach for him, wanting to comfort him somehow, but already it was over. The breath went out of him, and the gurgling of blood subsided.

Timothy Mulrennan had killed a man. Never, even in the darkest and most dangerous moments in Berlin or in the cold days of basic training at Fort Dix when he was often more scared than tired, had he imagined this moment in its stark emptiness.

"Dead," he spat. Sweat poured into his eyes, blinding him momentarily. Then the tears came.

Mulrennan allowed himself a moment to feel the full impact of what he had just done. Then he wiped away the tears—there would be time enough later to reflect on what had happened. Now he had to keep a clear head about him.

The priest stood back up, listening to the silence, wondering if the gunfire would have been heard back in the village. And if it had been, would anyone take notice or merely assume it was some distant skirmish of the war? In any event, he knew he must get out of there as quickly as possible. This soldier might not have been alone, and his friends might soon be in pursuit.

Before leaving, Mulrennan examined his wound and determined the bullet had done no serious damage but had passed through cleanly, missing the bone and any arteries. He could move his hand and fingers, though doing so caused quite a bit of pain. He tore away some cloth from the dead man's uniform and tied it around his arm, then started down the path.

He had gone only a few feet when he thought again of Ly Linh Sanh. A terrible fear came over him—an awareness, a certainty that she was in danger. The dead soldier had fired upon him without even making certain he was an enemy. Perhaps he had been following Mulrennan all the way from Ly's hut. Perhaps at that very moment Ly was being unmasked and arrested.

Timothy Mulrennan broke into a run back toward Dong Hoi, back to Ly Linh Sanh's hut at the edge of the village. It was more than a mile over dark, uneven ground, but in spite of his wound he covered the distance in eight minutes flat. He did not stop running until the little building came into view, the light of an oil lamp spilling around the door and through the slatted bamboo curtains.

Mulrennan slowed to a walk as he covered the final distance, listening for sounds from within. As he drew closer, he heard a muffled cry—unmistakably Ly's voice—followed by a low growling, grunting response. For a moment he was uncertain what was happening, but then he heard Ly cry out again. This time there was no mistaking her fear and pain.

Mulrennan eased the door open and stepped inside. There, in the yellowish flickering light of the lamp, he saw a Vietnamese man on top of Ly Linh Sanh on the floor. Ly was naked, her black silk pajamas torn and cast aside. The man's trousers were pushed down to his ankles, and he cursed as he thrust himself against her.

Ly saw Mulrennan, who in turn saw the pain, horror, and shame in her eyes.

Silence above all, he told himself. He must not let the entire village know what was happening here. He lunged at the attacker and, clasping one hand over the man's mouth, grabbed his black hair with the other hand and pulled him away from Ly. He saw now that the man was a Vietcong soldier. The woman understood the need to be quiet and stifled her cry of alarm and relief.

Mulrennan flung the soldier against the hut wall. The man's head banged loudly against the boards, and he slid to the floor, senseless.

"Are you all right?" Mulrennan asked, kneeling beside Ly.

She tried to hide her nakedness with her hands as she nodded. Then suddenly she gasped and gestured across the room, her eyes wide with terror.

Mulrennan spun around and saw that the soldier had revived and was struggling to his feet. The priest reached for his pistol, then remembered the need for silence. Instead he launched himself at the man, who shook clear his head and met the American straight on.

The two men collided with a jarring thud. Mulrennan's greater size gave him the advantage, but the soldier was wiry and athletic, and he dropped backward and sent the bigger man sprawling over him and into the wall. By the time Mulrennan recovered and turned around, the soldier was leaping past Ly Linh Sanh, headed for his AK-47 lying on the floor a few feet away.

Forgetting her modesty, Ly reached out and grabbed the soldier's pants, which were still around his ankles, bringing him down heavily onto the floor. The man gasped, the air going out of him. All the while he grabbed wildly for the automatic weapon just inches away. His fingers wrapped around the barrel, and he drew it to him, struggling to get it into both hands.

Mulrennan looked around frantically and spied a pair of scissors lying atop the sewing machine. Adrenaline and his army training took over, and he raced over and snatched it up. Across the room Ly was grappling with the man, who had rolled onto his back and was cradling the AK-47 against his chest as he jerked back the arming bolt.

In one swift, unbroken motion, Timothy Mulrennan hurled himself across the room, scissors outstretched before him, the dual blades dipping underneath the AK-47 and penetrating the soldier's chest just below the ribs. Mulrennan twisted upward, jamming the blades deeper until they pierced the heart. Hot blood seeped between Mulrennan's fingers as the man sighed heavily, gasped several times, then went limp, the weapon slipping from his nerveless fingers.

The gush of blood slowed as the heart stopped pumping. Mulrennan quickly put his hand to the soldier's neck to check for a pulse. There was none.

Ly gasped, "Is he? . . ."

Mulrennan held one hand against the soldier's chest and, with the other, yanked with all his strength and pulled the scissors free. The body jerked in spasm, then collapsed with finality in a heap.

He flung the bloody weapon across the room, then wiped

his hands on the floor, leaving smeared red handprints on the rough planking. Standing, the priest pulled Ly Linh Sanh up off the floor and into his arms, cradling her, protecting her as he would a child who had been violated. Her body was shaking, but he could feel in her tenseness that she would not let herself cry.

"They—they saw you when you left my house," she murmured, burying her face in his chest. "I—I thought I heard gunfire . . . far off."

"This one's friend caught up to me, but I . . ." He patted the pistol at his side, and she nodded in understanding.

Mulrennan led her over to the bed and helped her wrap a blanket around herself. She lay down on the mattress, hugging the blanket to her. Droplets of blood marked her bare skin like freckles. She lay with her eyes closed, perhaps hoping that she could thus become invisible.

As he wiped his hands on his fatigue trousers, she looked up at him and noticed the bandage around his arm, the fresh blood dripping down his sleeve. Instantly she was up, the blanket forgotten on the bed as she examined his wound.

"It is nothing," he said, but she insisted on treating it. She paused only to slip into a robe, then carefully removed his shirt and cleaned and bandaged the wound.

Mulrennan was seated on the bed as she stood in front of him, tying a fresh strip of cloth in place. He could see her body through the gauzy material of her robe, and he closed his eyes against the rush of feeling, against the closeness, the intoxicating aroma of her. She must have sensed his distress—his desire—for as she finished dressing the wound, she took his face in her hands and leaned close, her delicate lips touching his. In that moment she hated him and loved him for saving her life.

Mulrennan pulled her against him, felt the hardness of her bones beneath the magnificence of her golden skin. He leaned back onto the mattress, and she lay down beside him. They held each other close, rocking gently as he smoothed her hair with a blood-streaked hand. His lips trembled as he sought hers again, their kiss longer, more urgent. He tasted salt and blood and saliva from his mouth, mingling now with her own.

He started to speak, but she put her small hand to his lips.

"Be quiet, American priest. Just be with me now."

It was what he wanted—what he needed. Oh, how much he desired to forget where he was, all that had happened, and just let himself be, let himself feel. After all, he was a man, was he not? What would be the shame, the dishonor, the sin?

Somehow it was not a matter of sin, he knew. It was something else entirely—something he could not precisely comprehend. It had to do with love, with the very deepest aspect of love. And while after just twenty-four hours with Ly Linh Sanh he knew that he cared deeply for her—and that he desired her even more deeply—he also knew it was not love. Not the kind of love he felt when he stood in front of a congregation and said mass. Not the kind he imagined possible between a man and a woman—even between himself and the right woman. Perhaps if he felt that all-pervading love he could forget his vows, forget all that had happened, and . . .

"No," he whispered, pulling away slightly. She looked over at him, her eyes betraying her confusion. He smiled ever so gently and again whispered the word. "No, Ly Linh Sanh. I must not. I cannot."

He saw that she was afraid and disgusted—and relieved. But as they lay there, looking into each other's eyes, she seemed to understand his thoughts and feelings, and at last she, too, smiled. She gingerly touched his lips and made on them the Sign of the Cross.

Fifteen minutes later, Ly Linh Sanh was dressed and ready. She had understood and accepted at once when the American priest had told her what she must do now that her position in the village had been so brutally compromised. She was not upset as they packed the wireless radio into a canvas pack and prepared to leave the hut and her belongings behind. After all, this was not really her hut or her home. That home was three days' march to the south, where she had buried her family. This was merely a place of business, of survival, as she carried out the mission she had sworn to complete.

As they began their march, she did not even look back
at the hut with the body of the Vietcong inside. She walked
quickly alongside the tall American, leading him across the
fields. There was still three hours before his rendezvous. If
all went well they would be in the chopper and across the
Demilitarized Zone into South Vietnam before Dong Hoi
awakened and learned there had been a traitor—no, a spy—
within their midst.

As she walked, she kept hearing the strange words the
priest had spoken just before leaving the hut. They were
the same words he had pronounced over the grave of his
slain brother. Yet this time he had said them over the body
of the Vietcong who tried to kill them. Most curious of all,
his voice had held the same compassion, the same love, as
it had on the hilltop, at his brother's grave.

A strange man, she told herself, taking his arm as the
last lights of the village flickered into darkness. A strange
but comforting man, whose voice carried the kind of comfort she so yearned for—the comfort that was stolen from
her when she laid her own family in the ground.

She did not understand the words he had spoken, nor
why they seemed to touch her so deeply. But she heard
them still, in her heart, and as they played through her, she
imagined the American priest standing over the graves of
her mother, her father, her sister, her husband, her dear,
dear child. And for a moment, for the briefest of instants,
she felt that comfort deep in her soul:

*Memento etiam, Domine, famulorum qui nos praecesse-
runt cum signo fidei et dormiunt in somno pacis.*

*Ipsis, Domine, et omnibus in Christo quiescentibus, lo-
cum refrigerii, lucis et pacis, ut indulgeas, deprecamur. Per
eumdem Christum Dominum nostrum. Amen.*

He tugged at the jacket of the borrowed dress whites,
glanced down at the gleaming patent leather shoes that reflected the blazing light of the chandeliers. He shifted white
cotton gloves from one hand to another, nervously wadding
them in his fists.

The vast reception room of the American embassy
yawned before him, densely populated with uniformed men

and women in cocktail dresses. A protocol officer guided him by the elbow, then launched him into the shoulder-to-shoulder crowd.

Major Timothy John Mulrennan, U.S. Army, chaplain-at-large, wedged his tall thin frame toward the middle of the reception, seeking the American ambassador. He would pay his respects, have one glass of champagne, then leave. He was scheduled to depart Ton Son Nut airbase at 0700 hours the following day. As eager as he had been to come here to search for his brother, he now wanted to travel as far from this living hell as he possibly could get.

Floor-to-ceiling mirrors lined three walls, empire style, interrupted on one side by a huge marble and gilt mantel and a cavernous fireplace. Tall windowed doors opened to a terrace opposite the fireplace, and a long bar, attended by Vietnamese civilians in white coats and black bow ties, was set up on the terrace side.

Tim caught a glimpse of General Westmoreland at one end of the room, surrounded by a clutch of military aides, DOD officials, and civilians who he guessed were reporters probing for a story on the eve of the anniversary of the now-infamous Tet offensive. Carefully coiffed and bejewelled American women—diplomatic and military and business wives?—hovered behind the general. Tim pushed forward.

There were a score of Vietnamese beauties in Western-style gowns and beehive hairdos clinging to official-looking ARVN and government types. Was that Vice President Ky wearing the dark green aviator sunglasses, golden epaulets and gold braid on his tailored olive uniform?

The American priest inhaled perfume and pomade, cigarette smoke and boozy breath, as he squeezed through the throng. Before he reached the bar he saw a slender, slightly stooped Vietnamese man wearing the distinctive amaranth red zucchetto and black simar with the violet piping and fascia, or sash, of a Roman Catholic bishop. He recognized Paul Nguyen Van Binh, the Archbishop of Saigon, from his Council days. Two black-clad priests enclosed the primate like bookends. The prelate glanced toward the American in chaplain's uniform; Mulrennan pushed toward him.

"Your Excellency," Tim said, reaching for the arch-bishop's hand. He bent to kiss the amethyst-studded shepherd's ring on the prelatial finger. He introduced himself. "I worked for Archbishop Boland's committee at the Ecumenical Council."

"Our American taskmaster," Binh said, fingering his gold pectoral cross. "How is he?"

"He is healthy and vigorous, but the diocese is troubled."

"Your country is deeply troubled—because of us, I fear."

"We have our own demons, Excellency. Vietnam may be a symptom of graver ills that beset our people. I have lost a brother in this war."

"I have lost tens of thousands of brothers," the arch-bishop said.

Mulrennan wanted to crawl into a hole, but the Vietnamese prelate put his hand on Tim's arm. "I do not say this to trivialize your loss, Father. Only to salve my own wound. Your brother rests now in a place of perpetual light and grace."

"I know he does, Your Excellency. I did not take offense at your words." He closed his eyes for a moment and willed himself to forgive every living soul in a country that was pervaded by the odor of war, himself included.

"Father, have you met my friend from Canada?" Binh deftly turned Tim's shoulder. There stood Monsignor Henry Martin Vennholme: the same close-cropped salt-and-pepper head and black-rimmed spectacles, the ingratiating tight-lipped clerical smile, the neat black cassock and scarlet piping and sash of rank.

How had Mulrennan not seen him? He extended his hand. Vennholme clasped it softly, coolly, let go as quickly as he could.

The last thing on God's green earth that he wanted or expected was to meet this Canadian cleric who had left such an oddly bitter taste in Tim Mulrennan's mouth after their encounter in Rome. A sense of conspiratorial confidence emanated from the compactly built priest, evinced by a slight swagger of his shoulder. His stance, too, was combative, nearly like a boxer's.

"Father Timothy Mulrennan, you have changed little."

"And you not at all, Monsignor Vennholme."

The other priest was the cardinal's secretary, Michael
Ngo Dinh Thuan, a smiling, small-boned, brown-eyed man
who politely squeezed Tim's hand and murmured a greeting in French. He smelled of bay rum.

Mulrennan fumbled for a cigarette, pulled a pack of
Camels and a lighter from his pocket.

"The uniform suits you," Vennholme said sincerely. "I
am very sorry to learn of your brother's death."

"I hope you will remember him in your prayers. And
myself."

"Yes. I have often thought of you since our last encounter in Rome. The flame of faith burns ever more brightly
within, I assume?" Vennholme adjusted his glasses and
peered intently at Tim.

"If my actions were equal to my faith, I should be canonized, Monsignor."

The archbishop, sensing the tension between the two
priests, said: "You Western theologians are so very competitive." He then lapsed into French. "Perhaps that is why
you make the finest diplomats? Monsignor Vennholme represents the Holy See most ably in our besieged country.
We require all the faith, hope, and most especially charity
the Curia can spare."

Although Mulrennan was deeply curious about the spe-
cifics, he did not press for information about Vennholme's
mission. The singsong cocktail chatter swelled around him.
The native priest spoke softly to Archbishop Binh, whose
eyes narrowed knowingly.

"I have an appointment with the American ambassador.
Father Mulrennan, you will please excuse Monsignor
Vennholme and myself. It has been a pleasure."

Tim requested the archbishop's blessing and bowed his
head to receive it. The unusually tall prelate swept majes-
tically across the room, trailed by the smaller figure of the
Canadian diplomat.

Mulrennan turned to the priest, and blurted, "Father
Thuan, will you hear my confession?"

"Follow me, dear Father," Thuan said, and led Tim out

of the reception hall to a small private study a few steps from the embassy kitchen.

Mulrennan was curious. As the young priest closed the door and switched on a desk lamp, he asked, "How the heck do you know about this room?"

Michael Thuan flashed yellow teeth when he smiled widely. "I have spent much time here as a youth. My uncle was President Diem. Our family often were guests. I was a Boy Scout and explored the terrain!"

"The longer I'm here, the more Saigon seems like a small town to me."

"Small town, small country—with a long, bloody history. That is our tragedy: brothers and cousins fighting one another, entire generations dying at the hands of their own countrymen."

"And the Americans—what do you think of us?"

Father Thuan sat in a straight-backed chair and invited Mulrennan to sit on the softer chair next to him. "We have a saying in South Vietnam: 'My best friend is my worst enemy.' The Americans have been good friends to us in our fight against communism. Without your aid we would have lost this war to Uncle Ho ten years ago."

"I cannot account for the errors of my country, Father, but I should like to confess my own."

Thuan unfurled a purple stole, kissed its tiny cross, and placed it over his shoulders. As he leaned into Tim to hear confession, the heavy bay rum scent filled the American's nostrils.

"Bless me, Father, for I have sinned." Mulrennan found himself speaking French as he sought to unburden himself of his mortal trangressions. Thuan listened, eyes closed, fingers pressed to his forehead. Tim spoke about the path of deception he had trodden to discover his brother's fate, described the act of killing the two North Vietnamese attackers. "Father, after that—" He hesitated. "After that I nearly nearly violated the girl myself. I did not, but I wanted to. It was so wrong; I violated my vow of chastity, even if I did not engage in the physical act. I kissed her— after I murdered that man. . . ."

Thuan said, "Let me absolve you, Father, so that you

may put this out of your mind and make your soul lighter. This is a time of war. We all do things. The Almighty Father understands and forgives when we ask for His forgiveness."

Later, he stripped off his uniform and knelt by the hard bed in his cell in the chaplains' quarters. No rest for the weary. The meek shall inherit . . . Blessed are the peacemakers . . . *Please, God, let me sleep for an hour.* Tim Mulrennan climbed into bed and lay on his back with his eyes wide open, drinking in the darkness that could not slake his spiritual thirst. In the morning he would board the army transport plane to fly home.

Our Father, Who art in heaven . . . He closed his eyes.

"Tim, you holy SOB." Major Kevin Mulrennan, USMC, stood beside the narrow bed. There was no moon, no light, yet he was somehow palely illuminated. The lopsided grin that usually signaled the elder boy's triumph in a scuffle with his kid brother lay open like a wound across the square all-American face. "I hope you're praying for me."

Mulrennan's thoughts formed the words, but he did not speak them aloud: "God knows you need praying for. You went and got yourself killed. Dad is sick with grief."

"I know, but it's not like I planned it this way. I'd much rather be having a beer with the boys back home in the world."

"What happened?"

"It was ugly, brother. You have no idea—and don't want to. That gal you met, she knows more than I do. I lost consciousness somewhere along the line."

"She said they ambushed you, tortured you."

"Yeah, just like cowboys and Indians on TV. Only it was in living color, not black and white."

"Why you? Your tour was almost over."

"My second tour, and I would have re-upped for another if they'd let me. This is what I was born to do, Tim."

"I can't believe that."

"Believe it. You couldn't know—no one could who didn't live in my skin. Maybe another marine. God knows—and He ain't talking." Again, the calm, superior smile.

Tim seethed. His brother raised a hand in salute; he wore his spotless short-sleeved tropical worsteds with a breastful of ribbons. Tim noted the posthumously awarded Purple Heart.

"Kevin, we want you to come home." He knew the words were nonsensical, but his heart not his brain spoke, defying logic and reality. He raised his left hand to touch his brother.

Kevin Mulrennan crisply completed his salute. "You out-rank me now, brother, in more ways than one. Tell Dad I love him. And the girls. I was a damn fine big brother, wasn't I?"

Hot tears spilled down Mulrennan's cheeks. He choked on a throatful of phlegm and opened his eyes. He lifted his head and looked hard around the dark room. The sound of his own breathing. Nothing. What the hell—a dream? No one. Yet he felt Kevin's presence without a doubt. His own brother . . . his older brother and best friend . . .

Goddamn Vietnam—this stinking backward stubborn corrupt crippled country. Whose brilliant idea had it been to ship American boys over here to die in this godforsaken meatgrinder? Eisenhower? Kennedy? MacNamara? Johnson? Misbegotten politicians and technocrats. Military geniuses.

The woman whose life he had saved . . . the eyes, the glowing skin . . . her untranslatable murmurings . . . was she still alive? In one piece? Or had the communists revisited her hamlet by now and finished their task of terror? Tears turned to sweat, and he tossed back and forth between dreaming and wakefulness.

"When you get back to the world you've got to put this crap behind you," Kevin said.

"How the hell can I do that, after what I have seen—and what I did?"

"You have the one thing I don't, brother: time."

The words echoed through his somnolent, grieving mind. Kevin had faded from sight, but Tim heard him clearly— did not speak, but he knew that Kevin heard his thoughts.

"I can't take this—losing you. When Mom died it was a relief in a way. She was in so much pain, and so were the rest of us. Dad had to go through that—and now this. How could God allow this to happen to him—to you? Neither one of you deserve it."

"Ask Him. You're on speaking terms. You'll get an answer. You may not like it, but an answer will come."

Tim wanted to ask him so many things, but the presence faded quickly from the room. He sat up again on the narrow bed. He allowed that he could have imagined—probably did—the whole thing. He did not imagine, however, the gaping hole Kevin's absence left in his soul. He knelt on the bare cold tile floor and prayed once more.

CHAPTER TEN

Tuesday, January 30, 7:22 A.M.

Timothy Mulrennan remained in his room, praying and fasting through the long night and into the morning. He took a measure of comfort in his sparse, simple surroundings: a single bed, a small writing table, an electric teapot (a favorite gadget that had been a gift from his staff), a hard-back chair with a removable kneeling pad on the back, and the visitor's chair. Other than a small crucifix that remained in the room, the only decoration was a six-by-nine-inch framed picture of the Sacred Heart of Jesus, which he had carried with him from the seminary to Rome to New Jersey to Vietnam, then to New Mexico and to Jackson City, then back home and to every assignment he had ever held. Before the conclave it had hung in his bedroom within the cathedral rectory in Newark. These few objects represented a fair sum total of his current position: soon to be an outcast from the august company of princes.

He knelt behind the chair and folded his hands. The craving for a cigarette again urgently clawed at him. The desire to strike out at Cardinal Giannantonio—no, at his master, Henry Vennholme, and harm him in some way also taloned his being, but he resisted, imploring God to relieve him of these twin urges.

He prayed for clarity of thought and rightness of action. As angry and hurt and wronged as he felt, he would not act in any way to harm the Church or the Sacred College or his archdiocese. He rued the idea of a scandal for what effect it would have on others, but he was willing to pay whatever personal price God might exact from him.

At sixty-four, Mulrennan could look back at a vigorous

life dedicated to faith and service—and a life of error, temptation, and human emotion. What man on this earth was free of such defects? Yet in the context of Vennholme and Giannantonio's surprise attack, Mulrennan's missteps and shortcomings stood magnified a thousandfold. Accused before his colleagues like an errant child pulled up by his ear to the front of the classroom, there was no retreat from the past, no cover for his sins.

A bittersweet pang scored his breast as he knelt and opened his mind to the Creator. Had he betrayed his faith through actions that inevitably must lie exposed before his brothers? How to separate the falsehoods in Vennholme's indictment from the truth? And which truth? The innocent one in Newark, or those other darker truths that lay hidden so much deeper? Where would he begin to find the answers?

The Prayer of St. Francis came unbidden to his lips:

"Lord, make me an instrument of Your peace!
Where there is hatred—let me sow love,
Where there is injury—pardon,
Where there is doubt—faith,
Where there is despair—hope,
Where there is darkness—light,
Where there is sadness—joy.
O Divine Master, grant that I may not so much seek
   to be consoled—as to console,
To be understood—as to understand,
To be loved—as to love.
For it is in giving that we receive;
It is in pardoning that we are pardoned;
It is in dying that we are born to eternal life."

Father, who are in heaven, your will, not mine, be done. Amen.

There was no knock—or perhaps Mulrennan had not heard it. But when he looked up, he saw Cardinal Biagi standing in the doorway, an avenging archangel dressed in the red cloth of an earthly denizen, his eyes alight with anger.

The American looked up from his prayers and calmly greeted his friend. "Come in, Allo," he said, rising from his knees. "Would you care for some tea?"

"Don't you dare stand there and offer me tea, my friend. It is time to confront evil and defeat it." Biagi closed the door and moved into the room, wagging a finger.

"Unfortunately, Giannantonio's accusation—"

"Vennholme, not Giannantonio," Biagi interrupted. "If we speak of the devil, let us use his real name."

Mulrennan folded his hands soberly. "Okay, then, Henry Vennholme. His charge does have some circumstantial basis. I cannot deny or disprove it. Nor can this conclave become embroiled in my personal problems."

"But—" Biagi sputtered. "He must be stopped. I've concluded that you are the only viable candidate we have, Timofeo. You are the very best man for the job. The universal Church needs you."

"I am not very viable at the moment, my friend. The Church needs a shepherd who will lead us back to Christ. We know now that I am not meant to be that shepherd. I have decided to offer my resignation to our next Holy Father and retire to a contemplative community as soon as he is installed."

"No!" Biagi's voice echoed from the high ceiling of the small room that served as a secretary's cubicle in normal times. "You must fight to restore your reputation and your standing with the Curia."

"My reputation will survive that business in Newark. It already has. That rumor was circulated years ago, and nothing came of it."

Biagi paced nervously across the few feet of floor available to him.

"What is it, Allo?"

Biagi came to a halt in front of his younger friend. "I'm afraid this time it will be different. Yesterday's attack . . . it was only a preamble."

Mulrennan felt a dull ache in his stomach. "To what?"

Biagi reached out and took Mulrennan's hands. "I spoke with Vennholme this morning. He knows you had nothing to do with that murdered woman, and he even offered to make the rumor go away."

"Provided? . . ."

"Provided you agree to support the Evangelium movement if you are elected pope."

"Preposterous," Mulrennan muttered, pulling away and walking over to the narrow window. He gazed outside—unable, afraid to look back at his friend.

"I told him as much. That was when he revealed his true game."

Mulrennan's fingers tightened on the sill. His eyes closed to the sunlight outside, and he saw her standing before him, exquisitely beautiful. In his mind he called out her name—*Rachel!*—but he feared that giving it voice would somehow shatter the image, the memory in his heart. Instead he turned slowly, looked up at the Italian cardinal, and whispered, "He knows about her, doesn't he?"

Biagi said solemnly. "He said there was a Vietnamese woman."

"Ly Linh Sanh . . ." Mulrennan's vision blurred, and he dropped onto the chair heavily. Biagi's words came to him faintly, as if from a great distance.

"Your wife. He called her your wife. . . ."

After three days and seven ballots, a process interrupted by Gianntonio's indictment of Mulrennan, there was a single leading candidate, Pietro La Spina, who had built his total vote count to forty-seven, gaining a few more votes with each tally. He remained far short of the two-thirds level, but was building steadily toward a clear majority.

The already complicated path might become ever more dizzying and labyrinthine from this point forward.

The rules under *Universi Dominici Gregis* stated that if after three days the cardinals had still not elected anyone, the voting sessions could be suspended for one day for prayer and discussion among the electors. If the cardinal-electors chose to do so, this intermission would include a spiritual talk by the senior cardinal-deacon. Then another seven votes could take place, followed by a suspension of voting and a homily by the senior cardinal priest. Another seven votes then might be held followed by yet another pause and a spiritual exhortation by the senior cardinal bishop. Voting would then be resumed for as many as seven additional ballots.

If still no candidate received the required two-thirds after these series of ballots, the camerlengo would invite the electors to express their feelings about the procedure from this crucial point.

Here the late pontiff had dramatically changed the election process by allowing a simple majority (one more than half) of the electors to waive the requirement of two-thirds majority vote. Thus an absolute majority of the electors could decide to elect the pope by an absolute majority. They could also decide to force a choice between the two candidates who, in the preceding ballot, received the greatest number of votes.

In this second case also only a simple majority was required. As a consequence—an eventuality that Cardinal Vennholme and others had calculated to their advantage— if an absolute majority of the electors favored a candidate in the first ballot of the first day of the conclave, all they would have to do is hold firm for about twelve days through about thirty votes until they could change the rules and elect their candidate. There was no true incentive for them to compromise or move to another candidate. In fact, the incentive was reversed. The majority was encouraged to hold tight, while the minority was encouraged to give in since everyone knew that eventually the majority would prevail.

This change in the conclave rules allowing the cardinals to elect the pope with an absolute majority reduced the likelihood of a conclave going on for months. On the other hand, allowing a mere simple majority to elect a pope after about twelve days increased the likelihood of a conclave lasting that long.

Although there have been long conclaves in the past, a long one at the opening of the twenty-first century would be unusual. In the last 160 years, the two longest conclaves took only four days. One has to go back to 1831 to find a conclave lasting fifty-four days, or to 1800 for one that lasted three and a half months.

In the old days, Catholic monarchies could control or
deadlock a conclave with a traditional power of veto over
candidates the king opposed. In fact, this had happened as
recently as 1903: the *jus exclusivae*, or so-called right of
exclusion, had been imposed on the conclave by Emperor
Franz Josef of Austria-Hungary—resulting in the election
of St. Pius X. At this conclave, with such powerful interests
long dead and the papal states a thing of the past, national
interests were much less pronounced; regional and global
concerns were, however, more up-front than ever. In a
sense, the cold war and the threat of worldwide communism
on the Soviet model had checked petty politics. The threat
to the True Church had been globalized. Such an over-
arching threat had always precluded any serious consideration of a North American or any candidate from a
so-called superpower state. Hence Italian domination of the
papacy had continued unabated until 1978. After that Year
of Three Popes the old assumptions went by the boards.

Fewer than 18 percent of the cardinals in this Sacred
College were Italian, the rock-bottom lowest number in the
seven-hundred-year history of papal conclaves. Less than
one-third of this assembly was European. As recently as
1939 more than 56 percent of the voting members were
Italian, and more than 80 percent were European. Pius XII
had begun the process of de-Italianizing the Curia and ap-
pointing "foreign" cardinals at a remarkable rate. These
were the men who would eventually elect Pope John XXIII
in 1958, precipitating the Vatican Council.

As Timothy Mulrennan walked into the Sistine Chapel
with his fellow members of the Sacred College of
Cardinals, he felt the glare of many eyes. *Or*, he asked
himself, *am I being too self-conscious?* He thought it preposterous that any elector had ever seriously picked him as
the eventual winner. He felt strangely light-headed and at
peace with himself. He even smiled at Henry Vennholme,
who clutched a legal-size folder to his breast as he took his
place at a table not far from Mulrennan's.

Tim looked around at the men who filed to their seats;
few met his gaze directly. Very much like the people in his
own diocese, they were many colors and nationalities and

races, spoke a multitude of languages, came from every conceivable socioeconomic circumstance.

One man whose eyes engaged with his own was Jaime De Guzman, the Filipino archbishop whose flock numbered 2 million souls spread over eighteen thousand square miles and ten provinces, including the city of Manila. Tim guessed that the conclave, as tense and tedious as it was, was a kind of relief for this man: political unrest, violence, religious strife, Christian and Muslim sectarianism, economic instability—all added up to a roiling mix of troubles that no senior churchman could envy. Yet De Guzman, who had always impressed Mulrennan with his calm manner and easy, sincere smile, seemed unperturbed by it all. It was well known that, like the recently deceased pope, he spent many hours each day in prayer. In addition, friends and opponents alike admired his cool, precise administrative skills.

In 1997, when the cardinal from Manila had spent a few weeks in the States, he had visited Tim's archdiocese and concelebrated a well-attended Sunday mass for Filipino-Americans at St. Aedan's Church in Jersey City; the Filipino community numbered in the tens of thousands in northern New Jersey. As homilist for the mass, Cardinal De Guzman had exhorted his countrymen to participate in the life of the Church in their new land with all their hearts, but not to forget that their brothers and sisters in the Philippines also needed their support with prayers and financial contributions.

Mulrennan had never been to the Philippines himself but hoped one day to visit. He would like to see his friend Jaime in his native environment—and perhaps preach a sermon of his own in the old Spanish-built cathedral in Manila. The only time he had been in the Philippines was on stopovers to and from Vietnam. . . .

Cardinal De Guzman now lifted his hands, steepled as if in prayer, to Timothy Mulrennan, acknowledging the American. Deep brown eyes, friendly and frank, looked out at him from behind gold-rimmed glasses.

The Church in Asia needed such strong, holy, and humble men, Tim thought. And such leaders were good pro-

totypes for the universal Church. Since the passing several
years ago of Joseph Cardinal Bernardin of Chicago and,
more recently, John Cardinal O'Connor of New York, there
was no fellow American cardinal to whom Tim Mulrennan
looked for such leadership. O'Connor had been more conservative and confrontational, but an incredibly smart and
helpful colleague. Bernardin, while an able politician, was
decidedly more liberal or middle-of-the-road—and deeply,
obviously spiritual. Mulrennan had, in fact, taken upon his
own shoulders the mantle of conciliator and moderate
spokesman, irritating some of his conservative brethren in
the powerful archepiscopal sees of the United States. Some,
but not all. He saw to that, and he still counted most of the
bishops and archbishops of the United States—where he
was vice president of the national conference—and Canada
as personal friends.

   Why, then, did he now feel so deeply alone among this
gathering of men?

   To whom besides Biagi might he bare the hopes and sins
of his soul? He thought back to his conversation with De
Guzman on the night of Zimmerman's death: perhaps that
had been the only time Tim had felt a true brotherly bond
with a fellow conclavist. He loved De Guzman all the more
because of it. He recalled the same kind of feeling, the
stark, hard loneliness of the intelligence operative, from his
military assignment in Berlin. That had been more than
forty years before! He had been a green kid, a young Army
officer, charged with responsibilities that far outweighed his
experience. *How the hell did I pull it off—and survive?* he
thought with not inappropriate profanity. It had been right
out of a le Carré novel, improbable and ironic yet all too
real . . . a mission that put him face-to-face with evil in a
way he had seldom seen it before or since . . .

   In later years, during his official travels as well as the
time he had been asked by the first President Bush's national security team to undertake a covert mission in the
newly reunited Germany under cover of Church business,
Mulrennan never forgot the spycraft he had mastered during
those earlier, impressionable years. It amused him to strike
out alone in a strange foreign city, to test himself, to move

around via public transportation with no one knowing where he was. It was a private game. He did not take it seriously, but it was as much a part of his being as his faith in the Son of God to save human souls.

Perhaps a bit of that craft in this conclave might salvage his reputation and his career. His eyes swept along the rows of balding pates and bent shoulders of his fellow electors, gleaming crosses suspended at their chests. He smiled secretly to himself as his eye settled on the relatively young Polish-American archbishop of Chicago and his mind calculated the burden of financial and political issues that dominated his colleague's life. He wished the man grace and good fortune in a job that was, in effect, the equivalent of a CEO's position.

He knew more than a few tidbits about this fellow, and about the other Americans and the Canadians, and about more than a few of the sophisticated Western Europeans who, for the most part, so smugly considered the Church their private domain. The Archbishop of Cologne, known by most electors to be a homosexual who had lived with the same companion for decades. The man from Dublin, a ruddy, hard-drinking scion of one of the established banking families, reputed to have lost millions at the horse races, but those losses were covered from family funds, not the collection basket, thank the Lord.

What about the Africans? There the Church was growing at the fastest rate, giving millions new hope as famines and political chaos still claimed millions of victims. Had they no secrets? Were they perfect followers of Christ?

Mulrennan caught himself and turned away from this line of thinking. He was a man of God, not the Man from U.N.C.L.E. And his failings, no one else's, were on exhibit here. This he must accept as God's will. This he must deal with honestly. In fact, he knew what course he would take. All else was weak-minded fiddle-faddle and fantasy.

At this moment, only one pair of eyes burned into him, and he turned so as not to see the look of disappointment on the face of his old friend, Cardinal Biagi.

Mulrennan had not told the full truth to Biagi earlier that morning, and both men knew it. True, he had admitted that some of Vennholme's information about Ly Linh Sanh was correct. But he had refused to say more, to explain how it was that a man who wore the Roman collar could have taken a Vietnamese wife. How could he explain it to his old confidant? It was much easier to make his confession to the amorphous body of cardinals—to reveal the truth to the entire world—than to a close friend.

Mulrennan had his chance soon after the camerlengo brought the morning session to order and called for the first ballot of the day. Mulrennan rose from his seat, but it was Henry Martin Vennholme whom the camerlengo noticed first and recognized.

"My Lords and Brothers in Christ," the French-Canadian cardinal began, "I ask leave of our Lord Camerlengo to address you in regard to the charges laid before this assembly by my good brother, Pasquale Cardinal Giannantonio. It seems I did my brother a disservice yesterday when I questioned his character and motive in condemning our American brother, Timothy Cardinal Mulrennan."

He gave Mulrennan an almost dismissive glance, then picked up the folder from the table.

"Additional information has come to my attention that supports the charges made by Cardinal Giannantonio— charges, I might add, that Cardinal Mulrennan chose not to dispute. Is that not so?" he added, looking over at Mulrennan.

Seizing the opportunity, Mulrennan rose and declared, "It is my desire to answer those charges—completely."

Vennholme looked more than a bit flustered that Mulrennan had chosen to speak. "You will have ample time to do so after I—"

"Lord Camerlengo!" Mulrennan exclaimed, walking to the center aisle and toward the chamberlain, Carlos Roberto Cardinal Portillo, amid a rush of whisperings. "A point of order!"

It took a few awkward moments for the aged Portillo to lift himself to his feet and wave the assembly into silence. He turned to the American, his steel-wool eyebrows darting menacingly up and down. "What is it, Cardinal Mulrennan?"

Vennholme stepped forward and stood beside Mulrennan. "*He* is out of order, Your Eminence. He may speak when I am finished."

"He—and you—will speak when I say," Portillo admonished Vennholme, wagging a crooked finger. "We have sacred business to accomplish, my Lords. We must elect a pope. I ask that you do nothing and say nothing that will impede this body in its task." He turned again to the American and gestured for him to proceed.

"Yesterday Cardinal Giannantonio, and Cardinal Vennholme"—he looked pointedly at the latter—"made serious accusations against me, unjustified ones, I might add. Furthermore, Cardinal Giannantonio asked me to withdraw my name from consideration by this conclave. Today I claim the right to answer those charges and to address that request."

Vennholme started to object, but Portillo raised a silencing hand. When he spoke, his comments were addressed to Vennholme. "It is only proper that our brother cardinal speak to those charges before any additional matters are laid before the conclave." The camerlengo turned to Mulrennan. "You may address the assembly."

Again Vennholme started to protest, but Portillo directed him to his seat with a firm shake of the head. Vennholme stood in place a moment, looking at the faces of his brethren, then complied.

Timothy Mulrennan walked to the head of the room and turned to face the senate of holy elders whom fate, or perhaps Divine Will, had made his judges.

"My brothers and Lords," Cardinal Mulrennan began in halting but clearly enunciated Italian. "I was born a sinner and have remained a sinner all my life. I was born a child of God and have remained a child of God all my life. I am, as well, a servant of God. You have—most of you—known me as a priest and as a bishop during the past thirty-nine years since my ordination and service at the Ecumenical Council in this very place. Yes, I have committed sins throughout my life that no one but my confessor and God my Father know. I do have secrets from you, perhaps, but not from Him. If it be His will, and I sincerely believe it

is, I shall have no more secrets at all in the realm of man.
So be it."

The American cardinal glanced back briefly at Michelangelo's majestic rendering of the Last Judgment, which
graced the wall of the chapel behind the altar, where the
six cardinal-scrutineers and cardinal-revisers sat expec-
tantly, awaiting their duty. He remembered Biagi's lesson
about the painting.

The Sistine Chapel crackled with palpable but unseen
electricity.

"My fellow cardinals, I speak to you as if we were in
the confessional, for, indeed, you are yourselves holy
priests and confessors. I beg that you will hear me, judge
me as if it were Christ Himself who were my Judge, and
perhaps you will find it in yourselves to forgive me as He
has. How many times have I loosed the bonds of sin from
some wretched man or woman who, despite their sincerity
in the moment, will go home and do the same thing, be it
the most insignificant omission or the gravest sin, within
an hour of receiving absolution from me in the name of
Christ Jesus?

"And how many of us, sinners and utterly human beings
that we are, have done the same? 'Go and sin no more,'
the priest instructs us. And yet, we sin every day in act and
thought, by commission and by what we leave unsaid. But
let me not put any but my own transgressions before you."

Leandro Biagi fought down his conspirator's smile. This
American was clever indeed: asking for the seal of the confessional from his fellow electors, so that anyone who
leaked the story would be in violation of that sacred obligation.

"I must also add the caveat that I came here to elect a
pope, but not to be elected myself. Despite some very kind
but misguided electoral support—" Mulrennan turned to
face Biagi directly. "I have never for a moment considered
myself a papabile, a candidate to walk in the shoes of the
Fisherman. Perhaps a few others have, and again I am most
grateful to any of you who inscribed my name on the ballot.
Never, within my own soul, did I really desire to be chosen.
The late Holy Father, who was my friend—our friend—

once said to me that it was not yet time for an American
to be chosen to lead the Church, that if he were a cardinal
in this conclave he would probably vote for one of the
Italian brethren! Why? I asked him. 'Because it is always
important to balance change with continuity. And besides,
what harm would it cause if we adjusted the clock a few
seconds in our two-millennia hour?'

"Well, regional and political considerations aside, I cannot disagree with his analysis. Can you?"

Murmurs and rustling, like an impending storm front
touching a dense forest, greeted the American cardinal's
words. He had their attention, at least, but he knew he must
address the heart of the matter, the accusations against him,
if he was to hold the floor of the conclave among these
impatient politicians. As he spoke, he felt the sorrow and
anger lift from his shoulders, and he felt a lightness invade
his being. He fought the impulse to try to read their faces,
and thought, instead, of the image of the dark screen of an
old-fashioned confessional. *Bless me, Father, for I have
sinned. . . .*

"I believe in the Oneness of our God in the Persons of
the Father, the Son, and the Holy Spirit, and I always have.
I was called, as were each of you, to be a servant and
minister of Jesus, the Son, and upon my ordination I took
the sacred vows of chastity and obedience, promising my
fealty, my very life, to the service of the apostolic Church.
I stand here today to affirm those vows and to tell you that
I have never violated them—*ever*—by any action during
my priesthood." Tim paused deliberately to catch his breath
and heard many of the cardinals do the same. "I have come
perilously close in two cases, with two women, to breaking
my holy pledge of chastity—and many of you no doubt
have privately learned some of those details from my accusers."

Timothy John Cardinal Mulrennan, the disciplined altar
boy who had grown up to become a prince of the Roman
Catholic Church, strode to the center of the floor between
the tiered chairs of his peers, beneath the pigments of Michelangelo that portrayed the story of mankind from the
creation to the aftermath of Noah's flood, and looked up

briefly to contemplate the heart-stopping images that had witnessed the selection of popes for five hundred years. Behind him rose the virile Christ of the coming Judgment Day, welcoming the good and the penitent, damning the evil and hard-hearted who had turned from the promise of salvation. Tim put his long arms down against the sides of his elaborate cardinalitial choir vestments and stood as still and straight as he could manage.

"Know that I have been, and remain, a man of sinful thoughts and deeds. At one time I wanted so much to experience the love of a woman that I nearly threw away my commitment to Our Lord; but He would not have me do so, and He enlisted her in His battle to save me. He granted her the strength of character and clarity of vision to say no and to walk away from temptation. I love her all the more because she did that. But I have no lingering desire to fall back into that place. God Himself burned that out of me and tempered my soul to a hard, bright quality that bends but does not break. Yes, I did love her and lost her and thereby gained the precious gift of celibacy, which I prize beyond my ability to calculate.

"I will not use her name, because she does not belong here. I will tell you that I became very close to this woman, fell in love with her, in fact, and I put myself into a situation that looked terribly incriminating—for anyone who cared to look into it, and someone apparently did. But I can tell you, my brothers, with an honest and open heart, that I did not consummate that love in any physical form. My sexual instincts were not fulfilled—despite myself. I cannot claim credit, and here is my sin: I wanted to sleep with her badly. To this day, I pray that God may continue to bless her and to forgive me for causing her the pain and awkwardness of having to refuse me."

The memories of Rachel Séredi nearly overwhelmed him: her beautiful eyes, her scent, her God-given artistic talent, her warmth and humor . . . her compassion for a man on the brink of ruin. He squarely faced the assembly of cardinals.

"And the issue of my so-called marriage to another woman is a thorn that has resided in my side for more than twenty-five years, and perhaps you gentlemen will allow me to pluck it out and, if you are not repelled by the blood, reopen the wound. Then I shall ask your prayers to help me heal."

Tim Mulrennan folded his hands tightly at his midsection, touching the edge of the pectoral cross that dangled there.

"I lied to save a life. Not to do so might have been murder. I could not take that terrible chance; I made the choice, and I have paid the price for it, even unto this day. But I know that a human life was preserved because I acted as I did. What were the circumstances? After the American withdrawal, the war in Vietnam had turned against the South and they were lost; the communists were marching on Saigon. A young woman who had saved my life once, when I went to search for my missing brother, begged me to help her escape. If I signed a marriage certificate and proved my U.S. citizenship and veteran's status she would receive safe passage on a military transport. I forged the paperwork but did not participate in a ceremony, another man did that, using my name. So, we piled lies upon lies, deception upon deceit, in order to save one person's life. I regret the lies. I do not regret the life. She is a wife and mother and grandmother in California. Does God begrudge her this? Does He seek to punish me for the lies I told to preserve her life?

"The man we elect must not be, cannot be free from sin; that is an absurdity touching on impossibility—nor is it to be desired. For who among us, or among any synod of clergy of any faith, can claim to be without sin. Could this be said of the late Holy Father himself, whom many—myself included—would proclaim a saint?

"But it is not appropriate for me to preach a sermon here. We have heard about our sacred obligation from Cardinal Zimmerman; he ably and eloquently advised us of our duties before he died. And, frankly, if he had lived, it's unlikely that we would be engaged in this discussion. I would be less than a footnote to these deliberations, merely one vote for Cardinal Zimmerman's election. Apparently that was not the will of Our Lord."

He paused, swung his head slowly from side to side of the chapel, gazing into those faces of the 116 men who shared with him an awesome responsibility. He felt foolish and exposed, and at the same time elated to be able to unburden himself of secrets. This was the same process by which the troubled priests in the Monastery of Christ the Redeemer had found their way back onto the path of life. He smiled inwardly: he was a "victim" of the new age of confession and self-revelation.

"I stand before you naked and humbled. I renounce any claim on your approval, as a man, as a priest, or as a candidate in this conclave. I have never seriously held the thought of election in my mind, never even privately known such an ambition. You know more about me than my own diocesan flock, although I think that they will know soon enough." His eyes swept over Vennholme's enigmatic face and hooded eyes. "And I am prepared to resign my position and title and retire to a life of contemplation and manual work if it be the wish of the new Holy Father. I am a man, no more nor less, and I am an ordained priest of God, despite all of my many shortcomings. Only God Himself, through his representative on earth, can release me from my compact with Him; only you can place sanction or disfavor upon me as a brother of the Sacred College, which I am willing to bear."

Mulrennan turned to address one man in particular. "I thank our colleague Cardinal De Guzman for his kind words yesterday; his generosity has made me strive to be generous, his gentility and civility has made me want to be gentle and civil and forgiving toward my accusers. Why are we here if not to learn from one another how Our Savior would have us behave?"

His eyes flashed darkly; he felt a tinge of anger and humiliation, for he was a man accused unfairly but not completely without justification. As he let the anger dissipate and wash through him, he struggled to find the words that exactly expressed his position—his truth. He even felt a measure of compassion as he looked over at Vennholme, who sat stiffly without emotion, and Giannantonio, who looked as if he wanted to crawl under his table.

"Perhaps this was not the time nor the place for my brother cardinals to have put forward such serious charges, and there are those who have criticized them for doing so. However, I do not shrink from answering the accusations, point by point. But I will not begin with that baseless rumor that a woman was murdered because she was bearing my child. It is another woman whom I must speak to you about. I will tell you her story—and mine. And then you shall be my judges here on earth, as Our Lord is in Heaven."

Timothy Mulrennan looked from one man to the other, his gaze finally coming to rest upon his friend Leandro Aurelio Cardinal Biagi. To his surprise and joy he saw neither anger nor disappointment in the old man's eyes. Only love. A love that lifted and strengthened him—that gave voice to his heart.

CHAPTER ELEVEN

October 18, 1981, Jackson City, Missouri

Tim put his hand on hers. In her slender fingers that were roughened from hard work he felt the power and beauty of her art. She was a painter and sculptor, trained in Tel Aviv and Berkeley, with a modest but growing reputation. She had grown up in Budapest through the communist years, a difficult time for artists, let alone Jews. Her parents and younger brother still lived there, and her heart often called her back to her beautiful native city. One day soon, she promised herself, she would return . . . one day.

"I need some coffee," he said, lighting a cigarette and breaking their revery.

They sipped the hot, strong brew together in silence. They drank in each other's presence—she, mentally outlining the strong shape of his handsome head; he, marveling at the sworl and energy of her dark flowing hair as it framed her pale oval face. She whispered something that he did not catch, but he could not—dared not—ask her to repeat it. At times like this he found it nearly impossible to conjure words to express himself: how and why he loved her, how his life might be irrevocably changed if he were to break his sacred vow of chastity, where this affair would take them, when it would—as it must inevitably—end.

"Your Holiness," she said.

"Stop teasing me."

"You like being teased. I know it." Rachel smiled, and angels danced in his mind.

"You know too much," he said. "I don't know anything anymore."

She squeezed his hand. "You must not torture yourself.

God understands and forgives. Even if you do not."

He dressed, put on a jacket, and went into the backyard. The autumn air was bracing but not cold; leaves from a tall, dense stand of trees littered the earth, creating a brown and gold carpet that rustled beneath his thick-soled boots. He did not possess much of a "civilian" wardrobe, but luckily he always had some hiking clothes. He carried his breviary and began to read but stopped after two lines. He could not see the page because his mind raced beyond the words, shattering the hard-won discipline of twenty years of his priesthood. A crisp breeze blew, causing him to search his pockets for a tissue to blow his nose. Outdoors, away from the cathedral and the cares of his work, near this woman who had bewitched his heart, Tim Mulrennan was a different, more vulnerable man. It was a sensation unlike any he had ever experienced in all his forty-four years. Why, oh, why had it come to him now? As he walked into the copse of trembling trees he remembered himself as a skinny youth in the black cassock and surplice of the acolyte, serving mass hundreds of times at his home parish. What had happened to that boy?

Inevitably, thoughts of his family back in New Jersey tumbled through his mind: it had been five years since he'd left North Auburn, and in that span his own life had changed dramatically and his family's life had, as well. His mother was long dead of cirrhosis. There were some marriages, one divorce, more nieces and nephews, his father had finally retired, his young stepbrother, Stephen, had graduated from Yale and embarked on a career in New York City. He could not help thinking of his brother Kevin, dead nearly thirteen years. Those years had tumbled on, seemingly without surcease, yet a part of him remained the same twelve-year-old who served mass on Christmas Eve and prayed that the world would right itself, somehow, with God's loving intervention.

Since last summer he had often relived his first encounter with Rachel, remembering the Fourth of July picnic out in the country where an old friend from the seminary had dragged him, away from Jackson City where he had just come to be installed as bishop—only to postpone that scheduled ceremony when an assassin had attempted to murder Pope John Paul II. . . .

Father Joe Ricciardi, who as a burly Notre Dame tackle had terrorized all-American running backs on the college gridiron, took Tim Mulrennan in tow and pushed him through the picnicking throng to a table beneath a huge old live-oak tree that provided a delightful oasis of shade on this incredibly hot and humid July Fourth holiday. From the first fire engine to the last Shriner on a minimotorcycle, beneath a hellish, baking sun, the small-town parade had brought out everyone in the county, including politicians and merchants, beauty contestants and musicians, church ladies and middle-aged hobbyists with souped-up classic cars. Mulrennan had marveled, as he sat in a rickety folding chair in front of the town hall and drank gallons of iced tea, at the variety and intensity of patriotic fervor on display here in the middle of America. Of course, it was not very much different back in his home state or in any town you might find yourself in on this day of days; but he knew a secret thrill at the genuineness he felt here, the rightness of it all, the seeming lack of conflict or doubt, as if for one day, at least, these folks had agreed to have one hell of a good time being Americans.

Then there was the food. Father Ricciardi piled spare ribs—expertly prepared by the local Knights of Columbus— and potato salad and baked beans and pickles on Tim's too-flimsy paper plate and made him sit at the picnic table beneath the tree and eat every bite and drink another gallon or so of well-sugared iced tea.

"Now aren't you glad you came out today to see your flock, Bishop Tim?" Ricciardi prodded, his big tanned face smeared with barbecue sauce.

They were about forty miles southeast of Jackson City, in a small rural parish that fell under Tim's new episcopal jurisdiction. He was scheduled to celebrate a special mass that evening, before the county's fireworks extravaganza.

Before Mulrennan could answer, a woman came to the table, carrying a tray of sugar cookies. She spoke with a subtle accent that Tim could not quite identify: "You gentlemen need some of these cookies, baked by the Rosary

Society of St. Joseph the Carpenter Church."

"I'm afraid that's the last thing I need, Rachel," Ricciardi said. "But my friend Tim here wants to put some skin on his old bones, don't you, Bishop?"

An electric charge bolted through Tim Mulrennan as he watched and listened to this woman, and he hoped it did not show. He rose, dropping the plastic knife and fork, rubbing his mouth with a paper napkin, extending his hand in greeting.

"Hello, I'm Tim Mulrennan," he said in his formal voice.

"Rachel Séredi, artist and assistant baker. You're new in town."

Her brown eyes were flecked with amber and emerald, her eyebrows thick and nearly black; she wore no makeup to highlight her full lips and prominent cheekbones; golden hoops hung from delicate earlobes, and she had pulled back her thick hair in a wavy tail that hung between her shoulder blades. He did not notice what she was wearing, but he sensed her sturdy, slender body next to his as they touched hands.

In a stage whisper, the big priest said, "She's not even Catholic, but I swear I see her in church more often than some of our parishioners."

"I am absorbing the atmosphere of the church, looking at the beautiful stained-glass work of the windows." She lifted her hands to describe the shape of the windows in the humid air. "Father Joe has been so kind to allow me to come."

"Well, be careful, he may convert you," Tim uttered, desperate to think of something intelligent to say to her.

"Oh, he has tried." Rachel's eyes flashed, and she winked at Ricciardi. "My Jewish parents would have something to say about that, however."

Later in the summer, she attended his installation as bishop at the Cathedral of the Holy Trinity in Jackson City. Through the twenty-foot stained-glass windows of the one-hundred-year-old cathedral church the sun knifed in golden blades that filled the nave of the Gothic structure. It reminded Tim of his old parish, Our Lady of Mercies, in New Jersey: a magnificently high-vaulted house of worship. He felt at home from the beginning, when he celebrated mass and preached to his new diocesan flock. He had arrived nearly six months ago; now it was mid-October, cool for the season, a cloudless Saturday. The cathedral was packed with worshipers, fellow priests, seminarians, family, press, and the curious. The pageant unfolded with a procession of the diocesan and visiting priests in gleaming white albs, followed by the apostolic delegate to the United States, Henry Martin Vennholme, whom Tim Mulrennan had known since the Vatican Council in 1963. Archbishop Vennholme would consecrate Tim as bishop, with the Archbishop of St. Louis and several other midwestern prelates assisting. Rachel Séredi stood and strained for a clear view of the handsome new bishop who calmly strode up the middle aisle beneath a series of chandeliers, incense wafting throughout the open expanse of the cathedral. A local parish choir offered a beautiful Latin hymn. As Tim achieved the top steps and moved around the altar toward a thronelike chair next to that of the cardinal, several priests fluttered about him like awkward angels to guide and position him for the ceremony, as they had rehearsed two days ago. He smiled indulgently as he allowed them to do what they were required to do, and he thought it was a lot of fuss and feathers to endure, but so be it, it is the way of the Church.

Afterward, at a reception in the chancery, where he would live during his service as bishop of the Diocese of Jackson City, Missouri, Tim Mulrennan and Henry Vennholme greeted friends and visitors. He introduced Vennholme to his father and sisters and younger brother, Stephen, who had recently graduated from Yale. The nuncio was stiff but courteous, tolerant of his social duties but not enjoying them. When Rachel came through the receiving line, Mulrennan introduced her to his superior.

"Your Excellency, Miss Rachel Séredi is an artist from Hungary who has come to the U.S. to work and teach at the University of Missouri."

She took Vennholme's hand and shook it gently. It felt cool and oddly moist to her touch. She gazed at the large gold cardinalitial ring. "I am honored to meet you," she murmured.

"And I, you, madam," Vennholme said graciously. Then he probed: "Do you intend to become a citizen of this country?"

"I do not know—yet. Perhaps. If all the people are as kind as the bishop and the other Catholic priests I have met . . . they have made me feel so welcome—despite our differences of faith."

"Oh?" He wore the red biretta of his office and black cassock with scarlet piping and a wide, watered-silk progenta sash. He fingered the heavy, jeweled pectoral cross that hung in the middle of his breast.

"I am Jewish, Your Excellency," she said.

"I see," he muttered noncommittally.

"We are so pleased that you came today, Rachel," Mulrennan said. "Did you enjoy the ceremony?"

"Yes. It reminded me so much of the stories we learned as children, of Aaron and Melchizedek and the ancient priesthood. I might want to do some historical paintings based on those times."

As she moved past, Vennholme scrutinized her carefully. He said nothing to Tim, who grasped the hand of the next person in line. Rachel introduced herself to Tim's family and friends from New Jersey, shared a moment with Father Ricciardi, her "pastor," and slipped away without Mulrennan's noticing.

Three weeks later, on a Wednesday afternoon, the newly consecrated bishop drove out to Harrisonville to pick up Ricciardi for a long-planned golf twosome at an eighteen-hole public course. It was another picture-perfect day: sunny and moderate with warm breezes rustling the trees that stood on the verge of autumnal change, holding on to their greenness for the last gasp of summer.

They each shot a decent game, despite their rustiness, and enjoyed a hamburger at a little hole-in-the-wall joint on the outskirts of the city.

"Rachel has been asking about the Catholic faith, and I gave her a reading list. She has come to Sunday mass a few times. There may be some hope there." Ricciardi awaited a second burger and slurped his root beer. He grinned at his old friend. "If I weren't a priest . . . Do you

ever have regrets, Tim? I mean, about women? Sometimes
I wonder if I'm cut out for this celibacy thing."

"It's only natural, Joe. Yes, I have doubts and second
thoughts myself. I have to pray about it, work at it. I catch
myself thinking about the times I dated girls, remembering
the details—their names, what they looked like and smelled
like, where we went, what we did. I wasn't very adventur-
ous, to be honest. I was scared to death of females, really!"

The two men laughed. They finished their meal, and
Mulrennan drove the priest home. Then, as if the old blue
Mercury he had inherited from the previous bishop had a
mind of its own, he turned off the highway onto the country
road that led to Rachel Séredi's farmhouse. He had never
been there before, yet he knew, somehow, exactly where it
was. Had he asked her? Had Joe Ricciardi mentioned it at
some point? He could not remember; his mind was a blank
as he drove up the rutted dirt driveway and stopped beside
the old clapboard Victorian house. It needed some paint,
but bright curtains blew from the inside through open windows, and neatly tended shrubberies and flowers skirted the
front porch. Mulrennan honked the horn once and stepped
out of the car.

"Oh, Bishop Tim!" She pushed open the screen door at
the front of the house. "What are you doing here?" She
wore a multicolored scarf that bound her flowing brown
hair and made her face a pure, tanned oval, her lips curved
in a welcoming smile. Paint-splattered overalls hung
loosely from her lithe frame, and she moved like a dancer
across the porch and down the wooden steps into the yard.
He was stunned by her unaffected beauty and suddenly
ashamed of himself.

"I was in the neighborhood," he said stupidly.

She used a ragged old dish towel that smelled of turpen-
tine to wipe her hands. "I'm glad. I am brewing some tea.
Would you care for some, please?"

For the first time, Tim Mulrennan noticed the glottal element of her light accent, overridden to a degree by the
smoky musicality of her voice. Her face, her voice, her
hands, her work clothing—he drank it all in, answering any

thirst he might have felt. He realized he should respond to her invitation.

"Yes, that would be great. Father Ricciardi and I played a round of golf earlier," he added, not knowing what the hell else to say. "Wore me out."

"Oh, who won?"

"If we had kept score, I think he beat me by several strokes."

"I am surprised. You Americans are so competitive in sport. Friendly, but most competitive, I have noticed."

"I used to play my big brother one-on-one in basketball, started beating him when I was fourteen or fifteen. He didn't mind, much. Then once in a while I kind of let him beat me. *That* made him mad!" He followed her up the front steps, onto the veranda where she kept a few lawn chairs and a table with an ashtray, and into the house. It smelled of paint. He noticed flowers in every room. "Nice old house," he breathed.

"It has been nice to me. I have my studio over there, which is the dining room. Big windows, lots of light."

He stepped into the spacious kitchen, then looked to the left, where she pointed, saw the studio: a high-ceilinged room that would have contained a long dining table that could seat perhaps a dozen people, littered with canvases, prints, pots, empty frames, boxes, brushes, a sawhorse worktable. A tall vase filled with white asters sat in the middle of the worktable. Old tin cover, mixing bowls, and brushes were crammed onto the table, and her palette rested on a tall barstool near one of two large easels. An unfinished canvas, an abstract flow of colors, tilted precariously on the easel ledge, as if it had been hastily placed there.

"Impressive," he said. "This is where you paint." He could not help uttering the most obvious and inane things that came into his head.

"Paint and think. I also sculpt a little amount. It is a distraction, er, recreation, I think you would say." She went to a ten-inch clay model that looked like a tree trunk with short, thick branches. "Silly little thing," Rachel said. "I am teaching a graduate sculpture class at the university, so I must do something!"

Her smile illuminated the studio as no sun ever could—
from within. He felt the heat in his own gut and it made
him light-headed . . . or was it the fumes of the paint?
"Beautiful work."

"Thank you. Let's have some tea."

Tim Mulrennan had dated a few young women when he
was in high school, college, and the military. It wasn't that
important to him, just something he did, like other guys his
age. He took them to dances and movies and dinners; he
gave one girl his senior class ring, but they broke up over
the summer before he left for college. He had necked and
petted with some of them, and when he was overseas in
the army he had been to bed with an American girl whose
father was stationed in Berlin. She had provided the rubber.
He had felt guilty and disconnected from reality. Luckily,
he had soon been transferred to Seoul, and he left her behind. In later years he learned not to regret it, but rather to
be grateful that he had even some limited experience to
draw upon in his ministry to young people and engaged
couples.

Or had it left an open question in his mind? What if?
Why not? His vow of celibacy was ingrained in his soul, a
facet of his very being; he had taken it willingly and knowingly, and he believed that celibacy was a pillar of his
priesthood, that it made him a better, tougher, more focused
minister of the Gospel. Yet . . . there were moments, as he
had expressed to Joe Ricciardi, when he wondered about
the path not taken—the women he had never known intimately. He saw how his sisters grew and changed in marriage and motherhood. And they were great moms to his
nieces and nephews.

Stephen, he strongly suspected, was gay—or tended in
that direction. He had never known of a girlfriend or any
romantic relationship. Was this wrong? There were many
gay priests; he knew several and respected them tremen-
dously. He did not speak to them directly about their homosexuality, and he suspected that they—at least some of
them—were sexually active. Would he have to confront
this issue more directly as a bishop? He suspected he
would.

She served a strong black tea in fine white gold-rimmed china cups, and she placed a plate piled with freshly baked blueberry muffins on the table near him. He drank in the sight and smells of the kitchen: the neatly maintained domain of a single woman. It was a world alien and mysterious to him and he wanted to know everything about her, where she came from and what she did every day and what she wanted from life and where she was going and who was her family and what she had been like as a little girl and what she believed and why she was an artist and anything and everything she would tell him. Never in his life had he felt these things; they seemed to squeeze the breath out of him.

He tried to conjure the names of the girls he had dated long ago. He could think of only one name: hers. Rachel. She was Jewish, Hungarian. What did that mean? From Budapest, an ancient city in communist-ruled Hungary. How old? Thirty-five? Younger? Older? Her smooth features were ageless: wide-apart deep brown eyes, a large beautifully shaped nose, full pink lips above a sharp chin, high exotic cheekbones and dimples on each side of her smile. She smiled at him now, destroying his reverie.

"What brings you to my house, really?" she asked, point-blank.

"I just wanted to see you. I have been thinking about you. Should I go?"

"No. Please stay awhile. Drink your tea. You must have a muffin." She served him a mountainous blueberry muffin on a tiny plate, with the butter dish and a laughably small butter knife. "I will be insulted if you do not taste it."

"All right." He had never been tongue-tied like this. He had met with the pope and top-rank diplomats and politicians and intellectuals and people of all walks of life. Here, he could not put three words together in a coherent sentence.

She went to a portable radio that sat above the stainless-steel sink and turned it on. "I must listen to the news. I think I am what you call addicted. I have to know every detail, traffic reports, weather, wars, what the president had for lunch." She stood a few feet from him and he breathed in her light perfume, mingled with paint and country air. "Do you mind?"

"I am not contributing much to your knowledge of the world," he said sheepishly, a muffin crumb dropping from his lips. He caught it and put it on the plate. "I am curious, too. Haven't read a newspaper today, since we left so early to play golf."

Rachel sat again in the high-backed wooden chair. She looked directly at Tim. "You are a good man, I can tell. I have—" She searched for the right word. "Antennae." She smiled and the dimples scored her pretty face. He caught sight of a single strand of gray hair at her right temple and wanted to touch it. "I have been thinking about you, too. What brought a man such as you out to the middle of no-where to be a bishop. Oh—I shouldn't say it that way. This is not nowhere. It is where I want to be to learn and to work."

"Same with me. I go where the Church sends me. I was in New Mexico before, New Jersey before that. I grew up in New Jersey."

"You know, that sounds so foreign and exotic to me: New Jersey! I think of your George Washington crossing the Delaware River, that famous painting."

"I always felt there was so much history all around, when I was growing up. We were not very far from Mor-ristown and Springfield, Revolutionary battle sites. And Camptown was right next door. Do you know 'Yankee Doodle Dandy'?"

"Yeah, sure. We learned that song when we were kids. We always listened to Radio Free Europe and other West-ern broadcasts. I had it not badly when I was a child, even being Jewish. Religion was a minor thing, not even ac-knowledged officially. The government is communist, but the people don't trust the Russians one bit."

"I've always heard Budapest is a beautiful city."

"Yes. I will go back there one day."

"You're not married? No children?"

"I was married. He died. Pregnant once. Had an abortion. I was seventeen—not ready."

Tim recoiled. Her frankness startled him. Why? That was

how she was, and he liked it in her. He could see she was gauging his reaction. She had not intended to shock or offend him, but she had. He said, "I am sorry for you, Rachel."

"You need not be, Bishop Tim. Most girls in my country have it a lot worse than I did. My parents always supported me, helped me decide the right thing. I am grateful for them; thank God they are still alive and healthy, more or less."

"Please, Rachel, just call me Tim. I feel silly—I mean, I am not here as a bishop or a priest—just as a friend. Or, I want to be. I—think you are a beautiful, marvelous woman."

As he spoke he listened to the words that escaped his mouth. He could not believe he was saying these things to her. What the hell was happening to him? How had he gotten himself into this situation? He paused and tried to remember God and his vows and his own family and his responsibilities as a newly consecrated bishop. He stood, looking down at the unfinished blueberry muffin, the most beautiful he had ever seen or tasted, the shadowed pool of tea in the fine cup. He heard his own labored breathing.

"Sit down for a minute," she said.

He sat. "I'm sorry. I can't believe I'm doing this."

"What are you doing, Tim?"

"That I'm here—with you—that I came in the first place. I don't belong here."

"You are welcome here any time. I want to talk to you, to know you better. I think it is very right that you showed up. I was surprised. I am glad."

He clenched his hands, bowed his head as if in prayer—collected his thoughts. After a half-minute he said: "I want to come back, if I may."

"You may. I wish you to. Call first, though." She wrote her telephone number on the back of an envelope and handed it to him.

His lower back throbbed, nearly canceling out the horrific headache he had had since early morning, as he sat at his desk reviewing the financial printouts that had kept him up nearly all of the night before. He sat back and lit a cigarette, hating the taste and hating himself for smoking. He had quit three years earlier, when he was assigned to the Abbey of Christ the Redeemer in the New Mexican desert. Now he was back on the habit, having purchased a pack several days ago—just to calm his nerves.

It was not working. There was something gravely wrong with the diocesan balance sheet, but since he was not a financial professional he could not figure it out on his own. He had called in an outside auditor who sat across the desk from him, a tall, wiry philosophical-looking man in a gray suit, button-down white shirt, black-and-red striped tie. Jack Olsen of Dobbs, Dekker looked as if he had come from the Reagan Office of Management and Budget, just what Tim needed—an accounting hard-ass who cared little or nothing for the spiritual implications of the numbers laid out in front of him.

"Bishop, I can't draw any definitive conclusions until I spend some more time with the balance sheet and get into the bank accounts. We're looking at an annual budget of forty to fifty million dollars. There's plenty of room to maneuver in there."

"Well, you've got to tell me if there has been some 'maneuvering,' Jack. We're hemorrhaging by the bucketload, and it's just the second fiscal quarter."

Mulrennan rubbed his lower back. He would have to get back to the chiropractor—he needed help badly. And he hadn't run or played golf or tennis for weeks. He stubbed out the cigarette, which he had smoked nearly to the filter. He was forty-four years old, and he felt seventy; he had been on the job for six months and he was ready for a long vacation. Silently, and ruefully, he cursed his predecessor, Bishop Leo Goldsmith, a kindly muffin of a man who had died one night in his sleep, smiling, at age seventy-four, leaving a diocese in near-chaos, with no plan other than to start closing schools and hospitals as soon as Mulrennan could bring himself to do it. Bottom line: he never would. And during the interregnum between Goldsmith's death and Mulrennan's installation, conditions had only worsened. The children's hospital in central Jackson City—not the best of neighborhoods, locals whispered meanly—was literally falling down around the patients and staff. The suburban parishes and schools were actually thriving, but, again, in the city, the old urban churches (now mostly black) and schools (likewise segregated by white flight) were in decline, with contributions drying up and church attendance dwindling by double-digit percentages.

Tim could not understand how it had come to this precipitous point so quickly. God bless Bishop Goldsmith and his well-meaning, equally doddering chancellor, and the rest of the staff—but they had kept piss-poor books, scattered the diocesan accounts across a dozen banks, created a byzantine nonsystem of transfers and payouts and accounts payable that defied conventional expertise to understand and repair. By his own rough calculations, the diocese was owed in excess of $10 million in back assessments from the parishes, and in turn owed about $14 million to banks and suppliers.

When in God's name was anyone going to collect on what the parishes owed and pay the diocese's debts?

He had explained his frustrations to Olsen, who pursed his lips in a CPA's rictus-smile. "It will take weeks working around the clock for us to get to the root of this, sir. I would suggest you lean as hard as you can on accounts payable and beg for time from your creditors. I think they will give you some breathing room."

Mulrennan said nothing. He had already gotten extensions on the major bills, especially the mortgage on the cathedral property itself, two acres situated squarely in the center of Jackson City on a high bluff overlooking the Missouri River. It was a majestic, historic location, claimed by a zealous missionary immediately after the Louis and Clark expedition, when Jackson City was a trading settlement of tents and tepees. The cathedral itself had been build in the 1890s, added to and refurbished in the 1930s, now fallen into at least partial disrepair. The beautiful brick chancery offices and bishop's residence sat on a rolling lawn next to the big old church, and from his bedroom Tim could look across the big brown river toward the industrialized bottoms and rail yards that provided some of the city's financial muscle.

Jackson City had grown up as a rambunctious cow town like Omaha or Kansas City, and settled in its maturity into a capital of commerce and politics, spawning vast suburbs and linking small towns that stretched as far north as St. Joseph and south toward Wichita. There was a deep Catholic tradition that dated from Spanish conquistadors and French missionaries who roamed the hilly river country looking for gold and heathen souls. In the later years of the nineteenth century waves of Irish, Italian, and Eastern European immigrants settled here, having pushed out farther west from Chicago and St. Louis. A Democratic party machine with ties to the Church—and, it was said, to the mob—had ruled the city and the eastern half of the state for most of the first half of the twentieth century. Now Republicans sat in city hall, though the municipal elections were officially nonpartisan thanks to a wave of "good-government" reforms that followed a series of political corruption trials. The police department was relatively clean and professionally managed. The constantly merging privately held banks seemed to be in good enough shape, employment levels had remained stable, and there was even some culture: a second-tier art museum, dinner theaters, and a great Kansas City–style jazz scene.

When he had first arrived, Tim had met the mayor and liked him: an Ivy League–educated lawyer and Episcopalian. "Bless the old bishop, he was big into ecumenical efforts. There are more Baptists in this town than any two other denominations combined," the mayor told him with a smooth smile. "We need as much high church as we can get."

Well, there wouldn't be much of anything Catholic if Mulrennan didn't get his act together, he thought. He faced several weeks of parish visitations before the advent season and Christmas celebrations would keep him occupied at the cathedral. He enjoyed these visits more than any other aspect of his job—meeting priests and parishioners, listening to their needs and complaints. He fed on their faith to sustain his own.

"Your Excellency—" the auditor was trying to get Tim Mulrennan's attention. "I would advise you to bring an attorney into the picture as soon as possible. If we find anything, er, irregular in the diocese's accounting practices, you may face legal liability. Better to be prepared—just in case."

"Thanks, I will. Our counsel is Winston Albrecht. You must know him."

"The mayor's firm. Strictly white shoe, above reproach. At least they haven't ever pinned anything on him." Olsen peered at Mulrennan over a tall stack of printouts in his lap that reached nearly to his chin. "I'm just pulling your leg, Bishop," he added when he saw that Tim was not amused.

"Look, please straighten out this mess. If you do, your firm will go on full-time retainer with the diocese. I will gladly pay the highest fees in the city for some peace of mind."

"Smoking doesn't help, you know. Sorry to mention it, but I kicked it myself five years ago—I know it can be done."

"Thanks," Mulrennan replied. "I was off for about three years, but this has put me over the edge. I never should have picked up the first one."

"The devil made you do it?"

"Thank you, Mr. Olsen, for your time. Now if you'll let me get back to my worries and my bad habits . . ."

At 8:00 P.M., after a long afternoon of phone calls, a brisk, brief walk around the cathedral grounds, cheese and crackers and a bottle of beer for dinner, more phone calls and paperwork, Tim finally got away from his desk and went to an easy chair by an open window in his study and collapsed. He reached for a two-day-old newspaper; he had very little idea what was going on in the world outside the Diocese of Jackson City, Missouri. He remembered how Rachel had said she was addicted to news. How long had it been since he had seen her? Three weeks? Four? It was early autumn and there was a football crispness to the grass and golden-red tinge to the leaves. He turned to the comics pages of the newspaper, read Peanuts and Ziggy, smiled at

the simplicity and aptness of the humor. Life: a comic strip
. . . far from it . . .

He reached for the telephone. He knew her telephone
number because he had looked at it every day—several
times. It was an old black rotary telephone that resisted his
finger as he pulled each digit, making him work harder than
he wanted to. He wanted a drink but did not have the energy to get up from the chair to pour one for himself. He
finished dialing her number. He realized he was obsessed
with Rachel Séredi, a woman he barely knew; he had seen
her three times, and he thought about her, dreamed about
her every day since they had met. The connection took an
agonizingly long time. The first ring. Second ring. No answer. Was she out? Third ring. He would hang up.

"Hello," she said brightly.

"Hello, Rachel, this is Tim Mulrennan."

"Oh, Bishop—Tim."

"I have been wondering how you are. Since I saw you,
I—I hoped to see you again sometime."

"Tim, I don't think we should, really. I was so glad you
visited me, saw my workplace. I'm afraid you'll try to convert me."

"Oh, I hadn't even thought of that," he protested. And it
was true—he hadn't.

After a slight pause, she said, "I am joking."

He sat back in the soft leather chair and smiled, thinking
how stupid he was, like a pimply teenager calling the pret-
tiest girl in the class. He couldn't tell her what he *had*
thought of when he drove away from her farmhouse-studio.
In his mind he had taken her in his arms a thousand times.

"Rachel, I don't even know how to say what I want to
say to you."

"Perhaps it is better if you do not say anything, then.
You are not obligated to me. You do not know me. If the
situation were different, perhaps—In fact, I am flattered
that you even noticed me. But I do not want to interfere
with your work. I cannot do that."

"My work. I am buried in it. I don't know which end is
up. It is much more difficult than I imagined. I barely have
a staff, and I don't know who to trust. I will be spending

more time with lawyers and accountants than my priests before I can hope to straighten out this bloody complicated mess."

This is the second time I have walked up these steps, he thought as he took them two at a time. *But this time it is dark.* Black night clouds shrouded the quarter moon. He knocked lightly on the rather flimsy screen door, saw her come from the kitchen, wiping her hands with a damp dish towel. She wore an argyle V-neck sweater over a white T-shirt, old paint-dotted blue jeans. Her red-brown hair was pulled back from her face and held in a thick ponytail. As she pushed open the door he breathed in her scent; he caught himself looking at the line of her neck, from her hair to the whiteness of the T-shirt, and wanting to taste her. The door wheezed and slammed shut behind him.

She said, "Hello. Please come in."

"Hi. Thanks," he said as he stepped into the uncarpeted foyer.

The steep staircase to the second floor lay straight ahead. She veered left and led him into a cozy living room with floor-to-ceiling bookcases stuffed with a seemingly eclectic collection of paperback books in several languages. Two free-standing lamps shot bright white light toward the twelve-foot ceiling. On tables either side of the sofa and near a big reading chair, shaded lamps glowed like beacons. Magazines and spine-cracked books lay scattered on a long glass coffee table in the middle of the room. Three or four lipstick-smeared cigarette butts were piled neatly in the middle of a vast ceramic ashtray beside the reading chair. It looked as he would picture an intellectual's nest, a bit cluttered, but with no extraneous or showy object in sight. It suited her.

She plopped into the overstuffed chair and gestured for him to sit wherever he wished. He picked a corner of the sofa. He suddenly wondered what he was going to say to her without sounding like a tongue-tied teenager; he had never been—never put himself—in a situation like this before, as a priest. *And what situation is that?* he asked himself silently. The flats of his hands pressed into his thighs as he contemplated his own long legs.

"You look tired, Timothy," she said, breaking a minute's silence.

"Yes, I am that. There's no end to the work, and the problems have no bottom that I've been able to identify. I feel like a ditch digger working with a dull spoon." He looked at her. "Not complaining, but I had no idea—no conception of the scope—I guess I should have asked more questions before I agreed to come."

"Don't you like Jackson City?"

"Oh, very much. I'm surprised, actually, that I like it as much as I do. The people are superfriendly, don't seem to be in such a big hurry as where I'm from."

"I like the quiet, the privacy. I have done so much work in just ten months—more than the past two years back home. And I have learned so much. Not so much politics in everyday life."

"That depends on what circles you're moving in, I think," Mulrennan said with a smile, thinking of the earnest state senator he had met the day before, a Republican and Roman Catholic who was pushing legislation for tax-deductible school vouchers for private-school parents. His was a distinct minority position in the Missouri legislature, but he sought the bishop's blessing for his efforts, which Tim gladly gave him.

"Well, no communists, at least."

He felt small. Of course, that's what she meant by politics—Marxism. The piddling Democrats and Republicans, and their petty squabbles over patronage and money, must have seemed like merely unruly schoolchildren to someone from a Soviet satellite in which resistance had been crushed by tanks and show trials. He should know better. He had been there himself in the '50s.

"I think they're all cut from the same cloth," he said lamely. Why could he not complete a coherent thought when he was near her?

She rose and walked across the room and he followed her hungrily with his eyes. From a glass-encased breakfront she pulled two cut-crystal goblets and a decanter and poured two glasses of wine. She brought them over to Mulrennan, gave him one, and sat by him on the sofa; she lifted her glass in a silent toast and smiled as she took a sip. He also tasted the wine, slightly sweet, and it felt like fire when it hit his belly.

"Timothy," she said, "talk to me. Why are you here? I am glad—please don't get me wrong—I am very glad to see you."

"I haven't spent any time with women, really," he said. "I am not sure what to do or to say. I just wanted to be with you. I think I am falling in love with you." As he heard his own words he felt foolish, powerless.

"I think you are a wonderful man, but you are a priest. I have tried not to love you, Timothy. I think it is wrong, but I don't know. I don't know . . ."

He moved over to be closer to her. He reached for her hands, took them in his. They felt small and warm and alive. He lifted her hands and kissed them, touched his lips to her fingers and turned them and brushed his mouth over her palms. She closed her eyes and let him drink in her presence as he kissed her. She lifted her hands to his face and felt the stubble of a day's growth of beard, traced his jawline, then pulled his face to her own. They kissed.

It was the first time in more than twenty years that he had kissed a woman, and he felt her melt into him, become a part of his being. Rachel pressed herself hungrily against him, wrapped her arms around him. Mulrennan tentatively put his own arms around her slender frame, pulled her in.

After a few moments she pulled away from him, and they talked.

"My father was a student in Budapest when the war broke out. He wanted to be a lawyer, but that never happened. He went to France in early 1940, found his way to Paris, but the Nazis came in June, so he had to go into hiding. He nearly avoided capture. . . ." She had heard the story many times, told it many more. "He spent three and a half years in the death camps; he survived because he was strong and the Nazis put him to work: he accounted for the valuables they stole from the Jews—kept ledgers and records. When the Allies liberated the camps, he could barely walk; he weighed about eighty pounds. He walked back to Hungary like many refugees. Again he survived. He met my mother in Budapest after the war. She and her family had lived there—her father was a rabbi—and kept the flame of religion burning dimly for years. She nursed him, cared for him, fell in love with him. Like many intellectuals, he joined the party so that he could have a job at the university. I don't think he ever believed in Marxism, and he hated Stalin. He wasn't religious, either. I was born in 1949."

Tim heard the pain in her voice, saw that it was very painful for her to talk about her parents, especially her father. "I have a younger brother and sister." She brightened somewhat. "All of us are survivors, I think."

Not of her own memory, but her father's, in stories told and retold over many years, remembered, half-remembered, forgotten—only to be resurrected in the telling. This was how and why she became an artist: to tell stories, to give substance to images that represented lives, generations, dead souls, good and evil. Yes, she believed in evil, perhaps more than good. Images, memories, histories: Her father, Carl Jószef Séredi, born a Jew to devout parents, became a scholar and agnostic, aspired to the practice of law in a postempire Hungary. In Buda-Pest, the twin cities astride the Danube, he enrolled in the university before the guns of war rumbled through the streets.

Mulrennan felt a complete and utter fool and had no idea what had possessed him. Yet he could not—or would not—retreat from his absurd position; like the last soldier alive in a foxhole overrun by the enemy . . . he was haunted by the wasted lives of his comrades, determined to fight to the death. There was no common sense or logic in him, only the passion and the zeal of the damned.

"May I stay with you tonight?" he asked.

"Yes, if you wish to." She sat back and regarded him intently, her eyes bored into him.

"Rachel, I have not been with a woman in twenty years—since before I became a priest."

"But you are with women frequently, aren't you, throughout the day?"

"Yes, but—I mean, *with* a woman in an intimate sense. There was a time, in Vietnam when I saved a young woman's life—I happened to be there and was able to do it. I killed a man, two men, that night. Later, I think she fell in love with me. We signed fake marriage papers so she could escape from the country. I did it to help her, even though, looking back on it, I think it was the wrong way to accomplish a good thing. It has bothered me . . . I have confessed it and I know I have been forgiven, but I still think about it."

"Did you like her, this woman you saved?"

"Well, yes, I did. I respected her so much, for all she had been through, for her courage."

The image of Ly Linh Sanh came vividly to life in his mind, and he knew in that moment that he *had* loved her, that there were feelings he had never acknowledged before, ever—to anyone. He had confessed the overt sins of killing a man and "marrying" her in order to secure her emigration from Vietnam to the U.S. before the South fell to the communists. A means to an end, he had assured himself. His confessor had not suggested he undo the deed; eventually, even Archbishop Vennholme had found out about it, discussed it with Tim during the process of his selection as Bishop of Jackson City. The unresolved questions lay within himself alone; the issue went beyond right and wrong, sin and good works, life and death. There was the issue of his very soul and his identity as a man. He was proscribed from loving a woman and being with her sexually—this by his own vow of chastity as a priest of God. But with Rachel, more even than Li, he felt an overpowering need to throw aside his vows, his career if need be, to make love—to be a complete man—with her.

"This is crazy," he muttered aloud.

She stared at him quizzically, her dark eyes gleaming in the lamplight. She held the wineglass in both hands, balanced on a bare knee. He had never seen anything so beautiful, so sensual in his life.

Is this what it is like? he asked himself. He had no point of reference other than movies or novels, both of which he had little time for. What would Kevin do? He nearly laughed at the thought of his long-dead brother, who, Tim remembered, had an easy, natural way with girls; Kevin always had a girlfriend—at least one—and several calling and following him around. In fact, he had questioned Tim on this very subject when Tim announced he was enrolling in the seminary. Tim had not had an answer, as he recalled, to Kevin's intensive probing on the subject of sex and women.

"You sure this is what you want, kid?" said Kevin Mulrennan, soon-to-be-marine-officer brother. "Never get married and have a big Catholic brood? Never live with a girl or fool around with one when you want to? Never get your rocks off when you really need to—and, believe me, you'll really need to one of these days. I don't get it, little brother. I know you're holy and all that—and I like that about you, makes you different—but isn't this kind of extreme?"

"Yes, it is. And I don't expect it to be easy or fun. But it comes with the job."

Like many—even most—priests, Mulrennan had always considered priestly celibacy a unique gift and responsibility, a challenge, a grace. It set him apart from other men, though he never held himself up as superior to them. There were moments . . . such as this evening with Rachel, when he questioned the value of abstinence and the lack of a close, long-term sexual relationship in his life.

No such spiritual or logical thoughts inhabited his brain now. Her presence dissolved his long-built-up defenses, and he felt himself falling as if from a high precipice into an unknown depth of experience. He wanted to. He wanted to experience her in every way possible. Was it wrong? Was it unforgivable? Were his sacred vows so inviolable that he could never know this level of emotion? Was he not a human being?

She was so close that he could smell the lingering scent of shampoo in her hair and the patina of the day's perspiration on her shoulders. He felt the wine swim in his head, and all of his senses were acutely attuned to her physical being: his eyes limned her cameo against the soft lamplight and shadows of the room.

"You are far away from your family, too," she said.

"Yes, they are in the East, New Jersey and New York. My mother died about thirty years ago. My father remarried, and he's retired now. My three sisters are all married, and my younger brother, Stephen, lives in New York. I saw very little of them when I was in New Mexico, but we got together for Easter before I came out to Jackson City. I suppose it will be another long stretch before I see them again. I try to write at least once a week to my dad."

"It sounds like you miss them."

"I do. When I was working in my home diocese I could see them whenever I wanted—and even when I didn't! I talk to the girls on the phone regularly. Stephen works in New York City for a book publishing company. He's single and out there on his own, I guess. Haven't heard much from him recently."

"I wish I had sisters. I feel very lonely sometimes, even though I go home every year. It's very expensive to travel to Hungary, so I must live poor the rest of the time, as you can see!" With a laugh, she gestured to encompass the eclectic furniture and decor of the room.

"A vow of poverty, like many of my religious brothers," Tim replied. "But a lot more comfortable than the convent."

"I have been thinking about that lately. Perhaps it is not too late for me? As a little girl I thought about being a nun, until I found my true calling." Her voice washed over him in a soothing cascade of music. "I do believe deeply in my art—and in God—but probably in that order," she said somewhat sheepishly.

"An apostate? Perhaps there is some barbarian blood in your family?"

"Well, between my Jewish father and my atheist mother . . . at least there's some explanation."

"How, then, to explain your beauty and your talent? Tell me, who is responsible for those gifts?"

"I have no explanations other than my art, my movements, my life, my hopes."

"Then what do you believe? Do you have God in your life?"

"No—and yes. I think God does not care much whether I believe." Her smile radiated toward him as a slow breeze caught the curtains and swept gently through the room. "He has more important things to worry about. As you do."

"You are being dismissive. I am serious. I want to know you, inside and out."

"You already do. There is no more nor less than what you see. I put religion on the shelf, despite Father Joe's efforts. I am happy to attend church and to pray and to think about God once in a while. But what label should I put on the bottle? That I do not know. Your commitment is very impressive to me; I believe that you believe, and that is enough."

He sat back on the sofa and placed his fists on his knees. He seemed more gaunt than usual in the semiflicker of the candle and the lamplight. The shock of gray-white at his temples shone more pronouncedly. His eyes glowed darkly. "There is mystery in you. I think that is why I want to be with you, to learn the answer."

"I think you are stubborn—like all men. I tell you the truth, but you do not hear it. Ask me anything and I will give you my answer. I am not hiding or avoiding anything, at least not with you." She reached over and touched his wrist with her cool hand. "Even though it is truly none of your business, Bishop Tim Mulrennan."

The words stung him. "Why do you say that when I just want to—get to know you as a person?" He was amazed and appalled at how insipid he sounded. He simply could not express himself accurately to her; she dazzled and distracted him.

"Please speak the truth to me, Timothy. You are not very good at covering up your feelings."

"I want to—know you—to be a part of your life. I am deeply attracted to you, Rachel," he said.

"This is wrong," she replied.

"No, it seems right to me. I know I should not, but I must tell you. You asked me. I will not lie to you; I cannot do that. I don't know exactly what it is that I feel—it is new to me, different and strange." He unfolded his long frame and reached for the glass on the coffee table, saw the ring left there by the beaded moisture from the glass. He lifted it to his lips but did not drink. "Can you try to understand? Can you help me?"

"Yes, I will try. I want to know what is in your heart. But I do not think I can give you what you seek."

The wineglass felt heavy in his hand. "I love you, Rachel," he said.

"Timothy, you do not know what you are saying. You cannot do this." She leaned into him and looked directly into his eyes. "I fell in love with you the moment I saw you at the picnic, when Father Ricciardi introduced us—in the heat and confusion of the celebration. My heart nearly burst when we first touched hands." Tears brimmed in her brown liquid eyes. "This is very difficult for me, too."

"But how can you say you love me and not—"

"Be quiet for a moment, Timothy. Think of what you are saying. We are not free to do what we wish, like other people. You are 'married,' and if I am to love you, I am not going to share you with anyone. It is not possible for me, nor would you want it, I think. Yes, I hear the music that draws us to each other, but it is not destined to play for us forever. We would both have to change everything to be with each other—everything."

Tim Mulrennan struggled to find a foothold; he was like a drowning man in a shallow lake, near to the shore, but still too far, unable to cry out, flailing, alone, wanting not to die yet unable to pray for life, utterly afraid. He had never felt this fear in his life—not in Vietnam or Berlin or Korea or Newark or even in his darkest, most isolated days in the abbey in the New Mexican desert . . . alone in the presence of the most beautiful and desirable woman he had ever known.

"You say it is wrong for us to love each other because of what I am. But I am willing to sacrifice whatever I must . . ."

"Are you willing to give up your priesthood, Timothy?"

He sat quietly and stared into the opacity of the wine in his glass, twirling it gently, watching it crest against the crystal wall of the glass. Where was the answer? He was not willing to quit the priesthood, but he was willing to compromise, to go part of the distance required to have her in his life. Wasn't a partial relationship better than none at all? Couldn't she see that?

"I am in foreign territory, Rachel. To be honest, I really don't know what I want or what I am willing to do to have it. They did not tell me about you in the seminary." He attempted a smile, tried to meet her gaze head-on, but she looked down; he saw the tears running freely down her flushed cheeks, dropping from her chin onto the blue work shirt. He reached for her, touched her face, replaced the wineglass on the table and moved closer to her. He took her in his arms and held her to him.

She sobbed and trembled in his embrace. Tim buried his face in her fragrant curly hair. He held her like that for several minutes as she wept. He did not know what to do. He had caused this, and he was sorry—but he loved her, damn it, and her tears were his, too. He did not allow himself to cry, however, because he wanted to be strong for her, to hold her and rock her, to comfort her. In all his forty-four years he had never been in love with a woman and never held a woman like this and never known the deep, stabbing emotional pain that he felt at this moment and never been sorrier to cause another human being such pain. The sensation of drowning washed over him again, robbing him of breath and vision. Swimming, swimming, struggling, fighting for oxygen, desperate to feel the bottom of the dark pool. He opened his eyes, looked over the top of her head into the dark autumn night through the open windows: the unseen sky defined the end of the earth and the turning of time and called to him in a dark, womanly whisper. One of her candles flickered and died, sending a thin column of black smoke upward like the black ashy smoke of an ancient holocaust in the temple of Solomon. In that moment, with Rachel clinging to him, he reached back into the world of youthful imaginings. . . .

After a half hour of prayer and reading his morning office in Rachel's backyard, Mulrennan came in and lit a cigarette and sat at the kitchen table. She bustled about, fixing breakfast.

"I have never been with a priest in the morning," she

said without looking at him. "Do you always have these little rituals?"

"A priest is like an artist—he must cultivate and practice his faith every day. He must paint with it, or sculpt in it. Faith is his medium. Hope is his energy. Love is his genius. People can detect a false artist—so, too, they know a false priest. Likewise, they know a true practitioner."

"Timothy, I think you are a bit 'full of it.' " She smiled at his pained expression. "Did I not say that correctly?"

"Oh, you said it right. You might also say that I'm a horse's ass, trying too hard to impress."

"You have no need to impress me—I already am. I do like you a lot. To be honest, I didn't want to. I blame Father Joe; he said we would hit it off."

Tim laughed harshly. "Little does he know what he has done. I should banish him to another parish at the farthest edge of the diocese—teach the sonofagun a lesson."

"You wouldn't really do that—would you?"

The telephone rang, and Rachel moved across the kitchen to answer it. "Hello," she said brightly, listened intently for a few seconds, and handed the receiver to Tim with a startled look on her face. "A call for you. It is Father Ricciardi."

Mulrennan rose from his chair and took the receiver. "What a coincidence," he said to Rachel, then spoke into the phone, modulating his voice so as not to seem overly surprised. "Joe, this is Tim—how the heck did you find me?"

"Tim, I deeply apologize. I just kind of guessed you might be there. The office, I mean the chancery called. They are looking for you. For God's sake, didn't you go home last night? They're frantic. There is some sort of problem. I don't know how many people they've called, but I'm glad they got to me—it's still early. You better call right now."

"All right," Mulrennan said. He stubbed out his cigarette, felt his heart ball up in the middle of his chest. "Thanks, Joe. Just for your information, today is my day off—not that that makes a damn bit of difference. I should have called in myself. I know this must look bad, but it's really—"

"I don't want to know, Tim. I assume it's perfectly innocent. I hope you didn't spend the night at her house. Maybe you fell asleep in your car or something? . . ."

"No such luck, pal."

"Oh." In Ricciardi's silence, Mulrennan could sense the struggle within the man. "Well, call 'em back," he said gruffly.

"I'll do that if you get off the line, Joe. God bless you."

"Yeah. Thanks. 'Bye."

Tim Mulrennan immediately dialed his office, and the secretary put him through to Monsignor Thomas Mroz, the vice chancellor of the diocese, the bishop's chief aide and a native of the Jackson City area. He could hear the tentative yet accusatory tone in the priest's voice.

"Your Excellency, where—" But Tim cut him off.

"I drove out last night and kept driving. I needed to think and pray, Tom. I'm fine, and I'm very sorry I didn't call in to let you know that I was AWOL for a little while. Please forgive me."

"Yes, Bishop, of course. And I know this is supposed to be your day off. But something has come up—pretty bad, I'm afraid. The auditor called early this morning to tell us he has discovered an embezzlement problem. He said someone has been looting our accounts, very carefully and over a long period of time. It's hundreds of thousands of dollars, Your Excellency."

Jesus Christ Almighty, Tim thought, *this is a hell of a lot worse than I expected.* He had suspected something like this from the beginning, but not to such an astounding degree . . . and who could it be? He felt like cursing or throwing his coffee mug across the room. He contained his temper, thanks to years of training and discipline. He had not raised his voice in years: not since he was a basketball coach and had to yell to be heard above the noise in the gym. However, he had learned during his years at the abbey that he must not bottle up the bile, that it would spill over elsewhere—he would have to deal with it. Just as he must deal with his feelings for this woman. Oh, Christ, what had he stepped into?

He said to Monsignor Mroz, "I'll be there in an hour. Call Mr. Olsen and ask him to meet me at eleven o'clock in my office."

"Will do, Your Excellency."

Mulrennan turned to Rachel and gave her the receiver to hang up. "All hell has broken loose at the diocese."

"You better get back, Tim. I think this was a bad idea, staying here."

"Maybe it was, but we can't undo it. I'm grateful to you, Rachel, for everything."

"I didn't do anything. Just gave you a place to sleep and a cup of coffee."

"You did a lot more than that for me. I mean our conversation—what we talked about last night. I don't know where we're going from here, but I am glad I came."

He stood. She came to him, pressed herself against him, felt his strength and his need. He gingerly put his arms around her shoulders, hugged her. She kissed him on the cheek, felt his lips brush her temple; she drank in the scent and warmth of his body. They stood quietly together for a minute.

"If it was a mistake, I'm willing to pay the penalty," he said, his face pressed against hers. He felt raw and emotionally desiccated. "Whatever comes . . ."

"Timothy, nothing must come of this. We will not be together, cannot be together. Long ago, you chose a different path." She pushed herself from him; she looked earnestly, with longing at his handsome face. She wanted him more than anything in the world and forced herself to step away. "Go back. Don't come here anymore. I have work to do—and so do you."

His mind raced; his world spun off its axis. He gathered his car keys. He had not brought anything else with him, had he? Only his raw feelings for this woman. He walked out of the kitchen, into the front hallway, past the sitting room where they had talked for hours last night. His eyesight blurred with tears. The staircase that led upstairs to her bedroom . . . he did not look in that direction, but

headed purposefully toward the front door. She followed
him. He stepped through the screen door onto her porch;
the morning sunlight hit it directly and he felt its warmth,
saw the few scattered leaves that had blown up from the
yard. The dried leaves that had not yet fallen rustled in the
trees above. That was the sound of his soul. He could not
see, and he could not speak. She stood against the open
screen door with her arms folded. She watched him.

"Good-bye," he said without turning to look at her.

"Good-bye, Timothy," she said.

The car started easily. The gasoline tank was three-
quarters full; he could drive anywhere, in any direction for
hours. He could take her with him. . . . He pulled out of her
driveway and caught sight of her standing there, arms
folded, paint-spattered jeans, curly dark hair gilded in the
rays of the morning sun. It was autumn and he rolled down
the car window to feel the breeze on his face as he sped
away on the narrow county road that had taken him to her
last night.

CHAPTER TWELVE

Wednesday, January 31, 6:37 A.M.

The first faint light of dawn threaded through the un-shaded window as Leandro Cardinal Biagi took his place in the sitting room of his three-room suite, one of the more luxurious cardinalitial rooms in the Domus Sanctae Marthae, the St. Martha's Residence. He joined five other cardinal-electors who had come in secret and in silence, informed the evening before of this private meeting, this conclave within a conclave.

For ten minutes the six eminences did not speak: each praying in his own mind, in his own language, bare head bowed, hands clasped upon lap or tabletop. Biagi had suggested they attempt to clear the fears and biases from their hearts before they undertook a serious discussion of the events of the previous day.

The men here gathered represented every continent on earth, and they ranged in ideology across the ever-widening spectrum of theological thought that existed within the Church.

Francis James Cardinal Musselthwaite, the Archbishop of Sydney, Australia, was by far the largest of the group. At fifty-eight, he stood six feet seven and weighed in excess of three hundred pounds. But mere statistics revealed little of the man whose layers of guile—like his multiple chins—were legendary within the Curia and among his scattered Australian flock. He had once been a Rhodes Scholar; he had little use for scholarship or theology, was a committed moderate on doctrinal issues, and ran his archdiocese like a Fortune 500 corporation. He had difficulty keeping his hooded gray eyes closed at prayer.

Nicholas Cardinal Czeslowski, the unabashed Pole from Chicago, was one of the youngest and newest members of the Sacred College, having received his red biretta at the late pope's last consistory only a year earlier. Built like a wrestling champion—which he had been at Loyola University—he had just turned forty-nine. To call him a conservative barely hinted at the depth of his orthodoxy and pre-Vatican II inclinations. He personally celebrated one Tridentine mass per month at a different parish within his archdiocese of 2 million faithful. He chaired the nonpartisan Pro-Life Crusade in the United States and had as many enemies as supporters for that energy-consuming effort. The Curia smiled upon this young up-and-comer.

The cardinal from Hong Kong, who unofficially oversaw Church affairs throughout China, was a tiny, emaciated seventy-year-old with dark brown eyes behind thick gold-framed glasses and a sleek black pompadour. Matthew Su Cardinal Yuen had been nicknamed Merry by fellow Benedictines in his early monastery days—ostensibly because of his dour demeanor. He was valued by his peers, however, for his razor wit and pragmatic political mind—"flexible as a rubber band," a Curialist had once said. Was he a moderate? A traditionalist? A reformer? A reactionary? Yes—and no—to all of the above. Most of all, he was a survivor.

The handsome Chilean with a Roman nose, olive skin, and high cheekbones was Jorge Miguel Cardinal Ponce. Upon his golden bishop's ring were twelve emeralds, representing the Apostles, encircling a large blue diamond, representing God the Father. The polished ring sparkled in the room's light as he took a long black cigarillo from his pocket and lit it. He was the only man present who smoked. In his midfifties, though he looked like a lean and fit forty, he too was of the younger generation in the College; and he was among the most liberal, having grown up in Santiago during the repressive postcoup Pinochet era.

Like a sleek black cat, elegant and still, observing and absorbing everything around him, Mfon Cardinal Ibanga sat among his fellow eminences. The Nigerian, sixty-five, president of the Pontifical Council for Inter-religious Dialogue, attired now in a sweeping black simar, or house cassock, with a shoulder cape with scarlet piping and sash, placed his small black feet, sheathed in red stockings and black patent leather shoes, on a coffee table. His dark hands were folded comfortably upon his rising belly. Knowledgeable observers placed Ibanga squarely in the center on doctrine and gave him exceptionally high marks for empathy and diplomacy in his dialogues with Jews, Muslims, Buddhists, and others.

Leandro Aurelio Biagi, the lone Italian and only European present, gazed silently at his colleagues. These men could not all be considered allies in his earlier drive to elect Timothy Mulrennan; he doubted that more than one or two of them had voted for the American. Perhaps Musselthwaite, possibly Ponce. Czeslowski—even though a fellow countryman—and Yuen had probably backed other candidates. As for Ibanga the Impenetrable—who could even guess?

"Gentleman, thank you for accepting my invitation to this meeting," Biagi began. "I hope your prayers are answered—whatever they may be."

"A good night's sleep," the Australian grumbled.

"And for me, a sunny day at the beach," Ponce intoned wistfully. "I had scheduled a week's holiday, but it was not meant to be. . . ."

The cardinals fell into English as naturally as their native languages—with the exception of Merry Yuen, who struggled a bit with his word choices.

"Our depth of sympathy, dear brother, yes, is bottomless," the Chinese cardinal offered. "Let us elect a Holy Father who will bring sunshine into the Church for all the year, yes."

Ponce smiled and puffed on his cigarillo.

"This is what we must agree on, gentlemen." Biagi stood and paced across the room like a nervous expectant father or would-be kingmaker. "Not for ourselves, not for any particular political agenda, but for God's people."

Czeslowski blurted, "I've never known you not to have an agenda, Biagi. God will forgive me for saying so." His eyes rolled heavenward. "Let's get down to business."

"I appreciate your frankness, Nick, always. And I agree that we have no time to waste." To the room at large, Biagi said: "Whatever my motives, you must agree with me that this conclave is in crisis. No matter your political persuasion, you must see that we are being held hostage—that in fact we are being forced to capitulate—to the enemies of faith."

"Wait a minute—" Czeslowski smoothed his crewcut with thick sausagelike fingers. "We have no enemies within our own ranks, Allo. We may disagree sharply on many issues, but we are united by love of Christ and faith in His Church."

Ibanga spoke in a deep, measured voice. "We are truly divided, my friend, fundamentally and in some cases irrevocably. I agree with Cardinal Biagi, though I would not employ the word 'enemy' in my analysis of the problem."

"Will you share your analysis with us, then?" Musselthwaite asked impatiently.

Ibanga shifted his broad beam uneasily and planted his feet firmly upon the brown carpet. "I wonder whether my private opinions are relevant to this issue."

"They most certainly are," Biagi insisted.

"Wouldn't have asked the question, mate, if I'd thought otherwise." The florid Australian cardinal enjoyed the African's discomfort.

Czeslowski said, "Foul ball, Frank. None of us has to say a blessed thing we don't feel comfortable saying—and you damned well know that. Mfon is under no obligation to be here, let alone to spill his guts to you."

"Gentlemen—" Biagi interjected.

But Merry Yuen stepped into the discussion. "I agree with my American friend." He turned to the Nigerian. "You must not speak unless you do so of your own free will and fully confident that your words will remain in this room."

"What's the use, then, of this little soiree?" Musselthwaite grumped. "If we can't talk openly here, then where in God's name will we ever resolve these problems? Have anything to drink, Allo?"

"You have made an excellent point, dear Cardinal brother," Ibanga said. "I am perhaps discreet to a fault at times. In fact, I feel strongly that we have a severe problem, what might be called a cancer within the conclave." Bright pink palms were visible beneath the steeple of his fingers.

Biagi poured a cup of coffee and served Musselthwaite, then continued to pace the length of the sitting room. Ponce, the Chilean, smoked and narrowed his eyes. Yuen was a diminutive ramrod in his straight-backed chair. Each man gave his complete attention to Ibanga.

"From a twin perspective, as a congregational prefect within the Curia and as a priest of thirty-five years, I am convinced that Cardinal Vennholme has set this conclave on an incorrect course and has grievously wronged Cardinal Mulrennan. For your ears only, gentlemen: If I were in a position to do so, I would reprimand Vennholme and prohibit him from further canvassing for his candidate. I would request that he apologize to Cardinal Mulrennan and offer a mass of reconciliation to his fellow conclavists."

"I agree completely," Musselthwaite said. "Let's bounce the bastard right out of here!"

"Hold on a minute," Czeslowski blurted. "We're not lawyers, and this is not a Church court. I, for one, would like to speak personally to Henry and hear him deny he was the source of those news stories. Until proven—"

"Neither do American rules of law apply," Cardinal Yuen interjected. "We are in a game, if you will, with no established rules at all. We will find many cardinals in sympathy with Cardinal Vennholme's efforts, despite the questionable morality of such tactics."

"If I had my way," Ponce put in with a sly grin, "we'd bring back the old Spanish Inquisition just long enough to interrogate old Henry. But that's not going to happen, nor are we going to 'boot the offender out,' " he added, paraphrasing his Australian colleague. "So why not get back to the business at hand? I confess I was deeply fascinated by Cardinal Ibanga's suggestions." He turned to the Nigerian. "Mfon, do you really think a mass will put our house in order? If so, you must have a spiritual streak a kilometer wide!"

Ibanga flashed yellow-white teeth in a sincere smile. "It

must come from spending so much time among the Mu-hammadans."

"Continue, please," Yuen prodded Ibanga, eyes now alight with intrigue.

"I will simply conclude. Personalities aside, I feel we must not elect a Curialist, nor even an Italian. We shall be false to our conclave oath if we do not elect a shepherd to gather His flock—His entire flock—to retrieve the lost, and to recommit us all to the course of renewal."

"The last thing we need is more 'reform,'" Nicholas Czeslowski spat. "The late Holy Father set us on the proper course and kept us there, even in his long illness. I am no fan of Martin Vennholme and his cultish Evangelium cro-nies—but neither did I believe that Tim Mulrennan was the man for this job. We need a firm, knowledgeable insider, and I don't care one whit if he's Italian or not. If we do not elect a smart conservative, might as well flush two thou-sand years down the toilet."

"Bold words for a Pole—even an American one," Ponce quipped. The others laughed, including Czeslowski.

"Where do you stand, Jorge?" Biagi asked.

The lean South American stubbed out his smoke in a small crystal ashtray. As if he were dimming an electric light, he turned down the urbane charm and became gravely serious and priestly. "I could not disagree more with Car-dinal Czeslowski. I love you as a brother and respect your position, Nick, but you are dead wrong on this." He turned again to the others. "Perhaps I am the only one present who believes that our hierarchical celibate male priesthood ought not and will not survive another generation. Politics and sexuality are strangling our Church. Our enemy—if such a one exists—resides within our own breasts. The toxin that infects this very conclave springs from a poison well that has been dug for a thousand years."

Cardinal Yuen, who had been nursing a mug of black tea, pushed it aside. "Your words trouble me greatly, Em-inence," he said to Ponce.

"They are meant to, Don Merry, but only to illustrate the pain in my own heart. Many battles and a long slow march lie behind us. Now we have come to a new field of battle.

The enemy—invisible, powerful—is all around us and within us. Tim Mulrennan is a casualty because he was ill prepared for the fight. Vennholme, on the other hand, is a skilled general. I only ask, whose side is he really on? Not mine, I can assure you."

"Mystical claptrap," Musselthwaite weighed in definitively, surprising no one.

"Let us remain civil with each other, at least," Biagi urged.

The Chinese cardinal said, "We have had years to consider the problem of succession. Few of us are pleased that we must make this decision at all, yes, for it will be irrevocable. It is a heavy chalice to lift. We shall not please every person, even in the College, with this election. We must therefore try to please God."

"Who, then, do you suggest we support?" the Australian asked.

"Yes, I have searched my own mind," Yuen said. "To be frank, there is no one candidate I could vote for without reservation. But I feel very strongly that there is no Italian cardinal—especially not La Spina—who would be fit for election. Further, yes, Cardinal Vennholme must be dealt with according to the rules of the conclave, and Cardinal Mulrennan should be encouraged to remain in his archdiocese. He is a good man, and the Church needs him."

"We need priests who honor their vows," Czeslowski said bitterly.

"I daresay any of us would fall short on that count if pinned to the wall like he was." Musselthwaite swirled the coffee in his cup. "I know I am not beloved of you gentlemen, but I think we can agree on Vennholme. Even you, Czeslowski, cannot deny he has acted criminally and mortally wounded his own cause."

Biagi watched the young American cardinal's reaction. Nicholas Czeslowski scowled and folded his muscular arms over his chest.

"Who, then?" Ibanga interjected. "Cardinal Biagi, you did not ask us all here to debate, I think. Do you have a course in mind, or a candidate?"

"Why not Cardinal Ibanga?" Ponce suggested. "Mfon,

you are the kind of man, with the right background, whom we are talking about."

Ibanga laughed aloud. "We see the first American candidate with a realistic chance of being elected is destroyed, and now you suggest the conclave turn to a black African?"

"Perhaps we should wait and see what happens, who emerges on the next ballot," Yuen suggested.

All eyes seemed to turn to Biagi at once, and he seized the moment.

"That would be fine, Cardinal Yuen, if we had more than one ballot to decide. But I fear that our brother Cardinal Vennholme has played his hand deviously but well. With Tim Mulrennan out of the running, just enough will feel La Spina's election inevitable to throw their hand behind the apparent winner and thus secure future favor. If we are meeting here now, you can be assured that Vennholme has already met with others, making deals and promises to put his man over the top on the next ballot."

"Then why bother with this little get-together?" Musselthwaite asked, shaking his head and frowning.

"Because there is still a chance—a single chance, I believe. But we must make it united and at once."

"And that is?" Musselthwaite said impatiently.

"If we all back the same man, if we leave here and start contacting others—everyone we know, everyone who owes us favors—we just might forestall what now seems inevitable and give our brothers a real choice, a real candidate to back. But our campaign must be swift and unexpected by Cardinal Vennholme, which is why I waited until this morning to meet with you."

"This smacks of horse-trading and politics, and we all know that is forbidden in the constitution that governs the conclave," Czeslowski said. "And I'm not sure that La Spina isn't a good choice."

"You must forgive me, then, for my methodology, dear Cardinal, but not my intention. My conscience demands that I share what is on my mind—for the good of the Church."

Biagi paused, looking from one man to the other. He

knew he was skating on very thin ice here, that Czeslowski had said what was on the others' minds; but he felt he had no choice now, that there was too much at stake to dance around the issue or to adhere too blindly to the rules. He remained silent until the last moment, until they looked ready to spring at him, demanding that he reveal who he had in mind. And then he continued.

"I do not suggest a liberal reformer nor a doctrinal conservative. Instead I offer you a man few of us would have considered before. In fact, he himself will not have considered it and has no idea I am putting him forward—nor should he know until the vote is counted. But there is something about this man, something that could bring divergent people together, that could link North and South, East and West."

Biagi rose from his chair and walked across the room. Reaching the window, he gazed outside a moment, watching the growing light until he was certain he had their attention—and certain his instincts were correct. And as he looked out into the morning light, a sense of calm washed over him. He knew he was not speaking for himself but for the long line of men who had sat upon the Throne of St. Peter.

"Gentlemen," he said, turning back around. "My brother cardinals, I beg you to hear me not with your heads but with your hearts. I suggest—no, I proclaim—that our next pontiff, the next Vicar of Christ, is the man who addressed us so eloquently yesterday, our Filipino brother, Jaime Cardinal De Guzman.

The men looked from one to another, no one speaking, no one objecting. As Biagi watched their faces, he saw that his suggestion was not entirely unexpected—that somewhere, at some time during the past twenty-four hours, each had thought of the same man but had perhaps rejected the idea as too farfetched or too novel. Now, spoken from Biagi's own lips, it sounded simply inevitable—and right.

Even the cardinal from Chicago sat back with a look of bemusement that melted into a smile of agreement as he folded his arms across his chest. "Bingo!" he said.

Wednesday, January 31, 10:09 A.M.

Timothy Mulrennan was as surprised as any of his colleagues when he was chosen by lot as a scrutineer the
morning after his dramatic confession and attempt to withdraw from the conclave. He accepted the position without
argument, since it was truly the luck of the draft, sensing
in it perhaps some sort of divine consolation prize at having
been brought so close to the papacy before he came crash-
ing down.

As he and the other two *scrutatores* and three *infirmarii*
circled the chapel, handing out the ballot cards, he was
greeted with sincere smiles and an occasional comforting
pat on the hand. He did not return these private shows of
support, but solemnly continued about his business.

There had been no discussion among the electors before
balloting this morning. The entire assembly had wearied of
talk and debate during the fireworks of the previous days.
Instead, after a period of silent reflection and prayer, most
of the cardinals kept their heads low, intent on the single,
awesome purpose that had brought them there. Before each
man, on his green felt-covered desk, there was a Moroccan-
leather blotter, name holder, letter opener, and pens. His
scarlet biretta, the outward sign of his franchise and right
to be present, was placed atop the desk in full view.

Returning to his place with the scrutineers and revisers
on chairs that faced the entire assembly, Mulrennan looked
down at his own ballot card and debated what to do. He
had announced he would not vote but had been urged by
Cardinal De Guzman and many others to reconsider. He
held pen over paper, considering his decision. Finally he
put the pen aside and folded the card, still blank, waiting
for his turn to place it in the receiving chalice. He would
not vote—not this time, at least. A blank card would count
as an invalid vote but would not invalidate the entire ballot.
Perhaps on the next ballot, if one was required, he would
change his mind. He would remain open to that possibility.
When his turn came, he stood and deliberately approached

the chalice where each ballot card was placed. Holding his card over the it, he intoned, "I call to witness—"

Why is there no name? a voice whispered.

Mulrennan spun in place, looking behind him, as a wave of dizziness flooded through him. He was alone, the voice only in his head. He turned back around, saw the expectant faces of the cardinals waiting for him to finish the task so that the next man could vote. He looked toward the chalice.

"I call to witness Christ the Lord," he said, his voice quavering slightly.

The voice returned: *Where is your name?*

His vision blurred, and as he stood blinking his eyes, he saw a line of men appear before him. Each was waiting to place his ballot. It was a long line; he recognized only a few. And they were robed not in red but in white. Pius XII was in sixth position down the line, with John XXIII, Paul VI, and John Paul I standing in order in front of him. Just ahead of them was the late pontiff, not the old man so recently laid to rest but the vigorous, youthful one who had first donned the papal vestments, taking the entire world by surprise. He was not at the head of the line, however, nor was he the one who had spoken to the American cardinal.

Another stood in that place, his face largely hidden in deep shadows. Mulrennan tried to pierce that darkness, to see the recognizably blunt features of Pietro La Spina, perhaps, or an otherwise recognizable figure. But it was within a black abyss, a deepness that both frightened and comforted in kind. Like his companions, the stranger wore the papal vestments, but the white cloth bore streaks of red. Mulrennan wondered if it was blood, perhaps the Stigmata . . . or it could be a sign that the red robes of a cardinal had not fully transformed into white, just as the new pope's face was not yet revealed.

As Mulrennan, ballot suspended over the chalice cup, stared at him, the shadowed figure again spoke. The voice was clear but without distinct personality, like an echo ringing in Timothy's brain.

Walk with us, my son. Have no fear of what is past or what is yet to come. . . .

Mulrennan did not feel the card slipping from his fingers.

As it floated down into the chalice, he stepped forward, as
if in a dream, accepting the shadowed hand, walking with
the recently deceased Holy Father and the others as they
led him from the altar and back to his chair.

The vision—if that is what it was—passed as quickly as
it had come, leaving him empty and restless. Mulrennan
found himself seated back among the scrutineers as the final
votes were cast. He felt somehow embarrassed, as if he had
stumbled or fainted in front of the crowd. But no one
looked at him amiss, none seemed to have noticed that anything strange had happened. In fact, he himself began to
doubt whether he had seen what he thought he had seen
. . . heard what he thought he had heard.

Mulrennan was still in something of a fog as the voting
concluded and he and his fellow scrutineers and revisers
began to sort and count the ballots. The numerous votes for
Cardinal Vennholme's chosen candidate were not unexpected, but what surprised Mulrennan was that they were
not accompanied by random votes for a half dozen or more
new entries in the race. Instead, the balloting went back
and forth almost evenly between just two names: Pietro La
Spina and Jaime De Guzman. Somehow—and Timothy
Mulrennan could only guess how (Biagi? who else?)—a
concerted, last-minute effort had been undertaken to oppose
the candidacy of Cardinal Vennholme's designated man.

As the counting concluded, Timothy Mulrennan glanced
over toward Cardinal Biagi and tried not to smile, did not
want to reveal his feelings about the results. In earlier balloting, La Spina had captured nearly half of the 116 ballots
cast, with a minimum of two-thirds canonically required for
election. This morning he received sixty-two votes, a slight
increase but well below the required and expected seventy-
eight. De Guzman, meanwhile, who had received only a
few token votes in the earliest balloting before disappearing
from the field, suddenly emerged with fifty-two votes of his
own. This was a surprising and a formidable showing that
would signal to the conclave that the expected result—
Vennholme's result—was no more a foregone conclusion.
There was a new horse in the race, and all bets were off.

When the tally was announced, Mulrennan could see the

shock written on Jaime De Guzman's face. He searched
that face, as he did La Spina's, for some sign, some signal,
of whom the Lord's shadowed servant might be.

At least it isn't me—not any longer, he breathed in relief.
*No matter how it goes, no matter who is chosen, I can soon
return home to my family, my friends, and my life.* He
scanned the princely and political ranks in the chapel.

The aged Cardinal Portillo, who had struggled without
success to keep this rambunctious conclave under control,
slumped in his chair, visibly relieved. Biagi and some others in the assembly sat straighter in their high-backed thronelike chairs. Cardinal Giannantonio looked toward Henry
Martin Vennholme, who moved not a muscle, nor betrayed
any emotion with his eyes. La Spina, the stocky, dark-
browed politician from peasant stock showed spots of pink
on his high cheekbones and clasped and unclasped his thick
hands. And De Guzman, the Filipino bantam, whom nearly
everyone in the chamber respected after his speech of the
previous day, slowly shook his head in disbelief and stared
straight ahead. No one spoke, but the volume had been
turned up to maximum level.

The voting process was immediately repeated. The total
vote after the second morning ballot stood at forty-six for
La Spina and sixty-eight for De Guzman!

Now there was an electric sense within the conclave of
momentum toward a consensus winner. Leandro Biagi
jumped to his feet to request the suspension of the rules in
order to hold a third morning vote. But the camerlengo
wisely shook his old Jesuitical head. "Some of us need
sustenance," he said, with a thin, mottled hand pressed to
his breast. He rose unsteadily and led the college in a brief
prayer. "May the Holy Ghost continue to reside in our
hearts," he intoned, and he admonished his fellow electors
that there would be no caucusing during the brief break
for luncheon, that the time must be spent in quiet contemplation of their difficult responsibility. Even he knew,
however, that there would be urgent whisperings and horse-
trading during the next two hours. With a collective audible
sigh, the Sacred College of Cardinals adjourned to the dining room in the residence.

The noon meal was eaten in near silence by most of the electors, who then retreated for a quiet hour or so. Some of them paired off for consultations, but most adhered to Portillo's instruction. Henry Vennholme and Pasquale Giannantonio strode purposefully down the hallway together, then entered his apartment.

Vennholme closed the door almost too deliberately, as if he were holding himself back, afraid of his own emotions. He stepped to the center of the room where Giannantonio stood, downcast. The two cardinals had consumed their sparse lunch quickly and walked out together without exchanging a word. La Spina, to whom Vennholme urgently wanted to speak, ignored Vennholme's invitation back to his quarters. Vennholme silently cursed the man. Now he faced the one who had failed him in the most important mission that he—or rather, the Evangelium Christi movement—had ever undertaken.

"This is not a positive development," Giannantonio said feebly, with a helpless shrug. "I thought it would be over by now."

Barely acknowledging the presence of the other, Vennholme spat, "I do not think I can abide another pope who gets down on his knees to put his lips to airport asphalt. My stomach will not take it. At least De Guzman doesn't know how to ski! Or does he?" He shot Giannantonio an evil look.

"I know not, Your Eminence," the Italian sputtered. He saw his own career crumbling before him and felt the wrath of his mentor boiling up hotly, out of control.

"There will be no further communication with the outside about this—turn of events. Did you see the look on Merry Yuen's face in there? He certainly knows something. But what? Biagi? I can hardly believe he would support the Filipino . . . but it is like him to ride a dark horse. Our problem is, De Guzman is more than acceptable to most of the College. He has no enemies." The concept baffled Vennholme, who screwed up his face with contempt.

"If we had known, perhaps we could have identified some enemies—something. Surely he cannot be without some faults."

"No, he is a fallible and stupid human being, like the rest of us." Vennholme spoke the words without irony. "But time is short. If only I could reach my Evangelium brothers before the next ballot. Somehow, if we could delay the vote—" But he knew this was a near impossiblity. He checked his watch: only forty minutes to go until they reconvened for the tenth ballot of the conclave. His gut told him it was over, but he could not accept this as a fact, not after all the work and preparation and prayer by his colleagues in the worldwide Evangelium community. What would Frank Darragh make of this failure? Only the disgrace of Mulrennan would partially salvage their efforts.

"What can I do, Eminence?" Giannantonio asked, hoping beyond hope that his senior colleague would have some task he could perform that would take his mind off this debacle. Vennholme made his thorough displeasure as clear as cold, polished glass: he said nothing.

Giannantonio responded to a hesitant rap at the door. He opened it to admit Cardinal La Spina, who lumbered like a pitiful wounded bull toward Vennholme.

"I decided to come, after all," he said to the dour man. "Not that it has any purpose now."

"Do not lose hope, dear Pietro. Our brothers are perhaps reacting emotionally. They will still see that the best course for all of us is your election. Perhaps on the next ballot," Vennholme said, swallowing his ire.

"For *all of us?* For you, Henry, yes. But for me? I understand that you wished to be Secretary of State if I were elected pope."

"Only if the pontiff were to so choose. I am available to serve him and the Church Universal in any capacity." Vennholme glanced behind La Spina's shoulder to see Giannantonio lift his eyebrows heavenward. "I honor the constitution issued by our holy deceased brother that provides there shall be no agreements or quid pro quo arrangements made during the election. Have I ever made such a proposal or demand of you?"

"No, but it is said—"

"Said by whom, Pietro? Who would say such a false thing of you and me?" Vennholme subtly cast the net so as to be sure to entangle La Spina along with himself.

"Some of the Italian brethren do not like this idea."

"But there is no such 'idea,' " Vennholme countered. "Perhaps in their own minds, or—" He paused as the insight dawned. "Perhaps Cardinal Biagi has poisoned them with this thought. It is an evil thing for him to do this, do you not agree, my friend?"

"I don't know what is evil, or what is good for that matter, anymore." La Spina clasped his pudgy hands against his ample midsection; the black hair on his knuckles covered the sapphire of his cardinal's ring. In this moment he looked the part of the medieval prince who, after a lifetime of waiting, saw the anticipated throne slipping from his grasp. "I think it would be better to ask them to vote for the other man. He is going to win in any case."

"Only because you have given up, not because he is the better man. I can see that you have lost the will to fight for what is yours by merit and right. I am sad and ashamed for you, my brother."

Pietro Cardinal La Spina, a veteran of three decades of Curial and Italian-Church politics had shrunk visibly under Vennholme's withering words. What would his dearly beloved—no, worshiped—ninety-seven-year-old mother say about such treatment of her equally adored son? She, after all, had raised him to be as tough as a mule and as stout as a barrel. He felt that he had failed *her* somehow. And it was her judgment, after Christ's own, that he feared more than anyone's, even this would-be great elector.

The Tuscan countryside of his youth called to him in his troubled mind. There he had labored as a boy, beside his father, for the landlord. The sun beckoned him. He could count on one hand the number of times he had napped under a spreading tree on a steep hillside—and yet he drank in the memory of each stolen minute he had thus spent: a part of the very earth whence he, like Adam, like all men, had sprung. One earth. One God. One Church. Soon, one pope—and it would not be Pietro La Spina, the awkward peasant boy of sixty years ago, who assumed the throne of his namesake. He had already considered what name he would take if he were elected: Pius. The thirteenth of that

name and fourth within the past one hundred years. The
Church needed a pope of piety and strength, and he had
been ready—and Vennholme had been so certain.

"I am ashamed for you," La Spina responded quietly.
"As much as I believe—as you do—that our Holy Church
has been led astray by false prophets and self-concerned,
weak-minded theologians, I cannot think, however, that
Our Lord would abandon His children. We must have more
faith than that, and the humility to admit our errors and
allow the Holy Spirit to show us the truth. I am not afraid
to stand naked before God and man and let *Him* judge me."

"Naïve and pious talk, my brother. God does not will our
weakness; He abhors such lack of conviction in any Christian, but especially one of his bishops. We are his elect.
We show the others His way. We must be courageous in
the face of our enemies But I do fear for us all if we elect
the wrong man here today."

When La Spina hesitated to answer, to say anything,
Giannantonio moved closer to these two fiercely proud
churchmen. If God abhorred sin, Pasquale Giannantonio abhorred silence.

"Both cardinals are correct, of course, but I humbly suggest to the eminent Archbishop of Turin that humility *demands* obedience and putting aside one's own will in favor
of Almighty God's."

"A fine, if useless point, brother," La Spina acknowledged with ill-concealed condescension. "I am fully prepared to accept my Father's will as expressed through the
Holy Spirit in the decision of the conclave."

Vennholme felt the unmistakable stirrings of that old bottomless rage within himself. He fought to control his
tongue. He wanted to give this fat prick the lashing he so
richly deserved. He wanted to show the world—or, at least
the only audience he had, the hapless Giannantonio—that
this would-be pope was unworthy even to put the Roman
collar of the priesthood around his thick red peasant's neck.
He wanted so badly . . .

"Get out of my sight," he said viciously to the Archbishop of Turin. "And you—" He turned to Pasquale Giannantonio. "Tell our camerlengo that I am suddenly taken

ill, and I shall not attend the next balloting session. I must rest my tired body and pray—for the soul of Christ's Church."

La Spina glanced at Giannantonio, who looked like a stunned schoolboy whom the teacher has accused unjustly of some classroom malfeasance. Both men mumbled their inaudible good-byes and left to his own thoughts the trim, severe man who had helped shape their ecclesiastical careers. The door clicked shut behind the silent, departing pair.

Henry Martin Cardinal Vennholme, the desperately lonely orphan from Montreal, fell to his knees on the floor of his conclave apartment. "My God, why have You deserted Your Church in her hour of crisis? Are we not worthy of Your love and care? What wrong have I done to see our great plan in such a shambles? Why, O God, why?" Tears of rage and sorrow streaked his thin, sad face.

They gathered once more under the baleful eye of the wraithlike Spanish Jesuit who sat before them like a sacred gargoyle, bent and poised to spring from his makeshift throne upon any who displeased him. Cardinal Portillo was determined to bring this contentious conclave to an end— to elect a pope, for God's sake. Never in his career, not even in the 1978 conclaves when he was a comparatively junior elector in awe of these giants of the Church, had he felt the weight of responsibility so heavily. In those two pivotal elections he had seen the lions in action: maneuvering, bargaining, persuading, leading, arm-twisting. In this one the camerlengo sensed that the same thing was occurring, but away from his direct hearing, since he would rule it completely out of order and contrary to the letter and spirit of the apostolic constitution they had all sworn to uphold. He was troubled that Vennholme had chosen not to be present for the vote this afternoon. He somehow doubted the absent cardinal was really ailing. Perhaps it would be the final vote. De Guzman had come from virtually nowhere this morning to take a firm, possibly insurmountable lead. If he did not secure the needed total on this tally, however, all bets were off. And if La Spina fell off the chart, there was still time—please, God, let it not happen!—for another papabile to emerge. Portillo was quickly getting used to the idea of the quiet man from the Philippines as the next one. He might make a worthy successor to the old Slavic saint after all.

The camerlengo had sent one of the *infirmarii* to Vennholme's room with a ballot, as prescribed by the rules of the conclave, but it had come back untouched.

Timothy John Mulrennan, the all-American cardinal disgraced by scandal and innuendo, sat, outwardly calm, erect in his chair as a *scrutatore* for, he too fervently hoped, the very last time. The air within the Sistina was laden with expectation, as palpable as an extraheavy dose of pungent incense.

Cardinal Musselthwaite of Sydney knelt before the altar, then raised his immense bulk and approached the twenty-five-inch-tall golden chalice that for three hundred years had been used in this very manner, to elect twenty-five Successors to St. Peter, and placed his ballot upon the paten. He then lifted the gleaming plate and repeated the oath that had accompanied each vote of the conclave: *"Testor Christum Dominum, qui me judicanturus est, me eligere, quen secundum Deum judico eligi debere.* I call to witness Christ the Lord who will be my judge, that my vote is given to the one who before God I consider should be elected." He bowed deeply to the gold-and-bronze cast crucifix upon the altar and walked swiftly back to his place. He sat, hands folded, expressionless.

When all the ballots had been deposited the three scrutineers shook the chalice to mingle the folded cards. Mulrennan, as the third *scrutatore*, lifted out one ballot at a time, opened it, and announced the name inscribed on it. One by one, each of the other scrutineers also read out the name and noted it. Tim noticed that the handwriting of the electors was not disguised this time. They all must have felt there was no need on this round of voting. He read only one name for the first thirty or so ballots: *"Reverendissium dominum Cardinalem* Jaime De Guzman."

The vote tally was ninety-three for De Guzman, twenty for La Spina, and two for noncontenders.

Jaime De Guzman sat with his face buried in his hands. Applause and cheers rang through the high-vaulted Renaissance chamber, but the 263rd pope appeared to hear none of it. Mulrennan stood and applauded with the others, and he wondered what was going through the mind of the gentle soul who had just received the most awesome responsibility and greatest shock of a lifetime in service to the Catholic Church. He already had great affection for the pious Filipino, and now the man also had his heartfelt sympathy; he whispered a prayer for the new pontiff's health and well-being.

Tim Mulrennan caught his friend Allo Biagi's beaming visage. Biagi actually winked at him. This caused Mulrennan to smile ironically. There would have been no winking if *he* had been sitting in De Guzman's chair.

CHAPTER THIRTEEN

Berlin, January 17, 1990

The recently appointed secretary of the Sacred Congregation for Bishops, Timothy Mulrennan, waited in a tenth-floor hotel room in Berlin, the formerly walled-off eastern capital, for his appointment. A bowl of fruit and bottles of water on a table by the window contrasted with the heavy draperies redolent of smoke, and the desolate view from the window itself. The building had been erected in the 1970s, during the later years of the East German communist regime, and it looked and felt insubstantial, slapped in place, concrete and steel of dubious quality. God forbid there was a bomb attack or earthquake, the box would crumble to dust and take everyone inside with it. Shoddy socialist workmanship and drab decor, if it could even be called that . . .

Mulrennan was on a mission. Was it diplomacy or espionage? He smiled to himself as he sat near the window and looked out on the gray urban landscape of Berlin. There was already talk of moving the unified national government back to its traditional home, a once-magnificent and powerful city. But how could these people of the eastern bloc ever be given back their lives, the years that communism had taken from them? *And why the hell did I agree to put myself in the middle of this geopolitical mess?* he asked himself for the hundredth time.

He waited, his dark thoughts bringing him down. He thought of Rachel, of Jackson City, of the years of his life invested in turning around the troubled diocese, of the surprise Vatican announcement of his appointment to the Curia as an archbishop. Archbishop! He had never explicitly allowed himself to hope for such a thing. Yet secretly, within his homesick soul, he had wanted and wondered and once in a while let his mind wander in that direction . . . and now it had come true. As much as he would have loved to stay in Missouri or return to New Jersey, to his own home diocese, he had accepted his lot and set himself to learn the workings of the famously arcane bureaucracy of the Curia Romana, the collection of offices and agencies that implemented the work of the papacy. It was actually one of the most long-lived structures of government in the world, loosely based on the Roman system, which had evolved from the advisory councils that had served the earliest popes and been fixed in its current form, more or less, in the sixteenth century.

It would take years, decades even, Tim realized, to master such a structure—if that was even possible for a rank outsider like himself, especially an American.

A month earlier, after a high mass of thanksgiving at the National Shrine, celebrated for pilgrims from the Newark archdiocese, Tim Mulrennan—who had been visiting his family over the Christmas holiday—as well as the papal pronuncio, the current Archbishop of Newark, and several pastors who had accompanied him to Washington, D.C., were invited by President and Mrs. Bush to a White House reception. It was the first time Mulrennan had been inside the executive mansion since he toured the nation's capital with his senior class in high school. The day was gray and chilly; as busloads of New Jerseyans departed for home, the archbishops and several others rode to the president's house in limousines that deposited them at the famous front door.

Secret Service agents escorted them to a holding area where the men in black—the priests and their archbishop— were gingerly frisked. Then they were efficiently guided to the Blue Room where tea and coffee and snacks were served and they mingled with White House staff, several congressmen, and local Catholic, Protestant, and Jewish clergy who were nonplussed by the executive largesse. But Tim avidly drank in everything from the draperies to the china service. Then he saw his sister Kathleen and her husband, David Stanton, who was assistant secretary of defense for strategic affairs (whatever that meant!), and he greeted them both warmly and with relief at knowing somebody in this rarified gathering.

He hugged and kissed his sister. "Wow! So good to see you," he said, "and you look so elegant!" She was wearing a black suit over a silk blouse, and her hair was cut shorter than it had ever been; her pearl necklace and earrings were understated and absolutely perfect on her. He could hardly believe that his youngest sister was one of the most highly respected law professors at Georgetown University School of Law, married to an up-and-coming government official who was the darling of the conservative wing of the Republican party.

She had always been intellectually combative and ambitious, had stood out from the rest of the pack throughout her school career. And the two of them, brother and sister, had often clashed on social issues, debated and disagreed, sometimes bitterly. His heart went out to her—and her husband: they had been unable to conceive a child. Only recently, after a decade of tests and therapies, they had begun seriously to discuss adoption.

"And you are as handsome as ever," she allowed. Her teeth gleamed with perfection as she smiled. "We just flew back from ten days in Indonesia. David and I rarely come to any of these grip-and-grin fests, but we couldn't *not* see you today."

The archbishop greeted David Stanton, a stocky, shorter-than-average man in his middle thirties; he wore his hair in a brown helmet that added a couple of inches to his stature. His starched French-cuff shirt shone from beneath a dark gray suit, and his presidential cufflinks flashed as he gave Tim a double-handed shake. Stanton also flashed his expensive teeth, confirming, with his wife, their status of confident prosperity and influence in the highest circles of U.S. government.

"Your Excellency."

"David, I'm really glad to see you both—I can't get over the two of you. . . ."

"Neither can we," Kate said. "We're pretty impressed

with ourselves!" She disarmed her brother with a wink. "How are Daddy and Rosemary?"

Tim filled her in on family gossip with the latest on their father and stepmother, siblings, and nieces and nephews. They had seen each other over Christmas, but so much happened these days with the younger generation: from the smallest scrapes to the grandest achievements.

Kathleen looked at her husband as she spoke. "The president will be here soon, just for a few minutes probably." Then she turned to her brother, the tall prelate. "Tim, David would like to meet with you after the reception."

"Over in the Old Executive Office Building, with the president's national security adviser, Admiral Cummins."

Mulrennan sipped his lukewarm coffee and regarded the power couple over the gold-painted rim of the cup. He hesitated before answering Stanton. "I have to get back to Newark this evening."

"We can arrange a shuttle flight if that would help," the younger man volunteered. "It may take a couple of hours, the meeting with Cummins."

"Are you sure you can't stay and have dinner with us tonight?" Kathleen asked.

The air quality of the room changed perceptibly as the president strode in, smiling and shaking hands. Mrs. Bush worked one side of the room, the president the other. Tim remained in place, flanked by his sister and brother-in-law, as the president approached; he greeted President Bush with a smile and a firm handshake.

"Archbishop, thank you for coming over today," the president said. "Kate, David, I hope you've made him feel at home. Good to see you both."

"They are excellent hosts, sir," Mulrennan said. "It's an honor to meet you."

"It's good to get some religion into this old house," the great man said. "Barbara and I don't get out to church very often ourselves. Ask 'em over, she said. Okay, I said. So here we are." He was faintly befuddled at the whole idea, but very relaxed, seemingly right at home. An aide pushed at his elbow and he moved on. "Come back sometime," he said to Tim.

"Thank you, sir," Tim responded as the president moved on to greet a covey of Roman-collared priests. He did not want to stay any longer than he had to, but he had decided to give David a hearing. The national security adviser? What the heck did he want with a Catholic archbishop from the Curia?

Well, it turned out that the U.S. Department of State had already spoken to the Vatican Secretariat of State and received permission to send Tim on a mission to Berlin, to meet with a former top man in the East German security apparatus, Lt. Gen. Ernst Karl Schraeder, now retired and ailing. So, he waited with as much patience as he could muster. . . .

Schraeder was scheduled to arrive at 11:00 A.M. local time. Mulrennan consulted his watch: just a few minutes before the hour. His stomach churned; he was reminded of his previous assignment in Berlin, more than forty years ago. He had been a kid then, really, a green lieutenant better prepared to jump out of an airplane than to operate in the world of military intelligence, though both thoughts scared him silly. Schraeder, too, had been awfully young—in his early thirties, perhaps. They had been barely old enough to qualify as enemies . . . and now what were they—friends? The world turned inexorably, and man struggled against man only to stand together in the end for mutual survival. Isn't this what Christ taught: simply love God, and love thy neighbor? Look not for the differences but for the common needs and interests.

A knock on the flimsy hotel room door punctuated Tim's thoughts. He rose and went to the door; he lifted the chain lock, opened the door. There were three men there, but two melted away before Mulrennan could make out who they were. Ernst Karl Schraeder quickly stepped into the room and stood face-to-face with Mulrennan. Tim relocked the door, a poor piece of security but all there was. The two men looked at each other, the closest they had ever been, the American thought; they shook hands briefly, and the American led the German inside, to the fruit-decorated table by the window where they both sat.

Mulrennan drew in a breath of the stale air that filled the

poorly air-conditioned room. As it irritated his nostrils, he imagined it was the piercing cold of that January morning in 1955 when he had first awakened in the barracks at Fort Dix. That was thirty-five years ago, after two intense college years at Yale and before he realized his dream of attending seminary and becoming a priest. He remembered exactly how it had looked—the ten rows of double-stacked bunk beds that ran down each side of the open bay area on the second floor of the drafty two-story wooden barracks, heated only by coal-burning furnaces. But that first night the trainees had fallen asleep, the furnaces had fallen cold and silent. When the men were awakened at four, it was to the bracing chill and the white fog of their breathing. And to the even more frigid reception by Master Sergeant Avery Turnbull—later they would secretly rename him Turnbucket, due to his penchant for kicking over their full mop buckets to show his displeasure at their cleaning efforts. After that first night, it would be a long time before any of them fell asleep on duty.

Mulrennan had excelled at basic training and was accepted for AIT—Advanced Individual Training—at the Infantry School, Fort Benning, Georgia. This was the first time the college kid from New Jersey had ever been in the deep South, and he discovered that he liked it: eight weeks from mid-March until the end of May. Frequent rains turned the red Georgia dirt into big wet clay balls that clung to his feet on the ten-mile road marches. He excelled in AIT and was awarded the rare, coveted Expert Infantryman's Badge, which he wore proudly throughout his service career.

While at Benning, PFC Tim Mulrennan applied for Infantry Officer Candidate School, and because of his outstanding record in basic, as well as his two years at Yale, he was promptly accepted. He began OCS in June 1956, and his class number—he still remembered it clearly—was 57-01.

"Military candidate!" the tactical officer shouted at the top of his lungs, jabbing Mulrennan's chest again. "Did I just see you swat an insect, military candidate?" Spittle sprayed from the man's mouth onto the young candidate's face.

Mulrennan stood in the brace position, back flat against the wall, stomach and chin drawn in, arms held rigidly at his sides, eyes staring straight ahead locked in their sockets so as not to move, even as the tactical officer's face ranged back and forth in front of him.

"Sir, Candidate Mulrennan, sir! I just swatted a mosquito, sir!"

"Who gave you permission to swat that mosquito, candidate? That was an insect, government-issue, mosquito-type, specially trained and put here for the specific purpose of biting you and other lower-than-whale-sperm candidates like you in the ass! That insect, government-issue mosquito-type, was, no doubt, a husband and a father, and you killed him. Now, what do you have to say to the family of that hardworking, highly trained, government-issue insect, mosquito-type, candidate?"

"Sir, Candidate Mulrennan, sir! The family of that hard-working, government insect, mosquito-type, has my con-dolences and my most sincere apology, sir!"

"Not good enough, Candidate Mulrennan! You are hereby directed to assemble a burial detail. At oh-five-thirty hours tomorrow, you and your burial detail will dig a six-foot-by-six-foot-by-three-foot grave at the far end of the parade ground. You will then inter, rendering full military honors, that poor deceased insect, mosquito-type. Do you understand your orders, candidate?"

"Sir, Candidate Mulrennan! I understand my orders, sir!"

Thus, at 0530 hours the following morning, with the en-tire class of 57-01 assembled in khakis, spit-shined shoes, and polished helmet liners, a military funeral was con-ducted for said insect, government-issue, mosquito-type, M1A1, military occupational specialty: candidate ass-biting!

Twenty-two weeks later, Timothy John Mulrennan was commissioned a second lieutenant, then attended jump school, again at Benning, and graduated in another three weeks as a fully qualified paratrooper. At a "prop blast" party at the officers' open mess club he enjoyed the tradi-

tional send-off for jump school grads: booze, raucous singing, and general bravado.

From one training level to the next, over a total of nine
months, he had become a different person, a professional
soldier, a grown man. And throughout—amid the physical
pain and mental intimidation, from the first forced march
to the final parachute jump, with each new achievement and
each new friend earned along the way—the commitment to
his future vocation never wavered. He *knew* he was meant
to be a priest, convinced that God's purpose matched the
plan of his own heart. But before the seminary, there was
a war to be fought—a cold and clandestine one.

Now the man who sat with him in a faraway city where
he had once been stationed looked like a defeated soldier
of that bitterly contested cold war.

"I was assured that there are no devices in this room,"
Mulrennan said.

"I do not believe that, but there's no one to listen; perhaps a tape will turn up in the archives fifty years from
now—when we're both dead."

The German paused and pulled a pack of cigarettes from
the pocket inside his houndstooth jacket. His eyes, behind
the steel-rimmed glasses, focused on the cigarettes and the
lighter that he produced, flicking it, flaming the tip of the
cigarette. He breathed in deeply and exhaled a plume of
smoke toward the window. Mulrennan shifted in his chair.
The powerful nicotine urge exploded within him, then
quickly passed and changed to disgust at the foul smell of
the burning tobacco.

"I understand that you have a list you wish to give to
my government," he said.

"Yes, a list. This has historical importance, perhaps not
as much relevance today as it might have even a year ago.
It is a list of former agents, some German and some American, who worked for the people of East Germany and
against her enemies in the West. It is my understanding that
there will be no prosecutions of any former double agents
by your government."

"If that's what our people told you, then that's what it
will be. I have no authority to change any agreement, only

to take possession of the list and bring it safely back to Washington. They say you asked for me specifically."

"I did. I remember you from the old days." The merest shadow of a smile appeared on Schraeder's thin, dark face. "You were very sincere, very hardworking in those days."

"I hope I am the same now."

"We are older, more experienced in the ways of the world—politics, ambitions, reality—and we have seen the rise and fall of systems that we never dreamed would one day not exist. It is difficult to fathom—" The German's face knotted as he drew deeply on his cigarette and exhaled the smoke again. "I believed with every ounce of my being that we would prevail over the West."

"You were wrong," Tim said simply.

"That is very easy for your side to say now, however it was not always so, in fact, we were very right: the exploiters won the immediate battle due to their overwhelming economic power. We became embroiled in our own petty concerns and lost sight of the true goal of our struggle. Now, in my lifetime, there will be no victory for the people."

"Ernst, I had the highest respect for you; I even feared you in those days. You were part of an awesome espionage machinery that threatened our very existence. I remember that time we faced off over poor old Herr Busch, the shoemaker."

"Yes, he was trouble for our side. He fooled us by hiding microfilm not in the heel of the shoe, or even the sole, but in the tip of the shoelace! Very clever man. A dedicated capitalist and enemy of the revolution."

"We lost him to you," Mulrennan said, a dark, sick feeling rising in his throat.

Through the smoke haze from his god-awful–smelling cigarette, Schraeder regarded the Roman Catholic archbishop with an odd and contradictory mixture of curiosity, admiration, and contempt. He could not help himself: he had survived war and national defeat, been raised in the communist system and scarred by its bureaucracy. The price of survival for all these years was a heavy one. He had little to show but his memories of power and position,

the medals and insignia of his service to the state as a lieutenant general of the security services—and his lists of
names with which to bargain for petty favors. Perhaps this
one would buy his wife a coat, or just keep the rent col-
lectors from their door for a few months. They had never
had children . . . and now he was glad for that, because
there was nothing—less than nothing—to leave behind in
this brave, strange new world.

Tim Mulrennan clung to the flotsam of his own thoughts
and remembered history as the wave swelled and pulled
him out to sea. He could almost taste the salt and feel the
cold, wet, dangerous tide, the inexorable force of time and
memory. In thirty-three years the world had been killed and
cleansed and burned, like an ancient holocaust offering in
the temple. Now there remained ashes and smoke on the
sacrificial altar, and the priests in their robes standing by
ready for the next one. Who—or what—would it be, that
next sacrifice? How would this world be reborn? He and
Schraeder became less relevant with each passing minute;
their legacies were fading as quickly as they could speak
or write or attempt to pass on anything of note to an uninterested successor generation.

What of that old man, now long dead, Herr Busch? Tim
had been stationed in Berlin for just a few months when
the trickle of information from the shoemaker in the Soviet
zone had dried up, and he was given the task to find out
why.

He spoke with the civilian intelligence authorities, who
shrugged their shoulders: the source was not that important,
a few little items of interest once in a while, no exposure
to our side . . . not worth chasing. But he did some research,
found out the old guy had been a World War I veteran,
badly injured, mustered out with a minuscule pension by
the Weimar government, married with three children, all of
whom were lost in the next war, pension dried up, forced
to work in a clothing factory during the war years, learned
the shoemaking trade, eked out a living in the occupied
sector, recruited by a British agent to serve as a conduit for
microfilmed Soviet military-personnel files. Busch had not
ever met the agent face-to-face, took delivery of the con-

traband film in a dead drop near his apartment, hid the stuff in shoelace tips that somehow made their way into the British or American sectors—very clean, very impersonal, very efficient. Until it stopped coming. The British pulled the plug, and the Americans were about to, when Tim was asked to investigate. He was given just two days to come up with an answer. With the address of the old man's shop in the pocket of his civilian coat, he slipped across the line into the Soviet-controlled zone to see for himself. . . .

The cobbled street was spit-shine black in the damp October night, only haphazardly illuminated by a dim street-lamp or light from an open window. The drizzle settled coldly on his shoulders and on the felt hat he had borrowed from a clerk in the office; the cold seeped through the outer clothing into his bones. He was alone and afraid and almost turned back but for no good reason went ahead, walking deeper into the enemy's sector, following the occasional street sign, with only a vague idea of where he was going. His German was adequate—barely. It would be easy to pick him out as an American. He was taller and better fed than most, so he stooped a bit, trying to be inconspicuous, which was acutely difficult as he was virtually alone on the streets. The few passersby whom he encountered did not even look at him but went their own way. He walked past one policeman who nodded at him but said nothing. He shoved his hands into the coat pockets in a vain attempt to warm them. He carried no weapon; if he were caught he did not want to give them any tangible evidence of his intention. He had a thought: the address. He took the scrap of paper on which he had scribbled the information and put it in his mouth. He chewed it for a good long time as he wound through the deserted city streets. He eventually swallowed the paper and grimaced at the inky taste.

So this was what being a spy meant? He nearly laughed aloud at the comedy and inanity of it. He thought he must at least *look* like a secret agent in the absurd coat and borrowed fedora. He had been reading Eric Ambler stories, too many of them, and they kept him up nights. He was getting too little sleep, and he felt it now.

Tim Mulrennan, a year and a half out of OCS and just

a few months graduated from intelligence training, turned
into an unfamiliar *platz* that was too starkly lit and quickly
turned right onto another, narrower street. He followed the
cold paving stones to the next block where he turned left;
he had only a vague idea where he was now, but thought
he might be close. He searched his brain for the map details
that he had memorized. Confident that he was only slightly
off course, he circled left again, still avoiding the open
platz, and found the secondary allée that would lead him
to the street he sought. He stayed in the shadow as much
as possible and strained to make out the street numbers on
the buildings as he passed. Mostly houses, with a few non-
descript shops, mostly postwar construction, undistin-
guished, drab architecture. Occasionally there was an
elegant older building still standing, dwarfed by the failed-
grandiose newer structures.

He found the *strasse* he was looking for and followed
the numbers to a dark little shop with a walk-down entrance. He gingerly stepped down, knocked on the door,
got no answer; he tried hard to peer through the glass but
saw only black, not a stirring inside, nothing.

He quickly moved away from the door, walked a half
block east, slowed. His footfalls sounded like cannon shots.
He crossed the street and circled back to observe the shop.

Faintly at first, he hear the sound of an approaching vehicle bouncing over the cobbled pavement. The rough engine noise grew louder. Mulrennan walked quickly away,
trying to find someplace to turn off the street, out of sight.
Headlights swept the *strasse*, and the American turned to
face the automobile; it sped forward, then slowed. Tim's
first instinct was to run, but he froze as two men exited the
car and deliberately walked toward him. . . .

"You had the wrong address," Ernst Karl Schraeder said,
wrenching Mulrennan back to the present. "The shop was
half a kilometer away."

"I found that out later. I was a lousy spy," Archbishop
Mulrennan admitted. "I don't even know why I went in—
the risk far outweighed any reward."

"You were concerned about your source. That is natural
and right. But he was such a minor player. We did not even

arrest him. We simply put him under open surveillance and stopped the flow of information. He died a few months later."

"Your boys hustled me out of the sector. Why didn't they arrest me?"

"I was the driver of the car that night," Schraeder said. "They were Russians. They wanted to beat you, but I said no. I didn't want to create a mess because I was scheduled to be promoted, move into a larger office, get a secretary of my own—a pretty one. It was late, and I wanted to go home; I did not do my job very well that night, either."

Mulrennan faced the man who had driven him to the checkpoint and ordered the Russians to deposit him on the other side of the guardhouse. He was left standing there in his ill-fitting coat and hat as rain began to fall in cold hard pellets.

"So what was the point of the exercise? What did either side gain by it?"

Schraeder considered for a moment, puffing on his cigarette, which by now was an ashy stub, dangerously close to his brown-yellow fingertips. He, too, vividly remembered that night, the green American who had stumbled into trouble that could have cost him his life, as well as the life of his contact in the enemy sector. In subsequent years he had followed Tim Mulrennan's career, almost paternally, watching him rise within the Catholic hierarchy, wondering if one day their paths might cross again—as indeed they now had. Schraeder had thought his request to meet with Tim might be refused, was secretly astounded when it was granted.

"We gained knowledge of each other, which is the true value of intelligence. We did many things wrong, a few things right. Ultimately your side won because your economy was stronger; we never did figure out how to make socialism as attractive as personal and national prosperity. People's natural greed prevailed, you might say, over the common interest."

"Or the right won out against the wrong, is another way of putting it. Even your personal kindness to me back then was a victory for morality. And nothing forced you to behave that way; it is a natural human response."

"I thought of it as a moment of weakness," Schraeder said.

"Well, that's a refreshing thought. Blessed are the weak. General Schraeder, we should attend to the business at hand. I do not want to risk your safety in any way by detaining you too long. As much as I enjoy reminiscing about our previous encounter—and I do." The archbishop watched the old spymaster light another malodorous cigarette. It was painful to contemplate this cadaverous apparition in the process of killing himself. "You have something that I am to bring back to my government."

"Yes, business. Americans are very good at that—even the religious ones; perhaps they are the best of all, like your television preachers. Many of our people have become evangelical Christians in recent years, thanks to television."

"I think it has something to do with the message, as well," Mulrennan argued, silently kicking himself for getting drawn in to a discussion he did not want to have.

"All right, you are impatient. Well, I have two things for you. One is this—" He pulled a battered envelope from the same pocket where he secreted his cigarettes. He placed it on the table between them. "It is the list of our double agents, whom we ran in the U.S. from 1947 to 1989. It is very complete. Probably there will be few surprises, but your people will be glad to have it to confirm their own conclusions."

"Thank you, General. From the president and his National Security Council, we are most grateful." Tim touched the envelope but did not open it. "I appreciate personally what you have done, sir. Today and at our first encounter."

"I also have something else—for you, personally, as you say. This is not a document but a warning. I have cast a very wide net in my time, out of self-protection as well as the people's security, you understand." He raised himself with some difficulty and apparent pain to a straighter posture, gripping the cigarette with fervor. "I learned things, observed things, that came across my desk, and I sent my agents out to verify information. For many years I watched this group you call Evangelium Christi, a so-called lay organization within your Church. You are very familiar with this organization, I think."

"I am," he replied simply, trying to mask his deep curiosity.

"These people are your enemies. This I can tell you with certainty. They have spies everywhere, even in your own city. They have followed you, reported on you, for many years. You were in a place called Jackson City until recently, am I correct?"

"Yes."

"There were problems there, financial problems, were there not?"

"Yes."

"These problems were of much interest to the Evangelium spies and their masters. In Rome these problems were discussed—you were discussed. Your future was discussed. Oh, they are very interested in you, Herr Archbishop."

Tim said, "They must have better things to do than follow me around."

"They wish to control the policies of your Church through a few leaders of the Curia. They are very well financed and focused on their goals. They are to be much feared." Schraeder struggled to push himself upright. "I fear no man any longer, only death," he said.

Mulrennan moved toward him, grasped his hand, felt the coldness and sickness in the withered claw of a man who had been an avowed enemy yet who had spared him interrogation, torture, and perhaps even death.

"You need not fear even that."

"Do not try to convert me to your way at this late stage of my life, Excellency. I am an old atheistic dinosaur. My mother was a believer, until she died. She prayed for my soul every day of my life, I think. We shall see if it had any effect."

"Oh, I can tell you that it had an effect, Herr General. What you did today—probably there are countless little things that you kept from others, that she never knew. I know her prayers, and her example, shaped you."

"But does any of that outweigh the harm I wrought? I could list a thousand times when someone died on my orders, when a family or a career was destroyed. I had that kind of power, and I used it. For forty years I used it as naturally as breathing—which comes hard to me now." He smiled vaguely.

"How do you reconcile the inherent conflict in what you do? I mean, as a priest of God and a man of financial and political responsibilities? As a boy growing up I knew some priests, but they were scruffy aliens, the lowest on the totem pole, as you would say. You—well, when we knew each other forty years ago, you were a soldier and a worthy enemy."

Tim Mulrennan smiled wanly. "How do I answer that?"

"Not with a question, if you please. I am trying to understand you—and your world."

"We live in the same world, Ernst. Yes, we have been on different sides due to politics and religion. But in my sphere of activity, there is no room for hatred. Not that it doesn't happen; some Christians, yes, Catholics, hate other people: neighbors, enemies, different religious groups, God only knows who else. My job, however, requires that I love others—that I love you and every communist and every security policeman and every person in my diocese and my colleagues in the clergy—just as I profess to love God and to obey Him. I can tell you, I fall short of that ideal every minute of every day, especially when I'm driving." Schraeder and Tim both laughed. "Do you have crazy drivers here?"

"Germans drive too fast, but they obey the traffic laws. The competition is to see who is best at following the rules!"

"The conflict lies in being human, in having a choice as to how one behaves. I can be a terribly grouchy, demanding sonofabitch much of the time with my staff, but I try not to be when I catch myself, or when they call me on my stuff. I was an enemy of communism, as an American and a Christian, but that doesn't mean I have to hate every person on the other side of the wall." He pulled a pen from his pocket and fiddled with it as he spoke, tapping it on the opposite palm. "As a priest, and especially as a bishop, I see myself as a servant, not a ruler, of others. There are many important responsibilities, yes, that go with the office—property, money, employees, parishioners, fellow priests and religious, the duty to comfort and help those in need—and certain powers, especially in the sacraments. It's genuinely exciting and daunting; there's nothing else like it, being a part of the apostolic succession that dates back to Christ and the Fishermen of Galilee. You can look back on your ideological ancestors in the same way, I'd imagine."

"They have been discredited and defeated. Your Church has become more powerful in this century, after a long decline. How do you explain that?"

"The hand of God. And the hard work of men and women who believe in what they do. Leadership. John Paul II has given us the energy and direction we have been lacking since the Vatican Council. Yes, we have stumbled, often and badly and all over the world. But we have learned from our mistakes. And the people are coming to us, coming *back* in many cases. We have not relinquished one iota of the truth of our faith. We pray a lot, we talk to each other, we talk to our traditional antagonists. Look, you and I are sitting here speaking to one another."

"That is something, I agree."

Schraeder and his ghostly security detail left Tim Mulrennan alone in the depressing hotel room with a packet of information that contained the names of all the East German agents who had operated in the United States and Western Europe from 1947 through 1989.

CHAPTER FOURTEEN

January 31, 4:20 P.M.

Frank Darragh sat transfixed at the desk in his suite in the Hotel Columbus, staring at the screen of his laptop computer, reading the incoming E-mail message from his source within the conclave: "Unhappy prospect that De Guzman of Manila will be elected. Our work has been frustrated. And our prayers have gone unanswered. Release all information in hand about Mulrennan." There was no greeting or signature, and he was using a temporary on-line account under a false name, still, he was acutely discomfited by this turn of events. Where had Vennholme gone wrong? Why had the movement lost this battle? Well, there remained the war to fight.

He summoned Father Ciccone and entrusted him with a plain white envelope filled with "information" about Cardinal Mulrennan's tenure in Jackson City and his relationship with Rachel Séredi. The priest was charged with delivering it to Harry Benjamin, who knew what to do with it. Already there had been a series of stories over the last few days that Benjamin had written and leaked. The outside world had been transfixed by the papal election and fed eagerly on these scandalous tidbits about the American papabile. Vennholme had succeeded, at least, in destroying the man's reputation and preventing him from being elected. That was something . . . even if they would now be stuck with the Filipino as pope . . . half a loaf, indeed!

"You look unhappy," Ciccone said.

"It is an unhappy time. I fear for the Church. I fear for the faithful people of Evangelium Christi."

After the priest left, Darragh reread the E-mail message.

He stood and looked out the window onto the bustle of the Roman street, Mussolini's proud legacy, harkening back to the days of empire. Now automobile traffic clogged the wide lanes, and smog and noise and commerce replaced dreams of national glory. It was the way of the world; corruption and sin threatened to erase the gains made in Christ's most holy Name; it had been that way from the beginning, in the Garden of Eden. Yet Francis Xavier Darragh, and others like him, were dedicated—and now renewed their commitment—to reclaiming souls for the Church, to cleansing the earth of Satan and his works.

History records only two cardinals, both later canonized, who turned down their election to the papacy. If the cardinals have made a sensible choice, and the candidate is of good health (as Pope John Paul I apparently was not) and mentally competent, there is little to no chance of his refusing the decision of the conclave. It is the call of the Holy Spirit, and no man can turn away from such a call without an utterly compelling cause.

These thoughts occurred to many of the cardinal-electors as the camerlengo, accompanied by the dean of the Sacred College and the senior cardinal-deacon, approached De Guzman's chair. The men who had sat near the Archbishop of Manila parted, as if a magic wand had been waved over them, and the smallish man with black hair and gold-rimmed glasses, a red zucchetto affixed to his crown like a sacred bull's-eye, sat unmoving, his face still covered by his delicate, priestly hands.

"*Acceptasne electionem?* Do you accept your canonical election as supreme pontiff?" Portillo asked, in the formula that for nine centuries had been put to men great and small.

Jaime De Guzman, eyes brimming with tears, looked directly into the old Spaniard's gray-green eyes. There he saw the sympathy and love that the man held for him, just as the other members of the Sacred College did. At this moment there was a supreme pall of silence over the chamber. De Guzman held a wrinkled white cotton handkerchief in his left hand and removed his glasses with his right. He

wiped his eyes and unceremoniously blew his nose before
he answered.

"*Accepto*. Yes, I do," he said, barely audible to the others, and replaced his spectacles. "With a prayer to God
Almighty that He will make me worthy."

Then the camerlengo asked him: "By what name do you
wish to be called?"

The Filipino hesitated and breathed deeply. For the past
few hours he had been thinking about this question, considering the implications of such a choice, which had hith-
erto been a million-to-one possibility. He thought back to
his youth, the names of the popes with whom he had grown
up: Pius, John, Paul, the dual name adopted by the smiling
archbishop of Venice and his successor, the Pole. But he
reached further back into history, nearly three hundred
years, for the name that would represent his papacy. He
hoped that it might symbolize his vision of God's holy
apostolic Church.

He spoke just above a whisper, in Italian: "Innocenzo."

Mulrennan said it aloud to himself: "Innocent." He
smiled at the simplicity and symbolism of the choice. This
new man would wear it lightly, even with the somewhat
cumbersome numeral attached to it—XIV.

"My Lord Cardinals and brothers in Christ, our new Holy
Father will be called after a great virtue to inspire the faithful; in the historical line of succession from St. Peter he
will be the fourteenth of that name," Carlos Juan Cardinal
Portillo declared.

A scuttle of activity erupted amid a smatter of collegial
applause: from the Room of Tears behind the Sistine
Chapel emerged a clutch of assistants who awaited the
newly elected pontiff as the camerlengo's and other chairs
were removed from the altar area to be replaced with a
throne.

De Guzman, Innocent XIV, stumbled once as he took his
first steps as pope, descending the makeshift stairs to the
floor of the chapel. Arms reached out to steady him and to
touch him. He was taken firmly but discreetly in tow by
the whispering assistants and escorted to the Room of
Tears. There, as the Sacred College waited, he was un-

dressed, down to his shirt and trousers, and fitted with a
small-sized version of the pope's vesture: the white silk
simar, white moiree silk fascia without a heraldic device—
which would be one of a million decisions he must make
over the first few weeks of his papacy—a linen rochet and
red mozzetta of velvet; the valet handed him an embroidered stole, which the Filipino kissed with reverence and
placed over the mozzetta, as he had done thousands of
times before when donning mass vestments. His black loafers and scarlet socks were removed, replaced with white
silk hose and red moroccan-leather slippers. Later, clothing
would be tailored exactly to his slight frame, and this dressing ritual would be repeated at least once daily for the rest
of his life.

He chose one of three Fisherman's Rings that were proffered on a silken pillow; it fit him perfectly, eerily, almost
magically so. On the inside of this ornate gold ring prepared
by the papal jewelers was the image of St. Peter casting his
net onto the sea. Later, his chosen name would be inscribed
on it, as well. And eventually it would be broken at his
death by another camerlengo, and the process of election
would begin all over again.

Finally, a stocky man approached De Guzman with a
sheepish smile. "Your Holiness," he said with a gap-toothed
lisp. He held out the white zucchetto, or skull cap, delicately, as if it were made of the most fragile and elegant
crystal and would break if touched.

"My friend, what is your name?" the pope asked.

"I am Gregorio Castiglia, Holy Father," the man replied,
eyes downcast.

"A great pope's name, Gregory. Perhaps I should have
taken it instead of Innocent."

"No, Holy Father. God gave you that name. I hope it
will become as beloved as John XXIII was. Pray for me,
Holy Father."

"Please remember me, too, Gregorio, in your prayers."
He took the zucchetto and placed it on his black, wavy
crown. He gave his first papal blessing to the valet who
genuflected before him. "Up, up. Let's save our kneeling
for the Savior."

De Guzman returned to the chapel where his throne, an old gilt-edged chair with red cushions and a high, ornate back and wide-winged arms awaited him. Gingerly, glancing around the great chapel, he took his place there. He looked out on the conclave as he had on the first day when he had been chosen to be *scrutatore*. Would that he could turn back the clock and somehow change the events of the past few days.

He saw that Cardinal Vennholme had rejoined the ranks of the Sacred College, and his face betrayed no emotion at all, though surely he was churning inside. And there sat Timothy Mulrennan, the tall American with a deep sorrow on his handsome lined face, his hair a bit whiter. The deep black faces of several Africans, burnished yellow of his fellow Asians, pale paper white European faces, the ruddy mien of the big man from Australia: all of them now looked to the man from Manila as their spiritual father and leader. Leandro Biagi stood with the first half dozen cardinals who were to honor the newly elected pontiff; the majestic-looking Florentine seemed pleased with the outcome of the conclave.

Mulrennan awaited his turn and watched the aged camerlengo step forward, a bit unsteadily at first; then Portillo gathered his strength and, with a sweeping gesture knelt at Pope Innocent's feet. No longer did the Spaniard hold any authority of office, now that the Chair of Peter was occupied. The slender pontiff rose and went to embrace Portillo. "My brother and friend," he said. The Jesuit allowed himself to be lifted and received a kiss of peace, one brotherly peck on each cheek, from his Holy Father. "You had a very difficult task, keeping us in line. You put down the revolution very nicely."

"Not a revolution, Holiness, but a rambunctious Holy Spirit who seemed to want to have sport with us."

De Guzman's smile blazed like sunshine, seeming to illuminate the entire room. "Yes, and I am His joke. I hope we can all learn how to laugh about it."

The cardinal-bishops in order of their seniority, each a Curial power in his own right but for the moment brilliantly outshone by the most powerful peer of their ancient rite,

came before him, knelt, received his *embracio*, exchanged
a few words with him. Each also attempted to gauge his
standing in the eyes of his Supreme Pontiff; after all, the
politics of the conclave had divided the Sacred College and
forced the cardinals to take uncomfortable positions,
whether they had spoken a word about it or not. The
speeches and accusations of the past few days were sealed
in the annals of the conclave and in their hearts forever.
This event would bind them to De Guzman's papacy as no
other men would be bound; they must trust that he would
abide by the sacred Apostolic Constitution and take no pu-
nitive action against any who had not voted for his candidacy.

When Vennholme approached, the pope opened his arms
as he had for the others. The French-Canadian prelate knelt
and bowed deeply, his forehead touching the floor. "Most
Holy Father—" he began.

"My Lord Cardinal Vennholme, let's start off with no
bad feelings toward each other. It is a time to forgive and
to heal, for we must turn all our energies to the work that
must be done."

"The Church needs your compassion, Holy Father. I ask
your forgiveness and tolerance."

"I grant what is mine to give and know that Jesus Christ
extends his forgiveness to all of us who have sinned—
myself more than any other."

Vennholme looked down at the floor and stepped backward. He turned and walked away from the Filipino.

Cardinal Mulrennan was close to the hundredth man to
greet his former fellow. How majestic he looked in papal
white, Tim thought, how appropriate. Every emotion he had
felt since coming to Rome now flooded through his body:
sadness, anger, love, relief, and acceptance. He climbed the
altar steps with tear-blurred vision. He could not even see
De Guzman's familiar face. It was as it had been in his
vision: a red-streaked image, clothed in white.

He genuflected and stood, towering over the pope. "Con-
gratulations, Your Holiness. You have been chosen."

"I hope I will wake up from this dream and find out it
is not so." He hugged Tim Mulrennan, held his arms and

gazed into his face. "I expected a much different result. These fellows don't know what they have done."

"Oh, we know that we elected the best man."

"Stay near me when I go outside. I wish to speak to you later, please, Timothy."

"I will, Your Holiness, if you want me to."

"Yes, I do. And I want you to pray for me, starting right now and never ceasing. It could have been you standing in these shoes, my American friend, or another man. Why me?"

The priest-secretaries had removed the last ballots and notes and scraps of paper and had taken them to the stove that fed the sixty-foot pipe reaching through the roof. They sprinkled the detritus of the conclave with a chemical that guaranteed the white smoke that announced to the waiting world the conclusion of the election process. The sound of cheering penetrated the high windows of the chapel and many of the cardinals looked up. Pope Innocent then patiently greeted a score of archbishops, bishops, and priests— important *officiali* of the Curia and the papal household— who had been admitted by the master of ceremonies. He fumbled for a handkerchief to wipe his brow but found none in the pockets of his new vesture.

A young Italian priest sensed his need and discovered a box of tissues tucked into a niche behind the altar. De Guzman smiled widely at the young man and gratefully patted his brow with the tissues. "I suppose I am ready to see the people. But are they ready to see me?"

A few muffled clerical titters greeted the remark. Most freshly elected popes were more or less well-known by the people who cared about such things. The last new pope who had been virtually a complete surprise to the expectant crowds in St. Peter's Square—and to the world—was John Paul II, after the conclave of October 1978. Immediately, however, after his first words and his apostolic benediction, *Urbi et Orbi*, the Romans had eagerly embraced him.

What would the Romans think of their newest bishop? *Well*, Tim Mulrennan thought as he followed the Successor to Peter out of the Sistine Chapel and toward the Hall of Benedictions, the huge reception chamber that extends across the facade of St. Peter's, a salon worthy of any Renaissance prince or high king: *We will all know soon enough what the entire world thinks of this good and holy man.*

May he walk with God, and God with him. Amen.

The gray and oppressive sky lay heavily over the Piazza di San Pietro in the aftermath of a sudden Saturday downpour. Here and there a black umbrella dipped and fluttered like an angry crow shaking moisture from its wings. The crowd of more than a hundred thousand stirred restlessly, yet an unnatural hush blanketed the entire city of Rome. Caligula's Egyptian obelisk, ironically crowned with an ornate cross, stood irrelevantly behind a canvas-protected scaffolding that housed the ubiquitous cameras, witness to yet another apostolic succession—an unbroken chain that had more than 260 links. The usual chaos of horns and sirens was muffled by the unseasonable coolness and heaviness of the air as the Roman populace awaited this very first benediction upon *Urbi et Orbi*, the City and the World.

An overly imaginative eye might spy a wisp or two of white smoke curling above the stovepipe that protruded from the slate roof of the Sistine Chapel amid the Renaissance jumble of buildings that comprised the Palazzi di Pontifici, the Apostolic Palace. Over the course of the preceding days the twice-daily ritual of belching black smoke had effectively damped the enthusiasm of the faithful, and the crowds had dwindled to mere thousands. But this afternoon, when the first puffs of the *sfumata bianca* had billowed into sight, that historic column of white smoke had reverberated throughout the city and the world more resoundingly than the peal of a thousand church bells, closing shops and cafés, summoning the massed throng that stood before the papal balcony of St. Peter's Basilica.

Expectation—the yearning of these scores of thousands of souls who represented a billion others—washed over the square. The long curving rows of four-hundred-year-old Bernini columns, stamped possessively by a long-dead patron of the arts, Pope Alexander VII, embraced the gathered faithful. Everything about the piazza focused one's attention on the recently refurbished grand facade of the greatest

basilica in Christendom. Just a few years earlier Carlo Mad-
erno's magnificent seventeenth-century facade had been unveiled, after a three-year effort that had cost private
contributors $5.5 million. Subtle pastel shades of pink,
gray, and yellow now highlighted the famous baroque facing that stood beneath Michelangelo's impossibly huge
dome.

One by one the heavy draperies across the facade's windows had drawn apart. Red blotches were visible at every
pane. All cardinals, even those who had been ineligible to
enter the conclave or to vote for the Successor to Peter
because of their advanced age, were present in the Hall of
the Benedictions awaiting the pope's arrival.

An audible murmur swept through the piazza as Leandro
Aurelio Cardinal Biagi, the Archbishop of Florence and
great elector, upon the request of the senior cardinal deacon, who had been completely exhausted by the conclave,
appeared on the central balcony beneath the scarlet- and
violet-filled parabolic arch to declare, "I announce to you
a great joy. We have a pope!" In the ancient language of
the Church, and as prescribed by a formula that has not
been altered in six hundred years, the words rang out: *"Annuntio vobis gaudium magnum. Habemus papam! . . . Em-
inentissimum ac Reverendissimum Dominum, Sanctae
Romanae Ecclesiae Cardinalem—"*

The name stunned the assembly with an electric charge.
The name of one who would guide Mother Church through
what had already been a tumultuous opening of a third millennium of the Christian era. The elegant Florentine cardinal was a familiar sight to Vatican watchers and
something of a local favorite for his urbanity and intelligent, even acerbic humor. However, it was much less certain how these Romans and international visitors would
react to the new Bishop of Rome.

Several television cameras, pooled by networks from
nearly every nation on earth, recorded the tableau from a
media platform erected in the center of the paved square.
Radio and TV correspondents, as well as newspaper reporters, pushed through the throng wielding microphones
and hand-held cameras, some of them wearing electronic

helmets that fed directions and babbled questions into their
ears. Behind the scenes and far away across the wide ocean,
in the new pope's home country, reporters and camera
crews rushed to his diocese to snag interviews with family,
friends, and Church officials. Biographies of the new man
with as many pictures as could be gathered at this earliest
stage were being broadcast worldwide. Still, the unearthly
silence hung over all present.

Cardinal Biagi stood aside and the gold patriarchal cross,
carried by a violet-robed monsignor of the papal household,
appeared. Then the newly elected pontiff himself stepped
forward to the lip of the balcony, an alien to many, yet not
a complete stranger.

So very erect and full of energy, his image was a stark
contrast to that of the arthritic and Parkinson's-riddled old
man who had commanded the same balcony and the same
crowd so often in recent years. *Il Santo Papa*, as he was
already being called, had been a towering world presence
in this smallest state on earth, a presence that seemed to
increase in light even as his body shriveled and betrayed
him. Few here present remembered the vigorous younger
man, the first non-Italian pontiff in 450 years, who con-
quered Rome in the first moment of his election a generation ago. . . .

As if on command, the late-afternoon clouds parted
enough to allow filtered sunlight to bathe the square and
the wall of the great basilica. Harsh television lights struck
the enormous banner with the late pope's coat-of-arms that
hung below the balcony's rail. A surging roar erupted from
the piazza below as the new man raised his arms above his
head.

Two hours ago, immediately upon his election, when he
had answered in the affirmative to the age-old query, "Do
you accept your canonical election as Supreme Pontiff?"
the *Sede Vacante*, a canonical interregnum called the Vacant See of St. Peter, was ended and ipso facto the Bishop
of Rome assumed the full and absolute jurisdiction of his
office over the entire Church on earth. One billion faithful
followers now called him their Holy Father.

"I greet you, friends, brothers, and sisters in Christ, for

the first time as your shepherd and your servant," he said in Italian, bending toward the microphone that had not yet been adjusted for his height. "May the Lord Our God grant me the strength to serve Him through serving you. Please pray for me."

Frenzied voices and flashing camera lights obscured his words, flooded the senses, and he merely smiled in response. He adjusted the white cap on the crown of his head. He made a wide, sweeping Sign of the Cross to his right, another to the center, and a third to the left. He tried to speak again, but was silenced by the flood of cheers.

Habemus papam! We have a pope!

CHAPTER FIFTEEN

Wednesday, July 11, 6:10 A.M.

His day had begun with prayer: an hour of quiet time in the cool of the monastery's adobe chapel. How different from the high-vaulted historic Sistine was this little Chapel of Christ the Redeemer! Smaller, darker, less ornate, a single candle burning near the altar, the pews hard and squeaky. He loved being there, contemplating the primitive crucifix that hung above the simple wooden altar, breathing the air of the desert that mingled with burning wax and incense and the scent of humanity. He sat in the front pew with his eyes raised to the crucifix, listening for the voice within that signified his dreams and fears; it had taken months to quiet the conflict and chaos that ruled his mind since the January conclave. He was on indefinite leave of absence from the Archdiocese of Newark, and he was fully prepared to resign from his position and take anything the new Holy Father might offer him—or nothing, if that were to be the will of God. *I am Your servant, a humiliated and desperate sinner in the eyes of men, Your child, a failed and fallen son, Your priest, bound to obey Your vicar on earth in any assignment he might ask of me. Here I am, Lord, the potter's clay in Your loving hands.* Tim Mulrennan willed his mind to be quiet, to listen, to push away any thought of self. He read a passage in his breviary, then went to kneel before the altar. . . .

He had tried to slip away from the Apostolic Palace after the January conclave without being seen, but it was not to be. When he exited the residence, dressed in a plain black clerical suit and black raincoat, with his bag in hand, he

was met by a pack of reporters and photographers. He heard
English, Italian, French, and a few other languages shouted
in his direction. He could not avoid them; there was nowhere to turn. He stopped short on the steps leading to the
sidewalk. His secretary stood beside him; Cardinal Mulrennan handed his travel bag to the younger priest. He whispered something to him, and the man slipped away, leaving
Mulrennan to stand by himself and face the world press, or
this ragtag representation thereof.

"Did you have an affair with a woman?"

"Are you married?"

"Who did you vote for?"

"Why did the cardinals reject you as pope?"

"Do you support gay rights in the Church?"

"What do you plan to do now, Cardinal Mulrennan?"

"Your Eminence, are you going to resign?"

The last question came in English from a tall man with
bad teeth and a down-under accent. Mulrennan looked in
his direction. Cameras flashed and the voices broke over
him like an ocean wave. He blinked, held up his hands,
waited until the noise subsided somewhat before he spoke.
He wished he had prepared a statement of some kind, but
he had not anticipated this—what would he call it?—this
assault.

He thought about his family and his flock in the archdiocese: he felt small. Tim clasped his hands and bowed
his head, quickly said a silent prayer to beg for the ability
to speak with honesty and humility.

"My friends," he began, "I am sorry to say that I am not
fully prepared to answer all your questions today. We have
just elected a wonderful, holy man to be our universal pastor, to lead our Church into a new phase of her life. We
have lost one of our most esteemed brethren, Cardinal Zimmerman, and we mourn for him and for the Church of
Austria. We have been locked in conclave for four long
days, and I have been away from home for nearly two
weeks. Please allow me to get some rest and board the next
flight to Newark. I look forward to spending some time
with my family and my friends at home. I doubt that you

will be particularly interested in anything I do or say at this point."

"Cardinal Mulrennan, we are very interested in the information that has surfaced about your relationship with a woman named Rachel Séredi. Can you tell us about that relationship?" It was the persistent Aussie.

Microphones were thrust at him, and video lights glared. He squinted, unable to make out faces in the crush of bodies.

"I have known Rachel for almost twenty years, and we have been close friends during that time—although I haven't seen her for several years . . . I don't know what else to tell you."

"Were you lovers?"

"No, we were not. I love her as a sister, as a good friend. If you wish to twist the facts to fit a preconceived conclusion, that is your choice. But the fact remains simply that we are friends and have been for a long time. I have been blessed with many friends in my life, men and women; I have been blessed to have a large family, many people in my life. Further, I have been blessed with the strength and support of those people in fulfilling my responsibilities as a priest."

"What about the report that you were married to a woman in Vietnam?"

"I have been advised not to answer that question directly in public, primarily to protect the other party. I spoke in confidence to my colleagues in conclave about it; I will say to you that I acted in a spirit of charity to help someone who had saved my life years earlier. I consulted with my superiors beforehand, and I did not violate my priestly vows in any way. I regret that my actions caused this misunderstanding, and I know that my personal credibility has been damaged. But I will live with that. I will live with the results of anything I have done in this life. Like anyone, I must continually seek God's forgiveness for sins past and present."

"You are avoiding the question, Your Eminence. Were you once married?"

"I regret that I cannot answer that question with a yes or no at this time."

"What will you say to the Catholics in New Jersey when you get home? How do you expect them to respond to these alleged offenses?"

"I will ask for their charity and forgiveness for anything I have done to offend or confuse them. I, frankly, expect a very positive, Christian response from them. They have my deepest love and respect; they have taught me a lot over the years."

"What about gay rights? Are you in favor of gay priests? Is your brother gay? Are you gay?"

"I have to turn to the teachings of the Church on the issue of homosexuality. I believe that we are all children of God, that He loves us without condition or qualification. Every man or woman deserves respect, whatever their sexuality. I do not favor gay priests, just as I do not favor white priests over any other race of priests, nor brown-eyed priests over blue-eyed priests. I have gay friends and colleagues and relatives, and I hope they love me as freely and fully as I love them." Mulrennan felt like a wounded rabbit surrounded by hungry dogs. His heart sank as he looked into the faces of these reporters and cameramen. Is this what celebrity was all about? Did anyone really care what he had to say about these issues and accusations? Was anybody listening to his answers?

He added, "I have chosen a life of celibacy, and God has seen fit to accept my vow, to give me the strength to live it to the best of my ability and despite the natural human weakness that would take me in another direction. I give Him all credit for everything I have done or been, for everything I am and will be, and for everything I am not."

"Are you disappointed you weren't elected pope?"

"No. I am elated that the Holy Spirit led us to choose Cardinal De Guzman, a great and holy man. He will serve the Church with intelligence, love, and distinction. He will be a more than worthy successor to the late Holy Father."

"Did you receive any votes?"

"I am bound not to discuss the business of the conclave, now or ever."

"Was Cardinal La Spina disappointed? We heard that he withdrew from consideration when it was clear that he could not win a two-thirds majority vote."

"All of the cardinals tried to put aside personalities and politics to fulfill our sacred responsibilities within the conclave. I cannot speak for Cardinal La Spina, or any of the others, only myself, and I am sure he feels the same way. He is a very accomplished man, dedicated to the Church, a wise and holy man. Who knows what the future holds for him, or for any of us? The new Holy Father will have something to say, I'm sure, about the cardinal's future as a Church leader. We need Cardinal La Spina in whatever role he is asked to perform.

"Please," Mulrennan said in Italian, "I must catch my flight. Your press colleagues in the States must be waiting for me to get back!" He took one step down, toward the throng of reporters. The shouting and microphones came right at his face. He rubbed his jawline, grateful that he had shaved a second time that day.

"Did you speak to the pope?" A shrill, insistent questioning voice in English. He couldn't see the source as the lights waved and glared on every side of him. "What did he say to you? Did he ask you to resign?"

Tim Mulrennan took another step down, engulfed in a small sea of moving, shoving bodies. He looked up, held up his hand to protect his face from the bobbing microphones. He spoke in a normal tone of voice: "We had a brief audience, and I wished him well, offered my prayers and the support of the people of my diocese. He gave me his blessing and asked me to convey his love to the people of Newark."

The tall American pushed forward, away from the residence, toward the car, which he saw over the heads of the press mob. He felt his ribcage being squeezed, and he resisted the impulse to shove back, tried to walk slowly and steadily in the direction of the car. Never in his life had he experienced anything remotely like this scene, a politician's or movie star's daily fare. He swallowed his fear and humiliation and bent one shoulder down and pressed forward.

Miraculously, he reached the open door of the black lim-

ousine that would take him to the airport in Fiumicino, onto
the return flight to Newark, to whatever fate awaited him
at home among his own family . . . and he prayed as he had
not prayed in decades, *Your will, not mine, be done, O
Father—hear your unworthy servant. . . .*

As he knelt now in the Chapel of Christ the Redeemer in
the New Mexican desert outside of Albuquerque, Tim Mulrennan recalled the scene that was repeated on his arrival
at Terminal B of Newark International Airport: the scary
press of bodies and equipment and glaring lights, the
shouted questions and flashing cameras, the alien, disem-
bodied feeling that overcame him as he tried to be civil,
pushing through to another waiting car and a deep sigh of
relief as he collapsed in the backseat.

Now, almost six months later, he knew not what the next
twenty-four hours would reveal, and he felt liberated, however temporarily, from the oppressive responsibilities and
questions that had greeted him upon his return. Yes, there
would be an end to the respite, the Holy Father had assured
him, but the months of retreat and intensive prayer had
rekindled the fire in his soul. De Guzman had been wise,
and Mulrennan was grateful. He looked forward to seeing
the pope in September to discuss his long-term future. And
he would see his own family sooner, in mid-August when
he was scheduled to return to the chancery, meet with his
staff, and get a feel for what was happening there in his
absence.

At least once a week he hiked in the desert, in the foothills of Sandia Peak, often with an experienced guide who
led him on new paths that increased in difficulty and
beauty, always showing Tim some new flora or spectacular,
hidden vista; he left the city and the monastery behind on
these desert excursions; he tested and toughened himself
and learned like an eager child.

*God is good. God is my refuge. I am the child of
God. . . .*

He had also kept himself extremely busy with reading
and counseling work. He had dusted off his degree and
certifications and offered to help the director of the reha-

bilitation program who—no surprise—was chronically short-staffed. Working with others, focusing on their problems instead of his own, filled Tim Mulrennan with hope and gratitude. One-on-one counseling was a trying but rewarding job; he almost felt guilty that he enjoyed it and benefited from it so much.

He finished his morning office and quieted his mind for a period of meditation. He felt the dark hard pew and smelled the earthy scents of the chapel and heard the vague humming of life in the monastery and the faint animal sounds and the soft hot breeze as it moved over the earth. Papal politics and scandal and the affairs of the world seemed far away. He prayed for his friend and colleague Jaime Edgardo De Guzman, Pope Innocent XIV, a man with unfathomably huge responsibilities on his shoulders.

The day after the election, Tim Mulrennan had met with the new pope and told him what was in his heart: "Holy Father, I must resign as cardinal and archbishop, I can serve in other ways. I am willing to do whatever you ask of me—but you understand why I do this."

"You will understand why I cannot accept your resignation, Timothy," De Guzman had said mildly but firmly. He fixed his dark brown eyes on Mulrennan, who saw the love and empathy of the man's soul in those eyes. "I need you, and the Church needs you. Take some time away from your diocesan responsibilities, time to heal and be renewed in your faith. God has brought you this far; He is not finished with you yet. I know this."

"The Church doesn't need any more scandal or uncertainty. I would be asking a lot of the people and the clergy in my diocese if I were to return as their leader."

"You would be asking them to be good Christians, to forgive and to pray for you." It was clear that the new pope, gentle as he might be, was determined to have his way. "Give them some time to learn the truth and to respond to you with their prayers and support. Trust them, Timothy. Trust me. Most importantly, trust God the Father."

Mulrennan felt the new pope's hands touch his arms, and the weight of his burden lightened perceptibly. An overwhelming sadness welled up within him and brought the

image of the late pontiff into his mind. He contemplated
the apostolic succession from St. Peter to this kind and
humble man . . . from Christ to the people of the twenty-
first century . . . from God to one man, Tim Mulrennan
himself.

"Yes, Holy Father," he said simply.

So, he had returned to Christ the Redeemer, where he
had first come two-plus decades before . . . memory collided with memory in what seemed like someone else's life
in another time.

November 19, 1978

The gravid skies promised a pounding afternoon shower.
Monsignor Tim Mulrennan pressed the gas pedal of the '65
Ford Fairlane station wagon, accelerated as he swung into
the curves around the base of the foothills. He was in the
Indian pueblo country outside Albuquerque, returning from
the university to the old Benedictine monastery where he
now lived and worked. It was the site of the most frustrating
and challenging assignment of his priesthood.

He gripped the big wheel of the tanklike automobile and
felt the rebuilt six-cylinder engine hum with power. He had
bought the car from a mechanic in the city who had guaranteed him five trouble-free years with the old battle
wagon. Mulrennan paid for it out of his own pocket: he
was not going to be stuck out here in the desert without
reliable wheels.

That had been a month ago. He raced against time. Ten
more miles to the Abbey of Christ the Redeemer. Lightning
flashed to the northeast. He glanced back at the Sandia
Mountains—silent humped sentinels who stood darkly
against the sky.

He had felt poorly prepared to take over the operation
of Redeemer in a part of the country so far removed from
his home; and yet he knew when the archbishop had called
him in for a meeting in the chancery that it was time—past
time for a change. He had spent a total of eleven years at
Our Lady of Mercies parish, six of those years since his

return from Vietnam as pastor following Monsignor Froeschel's incapacitation by stroke. He himself had been made
a monsignor, an honorary papal title given to a senior
priest.

The years flashed through his mind like the yellow
center-line on the smooth blacktop. He checked the speed-
ometer: seventy mph. Over the new, lower speed limit, but
he needed to beat the storm if he could—to get home before
the new resident arrived. It was his self-imposed policy to
meet each new man as he was processed in. There were
nine residents currently, with a capacity for fifteen. He expected, sadly, a full house by the spring.

He had been selected for a "very special assignment,"
his boss, Archbishop Paul Garrison announced. Certainly
not an easy one: a task that would put the young monsignor
right in the middle of the most rapidly metastasizing crisis
within the American Church.

A monster raindrop exploded on the windshield. Thunder
tattooed against the distant sky. Then a heavy curtain of
rain fell across the highway, and Mulrennan drove through
with a clenched jaw and gritted teeth.

"The subcommittee of the national conference of bishops
has conducted a quiet but intensive search for the right man,
Timothy. I put your name forward as an experienced pastor,
a man of compassion and common sense, of spirituality,"
Garrison told him. Ten years earlier he had sat in this same
office—in the same chair—to receive instructions from the
previous archbishop during the Newark disturbances. A
more seasoned priest and administrator, and now a decade
older, Tim Mulrennan listened and wondered what God had
in store for him now. "After screening thirty or so qualified
candidates from around the country, we agreed on you as
first choice," the archbishop said.

"Father, you are called to be the director of Christ the
Redeemer Abbey Rehabilitation Center in New Mexico.
This is a former monastery converted for use as a facility
to minister to problem priests: alcoholics, drug users, gamblers, sexual aggressors, and the like. You will be their
confessor and pastor. You will have a small professional
staff to assist you. You will counsel them and evaluate their

fitness to return to the priesthood—or not, as the case may be.

"I will miss you greatly," the archbishop continued. "As will the people of Our Lady of Mercies parish. Of course, you will have the opportunity to consider this assignment, to pray about it. If for any reason you feel you cannot assume this responsibility, you must tell me immediately."

"Archbishop Garrison, Your Excellency—I don't know what to say. I—This is the very last thing in the world I expected."

"Surprises are good for the soul, Monsignor Mulrennan," the archbishop said.

Tim had prayed long and hard for a week. He looked back on his parish years and wondered if he had succeeded or failed, made any difference in the lives of the two thousand families who had been entrusted to his ministry. How could it come to such an abrupt end? And what lay ahead? If he had attempted to set himself the most difficult possible challenge—and one he had the least preference or affinity for—he would not have even approached this: working with fallen priests, drunks, pedophiles, criminals. He was not even certain he agreed that it was the Church's responsibility to provide for such men. After a determination of wrongdoing, the civil authorities should, he thought, become involved. Such a rehab facility—"conveniently" hidden away in a remote desert location—smacked of coverup and coddling.

I am no jailer, he prayed. *I am no psychologist. I am no spiritual guru. I am a parish priest, pure and simple. My ambitions to rise in the Church have been tempered by hard experience. Even so, this feels very much like a demotion, or at least a sidestep. . . . Should I not think about my career? Must I blindly accept such a farfetched assignment? Is this a test of my vow of obedience?*

After a few days of questioning and doubting, he decided to listen to the Holy Spirit. He visited Monsignor Froeschel in the nursing home, where the disabled, aged priest lived on tapioca and TV. He went to a Yale football game with his kid stepbrother, Stephen, a junior enamored of theater studies and English literature and undergraduate life in New

Haven. His own two years at Yale in the early 1950s (before the army, continued undergraduate studies at Seton
Hall and the seminary) had not been a particularly happy
time for Mulrennan. He had been acutely lonely, unsure of
his vocation, painfully young.

On the drive back to New Jersey late Saturday night after
the Bulldogs' loss, he remembered: he had actually cried
himself to sleep for the first two weeks as a freshman. Stephen, on the other hand, had a lively coterie of friends and
seemed to fit naturally into the Yale scene. At home, in his
study in the rectory, he knelt on the floor and felt the evening breeze through the open window.

It was difficult to think of a life apart from the parish—
his parish. After five years as a curate, that is an associate,
he had taken charge as pastor in a time of decline: but the
old man's stroke was merely one symptom of crisis.

Mass attendance, school enrollment, Catholic marriages,
vocations, conversions, financial support, all were decreas-
ing rapidly. Birth control, abortion, divorce, priests and
nuns turning away from their vows, drugs, crime, political
scandal, Curial obstinance, papal ennui, wars and famines
. . . a never-ending litany of decay and disaster.

The parish itself had provided a focus and a home. In
the particular problems and needs of his community, Mulrennan found purpose—he knew these people intimately,
had known many since childhood, ate and drank and celebrated and mourned with them. He had baptized at least
two hundred babies, claiming them temporarily for Christendom. The parish council and school administration
sought his approval for their progressive schemes. His father and stepmother often visited and beamed at him from
a front-row pew at Sunday mass. His older sisters' kids
flocked to him at family occasions. A capital campaign to
finance overdue renovations loomed on the near horizon.
They needed him, these parishioners.

Chastity and obedience and, although diocesan priests
were not required to take a vow of poverty, as some religious did, they certainly lived on very limited resources.
As he prayed for the strength to accept God's will he contemplated the meaning of those vows. Each and all had

been tested during his priesthood. He had succeeded, and he had failed. Because he had tried, as a human being, to live up to the highest expectations—his own as much as anyone's—he had been rewarded with God's grace in abundance. How could he now turn his back on this call to serve?

On his knees in the quietude of a comfortable study in the security of a comparatively well-to-do suburban parish, Monsignor Timothy John Mulrennan received the answer to his prayer. It was not the answer he wanted, not the course he had planned. He lifted his forty-year-old body and vigorously rubbed his knees. He went to his desk to write a letter of acceptance to Archbishop Garrison. Then he took a long walk through the neighborhood before he retired at midnight.

These many months later, driving in the desert, he prayed that his automobile would not be washed off the road in a desert flash flood. He pulled up to the front door of the abbey and ran inside with his briefcase tucked under arm. He was thoroughly soaked.

After changing into khaki slacks and a much-laundered Notre Dame sweatshirt he sat at his wide desk in the cavernous office of the abbot. A fragrant flame flickered in the fireplace. Books lined two walls, floor to ceiling. Before him sat stacks of files and correspondence. He chain-smoked as he read clinical and criminal reports on his charges. He expected a new man to arrive today.

Outside, the desert shower ceased pounding the earth. He pushed open the windows over the macadam patio. The afternoon sun splashed onto the wet surface.

A knock at the door. Brother James Impolito, a middle-aged Dominican and recovering alcoholic, wedged through the half-open door. He was attached to Redeemer through the end of the year; he had begun to get sober here nearly three years earlier. He wore the black-and-white Dominican habit. Mulrennan had immediately found him invaluable in the effort to learn the "rehab game." He had already attended several open Alcoholics Anonymous meetings with Brother James. He enjoyed the easy camaraderie and frankness of the sober, self-described "garden-variety drunks" he had met. He also adopted the favorite AA prayer known as the Serenity Prayer, in his own daily routine:

> God, grant me the serenity to accept
>   the things I cannot change,
> courage to change the things I can,
>   and wisdom to know the difference.
> Living one day at a time;
>   accepting hardship as the pathway to peace.
> Taking, as He did, this sinful world as it is,
>   not as I would have it.
> Trusting that He will make all things right
>   if I surrender to His will;
> That I may be reasonably happy in this life,
>   and supremely happy with Him forever
>   in the next. Amen.

Drug and alcohol abuse were just part of the problem, however. Deeper, darker psychoses had disabled the men of Christ the Redeemer—and brutally maimed the people they had touched, people who had trusted them as God's representatives. Could these men be forgiven? Should they be? Why had God allowed them to be born if others of His children were made to suffer because of them?

Within a few months of his appointment Mulrennan instituted a strict regime for the clients or "residents" at the abbey: two weeks of evaluation, including a thorough physical exam (plus detoxification at a local hospital ward for alcoholics and drug addicts); mass, prayer, and meditation daily; individual psychotherapy and group therapy each twice a week; "classwork" that included clinical study of addictions, compulsive sexual behavior, and mental illness; physical exercise daily (a program tailored to the needs and condition of each man); one-on-one counseling and follow-up evaluation; outside recovery meetings of Alcoholics Anonymous, Narcotics Anonymous, Gamblers Anonymous, and Sex Addicts Anonymous; discussion of career options (precious few for a defrocked priest who in other circumstances would be incarcerated).

After eight to ten weeks, Mulrennan and his counseling

staff wrote up their recommendations to the priest's home diocese. The course of treatment at Redeemer might continue for up to nine months, with the absolute minimum stay about ninety days.

The abbey "processed" three dozen men in Mulrennan's first year, including one Chicago priest on probation after an illegal weapons conviction and another, from Florida, who had been caught participating in a Satanic coven that had destroyed or desecrated several local Protestant and Catholic churches. . . .

The answers surely did not reside in the thick file folders arrayed before him. He was reading a report on one chronic child molester when Brother James interrupted.

"Monsignor Mulrennan, the new resident is here. Do you care to interview him now—or after supper?"

"Now, Brother. Let's process the sonofagun."

Impolito left. Mulrennan opened the thin legal-size file folder. Rev. Joseph M. Burgoyne, M. Phil., forty-eight years old, pastor for three years of St. Matthias's of Westview, Connecticut. Criminal charges of assault and endangering the welfare of a minor—brought by the county attorney, then dropped for lack of evidence. The alleged victim would not testify. Previous allegations referred to diocesan authorities by the parents of four different boys from the parish who claimed to have been touched, fondled, molested by Father Burgoyne, hearing scheduled, postponed, never rescheduled. Charges and letters of reprimand from two previous parish assignments—in Upstate New York and Massachusetts—covering a period of fourteen years. Burgoyne transferred out of diocese each time. Same issues over and over again: on overnight trips, visits to the rectory, in the sacristy after serving mass with the priest— Burgoyne was alleged to have fondled or sodomized the boys, a dozen in all who had come forward, and threatened physical and spiritual punishment if they reported his actions to anyone.

Twenty-one years a priest—wasted years? A life of hurt to others? Unredeemable? Privately, Mulrennan considered such a man as this unfit and unworthy of the priesthood. The damage he had caused to these children and their fam-

ilies, to his own immortal soul, and to the Church he represented, was irreparable. Why bother trying to save *him*?
What about his victims—who was mending them?

Finally, the Diocese of Bridgeport had pulled the plug,
relieved Father Burgoyne of all parochial and sacramental
responsibilities, shipped him out to New Mexico. They had
dumped him after only three years.

Joe Burgoyne, accused pedophile and Roman Catholic
priest, entered Mulrennan's office behind Brother James,
who directed him to sit in a comfortable chair facing the
desk. Mulrennan said nothing until James left the room.

Eyes downcast, fingers interlaced upon his lap, unshaven,
Father Joe Burgoyne spoke with what Tim thought of as a
"radio voice," deep and clear: "I have not done all the
things I am accused of," he said.

"Which of these acts have you done?" Tim asked.

"Perhaps some, not others."

"You must be clearer than that. If we are to help you,
you must get honest with yourself, with God, and with me."

"I don't remember everything—"

"What do you remember?"

"I remember praying to God for the strength not to do
it, not to harm anyone. He did not listen to me."

Mulrennan looked at the rust-colored crew cut, the pink
skin of the top of Burgoyne's shame-hung head. He felt
both compassion and loathing for this failed man, this sinful
priest. "You did not listen to His answers. The Father always hears our prayers, but we often do not hear Him reply."

"I believe He has abandoned me. I am alone with my
shame."

"I will share it; I am here with you."

"It's too late," Burgoyne said, raising his head briefly to
meet Mulrennan's eyes.

"It is not. You are here for a reason. You have been
given a chance, that you do not deserve, to make a new
start, to confess your failings, to learn how to live with
yourself. God has kept you out of jail, Father, and delivered
you into my care. I am responsible for you now."

"The Church has failed me—and, more importantly, has

failed these kids. I should have been stopped many years
ago. I wanted—to be stopped."

"Did you truly seek God's help? Did you ask for the
Blessed Virgin's intercession or Christ's mercy and guid-
ance? Did you confess to your pastor or a brother priest?
Did you take steps to seek professional help?"

"I was beyond help, earthly or divine." He hung his head
again. "Still am."

The silver rain began to fall again and etched the air
coolly. Mulrennan gazed through the open doors onto the
wet flagstones and saw the water drops hit and shatter into
glistening shards before they settled into shallow black
pools. The rhythm of the desert rainfall soothed his own
burdened mind.

He had begun to keep a journal upon his arrival at Christ
the Redeemer; he felt moved to record his thoughts and
prayers, his experiences in this assignment. It was so unlike
parish work, even more mentally and spiritually draining.

Mulrennan sat back in the tall leather chair and lit a cigarette with a paper match. He flung the used match into an
overflowing ashtray. In his right hand he wielded a ball-
point pen, in his left the burning cigarette. The rain
drummed to the earth, and a cool breeze swept into the
room. Within, a deep loneliness welled coldly and threatened to flood his entire being: for the first time in his life
he was unsure of his vocation, doubted the quality of his
faith.

Burgoyne was the hardest of hard cases. Full of denial
yet riven with shame and remorse, the priest had sat there
like a prisoner of war, refusing to divulge information except under threat (veiled) and cajolery (necessary).

Tim needed to gather his own inner resources to sum-
marize and consider Father Burgoyne's responses, to pray
about the man. He wrote in his journal later that day, recorded the exchange as best he could remember it.

The fallen priest had finally met Tim's steady, even look.
His eyes, behind black-framed glasses, were a limpid blue.
"I knew what I was doing but could not stop myself. As I
said, I prayed to be relieved of this horrible sin. I wanted

to change—yet I didn't. God must have known my reservations, must have seen that I got pleasure from my actions." Tears spilled from behind his glasses. "I did not intend to hurt. Can't you see that, Monsignor Mulrennan? I did not *choose* this way. I am cursed."

For Tim, the most difficult and painful cases were those of the child abusers like Joseph Burgoyne. He recommended the maximum term of rehabilitation for most, as he would for this one. He wondered whether the priest had an alcohol problem or other mental disorder, but the professionals would render such diagnosis, if any.

It became clear to the director of the rededicated abbey that Burgoyne's problem was singular and deep: he needed to have sex with youngsters in order to "live," to achieve power and purpose. According to his file, he had been repeatedly abused as a ten-year-old child by an older cousin, an experience that must have warped him mentally and physically. There was no question in Mulrennan's mind that Father Joseph Burgoyne should never again be entrusted with sacerdotal responsibilities. But could he ever be rehabilitated sufficiently to be allowed to rejoin society? And, if not, what should become of him?

Tim spoke again: "I cannot forgive you. I haven't the power. And doubt that I would. Only God has the infinite capacity for mercy and the power to bestow forgiveness."

"You have the sacramental authority to grant absolution."

"As do you. But the forgiveness I speak of is beyond absolution. It's a healing gift that comes directly from the Father. Most importantly, you must be prepared to receive it. You must also forgive yourself."

As Burgoyne sat before Mulrennan, a deathly stillness pervaded the room.

"You must become willing to undergo intense therapy, to accept the direction of the staff and of myself. God has called you to this place because He loves you—not despite your sins but *because* of them. His love is unconditional. That's why I say it is up to you to prepare for and to accept His forgiveness, which is readily given."

"What if I were to say I do not believe any of this claptrap?" Burgoyne muttered.

Just one month later Tim Mulrennan presided at the graveside of Father Joseph M. Bugoyne, who had hanged himself in his room. Another soul he had failed to save . . .

Wednesday, July 11, 10:34 A.M.

When he returned to his study after morning prayer a pink message slip lay on Cardinal Tim Mulrennan's desk. He immediately called the county sheriff's office, with a queasy feeling in his gut. It was about Father Dan Cade, one of his charges: he knew it without a shred of information. Then a deputy sheriff confirmed it.

INTERLUDE
Agnus Dei

Manila, The Philippines, Wednesday, July 11

The young woman in the brown nun's habit had arrived at 6:00 A.M. and waited at the park entrance by the national cathedral. She held a ticket that would admit her to the secure area most proximate to the target. A passing child greeted her with a happy *"Buenos dias*, Sister." She smiled, waved, and returned the salutation with a slight inflection that indicated she was not a native Filipina. She removed a pair of cheap plastic sunglasses and peered across the green expanse of the park. When she saw what she was looking for, she moved in that direction. It was by now well past seven. She put the sunglasses back on, wiped her perspiring forehead, then inserted her hands in the folds of the habit, allowing a heavy crucifix to dangle freely from her neck, and fell in behind the gaggle of similarly brown-clad women as they pushed through the ever-growing throng and made their way into the area reserved for local religious and clergy just below the magnificent outdoor altar.

By eight o'clock more than one million people blanketed every square meter of Rizal Park in the center of Manila, swarming around the great monument to the Philippines's nineteenth-century patriotic martyr and spilling onto broad streets as far north as the old cathedral and west to the openmouthed bay where a century of naval battles had determined the course of three empires. American-manufactured army helicopters soared and swooped noisily above the crowd. The faithful and the curious gathered beneath the cobalt sky in anticipation of the appearance of

Pope Innocent XIV on his first trip outside Rome since his
surprise election.

Security was exceptionally tight, both uniformed police
and military ringing the altar floor, and secret service–type
plainclothes officers fanning out to every section of the
open field. Helmets, sunglasses, auto-rifles, Kevlar body
shields, riot gear, radios, limousines, ambulances, a camera-
laden media tower, the majestic altar platform, the famous
and somewhat grotesque Pope-mobile . . . it all added up to
an event the like of which no one in this city had ever
witnessed. Not since Paul VI had come in the mid-1960s
had a pope set foot in the Philippines. And that visit had
been a near-disaster when he was attacked on the tarmac
of the airfield by a knife-wielding anti-Western zealot. Pope
Paul had escaped unharmed physically, but more crowd-
shy than ever.

At 9:00 A.M., Pope Innocent, Jaime Edgardo De Guzman, arrived in the bulletproof car that had carried his immediate predecessor to hundreds of such events over two
decades. It was now six months since a divided conclave
had chosen him, and after his installation he had faced a
crushing schedule of business that required his presence in
the Apostolic Palace: there were political and diplomatic
crises, petty Vatican appointments, financial decisions, Curial disputes, and local Roman issues that had lain dormant
in the previous pope's last, infirm years. He had spent much
of his time soothing bruised egos and salving thwarted ambitions among the Sacred College.

Finally, 168 days after his election, the pope had flown
the specially converted Alitalia 747 to Ninoy Aquino International Airport where he joyfully alighted and knelt to
kiss the earth and was embraced by old friends and priestly
colleagues.

According to the local meteorological forecast, the rain
would hold off until late afternoon. By then, following the
meticulously detailed plan that promised to be yet another
Vatican triumph, the mass would be long over and the people dispersed.

The Holy Father finished his circuit of the park in the
bulletproof automobile followed by a swarm of Asian car-

dinals and bishops and staff. The newly appointed Vatican Secretary of State, Leandro Aurelio Cardinal Biagi, the old Curia lion, mopped his brown brow with a white towel on this beautifully bright but sultry morning.

The pontiff walked to a tented high-security staging area behind the altar platform where he changed into his mass vestments. Liturgical song swelled from the mass of people in the park, led by a petite female cantor. When he emerged, the smiling pope was greeted with deafening, prolonged cheers. He was one of their own! He waved, blessed the assembly, signaled for quiet—which they did not give him. They were too elated not to let him know, from the very depths of their souls and lungs, how happy they felt, how much and truly they loved him.

The mass began, with the liturgy presented in Spanish, English, Tagalog, and Latin. Despite the intense heat, the Holy Father moved around the altar like a young athlete, agile and engaged, embracing his concelebrants and acknowledging his young altar servers, boys and girls, who stood in awe of him, barely able to perform their prescribed tasks.

He had never dreamed that he would be called to serve the universal Church as pontiff and the Servant of the Servants of God. Being a priest and later pastor had come naturally to him; he had studied hard as a seminarian and worked hard as a priest. He became known as a "people's priest," not an ideologue but a man who put the needs of his flock first, his own wants and comforts second—or third, or fourth—on the priority list. With a smile on his face and the Word in his heart, he gave unstintingly. Priest, bishop, cardinal, now pope: his parish was now the world.

After the Gospel reading the 262nd successor to the first Bishop of Rome addressed the throng. He spoke the first few words in English.

"My brothers and sisters in Christ—my people!" He could not continue beyond this point in his homily because a million voices erupted like a human volcano in a ragged, frenzied cheer. "My people . . ." he began again, after a few minutes, his hands lifted in supplication. A hot gust of wind whipped the white-and-gold chasuble against his lean body, and he touched the tall white papal miter to be sure it still sat securely on his head. He smiled widely, his eyes scanning the multitude through dark-tinted lenses.

The people would not allow him to speak. They roared and roared their love and approval, their renewed hope and joy. This Southeast Asian nation of seven thousand islands and 70 million people, bitterly divided by civil and religious strife, crippled by generations of colonial exploitation and corrupt government, and devastated by world war, beheld a savior who might use the power of his sacred office to quell the violent factions that threatened to destroy the still-young nation.

"Hear me, a voice crying out in the wilderness," the pontiff continued, shouting over the tidal wave of affection. The cheers finally subsided. Pope Innocent looked upward as he lifted the wood-and-brass shepherd's staff, so that the small figure of the crucified Christ was starkly limned against the virgin blue sky and the white "big top" canopy that roofed the altar. "I have come to preach to you of the One who loves you. He is your true salvation. He reigns in justice in heaven at the right hand of the Father."

He paused and looked down for a moment, gathering his thoughts, and the throng was ominously, miraculously silent. "Be an example to the world. Be chaste and respect the life of your neighbor. Seek unity rather than division. Love your brother who worships God in a different religion. Remember that God loves him, just as He loves you." Long decades of sectarian and political violence lay behind his admonition. The last few years had seen Muslim-on-Christian and Christian-against-Muslim violence reach horrific new levels.

"Mother Church calls you to be obedient and loving children, to lead the world to Christ! In this task, remember that I am with you always. I am with you even to the end of the world!"

The mass continued, through the offertory and the consecration of the host. A few handpicked congregants, most of them from wealthy and prominent Philippine families, some sisters from a local convent who worked with the poorest of Manila's streets, children from Catholic schools and orphanages, lined up at the foot of the altar to receive the host from His Holiness.

The nuns in their heavy brown habits moved excitedly toward the pope. They would receive communion from his hands! Never had such a remote possibility entered their minds.

Unnoticed in the moving knot of brown, the otherwise unremarkable woman wearing the dark sunglasses, her hands piously clasped the heavy crucifix to her breast, wedged in behind the others. She prayed that her compassionate God would give her the strength to carry out her mission.

More than two thousand priests took their stations on the field among the faithful who were to partake of the sacrament of the Eucharist. The people moved in orderly lines to receive the body of Christ.

A heart-sickening thud reverberated near the altar. Then a sudden, unearthly silence fell over the huge outdoor congregation for several tense heartbeats. Some tattered gray clouds moved across the otherwise clear and brilliant sky. A dirty smudge of smoke obscured the canopied altar. Bodies lay there, some bloodied and torn, others blown into unrecognizable bits. The Holy Father was nowhere to be seen, nor was the woman in the brown nun's habit who had just received the Eucharist from him. She had detonated the bomb as she stood just inches away from Innocent XIV. His miter had fallen about ten yards from the epicenter of the blast; his staff was shattered, the tortured Christ figure half melted by the concentrated blast. The pope's faithful aide, Monsignor Carlos Franzonia, lay dead, literally torn in two by the explosive. Dozens of others, concelebrants, altar servers, and faithful, lay on the earth wounded, dying. The scene of joyful reunion had been transformed into the carnage of a battlefield within a few violent seconds.

A plaintive, panicked scream rent the air and echoed across the green expanse toward the bay. Stunned security forces moved in, too late. Soldiers unshouldered their assault weapons, but there was no one to shoot. Mothers grabbed their children, men stood in helpless uncertainty, people ran like rabbits in every direction, trampling others.

Cardinal Biagi rose from his knees where he had been blown by the explosion and stood near the sagging floor of the altar, his face soot-streaked, the miter also blown from his bald head, his vestments spattered with blood and torn by fragments of the platform. The canopy over the altar now had a huge, gaping hole in the fabric. "Holy God in heaven . . ." He had somehow survived the tremendous blast. Why? Smoke and tears blurred his otherwise perfect eyesight as he looked out upon a universe of chaos and death.

Police and soldiers swiftly created a cordon around the explosion site, and the wounded Florentine cardinal stumbled away from the altar area. Reporters moved in toward Biagi with microphones and video cameras.

"There are no words—" he sputtered in English. "The Holy Father is dead. We have lost our shepherd—lost our way." The news cameras recorded the grief and horror on the face of the Vatican Secretary of State as he walked aimlessly into the remnants of the ebbing throng of a million souls who had witnessed the death of their native son and brother.

The gold Fisherman's Ring of Innocent XIV was never recovered.

Albuquerque, New Mexico, July 11, 5:15 P.M.

Another late-afternoon rain shower pounded the highway into the city like a million silver hammers and made driving treacherous, even in the 1999 model Ford Explorer that Tim Mulrennan manhandled at sixty-five miles per hour: too fast, he knew, but he was on a mission, perhaps to save a man's life. So this was his "vacation" from the Archdiocese of Newark! He tuned the radio to the local all-news station for the weather forecast, as if he needed to hear any more about the storm. He remembered the old station wagon that he had once driven on the same road, twenty-two years ago. It had rained then too.

He had come to the Abbey of Christ the Redeemer in February—come back, really, after a twenty-year absence—

seeking peace and renewal. He had volunteered to help local pastors when they needed a priest to fill in at Sunday
masses or other duties. Such work felt good; it felt right.
The long intervening years of diocesan administration had
taken him away from parish life: he found that he missed
it more than he thought he would. As a youngster, fresh
out of seminary, it had seemed so heartbreakingly routine;
of course, he had harbored ambitions then . . . not anymore.

The new Holy Father had reluctantly granted him a
year's leave of absence from his cardinalitial duties in
Rome and as a residential archbishop. He immediately
chose to come back to New Mexico, where he had once
served as the director of the rehabilitation program at the
Abbey of Christ the Redeemer: there his charges had been
drug addicts, alcoholics, pedophiles, gamblers, and otherwise fallen priests. He had built up a model program over
a four-year period, written a text that was still used in some
university courses, and forever opened a place in his heart
for disgraced priests. He believed that God, too, loved the
fallen brethren in a special way; he hoped so, anyway, since
he arguably qualified for that distinction himself.

It was now Wednesday, and Father Dan Cade had gone
missing from the little pueblo church about thirty miles
outside of town where he was pastor to a few dozen Jemez
Indian people and several locals who called St. Mary's their
parish. He had not shown up to celebrate 7:30 mass on
Monday morning, and a sweep of the church and his rooms
revealed the likelihood that he had taken Sunday's collection receipts with him. No one knew where, but the county
sheriff's department had been alerted and they swiftly located the AWOL priest's battered car in the parking lot of
a motel east of the city in a little one-stoplight hamlet in
the desert.

Mulrennan had asked for and received permission from
the sheriff to see the man first. He turned down the volume
of the static-marred radio and fumbled with a road map to
check for the exit he needed to take.

He gingerly guided the big automobile onto the exit
ramp, swerved to avoid a deep pool of water in a low-lying
stretch of frontage road dangerously close to an arroyo,

drove slowly as he looked along the roadside for the motel.
Within a few minutes he spotted it: a collection of cabins
under a sad, unlit neon sign that said, simply, U-Stay Motor
Lodgings. An ambulance and a sheriff's department squad
car were parked in front of the office. At the registration
desk he and a waiting deputy sheriff obtained a key to
number 7. Then they stepped out into the sheeting rain and
walked across the gravel drive.

The officer stood to one side. Mulrennan's hand shook
involuntarily as he inserted the key into the flimsy door
lock. He pushed the door open and was assaulted with the
stench of alcohol and sweat and dirty clothing. His heart
stopped as he saw the recumbent figure on the floor. It was
Father Dan, all right. Tim knew him from previous out-
patient counseling sessions at the monastery rehab. In addition to parish fill-ins Tim had taken on a staff assignment
as a counselor and was given three clients—enough to keep
him busy several hours a week, with one day off.

It was his profession, his calling, to minister to others,
to be available, to say the right thing, to manage budgets
and departments that tended to the well-being of a vast
Christian flock, to travel widely and chair committees and
see that good deeds were performed on a large scale. Yet
despite his training and experience of thirty-nine years as
a priest, his immersion in psychology and theology, he suddenly felt distinctly out of place. Here, faced with a fellow
minister of the Gospel, one-on-one in a cramped, filthy motel room, doubt seized him. This man needed his help. Was
he prepared to give it? What was he supposed to do? He
knew the answers, but also knew the pain and difficulty
that lay ahead. Almost mechanically, he stepped inside,
alone, leaving the door open to the cooling, cleansing
downpour. The deputy waited, as agreed, with his back to
the unpleasant scene.

Tim Mulrennan knelt beside the man's body, touched it,
detected breathing. Thank God . . . He slowly, carefully,
turned him over. A few days' growth of beard, uncombed
hair, desiccated lips, a torn T-shirt, dirt-streaked jeans, bare
feet: the priest, who was only forty years old or so, was in
very bad shape—but he was alive. A quart bottle lay empty

on the stained carpet beside the body. Vodka.

Gingerly, Mulrennan levered him upright, then lifted the deadweight: no more than 130 pounds, he guessed, but all arms and legs. The drunk moaned and flailed, making it even more difficult for Mulrennan to maneuver him onto the bed. Finally, he succeeded, and arranged the passed-out man's limbs and propped the head on a yellowish pillow.

Tim Mulrennan, a cardinal-archbishop of the Holy Roman Catholic and Apostolic Church, knelt on the filthy carpet beside the reeking bed and folded his hands in prayer.

First he felt it, as a powerful physical presence, then he looked up and saw it: a man dressed in white. Was he wearing a robe of some kind? He couldn't quite tell. There was something very human, yet otherwordly about the apparation, an aura or fire that came from within the strange angelic figure and illuminated his body.

As if it were a television picture or a holograph, the image of the man stood on the opposite side of the bed, looking down on Father Dan Cade. The face was familiar to Mulrennan, even without the gold-framed glasses. It was the smile, benign yet powerful, that betrayed his identity.

"Holy Father . . . ," Mulrennan croaked, barely able to spit out the words.

The figure did not answer, but put out his hands in a gesture of healing, first toward Dan Cade for a full minute, then over Tim Mulrennan himself. Mulrennan felt the renewing energy flow through his own body like electricity. He tried, but could not speak. He had so many questions. Why was this man, this angel here? He remembered that the pontiff had traveled to the Philippines for a pastoral visit. Was he still there? What did this mean? He knelt as if frozen to the spot, staring at the bright figure, drinking in the warmth and love that emanated from this man.

"I am with you," the figure said. Tim heard the words in his mind but there was no voice. "I am with you, even to the end of the world."

Mulrennan strained to listen, hoping for more. He watched the vision flicker, brighten, filling the room with a divine light.

The drunken priest moaned and shifted, breaking Mulrennan's concentration. He looked around the room. The apparition was nowhere to be seen. Then he heard the deputy call out to the ambulance driver.

Father Cade opened his eyes. "I really screwed up, didn't I?"

"Yes, you did. You took the money from the church. Do you realize that? You must have been in a blackout. The people in your parish are worried sick."

"I can't believe they give a damn about me."

"Oh, they do, Dan. And your bishop does. And I do."

"Christ, Tim . . . I mean, Your Eminence. I'm so sorry. I'll never do it again, I swear."

"For some reason I believe you—this time. We need to get you into the hospital first, to detox. Then you'll have to drag your ass back to your AA meetings if you're going to stay sober."

"I know—I really blew it—"

"You can stop whining now. I sure wouldn't want to have your hangover in the morning."

The pale, skinny, broken priest managed a weak smile. "You know, for all my troubles, I still wouldn't trade places with you."

"Now, that makes me feel good." Tim Mulrennan stood to his full height and smiled wanly. "I suppose we all prefer the devil we know."

He could not erase the powerful vision from his mind. His friend and spiritual father had been present—miraculously! Tim would have to call the Vatican, try to get through to him when he returned from his trip.

The officer and the medical team swept into the stagnant room and took over. The frail, sodden priest was taken away. Mulrennan answered a few questions for the deputy's report, then settled the bill in the motel office. U-Stay Motor Lodgings had a new vacancy.

He started the car's engine, noticed the gas gauge read Empty. Damn! He wasn't used to all this driving . . . must find a service station . . . He fumbled in his pocket to see if he had any cash left, pulled out seven dollars.

He was not listening to the radio, but the words cut through his mind like a knife through flesh: ". . . killed in a bomb blast at an outdoor mass in Manila today. Muslim terrorists are suspected by local authorities. Vatican spokesmen had no comment other than to say that an investigation is under way. Tomorrow the pope's remains will be flown to Rome, where funeral preparations are under way."

Dear Jesus, no! The Explorer felt as if it were hurtling out of control—and Tim Mulrennan jerked the wheel to the right, braking to a stop on the shoulder. The news broadcast moved on to the stock market; he switched stations, could not pick up any more news. He sat numbly, without thinking or feeling, as the fat, cold raindrops pelted his vehicle like so many unanswered prayers.

He cried like a child, sobs choking him, tears blinding him. How could it possibly be? No warning, not a hint. A bomb? He fiddled with the radio, trying to catch an all-talk or all-news station. Weather reports . . . sports . . . traffic—everything but the most important thing in the world . . .

Just a few weeks ago he had received a letter from the Holy Father. De Guzman had been very concerned, very solicitous of his friend's spiritual recovery. Tim Mulrennan had written back: "As I have gotten into the swing of activity here, doing my little bit to help the staff, I have been blessed to be assigned to a couple of difficult cases. It is very good to be needed, to be able to help, to get out of my own head and be of service to another human being. Not that the administration of a large diocese isn't service—of course it is. But one-on-one work with an addicted or otherwise troubled priest is satisfying beyond measure. One of the men I'm working with is a chronic alcoholic in deep denial, even after he was caught red-handed stealing from the collection basket and gambling in Las Vegas, drunk out of his mind. His bishop turned him out, not knowing what else to do. A local hospital detox found out he was a priest and referred him here. It took the bishop a month to respond to our request for his approval to treat the man. I don't blame him in the least: this priest is very far gone, a truly hopeless case. In other words, a candidate for a miracle. Yesterday he disappeared, tried to hitchhike back to Las Vegas, why no one knows. Please keep him—and the others—and me—in your prayers, if you can. And know that you are in ours, every morning and evening here."

Prayer. He had spent more time in prayer in the past few months than he had in decades, at least four times per day for a minimum of an hour. What had it gained him? He had never felt more devastated and alone than he did in this moment, abandoned by his God. . . . How could such hatred and violence continue to exist? Whether the target was a pope, a Muslim refugee, or a Jewish shop owner or an innocent tribesman, whether the perpetrator was politically to the right, the left, or simply evil, whether the world wept or turned aside with indifference—there was a grave human problem that had never been resolved and never would be until the final day of reckoning for all men and women. And what good was prayer? Mulrennan pounded the steering wheel as tears flowed down his face. What can any one of us do in the face of such evil? Why, God? Why?

He restarted the car, drove back onto the road and found his way back to the monastery, went immediately to his room where he turned off the ringer of his telephone and knelt in silence and grief for more than two hours. His mind had shut down, his soul numbly aching, and the words he wanted to cry out did not come to his lips. He had never known such a feeling of physical and spiritual paralysis.

In the late evening he returned a few phone calls from family and friends and called the chancery office in Newark to speak to his secretary and the archdiocesan vicar general. Both were stunned but businesslike, and both begged him to come back as soon as possible. He agreed to do so, and after notifying the director of the abbey, packed his few belongings and took a taxicab to the airport in Albuquerque, leaving his beloved SUV behind, a gift to the director and staff of Redeemer, who would put it to good use in their important work. It was a small token of his gratitude to the people and the place for making him welcome in his time of retreat, like a wanderer of old, a pilgrim far from home.

Home: he was needed there now. It was good to be needed by others in such a time. This was what he had trained and worked for, what he had been born for, he believed. The trip passed in a blur, and he found himself at

Newark Airport almost before he realized it; he greeted his secretary and driver with hugs and a silent blessing.

Home: as Mulrennan sat in the backseat of the sleek car that exited the airport and took the winding, rutted highway-access roads past the old North Terminal and toward the city. He saw asphalt and concrete and ghostly construction vehicles—a low, unspectacular skyline—intense traffic even at this Saturday evening hour in midsummer. He opened the back window and looked out and breathed in the humid city air and listened to the familiar ebb and flow of the highway and street noise. The summer of 1967 seemed very real and very recent in his memory. Copies of the day's *Star-Ledger* and *New York Times* lay beside him on the leather seat, untouched. The tragic headlines barely registered on him. He had not watched television or listened to the radio for more than twenty-four hours. He did not want to soil his mind with images of his friend's assassination and its aftermath. He had heard that the remains of the Holy Father, as best they could be recovered, would be flown to Rome for the funeral, then— in an unprecedented step—returned to his native Philippines for burial. The American archbishop smiled to himself at De Guzman's last act of independence; he would be remembered as a good and strong and holy pope, and a wonderful man. Mulrennan would always remember him as a staunch friend of the truth and his savior in the conclave that had shattered and rearranged both their lives.

"Your Eminence," the young priest beside him said, "do you wish me to prepare your things for the trip to Rome— for the funeral?"

"I suppose you must, but there is not much to prepare, just the usual clothes. Unfortunately, we have everything we need from the last time. . . ." He stared out the window as the big car turned from McCarter Highway onto Raymond Boulevard in the heart of the city near the old Pennsylvania Railroad Station. They were just a few minutes from the basilica and home.

Home: His brother and sisters would want to see him, and he them. He would call his stepmom. He would say mass tomorrow in the cathedral, speak to the staff, review the state of the archdiocese. He was back. He must try to wrap things up here within a day or so, then fly again to Rome. He could not imagine the funeral, did not even allow himself to try. He wanted to be home, stay close to home for a good long time. Perhaps he would, after all . . . The priest interrupted his thoughts.

"And for the conclave—should we make arrangements, Eminence? You know the drill." He was trying to be light in this dark moment.

"The conclave," Mulrennan said with some irony and even contempt in his voice. "I must speak to Cardinal Biagi. They will have enough electors to choose their new victim without me."

"What are you saying, sir?"

"I am not going into the conclave, Father. I have already been there."

CHAPTER SIXTEEN

Wednesday, July 25, 9:02 P.M.

Tim Mulrennan joined several young priests and semi-narians for a scheduled nine o'clock supper in the dining room of the North American College where he was staying, in a modest dormitorylike room. His decision not to enter the conclave had been reported and analyzed all over the world—a juicy bit of Vatican gossip for the scandal-addicted media.

One CNN reporter, an intrepid British woman who breached the minimum security measures on the College grounds, had found him at morning prayer in the courtyard and tried to persuade him to grant her an interview on camera; he declined, but eventually agreed to talk to her off the record. He was impressed with her pluck and her serious demeanor—and her apparent inside knowledge of the Vatican and the issues facing the universal Church. And she reminded him more than a little of Rachel Séredi.

"Cardinal Mulrennan, you haven't spoken to the press since January, after the last conclave and before you went on leave of absence from your archdiocese in New Jersey. Why?" Her name was Judith Freundlich, and she sat on a stone bench beside Tim, notepad poised to absorb his words.

"Off the record?" He wanted to confirm absolutely the terms of their conversation. She nodded to indicate her agreement. "The simple answer is, I've had nothing to say. I felt all talked out at the last conclave, and I spoke to the Holy Father, who instructed me to take time away from my duties as archbishop. The tentative plan that I discussed with him was to take several months and then discuss my return to Newark, perhaps in the fall."

"But you did not resign your cardinalate?"

"No. I remain eligible as an elector."

"Were you devastated by the accusations about your past that came out during the January conclave?"

"Devastated? I don't know. Hurt and surprised—yes, because everything was taken out of its proper context. I'm not making excuses. There's no question I have made mistakes and misjudgments as a priest, but I have never violated my vows, nor done anything illegal or unethical. I've had a lot of time—the past six months—to look back at my life, the decisions I have made, the sins I have committed, the good things I have done. On balance I'd have to say that I qualify as a human being."

"What did you do during your time away?"

"I returned to New Mexico, to an abbey outside Albuquerque, to work with troubled priests. I had been director of the treatment center there twenty years ago. It was greatly therapeutic and restorative for me, and I hope I was able to help some of the men there. One of them was a very special case—and I pray for him every day.

"I ask myself: Have I been a good steward of these abundant gifts from my Father? The answer is, I can do a much better job—and I will. I have decided to ask the next Holy Father, whomever he may be, to allow me to resume my work for the church of Newark. You know, there are now nearly two million Catholic souls there, and it is my home. I hope to serve the community of the faithful there, for as long as I live."

The morning sun had limned the roofline of the buildings that surrounded the courtyard. As they sat there, Ms. Freundlich scribbled notes while the American cardinal spoke. He was more voluble than she had expected. She also noted the austere and serene setting of the North American College—called by some the West Point of the Catholic Church; she would need more background on that institution, she realized, her curiosity piqued. She liked Mulrennan, and she could understand how some of the old sourpusses in the College of Cardinals might be jealous of this rather handsome and charismatic man. Even in the black soutane with the scarlet sash and piping, the stiff white Roman collar, the pectoral cross, the red zucchetto cocked back on the crown of his gray head, and the plain black penny loafers, he exuded masculinity and empathy.

"Do you expect him to agree to your return?" she asked.

"I have no expectation whatever, and I'm willing to do whatever he asks, to go wherever he needs me."

"Who will be elected pope this time?"

Mulrennan's laugh was a sharp bark that echoed off the surrounding walls. "I have absolutely no idea. I will find out when you do. If I were to bet, I'd put my money on Cardinal La Spina."

"But he dropped out last time, according to stories I've read."

"True, but he had—and has—substantial support. I cannot say more than that without violating the secrecy of the conclave. Also, he is very conservative, perhaps traditional is a better word, and the cardinals always most naturally lean in that direction, unless forced to consider another direction by circumstances—or by the Holy Spirit!"

"You are teasing me now, Cardinal Mulrennan," the reporter protested.

"No—I am very serious. I believe in the Holy Spirit, and not just because it's a job requirement. I have seen His influence in my life, and within the conclave itself. The election of De Guzman as Pope Innocent was a direct manifestation of the Holy Spirit. Ask even the most cynical Catholic whether or not he believes it so."

"You admit, then, that there is cynicism and disenchantment within the Church? Isn't this especially true in the States?"

"Possibly. It is so unfortunate that the pope was taken from us so quickly. He had begun to win back the trust and affection of so many Catholics—and other Christians."

"On what do you base that conclusion, sir?"

"Well, on common sense and observation and reading the newspaper and watching CNN." Tim smiled wanly. "In my bones I could feel it. Pope Innocent connected immediately with all kinds of people. He was what we Americans

call a regular guy. Given time, he would have reached out
to the Muslim world the way his predecessors reached out
to Jews and to other Christian churches. Remember, he
came from the Philippines, which is still a very volatile
place—especially between Muslim rebels and the Catholic
majority in the cities. It is possible he could have secured
peace in his native region the way John Paul II did in Eastern Europe."

"Who do you think killed him?"

Tim Mulrennan reached for the breviary that he had lain
beside him on the cool stone bench. He touched the black
tooled-leather cover of the book, felt the worn, pebbly surface, tried to touch the truth and holiness contained therein:
the prayers he read every day of his life as a priest, the
words that drew him into his Father's loving presence. . . .
Who had murdered Pope Innocent XIV? The deep sorrow
and rage that he had known in the hours after he had
learned of the pope's assassination welled within him again,
and he was powerless to dam the flood. He turned his face
away from Judith Freundlich, who sought a headline and
not the underlying truth. Who had murdered his friend, the
gentle priest from Manila? Who had erased the embodiment
of hope from the earth? This was an act of pure evil by
evil men. Cardinal Mulrennan fumbled in the folds of his
cassock for a handkerchief and retrieved it. He stood and
blew his nose vigorously, unashamed.

"If you'll forgive me," he said as he stood and faced the
reporter once again. "I don't know who killed him. The
investigation will tell us, I'm sure—and I don't want to
speculate, even off the record."

She stood, taken aback by the American prelate's emotional reaction. "Sorry to upset you. I didn't mean—"

Timothy Mulrennan shook his head. "You have every
right to ask the question, but I do not have an answer. I
must return to my morning routine. I am scheduled to say
mass soon, and I can't be late for that—bad example for
the seminarians."

"One last question, if I may: What is your opinion of the
Evangelium Christi movement? They were rumored to have
opposed your election in the last conclave, and to have been

unhappy with the ultimate choice of De Guzman."

"Some of my best friends are Evangelium Christi," Tim joked. "I have even had dinner with them on occasion. And that's *on* the record if you like. Now, I really have to attend to business, Miss Freundlich."

At the supper table that evening he invited one of the seminarians, a thirty-year-old ex–public-interest lawyer from California, to offer grace. As they prayed Tim replayed the inteview and various other events of the day in his mind. He tried to put aside any thought of the current conclave, but it was nearly impossible; he felt like the kid who stays home sick during the school's biggest game of the season. But this was his own choice, he reminded himself.

The young men attacked their salads with gusto, keenly aware of Tim Mulrennan's presence among them. It was clear to him that they were too uncomfortable to start a conversation, so they focused on their plates. He nibbled at his own greens, then paused to refill everyone's glasses with iced tea—a real taste of the good old U.S.A. The evening news on the major Italian television network had focused on the investigation of the assassination: the Philippine national police had requested help from the FBI and Interpol, clearly signaling a theory of international conspiracy.

The American seminarians all seemed to agree that it had been orchestrated by terrorists for maximum news impact and disruption of the Church worldwide. It had certainly been a successful effort. Nearly two dozen people had died, and another forty were injured, some severely maimed. Cardinal Biagi had emerged with barely a scratch, but deeply wounded emotionally and spiritually. Likewise Vatican security forces, who generally teamed up effectively with local law enforcement and intelligence agencies, were shaken beyond enduring. No pope had been assassinated for three hundred years, since the imperious Boniface VIII, who had died after capture and torture by his French enemies in 1303, ending a nine-year reign. The nearly fatal attack on the pope in 1981 had caused the Italian police and the Swiss Guards to implement strict professional tactics that had

proved successful for twenty years as they guarded the most
public and peripatetic pontiff since Peter himself. But a
.500 batting average was in no way acceptable or excusable
when it came to protecting a pope's—or any man's—life.

"Did all of you attend the funeral mass last week?" Mulrennan blurted, nearly choking on the ominous silence. The
men nodded, looking at each other in vague embarrassment.
That was the correct answer, wasn't it? One of them, an
ordained priest studying for his doctorate in theology, mentioned that he had distributed the Eucharist, one of several
hundred priests recruited for that sacramental task.

Tim Mulrennan smiled. "I was a newly ordained priest
here in Rome in 1963, just taking on an assignment for the
Council, when Pope John died—I remember his funeral
very well. A sad but majestic occasion." And the immediate
aftermath, the knowledge that he was at the very center of
history . . . not something a young man—or his older version thirty-nine years later—would ever forget.

Rome, September 17, 1963

The small Roman gymnasium had only three grimy windows, barely cracked open, near the ceiling. The air inside
was dank and malodorous with male perspiration.

The two men darted across the basketball court in pursuit
of the brown leather ball. Twenty-six-year-old Tim Mulrennan, tall and skinny, clad in a sweat-soaked T-shirt and
dark blue trunks, secured the ball in his large hands before
it bounced out of bounds. His opponent, the forty-three-
year-old Polish bishop he had met just a few days ago,
screened Tim from the goal. The American priest pivoted
expertly, playing to his left, dribbling hard around the bulky
Pole.

Mulrennan gulped for breath. The Pole waved his long
arms to prevent a shot. Tim dribbled to the opposite side
of the foul lane, stopped abruptly and faked a shot. The
bishop jumped to block it. Then the young American gently
lofted a set shot that arced high and whispered through the
hoop. The tattered net arrested the ball for a split second

before allowing it to drop to the uneven floor.

The two players bent double, holding their knees, heaving for oxygen. Mulrennan had triumphed in this one-on-one match, 20 to 16.

"Your Grace—" Mulrennan wiped his face on his shirt. Tim had won three of their five games to twenty points, none easily. "If you wish to quit now—I'm happy to claim victory."

The Pole stood just under six feet and wore khaki slacks and all-black athletic shoes, vintage Stalinist-bloc 1950s. His short-sleeved shirt stuck like Scotch tape to his damp torso. His black-framed glasses gave him an intense scholarly aura that belied his athleticism. He had lost weight during a recent bout of mononucleosis brought on by chronic overactivity. He gave Tim a yellow-toothed smile.

"I do not accept defeat so readily. Best five of eight?"

Mulrennan could not help grinning and shaking his head. This man who appeared so deliberate and stolid would probably play thirty games, if that's what it took to beat a respected competitor.

"I'm so out of shape—" Tim gasped.

"You do not look that way to me."

"I feel it. I've been behind that desk all summer."

The two men went to the bench where they drank from the bottled water that they had brought and toweled themselves.

"I am tired and must go back to my room to finish the paper I am drafting for review by the council," the bishop said in precise English. He sat on the bench beside Tim.

"Which one?" Mulrennan toweled his sweat-soaked crew cut. He looked admiringly at his elder colleague. Karol Jozef Wojtyla, an auxiliary bishop to the See of Krakow, stood knee-deep in the middle of some of the most important and controversial work of the Second Vatican Council.

Tim Mulrennan, on the other hand, was a secretary-clerk for the Archbishop of Newark who headed the Bishops' Study Committee of the Ecumenical Council. He virtually lived in a cramped Vatican cubbyhole with a typewriter, electric coffee percolater, overflowing ashtrays, and mountains of paperwork to process. He knew that, even so, he held a privileged position—a brand-new priest among the Church's leaders and legislators gathered in historic session.

"A message on artificial means of birth control," Wojtyla replied. "A most interesting topic for a celibate."

Tim smiled. He had been in Rome for less than a month when the Vatican press office announced the death of Pope John XXIII, the beloved former patriarch of Venice, after a lengthy illness. In just five years as pope, Roncalli had single-handedly propelled the Church into the present century by summoning the first Ecumenical Council in nearly a hundred years. The Council's first session began on October 11, 1962, and the second session was scheduled to open in ten days. Cancer had taken the old pope's life. The clarity of his faith and the simplicity of his spirit would ensure his place in Church history forever.

Father Tim Mulrennan, scribe and paper pusher, played his own small role in John XXIII's legacy. He was curious to know more about his opponent's assignment to a very controversial subject. But before he could quiz the Polish prelate, Wojtyla spoke.

"I am very interested in your United States. Tell me about the section where you live."

"New Jersey—it is called the Garden State because of the many farms, woods, and mountains. But where I live is a large urban center near New York: industrial, grimy, crowded. My family has a home in the suburbs, and my father takes the Lackawanna railroad line into Newark. We are very typical Americans."

"Even as Catholics? In Poland, of course, more than ninety percent of the population is Roman Catholic. I have read that there is much intolerance of Catholics and Jews in the United States."

"By some people and in some places—yes. Bigotry against Negroes as well. That, I'm afraid, is pervasive. In the South there are Jim Crow laws and practices that date back to slavery times. In the northern states the prejudice is less open but still a fact of life, especially in the major cities with large black populations."

"Your black people are artists and laborers, are they not?

They contribute so much to the American society."

"I cannot explain the situation rationally," Tim said, "especially to a non-American. I believe slavery caused a terrible wound in our nation that has not yet healed—and it may never heal."

The Polish bishop grasped his towel in both fists and hung it from the back of his neck. He stood. "War and persecution are human conditions in every age and on every continent. See what we did to the Jews in the last war. I say 'we' because you and I are responsible as Catholics and as men for the actions of our fellow men. It is our task to correct these wrongs, to lead the Church in action."

"You fight the communists in your own country. Is it difficult?"

Wojtyla smiled like a schoolboy. "I do not fight. I surrender every day to the atheist bureaucrats and humbly render unto Caesar his due." His words were meekly Christian, but his stance was combative. "What the state 'allows' me to do—tend to my flock—I do vigorously: I mobilize them in their faith and strengthen their confidence; I keep them busy in their parishes. We Poles, too, are artists and laborers. We labor at our arts and make art of our labors. In fact—" His voice rose to the gymnasium rafters as he became more comfortable speaking in English: "Our greatest art and labor is our faith in the Gospel of Christ and in the glory of His Mother. She gives us the strength daily to render unto God *His* proper due."

He shrugged those powerful athletic shoulders. "We work, we pray, we survive. God is good to us, and one day He will open the eyes of the atheist bureaucrats. And on that day—" The bishop glanced upward and fell silent.

"During the war," Tim asked, reluctant but curious, "what did you do? And your family?"

"My entire family was gone by the time I was twenty-one. My younger sister died when she was a baby, my mother when I was eight. Then my older brother three years later. I lost my dear father in 1941. He died of a heart attack. I was not there. He was sixty-two. The war killed him.

"I alone survived. I was a forced laborer. God carried

me through the experience. I often ask, Why me? Why not my father or mother? Why not the Jews who were our friends, or the many brave Polish soldiers who fought the Nazis?"

Tim immediately regretted having raised the subject of the war. He had been a child in the States, far from the horrors this man had lived. He had asked because he wanted to know more about Wojtyla, not to dredge up the pain and the horror of the past.

The Pole surprised him. "Tell me about your family," he said with genuine interest, and perhaps to change the topic of their discussion.

"Three sisters and two brothers. My mother died when I was fourteen, and my dad remarried. My younger brother is really my stepbrother. Pretty boring, except it was very tough on all of us when Mom was sick. She had a drinking problem and—she died of cirrhosis."

Tim Mulrennan remembered the smell of the hospital corridors on that last visit to St. Michael's Hospital in downtown Newark. With his sisters and elder brother he attended her bedside as she was eaten up from inside by the alcohol she had ingested for many years. He feared her death and resented her abandonment of the family. He prayed to God and to any saint he could conjure to cure her and bring her home to Dad and the Mulrennan kids who needed her, that she would be miraculously struck sober. With the hospital chaplain and the nuns, they prayed the rosary in the hospital chapel. His elder sister, Theresa, knelt with him in the dingy wax-scented chapel; the others had little patience for the intricate time-consuming ritual of the rosary, though Madeline Mulrennan would have wanted them to pray for her this way. Even Tim's father rarely lasted for the entire five-decade cycle of Hail Marys, punctuated by the Our Father, and the Glory Be.

Prayer and sorrow mingled in the boy's mind. "Blessed is the fruit of thy womb" became a weirdly significant refrain that transported Tim back to the darkness of his own origin and gave him a deeper identification with the humanness of Jesus.

"Born of the Virgin Mary . . . was crucified, died, and

was buried." So the Master had been a man and had known suffering and death—and He promised every Christian triumph over these travails. "On the third day He rose again, in fulfillment of the Scriptures."

Sore-eyed and wearing a new navy blue suit, at his mother's funeral mass, Tim knew he wanted to be a priest. He wanted to get as close to God as he could so that he might ask Him why He had twice taken Madeline O'Casey Mulrennan from her young family: first, as a drunk, and secondly, through death. He trusted that there was an answer—and that it was God's right purpose. But it hurt so much for her to be gone. He also felt relieved for everybody. He didn't know what he felt . . . he ached from crying, and he had not spoken more than five or six words in the few days since her death.

Theresa sat by him in the front pew. The two smaller girls, Gertrude Anne and Kathleen, clung to Daddy. Kevin, a handsome eighteen-year-old with a fresh crew cut and a violet carnation in the lapel of his black suit, was a pall-bearer and sat with Madeline's brothers and cousins. There was room in Tim's bursting heart for jealousy of his brother's maturity. Tim did not want to be a "little boy" in the custody of his sisters but a man and a priest with a role and a voice in the mourning ritual.

His father hugged the little girls, just two and three years old, tightly to himself. Tim also yearned for Dad's steely attention. He rarely spent any time alone with Dad—which was to be expected in a family of five kids. Dad was distant and benevolent: Ted Williams and Santa Claus rolled into one tall, broad-shouldered, hardworking man.

The incense pricked young Tim's nostrils. No sun shone through the elaborate stained glass of the cavernous church. It was a chilly, overcast October day, a damp gray eternity. The boy shivered and shifted his butt in the hard pew. Theresa reflexively hushed him, but he ignored her maternal blandishments. His mind remained focused on the priest's movements before the altar.

There was no seeing beyond this day to a time when Mom would be absent from the family. This trial, to be motherless, Jesus had not endured: His mother had been

present at His death and had survived for a while before
she was taken into heaven to be with Him forever. Tim
believed this fervently and hoped that he, too, would somehow, someday be reunited with his own mother . . . that he
might ask, *Why?*

He knelt for the consecration of the bread and wine. As
the priest lifted host, then chalice above his head the altar
bells tinkled dimly. Tim's knees and back were sore as he
held himself attentively in the prayerful position. He anticipated the taste of the wafer on his tongue. He had fasted
since the night before, and his mouth was dry, his belly
empty.

Outside, between the church doors and the sleek black
funeral car, Tim stood in the cold October drizzle as his
mother's coffin was borne to the hearse.

He did not tell the Polish bishop all these things, but the
unspoken sorrow and hope were communicated as clearly
as if he had presented a treatise on the event. He bowed
his head and felt the bishop's silent blessing.

"Survival is not an end in itself, Father Mulrennan. Yet
I learned from the—what is the correct word?—*process*,
I think. Yes, I learned that hard work and discipline will
prepare one to receive God's grace. This is what happened to me. Many times I was stopped by soldiers who
demanded papers, identification, what was I doing there?
Each time I passed the test—I survived until the next
time." A shadow of sadness passed across the bishop's
ruddy face. "Why me? This is the question we survivors
ask ourselves."

"Don't you believe there was a purpose behind it all?"

"Oh, yes, I do. And I no longer have any doubt as to
God's will for me, nor that He took my family into his
bosom. They are at peace. There is no peace for me except
in prayer." He wiped the fog from the lenses of his glasses,
smiling.

Mulrennan's body ached, but his spirit soared. His own
large family had been virtually untouched by the war. With
five children to care for, Tim's father had not been drafted
but remained at his job and was able to support his brood
from Pearl Harbor to V-J Day and thereafter.

Survival. Perhaps he did not know the true meaning of the word, at least not as Wojtyla knew it from bitter wartime experience. Yes, he had lost his mother; he had failed a few school exams; he had lost some close baseball games; but what were any of those things? He himself had yet to be threatened with physical or mental extinction. One day he would be tested. He was certain of this. When? He could not know.

"I will remember you and your family in my prayers," Mulrennan promised.

"Thank you, Timothy. I shall remember your mother in my prayers to the Blessed Virgin." Wojtyla added: "I will whip you soundly the next time we play."

"That'll be the day," Tim muttered good-naturedly.

As Mulrennan looked up from the narrow players' bench he could not know that before year's end this man would be elevated to the post of Metropolitan Archbishop of Krakow, but he keenly sensed that he was in the presence of one of the most dynamic human beings he had ever known.

Cardinal Mulrennan did not share all the details of this encounter with the Americans at the supper table. He and they ate spaghetti Bolognese for a main course and winced through a soupy canned fruit cocktail for dessert. He sensed that his presence was a burden and something of an embarrassment to them. *Why isn't he with the others in the conclave, where he belongs?* they were saying silently, accusingly, to themselves.

How could they know the agony that his decision had caused him? They would never, could never understand truly. No man could. Except his old friend Cardinal Biagi—Allo, the self-described Vatican war horse and great elector. Tim could see him clearly and hear his silky politician's voice as he worked this second conclave within six months. After all, he had perfected his craft well enough to be named Secretary of State and camerlengo pro tem by the late pope, who surely recognized and needed Allo's gifts. Oh, leave it to Allo—he would get results, all right! His Eminence Leandro Aurelio Cardinal Biagi

would ensure that the promptings of the Holy Spirit were
understood clearly and acted upon unhesitatingly by the
114 electors now present and accounted for in the Sistine
Chapel. (Two cardinals had died in the spring, and Pope
Innocent had named a Filipino bishop to succeed himself.
He had not yet held a consistory, nor named any other
new cardinals.)

"Gentlemen, I must walk off this magnificent repast. Are
any of you free to join me?" None were—and just as well,
Tim needed some solitude.

"Your Eminence, will you give us your blessing,
please?" the sandy-haired Californian asked.

The young men bowed their heads and received the cardinal's blessing, then melted away to their rooms and the
college's library to hit the books. Tim stood, alone, and
went outside. The night was close and very warm, and he
was conscious of the sweat beading on his temples and
dripping from his armpits as he trod briskly through the
neighborhood, dodging cars and paying no attention to his
destination. In fact, he had none; he simply walked and
walked and glanced at his watch and walked some more,
losing himself in the ancient urban maze, breathing and
perspiring and forgetting—or trying to forget—his own
predicament.

He turned his mind upward to God and outward to others. . . . "For it is by self-forgetting that one finds. It is by
forgiving that one is forgiven. It is by dying that one awak-
ens to eternal life."

He prayed for Dan Cade, that he might find peace; for
Father Burgoyne, the pederast and suicide; for Cardinal
Vennholme, the manipulator and conspirator; for Rachel
Séredi and Ly Linh Sanh and Rita Kearney, who each had
shared with him a woman's heart; for his mother, an alcoholic long since dead from hopelessness; for the pastors
and teachers who had shown him how to be a man and a
priest; for his beautiful sisters and brothers, the gifts of a
loving God in his life; for his army comrades and his "enemies" in the war that had been fought silently and clan-
destinely, for the men who had tortured and killed his
brother Kevin in a terrible, brutal war—now thirty long

years ago; the man who had raped Ly Linh Sanh, whom
he had killed; for his dear father, a man who had worked
hard and tried his best to live a Christian life; for his stepmother who had tried her best to be a friend to him; for
the men sequestered within the Apostolic Palace this very
night who had accepted the responsibility to choose the
next Vicar of Christ, and for the man who would be chosen—may he truly love God and his fellow man enough to
take such an impossible burden upon his shoulders. . . .

As if it were a radio or loudspeaker blaring in his brain,
he remembered the words of the sainted Holy Father during
his visit last year, before his death in January: "When He
calls you must answer. You must say *yes* to God." Startled,
admonished, Tim Mulrennan replayed those words over
and over in his mind. Had he made the wrong decision?
Had he selfishly denied his responsibility to God and the
Church? Was it even his choice to make—or a matter of
humble obedience?

It was nearly midnight when he returned to the residence. He was ready to collapse, but when he went to ask
for his room key there was a message for him at the desk;
the night clerk said it had been hand delivered—by a
woman.

She was staying at the Caetani House, a pensione located
about a quarter mile from the Colosseum; he knew it well
because several family members and friends had stayed
there when they had visited him in years past. He phoned
but could not reach her directly. He left a message that he
would be there in about an hour. His watch read 11:54 P.M.
He took a quick shower and changed his clothing, putting
on a dark green polo shirt and black slacks. He called for
a taxi.

She awaited him in the small lobby of her hotel: Rachel.
Tim Mulrennan had not seen her for nearly fifteen years,
when she had left Jackson City and returned to Hungary.
They had corresponded intermittently, but no communication for at least five or six years. She stood, and he went
to her wordlessly. They embraced. He felt an immense sadness and a wonderful relief to see her again.

"What are you doing here? Why—?"

"Oh, Tim, my friend," she breathed, holding him tightly, her artist's hands pressing into the middle of his back.

It felt so right to hold her, and she fit comfortably into his embrace, her compact body against his. Yet it was not a sexual, or even a merely sensual experience for Mulrennan. It was pure unconditional love, as he had never quite felt it with anyone else.

They walked and talked like a pair of teenagers, catching up on lost years. Rachel was now in her fifties, lithe and animated, with streaks of silver in her hair that framed her strong face and jaw. She wore a white silk blouse and baggy gray pants above a pair of rope sandals. They wandered over toward the Colosseum that was illuminated even at this late hour for tourists. They bought cappuccino in paper cups and drank as they strolled. He could not believe his eyes.

"I had to see you, I'm not even sure why. I have established a good career in Budapest, my own studio, and students, the occasional exhibit. I am working in acrylics and multimedia, a few watercolors on the side." She smiled—watching his reactions, just enjoying his presence near her.

"I don't think I have to fill you in on my career moves," he said sardonically.

"I'm sorry they hurt you, Tim. That was very ugly, what they did."

He thought back to the days in Jackson City—his infatuation with this beautiful woman, the financial trouble in the diocese, his brother Stephen . . . how all of these crises had merged and crashed over him at the same time.

Jackson City, Missouri, October 21, 1981

Monsignor Mroz paced the floor of the bishop's office like an expectant father. Tim Mulrennan was at his desk poring over the auditor's report, and the counsel to the diocese waited outside. It was a bad day all around, and no one was kidding about it. Putting every inkling or image of Rachel to the back of his mind, the bishop did his very best to focus on the papers in front of him, which more or less proved that a lay administrator in the financial office had been embezzling funds for several years; the total amounted to more than $300,000.

"So where is he—Bill Mackey? Have you seen him?"

"Not for the past two weeks," Tom Mroz said. "He hasn't been in the office since you called in the auditor. No one knows where he is. His family lives in St. Louis, but they're not saying anything."

"I must call the archbishop. He will need to know about this." He dialed the archbishop's office in St. Louis, but the archbishop was not available at that moment. He left an urgent call-back message with the secretary.

Half a minute later the intercom buzzed and Mulrennan picked up the receiver. It was his secretary again: "Your Excellency, a visitor—he says he is your brother, Stephen, and that it is very important that he see you."

Stunned, pleased, worried, distracted, the bishop bolted from his chair and went out to the reception area where his younger brother stood anxiously, a tentative smile on his face. Stephen Mulrennan was a slight, handsome man in his late twenties, not nearly as tall as Tim, with hazel eyes and pale skin, lightly freckled. The older man embraced the younger and squeezed him hard. "God, it's really great to see you. What brings you all the way out here? Why didn't you call? Is something wrong?"

Stephen smiled as he gently pushed himself away from his brother. "I just needed to see you, that's all. I drove all the way from New York—twenty-four hours straight through."

"Well, then you've got to be exhausted. You'll stay here with me. But why didn't you call me, let me know—?"

"It's better face-to-face. Some things I have to tell you. I hope you don't mind, Tim—I had to do it this way. I know that you must have a million things going here, running a diocese and all. I took some time off work so that I could come out here . . . I really hope I did the right thing."

"Of course you did." Mulrennan could tell that Stephen was deeply troubled, having difficulty bringing himself to say what was wrong. He would not press the young man, let him get settled in a bit, rest and relax. "You've met Jenny, our secretary. She's the real boss around here. She'll show you to the living quarters, and you can take a shower, change clothes, get a bite to eat, whatever you need to do. I'll take care of some business first, then join you for dinner—early. How's that?"

"It's great, Tim. Thanks. I—" Stephen turned away to retrieve his single bag.

That evening, after a series of meetings but with the problems still far from resolved, the bishop ordered Monsignor Mroz to go out for a drink or to a movie to take his mind off the situation. He found his brother alone in the small guest room on the second floor of the chancery of the Diocese of Jackson City, as unlikely a place, he thought, as Albuquerque or Saigon or Rome itself for him to be. He considered the notion that God's plan was rarely obvious until it was too late for a mere human being to do anything about it. He wished he could wash away his feelings for Rachel and the tension caused by the diocese's financial crisis and his own doubts and insecurities, to reclaim some control over his own life. But he knew better: he knew that Almighty God was in charge, and that he, Tim Mulrennan, was a subject and a soldier and a servant whose duty was to report for duty and let the chips fall where they may. *Dear God, is it like this for every American male in his midforties? Where do I go from here?*

He decided to take Stephen out for dinner to a favorite barbecue restaurant in a depressed section of town. He was becoming well-known there among the largely black clientele and by the owner, a retired railroad porter now in his eighties who had opened this little hole-in-the-wall joint to keep busy and provide his countless relatives with paying jobs. No one worked harder than the owner, who seated Tim and Stephen at a wobbly table with a view of the black-and-white television that flickered inanely with the volume turned completely down: a silent rerun of *Three's Company* filled the small screen.

The brothers toyed with their food, though both were very hungry. Their minds were preoccupied by unspoken

problems; they talked about family and Stephen's career in
New York City and books they had recently read—everything but the burden Stephen seemed to be carrying on his
shoulders like a five-hundred-pound deadweight.

Finally, the elder brother said: "I'm ready to listen. Do
you want to talk here or someplace else?"

"You sound like you're in your bishop mode."

"I guess I can't help it. But I just want to be your brother,
if that is what you want. I know something is bothering
you—and I know it will help to talk about it." He regarded
the lines and contours of Stephen's face: the younger man
was obviously in some kind of pain.

"I want to, Tim. It's so hard. I haven't been able to—"
The young man burst into tears, looked down at the table,
his shoulders shaking.

Mulrennan reached across to him, touched his shoulder
and felt the surge of emotion that racked his body. As a
brother and a priest Tim wanted to take Stephen in his arms.
"Should we go someplace else?"

Stephen shook his head deliberately. "No," he managed. "I
might as well just tell you here. It doesn't really matter—"
He lifted his tearstained face. "Tim, I'm gay. My best friend
and lover is terribly sick, and I don't know what to do,
where to turn. I was afraid to come to you because—just
because I thought you wouldn't understand, that you'd condemn me. But I can't keep it inside anymore; I didn't know
who to tell."

Mulrennan sat back, rocked, breathless, as if his lungs
had been punctured. Oddly, he felt shocked but not surprised. Suddenly all the subtle indicators and signals that
Stephen had sent out over the years all made sense. He felt
guilty for not picking up on them before, not being available to Stephen who must have wanted to talk to him but
felt intimidated, put off by his clerical status, by the Church
he represented. He reached across the table and touched his
brother's hand.

"You could have told Gertie Anne, surely. You two are
close. Not that you couldn't have come to me."

"Oh, she's always known. That doesn't really count."

Stephen Mulrennan smiled through his tears. "She knows everything."

Tim could not hold back a chuckle. "Of course. God, I must be the stupidest person alive. Forgive me, Stephen. You know I love you, and nothing will ever change that— nothing. Let's take a ride."

The brothers drove around Jackson City and out into the country for hours, stopping only for gasoline for Tim's car. Stephen's lover had some type of virulent cancer that had struck suddenly: he was only twenty-eight. He was dying, and Stephen was angry and afraid. Tim put aside his priest's stole and years of academic training in theology, canon law, and even psychology, and just tried to be what his elder brother, Kevin, had always been for him: available when he was needed, an example of unqualified, unambiguous love of one brother for another. He had no doubt that Kevin, tough marine that he was, would have embraced and supported Stephen with ever fiber of his being—if only he were here. . . .

"Steve, let's make a pact," Mulrennan said when they returned to the bishop's residence and parked the car and went into the kitchen for some lemonade. "We will talk to each other at least once a week by telephone. Pick a time— or it could be any day of the week. But let's commit to ourselves that we'll do it."

"Don't you think I have done wrong? I really expected you to want me to reform somehow."

"I want you to be who you are. I cannot condone sinful behavior of any kind, in myself or anyone else. But I am not going to judge you one way or the other or require that you change before I love you. If your heart is open to God, you will know what is right and what is wrong. He created you, I didn't. I'm just glad to be your brother." He embraced Stephen again.

"I dreaded coming out to you, Tim. I was sure you would want to have nothing to do with me. I'm sorry I doubted you."

"You have nothing to be sorry for on that count. But I will be very angry with you if you don't stay in close touch.

CONCLAVE 355

I mean it." Mulrennan clasped his large hand on his brother's slender shoulder.

In the early hours of the next morning the bishop awoke to the shrill ring of his bedside telephone. It was the indefatigable Mroz—did the man never sleep?

"We've located Bill Mackey. He's in St. Louis. He went directly to the archbishop. He has been granted sanctuary of a kind, according to the archdiocesan chancellor—orders from the papal nuncio in Washington."

"Vennholme?"

"Yes. Seems like Mackey is a staunch Evangelium Christi member, and he ran to the 'big boss.' But I don't get it. I would have thought he'd go anywhere else."

"Neither do I. I'll call Archbishop Vennholme myself in the morning. There are legal issues now. Sounds like he wants to take this upon himself."

"How's your brother?"

"Much better, I think. We had a long talk last night. He'll be driving back to New York in a few days."

"Busy day ahead. Sorry to call at this hour, but I thought you'd want to hear."

"You were right. But you need to get some sleep yourself, Tom."

"I'll try. Can't promise."

Mulrennan himself lay awake until sunrise. His brother Stephen. Bill Mackey. Henry Vennholme. The diocese. Rachel Serédi. The timing of all these events . . . a grand tragicomedy of coincidence. Or was it?

Tim and Rachel walked and talked for hours without stopping. They found themselves back at the North American College, and he was flustered, not wanting their conversation to end, to lose her again. A priest came out from the reception hall and approached him. At first Tim did not realize that the man wanted to speak with him. Rachel, though, understood what was happening.

"Your Eminence," the priest said. "Cardinal Biagi sent me. He urgently asks you to join him in the conclave."

For an agonizing, soul-exploding moment he felt whipsawed—between emotion and duty, between the past and the present, between earth and heaven—yet he knew what he would decide, what he must decide. His God had called him to be a servant and a fisher of men, and he had committed himself to the priesthood; there was nothing more important—no personal need or comfort or instinct, no person or relationship—than this vocation. He could hear Monsignor Froeschel's voice in the old pastor's study at Our Lady of Mercies: "Be patient, be grateful for your vocation. Few men can know what we do—about the souls of people, about the will of God. If you serve the faithful, the children of Our Father, they will give back to you more than you could ever hope for. That is the greatest and most secret joy of being a good priest." A good priest . . . could he still be one? How would going into the conclave now, at this late hour, accomplish anything? He suspected Cardinal Biagi's motive—surely it was political. Did the Florentine need one more vote to push his candidate to two-thirds? A harsh wind of doubt swept through his being, chilling his soul. Had he been wrong to stay away in the first place? And what was the almighty hurry now?

He immediately made a decision, surprising himself with its rightness and clarity, against his every instinct of self-interest. He did not want to, but it was a matter of sacred duty; in a sense, he had no other choice.

"I must go," he said to Rachel. He looked directly into her brown-flecked eyes.

"I know, Tim. I do not wish to hold you back—I never wanted that." She reached for his hand. "You have always been a man called to do great things for God. I just wanted to see you for a little while before—" She did not finish her thought but looked down at the floor.

Tim Mulrennan touched her chin gently with his finger and lifted her head so that her gaze met his; they were both cried out, emotionally drained.

"It means so much to me that you are here, that you understand. Rachel—" He struggled to find the right words. "You are the only woman who ever touched me in that secret, sacred place in my heart . . . the only one who ever will."

"I wanted to do the right thing, even though it hurt so much, Tim. It still hurts after all this time."

"You gave me the greatest gift you could have given, my lovely Rachel."

"Go, go." She released him, stepped back to look at him.

"Good-bye, Rachel. Please keep me in your prayers."

"What would my Jewish parents say about that?"

"They would say you are a wonderful daughter—the best."

"Good-bye, Bishop Tim." Rachel Séredi walked quickly away in the night.

When she was gone, Mulrennan turned to the priest who stood nearby, mouth agape, wondering what in the world was going on here. The American addressed him briskly and in his best businesslike matter: "I will grab a bag and come right back. I'll be just a few minutes."

He was as good as his word. He threw a change of underwear, a pair of socks, toiletries, his black cassock, and his breviary missal in the overnight carryall. The priest-escort guided him to a waiting car, and they drove off toward the Vatican. In just a few minutes they entered the Domus Sanctae Marthae, and Tim, despite the hour—close to 4:00 A.M.—and the suddenness of the summons, easily found his way to the assigned room: the same one he'd had during the January conclave. A strange sense of inevitability gripped him as he lay, fully clothed, on the familiar too-narrow, too-short bed. He closed his eyes and folded his hands on his chest and silently recited the Hail Mary and breathed deeply of the centrally cooled air of the residence and asked God for some serenity of mind in this hour of haste and uncertainty.

He slept for about an hour, then awakened as was his habit at five. He had just splashed water on his unshaven face, still wearing the clothes he had slept in, when there was a hard rap on the door. He had no doubt who it was.

"Timofeo, my son—you came. You are needed here." Biagi stepped into Mulrennan's room and gave the younger man a tight, paternal hug. "You look handsome in mufti," he remarked with a question in his voice, eyeing Tim's nonclerical clothing.

"Well, it's just what I was wearing when you called for me. Take me as I am."

"Gladly," Biagi said. The Italian prelate still bore the marks of bomb-strewn debris on his face, and he looked rather gaunt, as if he had just returned from a faraway battlefield. "Just as you are."

CHAPTER SEVENTEEN

Thursday, July 26, 9:47 A.M.

Five hundred years of incense, burning candles, and pilgrims' perspiration, to say nothing of the ghosts of long-past conclaves, assaulted Tim Mulrennan's senses as he walked from the Pauline Chapel, after the opening-morning Mass of the Holy Spirit, into the Sistine Chapel at the tail end of the assembly of cardinals. For the second time in six months, he was an elector, albeit a reluctant and uncertain one. But the obligation of his cardinalate, the strictures of the Apostolic Constitution he had previously sworn to uphold—these responsibilities outweighed, negated his personal discomfort. It was not, after all, about *him*, as much as it sometimes seemed that way in his private mind. Still, he felt the tug of his conscience and distaste pulling at the long black sleeve of his plain priest's cassock. Only for Biagi, dear Allo the inveterate politician and spiritual Dutch uncle, would he endure the emotional anguish it cost him to be here. Then he chastised himself silently: *Why don't you just shut off your brain and be grateful that you're alive and had a choice whether to be here or not.* Perhaps it would go quickly this time; perhaps the Holy Spirit would blare His message to these men with unmistakable clarity and volume; perhaps the Sacred College would announce its choice by suppertime. Perhaps St. Peter's would ascend from the earth into the clouds. . . . He smiled wanly at the image of Christendom's greatest basilica as a latter-day extraterrestrial ark.

He felt their eyes on him as each cardinal took his place in the double-tiered rows along the walls of the chapel. There were a few changes in position in the less-senior ranks of the electors due to the absence now of De Guzman, Zimmerman, an ailing old Italian who had passed away, and the Spanish Jesuit, Portillo—the presence of the newly created Filipino cardinal who sat in dazed and silent awe among his fellow princes of the Church—as well as Biagi's assumption of the camerlengo's role. There were two fewer electors than in January, yet it was remarkable how much was the same, how similar it must be to every conclave that had ever been held here; there were more dark faces, fewer Italians, many more native languages, but tradition and history prevailed: these successors to the apostles and the bishops of the ancient Church shouldered much the same spiritual and temporal responsibilities as their predecessors. They gathered under the constitution promulgated by the assassinated pope's predecessor; Innocent had not lived long enough to reconsider the process of electing the Roman pontiff, and it was doubtful that he would have wished any changes at all.

Cardinal Mulrennan had been admitted to the conclave late, but before the seal had been applied to the sacred proceedings, after the camerlengo had polled the assembly to be assured that a majority did not object, which caused some whispering among the 114 other electors and a few challenging looks during the mass from some of the bolder conservatives. Tim had barely had enough time to shower and shave and comb his hair before rushing to join the others; he caught his breath and gathered his thoughts during the homily, and his mind lifted to a more spiritual plane as the electors had processed into the Sistine with the chant of the *Veni Creator,* setting a decidedly medieval tone for the gathering. It was like being transported back and forth in time, only affirming the apostolic connection between this twenty-first-century conclave and the earliest synods of the Church elders in Jerusalem . . . a time when the Holy Spirit was manifested in tongues of flame and a faith that took the early apostles to the very ends of the earth, as they knew it, to spread the Gospel.

Mulrennan's mind was heavy with doubts.

Are we worthy successors to those men and women of the ancient days? Will the Spirit come again to us, despite

*our terrible sins and lapse of faith? How can we choose a
successor to the martyred pope who walked among us in
this very place only months ago?*

Francis X. Darragh stood at the window and looked out at
the brilliant summer morning, one of the hottest on record
in Kansas City: and it could get awfully damned hot and
humid in this part of the country. Frank Darragh's quarter-
acre front lawn was a green carpet dotted with manicured
shrubbery and pin oak trees that maintained some privacy
for the big house. The high-tech sprinkler system worked
overtime after dark, and the landscape crews came twice a
week to trim and weed the grassy expanse. His mother had
retreated to her room after morning mass, and she would
enjoy the centrally cooled comfort of the house until evening when she and her son might drive over to the park for
a short walk among the magnificent roses that had, so far,
and with an enormous amount of attention, survived the
brutal heat of July.

Darragh had chosen not to fly to Rome for the second
conclave. His private office was, instead, wired to the max:
E-mail, Internet, television, several telephone lines, fax ma-
chines, video-conferencing capability. He received hourly
bulletins from the Vatican news service, and Father Ciccone, who had traveled to Rome and taken the suite at the
Hotel Columbus, phoned three times daily with news from
their Evangelium sources within the conclave.

He mouthed a silent prayer: *Let Your will be done among
the men gathered again to choose the Successor to Peter.
Let the Holy Spirit speak to them this time without interference from the forces of the Antichrist who had corrupted
the last conclave and thwarted the ability of the cardinals
to make the correct decision. Bless Cardinal Vennholme,
and give him the strength to prevail in the face of certain
opposition and criticism. Open their eyes and their hearts
to the truth, that they might repel the minions of evil. . . .*

The harsh ring of the telephone startled him from his
musings, and he went to the wide glass-topped desk and
pressed the blinking orange button, which activated the
speaker phone. "Darragh," he barked preemptively.

"My old pal," came the cocky greeting. The voice was unmistakable: Harry C. Benjamin. "Haven't heard from you in a long time, so I thought I'd give a ring. How've ya been?"

Darragh switched from speaker to hand receiver. "Our business was concluded several months ago, satisfactorily, Mr. Benjamin. We have nothing to discuss."

"Oh, I beg to differ, sir—with all respect, mind you. I invested your generous financial support in some world traveling. Had a blast, I don't mind telling you. Went back to my old haunts in Aukland, saw a bit of Asia—beautiful and frightening place, I can tell you candidly. And I stopped off in Manila for a few weeks. Did some snooping there, following my nose for a story. I was blessed with keen instincts, I was. That's why you employed me in the first place, I think—wasn't it?"

"You are not in my employ anymore, and I am very busy at the moment. Good-bye."

"Not so quick, Mr. Darragh, sir. I think you might want to hear about what I turned up in the Philippines."

"I can't imagine why I would be interested in anything you have to say."

"Well, I hope you're taping this, because you certainly will want to listen to it again. I don't expect you to take what I tell you at face value." Benjamin chuckled conspiratorially and coughed. "Anyway, it does have some value, though. I would put it at about a million dollars U.S."

"What are you talking about?"

"Give me your fax number, Mr. Darragh, and I'll send you the first page of a story I'm writing. This is legitimate news, and I imagine the TV people or even the *New York Times* would love to get their paws on it. Speak slowly and I'll write down the number."

Despite his impatience with this charlatan, Frank Darragh gave him the fax number and hung up. Within a minute the machine spit out a single page, which he snatched up and read. Anger gave way to fear and hatred, and he paused before picking up the telephone as it began to ring almost immediately.

It was Benjamin again, of course chuckling merrily.

"You are insane," Darragh said by way of greeting.

"I frankly don't know what sanity is anymore. Is assassination sane? Is funneling money through Evangelium Christi accounts to Muslim extremists sane? Is expecting to get away with it sane? You tell me, sir, what is sane or insane."

"You cannot prove any of this garbage," Darragh blurted.

"Close enough. There are a few pieces of the puzzle I haven't been able to fit in. But the big news organizations have the power and the money to investigate, as well as the cops, and the Vatican too—they will be very interested to find out the truth."

Darragh saw on the caller ID read-out that Benjamin was calling from Rome. It would be easy enough to track him down.

"I will wire you a payment today. Where can I reach you?"

"How much?"

"One hundred thousand—to start."

"Not enough. I want two hundred as a first payment toward a million U.S. And don't tell me you can't. I'll give you an account number in London for this one. Different accounts for future payments."

"Send me the rest of the story. And I will need evidence that you have destroyed all your notes. Also, I want the names of your sources, everything you have supposedly found out and from whom. Understood?"

"I understand English pretty well, Mr. Darragh."

Darragh's head churned with anger and resentment. How dare this worm of a man threaten him—and the Evangelium movement? Little did Benjamin know with whom he was dealing . . . and how swiftly he would be dealt with in turn.

After the January conclave, Darragh had retreated to his home to pray and seek God's guidance for him and for the movement; he consulted with Evangelium leaders from around the world to determine what their best course of action should be. He even met with Cardinal Vennholme, now disgraced and headed toward retirement or exile, at the Vatican, to ask for his counsel. The cardinal had merely advised caution and a watchful stance; the new pope did not have a reputation for extreme liberalism or impatience—rather, he had always been a politically cautious doctrinal moderate, leaning to the conservative position whenever pressed to the wall. His strength had been his pastoral commitment to his diocese and his region. He had served throughout the tyranny, revolution, democratic reform, and the inevitable corruption that had followed; and through it all he always took a quiet middle path for the Church. Yet his first statements after ascending the Throne of Peter were disconcerting to staunch Evangelium adherents like Darragh.

Had the electors of the conclave made a mistake? Had they ignored the promptings of the Holy Spirit? Had La Spina been pushed aside unjustly? Had De Guzman usurped the papacy in a coup engineered by Biagi? Was Mulrennan the bait, the distraction that enabled anti-Evangelium forces to prevail—this time? The philanthropist's mind traveled many a circuitous path to reach a verdict of conspiracy and collusion. The next question was, what to do about it?

Books would be written, newspaper stories printed, claiming a countercoup by conservative forces. This had happened after the death of Pope John Paul I in 1978. It was inevitable, and Darragh and his comrades in the movement must accept that and live with it, for it was the way of the world in this post-twentieth-century world. People would chose to believe the worst. A fact of life. He rubbed his temples to ease the throbbing pain.

God, may the light of Your righteousness shine upon Your chosen people. May we do Your will in a world infested with evil and error. May You grant us the courage to act, to preserve Your Church, to protect life—and, yes, to take life if it becomes necessary to do so . . . for the good of Your people.

Frank Darragh hung up the telephone in disgust. He felt like taking a shower—after he called Father Ciccone to report on this latest untoward development. The young priest would know what to do about Benjamin. . . .

Darragh himself would never, ever relinquish his dream for the Holy Church! With the power and clarity of the visions the apostles themselves had experienced, the man from Kansas City had seen the risen Christ and heard His voice calling him to act in the name of the Lamb of God. He had been astounded at this event, kept it to himself for fear that others would not understand or believe him; he took it as a sign of favor from God, a sign of his specialness in the sight of the Creator, although he would never claim sainthood for himself or his fellow laborers in the Evangelium movement. Perhaps his mother qualified, having raised an unruly brood the way she had—with faith and selflessness—and served the Church in so many quiet, heroic ways through prayer and anonymous gifts. Yes, she was a saint in his heart and, he was sure, in the mind of God. He was so grateful she was still alive, with him!

Sometimes he felt dirty in her presence. There were things a man had to do that were unpleasant, even nasty, things that might seem wrong to others who did not accept a greater purpose. She would not understand . . . and he would maintain a wall of secrecy to protect her from things she need not know about. Just like Jesus had protected His mother, the Blessed Virgin Mary, from the grinding work of His ministry. How she had suffered at His death, rejoiced in His resurrection, and ultimately deserved her own assumption into heaven to be with Him, and the Father and the Holy Ghost!

Frank Darragh punched in the long-distance codes and the number of the Hotel Columbus. Father Ciccone picked up on the first ring. Darragh heard firsthand that Cardinal Tim Mulrennan had decided at the last minute to enter the conclave after all.

Leandro Biagi, as camerlengo, read aloud the now-familiar oath that all the electors must take, and Timothy Mulrennan listened to the prescribed formulation, as he had in January:

"We, the cardinal-electors present in this election of the Supreme Pontiff, promise, pledge, and swear, as individuals and as a group, to observe faithfully and scrupulously the prescriptions contained in the Apostolic Constitution of the Supreme Pontiff . . . We likewise promise, pledge, and swear that whichever of us by divine disposition is elected

Roman Pontiff will commit himself faithfully to carrying
out the *munus Petrinum* of Pastor of the Universal Church
and will not fail to affirm and defend strenuously the spiritual and temporal rights and the liberty of the Holy See.
In a particular way, we promise and swear to observe with
the greatest fidelity and with all persons, clerical or lay,
secrecy regarding everything that in any way relates to the
election of the Roman Pontiff and regarding what occurs
in the place of the election, directly or indirectly related to
the results of the voting; we promise and swear not to break
this secret in any way, either during or after the election of
the new Pontiff; and never to lend support or favor to any
interference, opposition, or any other form of intervention,
whereby secular authorities of whatever order and degree
or any group of people or individuals might wish to intervene in the election of the Roman Pontiff."

Then, Mulrennan was required to take in hand a book of
the Gospels and affirm the oath as an individual elector:
"And I, Timothy John Cardinal Mulrennan, do so promise,
pledge, and swear. So help me God and these Holy Gospels
which I touch with my hand."

"Welcome back, Timofeo," Biagi said to him with a
smile, grasping the American by the shoulders. "Now we
can truly begin our work."

The camerlengo then spoke from his chair beneath the
altar, reviewing the outline of the scrutiny process. Ballots
were distributed among the electors by the master of ceremonies; nine cardinals, three scrutineers, three *infirmarii*,
and three revisers, were chosen by lot by the junior cardinal
deacon. Immediately the secretary of the College of
Cardinals, the master of papal liturgical celebrations, and
the master of ceremonies left the Sistine Chapel, closing
the door behind them, to allow the cardinal-electors complete secrecy for the balloting. The methodology, so familiar by now to these men, and yet so strange for the fact
that they were gathered only six months after the last conclave, under such horrible circumstances, went off like
clockwork. Each ballot was dropped into the huge chalice
with the elector's oath ringing through the vaulted chapel:
"I call as my witness Christ the Lord who will be my judge,

that my vote is given to the one who before God I think should be elected."

As the final scrutineer read out the individual ballot, he pierced it with a needle through the word *Eligo* and pushed it onto the thread with the others.

There were 115 eligible electors, and all were present and voting. Benignly, Cardinal Biagi presided, casting his own vote in the order of seniority, nodding almost imperceptibly to each of the other cardinals as he walked to the altar to deposit the folded paper in its proper place, sitting as still and self-satisfied as a cat as the votes were counted. One almost expected to hear a purr of contentment from the camerlengo's chair. His slitted eyes swept the room as the tally was announced.

"Cardinal La Spina, forty-one votes; Cardinal Biagi, thirty-one votes; Cardinal Mulrennan, twenty-seven votes; Cardinal Fallaci, thirteen votes; Cardinal Ibanga, four votes."

In the silence, there was a heavy, expectant collective intake of breath. Tim Mulrennan could not believe his ears, and he nearly bolted from his chair.

"We shall immediately proceed to a second ballot," Biagi announced. He glanced toward Mulrennan, his cat's eyes slitted, a vague smile on his brown face.

What had the old Sly Boots been up to? Mulrennan wondered, panic and sadness welling within him. Perhaps there was a sentimental feeling among some of the cardinals toward Tim . . . a nice gesture to salve some of the hurt feelings when the American had been trashed by enemies in the previous conclave . . . perhaps because he had been a good friend of the dead pontiff, had been identified with him as a moderate-progressive who wished to build bridges rather than condemn error. *Who knows? . . .*

It took two excruciating hours to achieve the next tally. "Cardinal La Spina, forty-four votes; Cardinal Mulrennan, thirty-nine votes; Cardinal Biagi, nineteen votes; Cardinal Fallaci, eleven votes; Cardinal Mercer, two votes; Cardinal Ibanga, one vote."

Both Mulrennan and La Spina had gained supporters. The tension only increased as the results were absorbed by the assembled conclavists. At least one, Tim Mulrennan, felt physically ill.

Friday, July 27, 8:22 A.M.

"You must do what you can to stop this."

"Only you can take your name from consideration."

"I don't see why I shouldn't."

"I do—the workings of the Holy Spirit."

"This cannot be happening. Maybe La Spina will continue to pick up more votes."

"I am going to request that any who voted for me not do so on the next ballot and suggest they vote for you instead. That would give you about sixty votes. Unless La Spina picks up a substantial number next time, he is going to fade."

"You can't instruct anyone; it's against the rules."

"Not instruct, merely suggest."

"You think you have this one figured out, don't you?"

"Yes, I do, my friend. Two more ballots. Three at most."

There seemed to be no way out, no alternative but to sit quietly and pray that the worst—his own election—would not come to pass. It was absurd even to think about it . . . he had been certain that the air of scandal, no matter how unjustly manufactured, had eliminated him from any serious consideration . . . hadn't it?

"I am going to vote for you, Allo, no matter what."

"Stubbornness can be a virtue—or a mortal sin. You wouldn't want me in St. Peter's chair, I promise you." Leandro Aurelio Biagi, the master politician, had turned out to be a superb Secretary of State during Innocent XIV's brief pontificate. The next pope would be smart to keep him in that position and thereby use his talents in the most suitable and beneficial way possible.

Tim Mulrennan recognized that. He said: "I am simply not qualified, and they know too much about me. It would cause a scandal."

"It would cause a scandal if they did *not* elect you, dear

boy. Be quiet and eat your breakfast. And consider what name you might want as pope."

Cardinal Vennholme had been silent throughout the conclave; he had listened attentively to the homilies and instructions; he had taken his meals with Cardinal Giannantonio, but without conversation of any kind; he had not spoken to La Spina, nor to any other of the electors in the *prattiche* before the voting. The first night he had gone to his room immediately after supper and slipped in like a mouse, locking the door behind him. He had betrayed no outward emotion during the four votes of the first day, nor had he commented about Biagi's maneuvering to get Mulrennan into the conclave before it was sealed. Tim tried a few times to make eye contact with Vennholme but did not succeed. It was clear to Mulrennan and to Biagi that Vennholme had abdicated his role as the voice of the Evangelium movement within the conclave. But why? Had he been so wounded last time? Had the assassination of Pope Innocent taken the fight out of him? Did he expect his fellow electors to see the light this time without any explicit direction from him? He seemed to have lost weight and become somewhat stooped in the last several months.

Before joining the others for the second morning session that would start with the fifth ballot, Henry Martin Vennholme looked at his own face in the mirror. He toweled his jaw and chin after shaving and briskly brushed his short-cropped hair, which stimulated his scalp and made him appear more human and more alive. But he did not like what he saw.

He had vowed to himself—and for himself—to maintain an attitude of watchful silence for the duration of this conclave: *God, in His own wisdom and purpose, has brought us here again, perhaps to correct the mistake of the last conclave—perhaps to listen more carefully to Him this time. Yet,* Vennholme considered, as he regarded the seventy-one-year-old man in the mirror, *the voting indicates that we have not learned our lesson. We are again taking the path of least resistance, of sentimentality and weakness. Why, God, why? Your apostles have fallen asleep in the*

*garden—again. And there is nothing I can do to stop them
but to pray and to cast my own vote for the strongest,
soundest candidate, Cardinal La Spina.*

The harsh memories of those cold, lonely days of his
youth washed over Vennholme, drowning the acute pain of
the present with the dull, numbing pain of history: he closed
his eyes to veil the images that haunted him, ever tormented
his immortal soul . . . the orphaned, solitary boy who sought
light and love and found neither; the young man eternally
scarred by abuse but equally certain of salvation; the priest
consumed by a burning ambition to do right and represent
the Savior in a dangerous, corrupt world, to stand against
the armies of evil; the tireless nuncio, prince of the Church,
successor to the apostles who could never rest as long as
the magisterium was threatened from within the Body of
Christ by weak-minded wafflers, Marxist-influenced addicts
of liberation theology, and Satan's followers in sheeps'
clothing. But when he opened his eyes Cardinal Vennholme
saw only an old man with bitter eyes and a sternly set
jawline.

For the past six months he had endured the utter humiliation of the pope's overt attitude of indifference. He had
not been granted a single audience with the Holy Father
subsequent to the coronation of Innocent XIV; his letters
and memoranda had gone unanswered; his imminent re-
moval from the Curia to a lesser diocese in western Canada
was rumored. Fewer social invitations signaled the wide-
spread opinion that he had ceased to be a major player in
the Vatican power game. He felt more and more isolated
with each passing month. Only Frank Darragh, his staunch
American friend and fellow member of Evangelium Christi,
had stood with him, supported and encouraged him with
weekly telephone calls and visits, including one several
weeks before the pontiff's death.

Henry Vennholme had rehearsed the events of that meeting many times in his memory, replaying the words and
gestures and personalities as vividly as if they were images
on film. Darragh had come to the cardinal's private apartment in Rome, accompanied by the young priest from Philadelphia, Ciccone. Vennholme had sponsored the priest's

application for a promotion to monsignor through his contacts in the Congregation for the Clergy. He was unhappy that the process seemed stalled—that would not have been the case several months ago. Another sign that Vennholme was in disfavor?

"You are gracious to receive us on such short notice," Darragh had said as they settled into the comfortable chairs before the tall, open windows in the cardinal's sun-dappled parlor. "You look well, Your Eminence."

"Both of you gentlemen are always welcome to visit— at any time," Vennholme assured them warmly. He smiled, but with difficulty. The tension and uncertainty he had been experiencing had taken a toll, physically and emotionally. He sipped some prime-vintage Tignanello from a tall cut-crystal goblet. His guests drank only inexpensive bottled water. *Americans* . . . "I appreciate your friendship immensely."

"Cardinal Vennholme, we have been alarmed at the drift of events in recent months since the election of the new pope. Many in the United States—and not just members of our society—feel that the Holy Father has not addressed the issues of faith and morality that are festering within our Church; in fact, he seems unwilling to acknowledge the depth of these problems."

Father Ciccone could not refrain from adding his own perspective: "I fear for the soul of our Holy Mother Church. The devil is at work in the world, winning more souls and destroying the fabric of the Catholic faith. You have seen firsthand the state of the Church in America, as well as the rest of the world. I believe we must act to stem the momentum of the Evil One."

Henry Vennholme listened appreciatively to the young priest. He saw a reflection of himself there, in the earnest face, and heard a youthful echo of himself in the urgent voice. "I know, Father," he said soothingly. "And the clergy and laity within the Evangelium all agree with you. I must take a large share of the responsibility for this current state of Church affairs, because I was unable to persuade my fellow electors in the last conclave to follow the right course. I believe they closed their hearts to the Holy Ghost and listened instead to the soft, sweet promptings of pastoralism, and they felt the need to kowtow to diversity and ecumenism—which are twin evils disguised as virtues. Where did they think this decision would lead?"

"The problem is, they didn't think—they didn't pray, they didn't look beyond their own noses or their own interests. Certainly De Guzman is a very pleasant and presentable man—but he is not the man God requires of us, not the man we require of God!" Darragh propelled himself from the comfortable damask-covered chair and paced over to the window that opened onto a lushly green courtyard. But he saw none of the beauty, heard none of the irony in his own words. "We all agree on the serious danger of this papal . . . situation. My question is: What are we going to do about it?"

"Please lower your voice, Mr. Darragh," Vennholme said. "It is in God's hands. What are we going to do? Work and pray. Work and pray for an opportunity to correct the error His Church has made. It is not the first, nor the last time we have strayed from the path of righteousness."

"Your Eminence—of course, you are correct, but—"

"Do not say anything more," Vennholme interjected. He looked from Darragh to Ciccone. "I am not in a position to remedy the problem. I will probably be reassigned by His Holiness, sooner rather than later. My last direct conversation with him was immediately after the election. Since then—" He paused, folded then unfolded his smallish, pale, manicured hands. "I await his pleasure."

Frank Darragh swallowed a curse. He swung around and popped his fist into the opposite open hand. "Damn him to hell," he spat. "Forgive me, Eminence, and Father, but I don't think we can afford to wait—our people cannot wait. We must make things right—now!"

Vennholme said nothing. Ciccone looked at his well-polished shoe tops. A pregnant silence filled the cardinal's apartment. Outside, a hot breeze touched the tall trees in the courtyard. The early summer sun burned into the room through the windows as the three men stood frozen in a silent tableau like chess men awaiting an unseen hand to move them.

When the visitors had left him alone and the Roman sky turned a rich sarum blue and Vennholme had drunk another few glasses of wine, his heart constricted painfully and he instinctively knew the curtain of deepest night had fallen on the papacy of Innocent XIV, and he hated himself for the knowing. He found it impossible to pray.

La Spina looked very much the Italian peasant, as had Angelo Roncalli who had been elected Pope John XXIII in the bitterly difficult and divisive conclave of 1958 forty years and four popes ago. . . . Privately, La Spina had asked Biagi to recognize him so that he might speak to the conclave. He had spoken to no one else about this. The Archbishop of Turin, whom cardinals Fallaci and Giannantonio had again promoted among the Sacred College in the *prattiche* of the days and weeks leading to the conclave, was clearly uncomfortable addressing the conclave. For more than a decade he had usually read his sermons and pronouncements from a dense, much-edited script provided by his staff, with assistance from men of the Curia. He was notorious for grammatical, Freudian, and even theological slips of the tongue when he spoke extemporaneously. So, as he stood before them, he hesitated, not wanting to say the wrong thing, trying to find the courage and the proper words to say the right thing, forcing himself to say anything at all. He did not even glance in Vennholme's direction.

"My brothers in Christ," he began, easing into his remarks with the familiar formulation, "I am not an orator. Even less am I a pope. How may I express my gratitude to you who have entrusted me with your votes? This is the second time, unfortunately, that we have come together to elect a new pope. I am sad because of this. Our murdered pope should have reigned for a long time. This was a cruel and sinful act, to rob the Church of her leader. Whoever is responsible must be caught and punished to the fullest extent. I pray for this every day.

"I also pray for the discernment to make the correct decision for the Holy Roman Church, and that you, my brothers, will see the light of the Holy Spirit in your minds when you cast your votes. I know that I am not the right choice for you, for the universal Church. I am not meant by God to be your pope. How do I know this? In my heart—right here." With his large fist he touched his breast.

"I ask you, in the name of Jesus Christ, Our Savior, do not continue to vote for me. I will not suggest another, nor tell you who my vote has been for. Please erase my name from ballots, but keep my name in your hearts, as I do yours—all of you."

A thunder of applause rose from among the seated electors, unusual in this generally quiet, deliberate, ceremonial group of men. Cardinal La Spina was stunned at the response, swung around and returned to his place, fighting to keep his face expressionless. Finally, he looked toward Henry Vennholme and saw the Canadian applauding with the rest, but with decidedly less warmth and enthusiasm. Then he glanced over to where Timothy Mulrennan, the surprise American candidate, sat. Mulrennan was not applauding; instead, there were obviously tears in his eyes.

Thus the fifth vote began on the second morning of the conclave in a rather stuffy Sistine Chapel. The cardinals shifted uncomfortably in their seats under the watchful stage direction of Leandro Biagi. Mulrennan avoided eye contact with the Florentine prelate. In fact, he could barely hear the proceedings as each elector cast his ballot: his mind was filled with the music of fate that thrummed through his bloodstream to the beat of his heart. He worried a hangnail on his finger and tried to pray. Soon it was his turn to deposit his ballot in the chalice on the altar. He felt the eyes of his colleagues on him, again, on the long walk up to the altar. Biagi watched him impassively. Tim Mulrennan cast his vote and returned to his place and sat in silence; he prayed. What else could he do?

While on leave in New Mexico he had focused intently on his prayer life and reopened that channel to God, spending as much as four or five hours on a given day in prayer and contemplation. It clarified and simplified one's life so much to turn every thought and problem and need toward the Father, to listen for answers rather than demand results, to emphasize gratitude and faith throughout any given day. And in his liturgical life he had stripped down the daily celebration of the Eucharist to its barest essentials: he enjoyed the simplicity of sharing a meal with the Lord and his fellow communicants, often just a handful of people, in contrast to the vast staged events in the basilica in Newark or in the parishes of the archdiocese. He felt that he had become a better priest in the process.

To be a priest . . . to be a pastor . . . to be the representative of Christ and successor to His apostles . . . this is what he had been called to be in his short time on earth.

His brother and sisters loomed large in his mind, and he wondered what they were doing at this very moment—probably still sleeping or just rising in the early morning to face a hot, busy midsummer day. Theresa's and Gertrude Anne's children were now grown, and there were great-nieces and -nephews. Stephen, of course, had no children, nor had Kathleen. They had all been staunchly supportive of Tim during the time after the last conclave, through his sabbatical. And after he returned to Newark for a twenty-four-hour stopover, he had spoken to each before he departed for Rome on this trip.

Stephen, especially, had touched him. From across the Hudson River in Manhattan, the sincere voice conveyed the younger man's feelings: "I know this is a difficult time for you, Tim—maybe even tougher than the last time. Is there anything I can do for you?"

Sitting at the familiar desk in his chancery office, Cardinal Mulrennan had felt at home for the first time in several months and he did not want to leave. He would rather invite his brother over for a drink and talk face-to-face. He said, "Just pray that I might have the strength to do the right thing."

"What the heck do you mean?"

"Well, I'm not sure that I want to be a part of this conclave." The words sounded hollow and prideful in his own ears.

"You are flying to Rome, aren't you?"

"Yeah. But I haven't decided what to do when I get there."

"Did you crack up out in New Mexico? I don't get it. It's your responsibility to be there and to cast your vote."

"I am so angry, Steve. I don't know if I'm capable—"

"Bullshit! You don't have a choice."

"I think I do."

"Tim, you have always been an example to me, always been there to advise me when I needed you. I can't believe you wouldn't do the right thing here. That's what you'd tell me—I know it."

Mulrennan laughed. "I would. I'm pretty good at dispensing wisdom to my fellow man, aren't I? But it's tough to hear it when it comes back at me."

Our Father, who art in heaven . . . Thy will be done.

When he had accepted the call to a vocation in the priesthood, some forty years ago, Mulrennan could not have anticipated this moment. Was *this* God's will for him? It had seemed so clear in January that it was not—that he was unready, not the best available choice of the conclave. Was he so different now? Had *he* changed, or had circumstances and needs changed? Had the cardinals changed? What must Vennholme be thinking right now . . . and his allies among the Sacred College? Was this a great joke upon them?

He could not manage a smile. Mulrennan stared at the blank white ballot on the desk in front of him, fingering the smooth surface of his pen, hesitating before he began to inscribe a name on the hairsbreadth line. Whose name? Or no name at all? Who would truly be the best shepherd of this widely scattered flock? He had written Biagi's name on each of the previous four ballots; this time, however, it was a different name. As he wrote it felt both easily familiar and very odd, indeed. Quickly he put down his pen and folded the paper ballot once. It absorbed the perspiration of his fingertips.

God, forgive me. God, guide me. God, help me.

The laborious ritual of voting proceeded. Again he waited with as much patience as he could muster, controlling the impulse to fidget in his seat like a grammar school student before the dismissal bell. Before long it was his turn again to cast his ballot, which he did, praying that it would be the last. Again: the long, silent walk back to his place among his fellow electors.

As the vote continued, Tim Mulrennan watched the

seeming distant faces of the scrutineers and revisers, still avoiding the gaze of the camerlengo, Cardinal Biagi, not wanting to hear the numbers. He did not believe that his own vote total would increase, let alone approach the number required to elect: seventy-seven. It was, to him, a fantastical and nonsensical notion.

He turned to look toward the rear of the narrow, high-vaulted Sistine Chapel, away from the altar and the mural of the Last Judgment. He was astonished to see the stark, solitary figure of his friend Jaime De Guzman, who had been Pope Innocent XIV, and who had been so brutally erased from earthly existence sixteen days before. As he had in New Mexico, the specter of the dead pope gestured to Tim Mulrennan. *Come, walk with me,* the apparition seemed to be saying.

He was dressed in the distinctive white simar and red mozzetta of the Roman pontiff, and he appeared much taller than the Innocent whom Mulrennan had known, more physically powerful. The voice, now silenced, had turned the last conclave from a course of destruction and disaster. The eyes, now closed forever, had looked upon Timothy Mulrennan as a brother and a friend, with kindness and understanding. Now the figure gestured, his hand uplifted, pointing toward the ceiling of the chapel. Was he going nuts with these visions? he wondered.

Tim raised his eyes: he saw the portrayal of the expulsion from the Garden, the temporary triumph of Satan. He felt the crushing burden of failure that Adam and Eve, magnificent specimens that they were in Michelangelo's brushwork, carried on their shoulders. Defeat. Yet there was the power and the promise of salvation by a loving God—as disappointed as He was in the sins of mankind—always available, even to the lowest, most abject of His creatures. *Even for me . . .*

He looked for the ghost of the murdered pope, but it had vanished. The moment passed, and the American folded his hands and straightened his spine. He knew he was not alone—De Guzman still watched over him. . . .

In a blur of time and sound and subtle motion, Timothy Mulrennan absorbed the tally of votes as each was recorded

and announced. He did not write down the count as most
of the electors did—to keep themselves busy, if for no other
reason. They marked each name and each vote. Mulrennan
heard his own name over and over again. La Spina was the
only other name spoken for several minutes, despite his
withdrawal. Then one surprising name that caused the assembly to gasp. About halfway through the count it became
clear to all who were present: this was the final ballot. *Habemus papam . . .* we have a pope. But that did not halt the
process. Inexorable and tedious and tradition bound. It
might have been the thirteenth, or the sixteenth, or any
century, but for the number of electors—so utterly timeless
was the moment at hand. Already the sense of inevitability
infused the conclave.

His mind veered off in trivial directions: *How many
masses have I celebrated since my ordination as a priest?*
A quick mental calculation put the number at fifteen thousand—conservatively. Could it be sixteen thousand? More?
And how many communicants, members of the community
of the Catholic faithful, had he personally touched since he
had been a bishop and archbishop for twenty years? He
could not even begin to count. And how many confessions
heard, babies baptized, young people confirmed, couples
married, funerals preached, priests ordained? How many
souls saved? *And my own? For what doth it profit a man
should he gain the whole world? . . . My own immortal
soul—it has been in daily jeopardy, God certainly knows.
Yet He has seen fit to carry me through up to this very
moment—*

*You are the source of my strength. You are my refuge. I
am the child of God. I am the servant of God.* He prayed
in this moment as he had never prayed in his life, yet his
very soul seemed caught in his throat, nearly strangling
him.

Barely perceptible to Tim Mulrennan, amid the clanging
din of his own destiny, the vote total was announced in
simple, unadorned words: "Cardinal La Spina, thirty-six
votes; Cardinal Vennholme, one vote; one blank ballot; and
Cardinal Mulrennan, seventy-eight votes." Silence, utter
and devastating, swelled within the sacred chamber for

about twenty seconds. A wave of applause, at first a polite smattering, then an enthusiastic crescendo, broke over Timothy Mulrennan, and all of the cardinals rose as one from their benches. Gone were the days of the canopies that each of the cardinals lowered in tribute to the one elected. Mulrennan remained seated for a moment, stunned, barely able to see clearly through a mist of tears, his breathing labored. The benign applauding figure of Cardinal Biagi was a white-and-red blur, but Tim knew he was beaming like a proud father—no, great elector, again! The American felt paralyzed, trapped in a sucking, bottomless bog of time.

He could not speak or smile or even acknowledge his colleagues, so he breathed a silent prayer: *O Father, I am an unworthy pilgrim, a prodigal son whom You have never, ever abandoned, even in my own doubts and failings. Please, God, send Your only-begotten Son to guide me on this path and to protect His Church in our time of greatest need.*

"By what name shall you choose to be called?" the camerlengo asked him.

"Allo, my friend, I have no idea. I did not think—"

"Ah, but thinking is not allowed."

The nearby cardinals listened to this exchange between the two old friends and smiled knowingly among themselves, conscious of the value of the moment they were witnessing.

Truly, he had not thought at all about a name. He had sincerely not believed it possible that he might be elected. Yet, in the back room of his mind he had allowed a small seedling of a thought to take root and to grow ever so tentatively in a little clay pot on the sill of the window—there in that secret place. Perhaps it had been prompted by God, through the intimation of the Spirit, through the intercession of the Son. Tim Mulrennan now recognized it as not a conscious thought or choice but as an inspiration from a source or power outside himself. He questioned it, however, for a fraction of a heartbeat; he somehow doubted that it was right: after all, he had not given this decision—which would change and define his entire life—more than this moment's consideration. Finally, he pushed aside the whisperings of doubt and said the name aloud.

"I will choose the name Celestine." Murmurs of surprise and approbation greeted his announcement. Biagi smiled. "For one thing," Mulrennan said, "It has been a while."

"Of the heavens—and the name of the pope who resigned the throne of Peter rather than countenance the corruptions of Rome," Biagi remarked. "There have been only five of your predecessors with this name."

Celestine V had reigned briefly, from August through December in 1294. He had been an exceptionally pious hermit, selected by a desperately divided conclave of a dozen worldly cardinals who could not come to agreement otherwise. Poor Pietro del Murrone, later sainted, never even saw Rome as its bishop; he was ill-equipped for the task of Church governance, possessing only extraordinary holiness, but no knowledge of Latin or political administration.

Like the name John, which Angelo Roncalli chose in 1958, and which had not been used since an antipope claimed it some 550 years earlier, the name Celestine hadn't been seriously considered by subsequent pontiffs. St. Pietro, Celestine V, lived about a year and a half after he abdicated the papal throne to Boniface VIII—who turned out to be one of the most accomplished politicians ever to wear the triple tiara.

Did this American, then, have an underlying message in the choice of name? A predecessor who had resigned the papacy . . . a simple mystic who had thrown off the trappings and pretensions of the Holy See and all its earthly attachments . . . a saint who chose to live out his life in exile rather than to wear the shoes of the Fisherman . . . these were some of the possible clues that the press and other Vatican watchers would cite as proof of one argument or another. On a day of surprises, then, here was just one more.

"Then maybe the sixth will be graced to lead a return to more heavenly concerns." The new pontiff said this quietly to the camerlengo, and then as he spoke he realized that surely some clever or cynical journalist would comment on the irony of his reaching back seven hundred years to select such a long-dormant and unusual name.

But Biagi was not listening. He turned to the assembly of cardinal-electors with a smile of triumph on his smooth, nut brown face. "My Lord Cardinals, our brother, Timothy John Mulrennan of the United States, has consented to his canonical election as the Supreme Pontiff of the Roman Church and the Successor to Peter. He has chosen to bear the name of Celestine, after five predecessors. Let us pray for him and for Christ's Church."

The cardinals' applause resumed, and Timothy Mulrennan, now to be called Pope Celestine VI, stood to his full, commanding height and faced the men who had elected him as their servant, their pastor, their pope. He struggled to control the tremulousness in his voice.

"I ask, first and last, for your prayers, for that is how brothers in Christ have always helped each other. Brothers, forgive me for my personal failings and help me with your prayers. If I had known the outcome, I might have *really* stayed away." He smiled through the tears and thought to himself, *I am becoming a crybaby in my old age....* "I have no agenda other than to listen and learn. I pledge to you and to God that I shall try my very best to be worthy of your trust, to earn that trust through my actions more than my words.

"No one among us has any earthly or spiritual right to challenge the Holy Spirit's role here, whether or not he thinks that we, as men, have made a mistake. I have my own personal opinion about that. I say this because I believe that certain forces within the Church did not acknowledge the legitimacy of my predecessor—when each and all of us who were present for his election *know* that it was valid and proper."

The magnitude of the event, the crushing responsibility of the office, struck Mulrennan like a blow to the face.

"Every man in this room knows that I am unworthy to stand before you—and before the world—to claim the apostolic succession to St. Peter." He paused and swallowed hard, looking into their faces. "Yet, as has been true during my entire life, this is the mystery and the miracle of Christ's love for us—He raises up the least of us to sit with Him at the banquet. He builds his kingdom with materials rejected and scorned by others. Do you remember whát St. Patrick, the Apostle of Ireland, wrote about himself? It is something like this: 'I was like some big stone lying deep in the mud; and He who is all-powerful came and in His mercy lifted me up and raised me aloft to a place on the very top of the wall. Therefore I should cry out aloud and so also render something back to the Lord for His great benefits here and throughout eternity—gifts that the simple mind of man is unable to comprehend.' "

He had read St. Patrick's *Confession* many times and been impressed with the missionary bishop's zeal and humility.

"I will seek your counsel and support in every aspect of my leadership. I will seek to involve both men and women, religious and the laity in Church governance. I will seek to bring the churches of Africa and Asia into closer union with Europe and the Americas, to create a greater cohesion within the universal Church. I fear that our more conservative brethren in the Roman Curia will naturally oppose me on many of these important issues—and I know that is a very controversial thing to say, especially in my first address to you, my brother electors. However, I tell you that I understand and respect such opposition, and I do not wish to prevent its expression. We will engage in healthy and open debate among ourselves and with fellow Christians and members of other faiths, as well, especially Jews and Muslims. I ask only that any who oppose me do so sincerely and openly, for the good of the Church we love so much.

"Remember that Peter himself failed Our Lord in His hour of suffering, yet Jesus entrusted him to lead the Church—but not alone. No pope, no priest or bishop, no elder or wise man should 'rule' any other man as a dictator.

"You have elected me anyway, and no one is more surprised than I. You have elected an American for the very first time, a man of the New World with only the most tenuous connection to the old Roman ways. This break with the past signals the openness that was asked of us by the

Council Fathers of the last generation. But more important than any overt new direction is the apostolic continuity and our constant recommitment to the Gospel of Jesus Christ. It can be, and should be, as simple as that—for all of us." He scanned the faces of the cardinals as they stood before him: among them were brothers, colleagues, sometime antagonists, fellow believers, stubborn bureaucrats, closet mystics, men with strengths and failings, men just like him.

"I hereby put aside any personal doubt that I may have held in my heart before this conclave. I do not pretend to understand, but I *accept* the will of God, and let it not then be said of us in what we do and how we treat one another that we failed to preserve and pass on the Gospel to our sons and daughters, for unborn generations to come."

The soul-memory of the altar boy he once was, the twelve-year-old with sore knees from the hard marble, the scent of incense and hopes of Christmas Eve, the fear and love for his mother and prayers for release from the pain that afflicted the entire family . . . the faces of his father and mother and brother . . . all these things came to Tim Mulrennan when he stopped talking and sat for a brief moment of reflection. *Dear God, be with Your son in his hour of need. . . .*

POSTLUDE
Urbi et Orbi

Rome, Friday, July 27, late afternoon

Timothy John Mulrennan, lately the Archbishop of Newark, now the newly elected Supreme Pontiff of the Holy Roman Catholic and Apostolic Church, received the members of the Sacred College of Cardinals from the gold-covered chair that served as his throne. He still wore the plain black cassock of a priest, which he had refused to change during the conclave and in the immediate aftermath, to the horror of the hastily gathered attendants and tailors. There was no precedent for this. An American, no less! Their heads were spinning. The cardinals, similarly, were taken aback by Mulrennan's decision. They came to him as humbly and hopefully as they were capable of being.

The outside world knew that a decision had been reached. The chemically manufactured white smoke of centuries-old tradition spewed from the chimney atop the Apostolic Palace, beclouding a brilliant blue summer sky and causing the men and women gathered in the Piazza di San Pietro to applaud, though they did not know who had been elected. Then they settled in to wait. The international press shifted into gear, television and radio networks broadcasting headline bulletins around the world, but without the complete story. A torpid blanket of heat lay upon Rome, the age-old city of pagans and martyrs. The cynical citizens of this world capital would feign indifference, though in their hearts they would thrill to the news that they had a new bishop, a new target for their tired jokes and complaints, for their reluctant respect. Then life would return to normal—whatever that was—as it had for centuries beyond memory.

Within the Sistine, the cardinals in their choir dress, a magnificent line of red-and-white-clad figures, approached their new leader for his blessing upon them, each perhaps hoping for a personal word, a first chance to connect with the man who would personally and powerfully govern the direction of their lives and careers. They approached with smiles, with fear, with joy, with uncertainty. Would he guess who had voted for him and who had not? Would it matter? They read his face and his body language like the front page of a newspaper or the introduction to a book, of which Chapter One had yet to be written.

Cardinal Vennholme was among the first score of electors to pay obeisance to the new pope. After the first awkward genuflection before him, Mulrennan had smoothly and expertly shared a very few words with each man, firmly clasping the hand, gently pushing him aside with a hand on his right arm, an old politician's trick he had observed many times. He saw Vennholme standing a few places down the line. He girded himself, hastily wrote a script in his mind, then abandoned it as he reached forward to take the older man's hand to lift him from the kneeling position he had assumed.

"Please, Your Eminence, you needn't do this. I have been worried about your health since I saw you the other day; you don't look well."

"I do not feel well, Your Holiness. I feel—I carry a heavy burden that I hope you can relieve. I ask for your indulgence and your forgiveness."

"What? Why? We have disagreed on many things. But I know that your motives have always been true and pure. Even during the last conclave . . ." He felt the anger and sadness rise within himself, but he fought to allow compassion override the negatives. He understood that in some profound, painful, and mysterious way, Vennholme's attacks had made Mulrennan stronger. "I have put all that behind me, because I must. You should, too."

"I have never hated—you must understand—never hated you, nor De Guzman. You must believe me." He looked up into Tim Mulrennan's eyes, as tears spilled from his own. His face was an ashy gray, with purple splotches rimming his eyes as if he had been in a fistfight. Beads of sweat shone on his pale forehead just below the hairline. "I never wished harm upon either of you. You must believe me."

"I know, Henry. I know. Did you wonder who cast a vote for you on that last ballot?" He still clasped Vennholme's somewhat clammy hand.

"You?" he whispered, astonished.

"Pray for me, Henry, please. I need your prayers."

"Forgive—"

A cloud passed over Vennholme's eyes, and he seemed to lose focus, as well as his balance. He lurched to the left, sinking like a deadweight in water. Mulrennan leaped from the throne, held on to the limp hand and reached out for Vennholme's torso, trying to ease his fall. His long-ago Boy Scout and army first-aid training came back to him as he eased the fallen man to the hard cold floor of the chapel. He put his ear to Vennholme's chest, felt the man's breathing and heard his faint heartbeat. Already one of the security aides had summoned the Vatican physician who quickly took over as the men in red and one man in a black cassock stood by. Within a few minutes Vennholme was on a stretcher that seemed magically to appear, and an oxygen mask was strapped to his face. The doctor led the emergency personnel to the exit behind the altar, taking the now-unconscious man to an ambulance.

The moment seemed eerily familiar to the assembly, most of whom had witnessed Cardinal Zimmerman's demise in January.

"Gentlemen, my Lord Cardinals," Timothy John Mulrennan, the pope said, his hand raised, "let us say a prayer for Cardinal Vennholme." He stood by the chair and made the Sign of the Cross over the College of Electors. "May Our Father keep and protect the life of our brother Henry Martin Vennholme who has given himself so completely to the service of His Church. Almighty God, may it be Your will that his health be quickly restored and that he rejoin us in service to You and Your Church on earth. We ask this in the name of Mary, the Mother of Your Son, who sustains us all through her example of sacrifice and pure love and through Jesus Christ." Those present joined the newly elected pontiff in a resounding "Amen." Calmly, Tim Mulrennan resumed his position on the temporary throne, his hand extended. The episode had taken about twenty-five minutes, but no one seemed in a hurry to leave the Sistina; perhaps they found some security among themselves here, in this place, that would not be available to them outside the Apostolic Palace.

One by one they came to him, chastened and rather frightened by the collapse of one of their own number as the world seemed to cinch in a bit more tightly upon each of them.

To Cardinal Giannantonio, who approached tentatively, he said in an even voice: "We will take good care of our beloved friend, you can be sure. I think he will be all right. It was just too much for him—a terrible strain."

"We are all concerned about him," Giannantonio said noncommittally, genuflecting properly before the man he had denounced in January. He rose and eyed the new pontiff warily, his bureaucrat's flat eyes sizing up the threat to his own career represented in this man from New Jersey, U.S.A. Like Vennholme before him, his heart was doing strange flip-flops and he wanted desperately to lie down somewhere quiet and hope to awaken from this terrible dream.

Cardinal Czeslowski of Chicago marched forward when it was his turn to pay homage to the new Supreme Pastor. The wide-shouldered American was still the youngest member of the College, and already he had participated in two conclaves; chances were, he would vote in at least two more before he turned eighty and became ineligible. He smiled as he rose from his knee and received Mulrennan's *embracio* and Kiss of Peace.

"Well, Nicholas, I guess the Irish have something to cheer about for a change. Now they'll know how the Poles felt for all those years."

"Your Holiness," Czeslowski blurted, "I must confess that I didn't vote for you."

"That's not very politic to admit such a thing. I thought

you were from Chicago . . . we Americans have to stick together— don't we?"

"Like the Democrats and Republicans?" Both men
laughed. "We'll work together for the good of the Church,
Your Holiness, I promise you—and it is a historic day for
the Church in America. You're the first!"

"I can't say I'll miss those interminable bishops' meetings, Nick."

"Oh, we'll miss you."

It took another hour to greet and bless each of the remaining electors. Although he was already emotionally and
mentally drained, Pope Celestine faced another task: his
first apostolic benediction, *Urbi et Orbi,* upon the city and
the world. Biagi escorted him first to the Room of Tears
behind the Sistine Chapel where he tried once more to convince Timofeo to don the familiar sacred vestments of the
Roman Pontiff, white silk simar and red mozzetta, along
with the white zucchetto. The new pope chose to wear a
beautifully embroidered stole and the zucchetto, but none
of the other traditional vestiture. The Master of Cerermon-
ies and the other assistants were shocked into silence as
Mulrennan blessed them and requested their indulgence and
departed with Biagi, then walked to the Hall of Benedictions.

He remembered following De Guzman into the ceremonial Renaissance hall six months ago, along with the
others of the Sacred College. Now they awaited him. He
entered, wearing his plain black cassock, multicolored stole,
and white cap that lay slightly askew upon his neatly
combed gray crown. He blessed them all again, not knowing what else to do, as he awaited Biagi's announcement
from the central balcony. Timothy Mulrennan, Celestine
VI, heard the Latin words as if in an echo chamber, distant
yet resounding within his own physical being:

"*Annuntio vobis gaudium magnum.* I announce to you a
great joy. *Habemus papam!* We have a pope! *Eminentis-
simum ac Reverendissimum Dominum*—His Most Eminent
and Reverend Lordship, Timothy John *Sanctae Romanae
Ecclesiae Cardinalem* Mulrennan. *Qui sibi nomen impsuit*
. . . Who has chosen for himself the name of Celestine . . ."

He then stood amid the cheers and shouts in the dying light of the summer day, looking out from the impossibly tall-windowed balcony, and he spoke to them from his heart and soul.

"To the people of Rome and the world, to my family, now expanded beyond comprehension to all brothers and sisters in Christ, to the friends of the Holy Church and to its enemies, to my dear people in New Jersey, and to all priests and men and women in religious orders: I greet you and bless you in the name of Jesus Christ, the Savior of the world, with deepest humility and certain knowledge of my own inadequacy in this moment, my sins and my"— Pope Celestine paused, his gaze sweeping over the mass of people in the square before him—"surprise at the electors' choice. I think they believe this is the most fitting penance for my numerous sins." There was a smattering of laughter and applause among the assembly in the piazza. He spoke in English first, then switched to his halting Italian. "I feel especially unsuited to be the Bishop of Rome, for like St. Peter I come from a place far away from this most sacred city. But I shall do my best to serve you as bishop, to earn your love and support not ex officio but rather by what I do, whether it pleases or displeases you. I shall try to improve my use of the Italian language so that I may hear your kind criticism of me firsthand."

The Romans in the crowd roared in response to Mulrennan's statement. They saw before them something wondrously unique yet very familiar: the 264th man to claim legitimate apostolic authority over them. They were inclined to be generous to the "new man," until he proved himself unworthy of their affections. It was the same in each generation, in each papacy.

"As your bishop and pastor," he continued in English, "I bid you, the men and women of Rome, and the entire Body of Christ, to open wide your arms to our brethren of different faiths—and of no faith—in the spirit of Jesus Himself who was no respecter of persons in carrying the love of His Father, Almighty God, Creator of us all. The deposit of truth in which we as Catholic Christians find the basis of our faith, is what we know and believe, what we preach and protect with our very lives. But we may find in each other's hearts the manifestation of the Holy Spirit—if only we seek it. Open your arms and your hearts to those who are different from you, for, indeed, Almighty God created those differences, too. Do not think that you are right and that it is *your* work, but rather, that you are blessed to participate with Christ in *His* work. No one of us has a greater claim on His love than any other."

He took a half step back and looked over his shoulder to the upturned faces of the men who had just elected him. *This is going to be one hell of a difficult job,* he thought to himself, unable to read their thoughts in the political and theological masks that they had effortlessly put on for the occasion. *That is what I must do,* he considered silently: *do my best to learn their hearts, not what they say but what they really think.* They—the institutional "they" of the Curia and the College of Cardinals—would be here long after he was gone. Wasn't it always the way? Who was the pope, anyway, but the temporary human representative of the Son of God, whose own ministry had lasted only three short years. Now for the first time in two thousand years, a man of the New World stood as His vicar on earth. Had they made the right choice? It was a question that Timothy John Mulrennan, Pope Celestine VI, was the least qualified to answer.

"It is my responsibility, as I see it, to love you, each and every one, with every breath and ounce of energy that Almighty God sees fit to grant me. For He has not brought you and me to this place to abandon us. He is with us—always."

In the receding flood of the awesome assemblage of Romans, tourists, pilgrims, curiosity seekers, journalists, religious, parents and children—sinners and needy souls all—Father Anthony Ciccone, dressed like an American visitor to the Holy City rather than a priest, scanned the fast-moving faces on every side of him. Thank God there was still daylight. Even so, his was an impossible task: find Harry C. Benjamin, the irritating scandalmonger from New Zealand. Although he carried press credentials, Benjamin was not exactly welcome in any of the official international press pens that the Vatican had provided in various spots around the vast square.

Ciccone sensed that he was on the trail of his quarry, just felt it in his bones. He tried to put aside his consuming anger at the sight of the man in a plain priest's cassock who had just spoken to the people in the piazza and throughout the world. What must they think of this man who mocked the traditions of the Vatican in a time when it would only weaken the status and strength of the papacy? Mr. Darragh would be devastated. He did not relish his next conversation with the philanthropist. When he got home he would request a parish assignment as soon as possible. He was tired of intrigue and "high Church" politics; mere breathing in such an atmosphere had become difficult lately. First, though, he must finish the job at hand.

He took a few steps to the left, toward the towering colonnade that had never seemed to him so immense as now. He forced himself to maintain his focus on the faces of the people in the crowd, looking for the distinctive pasty pink visage of the tabloid reporter. He mouthed a quick prayer to the Blessed Mother. It would be a miracle if he found him.

There! He spotted Benjamin about twenty yards away, sidling through the crowd, incongruously wearing the battered trenchcoat that Ciccone remembered from their meeting in the dead of winter. *He must be sweating like a pig,* the young priest thought. *But probably no more than I am. . . .*

He pushed forward, heedless of anyone else but Benjamin. What would he say to the man when he caught up with him? Or should he just follow him and find out where he was staying, approach him directly later? Mr. Darragh had not been very specific. "Find him and find out what he knows, who his sources are. We've got to stop him from printing anything about the pope's death."

Ciccone stepped into an opening as the mass of bodies thinned briefly and dramatically, gained a few yards on Benjamin, approached him from an oblique angle as the reporter seemed to be headed for the first cross street along

the Via della Concilliazione. The American priest tried to
remember the name of the street but could not bring it to
mind. Then Benjamin suddenly disappeared behind one of
the giant travertine columns and Ciccone scrambled and
pushed ahead, zigzagging through the crowd. He regained
sight of the pink head and sprinted toward it.

Nearly breathless, the priest from Philadelphia found
himself shoulder to shoulder with Harry Benjamin, who
turned and saw him but at first did not recognize him, since
Ciccone was not in clerical clothing. Benjamin stopped and
looked around for a policeman, but saw none. He stepped
backward as the priest reached for him.

"It's me, Father Ciccone," the American said. "Remember, we met before."

"With Darragh. Yeah, I remember now." He still did not
comprehend what the hell this fellow might want with him
and he kept himself at arm's length. "You're not dressed
up like a priest, like you were then."

"Let's get a cup of coffee, Mr. Benjamin."

"I've had enough coffee today. I've got to get a story
filed right now, you'll understand, Father, eh?" He fingered
a floppy disk in his coat pocket.

"You must understand my position, sir. We will first find
a quiet spot to have a coffee. Mr. Darragh insisted that I
treat you."

"Oh, he did. He's a high-and-mighty beggar if there ever
was one. Who does he think he is, Rupert Murdoch?"

"No, he's just a servant of the Lord."

"He's no bloody servant. He likes to order other people
around too much—like myself, if you take my meaning,
Padre."

"Let's have this conversation more privately, Mr. Benjamin." He gripped the journalist's arm firmly, feeling skin
and bone beneath the fabric of the somewhat threadbare
coat. "Come this way," Ciccone began, steering Benjamin
into the street.

"Ouch! Careful there, you're hurting me." He resisted
for the briefest moment, then allowed himself to be guided
forward by the younger man.

"Come along. I don't mean to hurt you, sir, though I'm

not sure Mr. Darragh feels the same way. I'll have to report back to him on our conversation—after we have it, of course."

"Oh, he's a very nosy, meddlesome fellow, I'll give you that. I've a few things I'd like for you to tell him—for me. A few things to get off my chest."

"You'll have every opportunity," the priest said.

Father Anthony Ciccone loosened his grip on Harry C. Benjamin and walked beside him toward an anonymous café just a few blocks from the medieval walls of Vatican City. Soon Benjamin would leave no further earthly worrier; and Darragh, too, could be assured of a restful night with his secrets secure.

His Holiness Celestine VI had instructed the papal telephone operator to put through a long-distance conference call at 11:00 P.M. Rome time, so that he could speak to his three sisters, brother, and stepmother, Rosemary Mulrennan, who at eighty-eight lived in an assisted-care home in West Auburn, New Jersey, not far from the house where Tim Mulrennan had grown up. It was a late deep-summer afternoon back home in the eastern United States. Each family member was on the line when he picked up, and he could hear some of the great-nieces and-nephews in the background, too, and he was overwhelmed with their jubilant greetings. He could not contain the tears, but he tried as best he could to control his voice.

"You've all got to come to Rome for the installation. I can't wait to see you. I already miss you all, and the kids." He could see barely a foot in front of him because of the torrent of tears.

"We're there with you, Tim. We'll always be there, like you've been for us," Stephen said, and the women echoed his statement.

As surely as he felt the presence of his predecessors in this room in the papal living quarters, he felt Madeline and James Mulrennan beside him, perhaps shaking their heads in sympathy and amazement at what they had wrought— and Kevin, with the cocky big-brother smile and slug on the arm.

"Pray for me," he asked them all. It had become his mantra in the past twelve hours. "I've never needed it more than I do today. I feel as if all of the planets and the stars have fallen in on me."

"And you—keep us all in your prayers, too, Tim," Gertrude Anne said, her musical voice distinct among the others'.

The loneliness he had often felt as a celibate priest, and never more distinctly than today when Biagi had asked him whether he accepted his election, dissipated for a moment, and he felt at one with his family, at peace with being a Mulrennan, a brother and son and uncle . . . a human being among other human beings, all children of a loving Father. He said good-bye and hung up the phone and thought, *So, this is my vocation: to be a part of a greater whole, not separate and distinct and alone. This is what it means to be a priest: to be brother and friend, not master or superior. God, please keep them ever in my life, and let me remember that I am always Tim in their eyes, no more nor less than that—Timothy John Mulrennan, a kid from a small town in New Jersey. Never let me forget where I came from. . . .*

He called the hospital for the third time that evening and was relieved to learn that Cardinal Vennholme had come through his crisis; he had suffered a mild stroke but there probably would not be any long-term damage to his system. Yet he remained in a fragile state and would take some weeks to recover fully.

"Please let me speak to him for just a minute," the pontiff asked.

"Yes, Your Holiness, but literally for a minute and no more. He is still very weak."

When Vennholme came onto the line, Mulrennan said, "Henry, I am so sorry—I hope I did not contribute to your condition by what I said."

"Your Holiness, it is very good of you to call me." The voice was raspy and faint, but it was Vennholme, all right. "You said—"

Pope Celestine interrupted the ailing cardinal. "I did not

cast my ballot for you, either. Mine was the blank ballot.
Earlier, I was only speaking rhetorically. I have no idea
who it was. Cardinal La Spina, probably."

"It is not important," Vennholme breathed.

"Get some rest, Your Eminence. You will need your
strength if you are to oppose me."

"I don't—I can't—"

"You will because you must, my dear Cardinal Vennholme. But let's call it the loyal opposition."

"Holiness—"

"We shall see, Henry. We shall see. Good night. You
are in my prayers—always."

"Always—"

Mulrennan cradled the telephone receiver. No more
calls tonight. He would call back the countless well-
wishers, including the president of the United States, tomorrow. He simply could not handle any more right now.
His ears were ringing with words, too many words and
too many emotions today. He turned to try to absorb his
new surroundings, his new residence. He sank into a
leather chair and allowed it to take him in, as if in an embrace. His old friend, the late, sainted pope, had sat in
this very chair at their final meeting. Less than a year ago
. . . almost a lifetime ago.

Sleep would not come, and in truth he did not want
to sleep, though his body screamed out from exhaustion,
as if he had just survived a grueling triple-overtime
championship basketball game. But had he won? Had his
team prevailed? What was the final score? He smiled at
the absurdity and the mystery of it all. He wanted to remain awake, alive, to smell and touch and know everything.

Outside his open window the roar of Roman automobile and motorcycle traffic had finally died down, the ebb
tide of human activity on the shore of St. Peter's Square.
Timothy John Mulrennan, the Vicar of Christ, loosened
the top buttons and the collar of his cassock, fell to his
knees in the deafeningly quiet study of the papal apart-

ments, his home from now until his death, and prayed not for the answers but that he would be granted the grace to ask his Almighty Father, the Author of all, the right questions.

AUTHOR'S NOTE

Inevitably, some readers will wonder why I chose to write a novel about a priest of the Roman Catholic faith and set much of it within a papal conclave—and how I came up with the idea in the first place. Also, they will ask, are my fictional characters based on real-life people?

The characters in this novel, *Conclave*, are wholly the product of my imagination, with the exception of some historical figures of the past fifty years. Timothy Mulrennan, in particular, is not based on any one person or any one priest, but he represents my personal knowledge of Roman Catholic priests since childhood. As a young curate, a mature pastor, and a bishop, his experiences may represent those of others who have held those offices—or they may not. His character grew, along with the story, in my mind as I wrote the novel and reached back and forward in time to explore the secular and religious issues such a man would face in real life. I imagined him to be a man I would respect and like to spend time with.

Of course, one inspiration for this work is that monumental novel that was published in 1950 by the American author Henry Morton Robinson, *The Cardinal*, a paperback edition of which I found one day by chance while browsing through used books in a (Protestant!) church rummage sale. I reread it with awe and delight. Paraphrasing Robinson's Foreword, I offer my own caveat for the novel you have read:

I am a Roman Catholic layman, having been born into, baptized, and confirmed in the apostolic faith of my Irish-American forebears. Whether or not I am a "good" Catholic

is surely a matter between me and the God of my understanding (although my pastor, my family, and fellow parishioners might have an opinion). As a child I thought
seriously (as seriously as a nine- or ten-year-old is able)
about becoming a priest. It never happened. As both a com-
municant and a writer, I (like Robinson before me) have
always been struck by wonder and awe at the priest's function—the priest in the Roman religious tradition especially.
In *Conclave* I have attempted to describe the interior and
exterior lives of a particular priest who participates in some
of the most crucial human experiences of the second half
of the twentieth century and faces the unknown terrain of
the third millennium since Christ.

Further, I fully expect to face criticism from some readers for some of my choices (or perhaps for all of them):
how can I, as a layman, truly understand the mind of a
priest? would such a man as Timothy Mulrennan fail his
Church and his God in the ways I have described? would
he, on the other hand, be as resilient and virtuous as I have
portrayed him? in a time of crisis in religious vocations,
how could I put forward such a picture of the ecclesiastic
life? Well, even if I can anticipate such questions, I cannot
attempt to answer them, only to commend the reader to my
story and beg some tolerance of the license implied and
required in a novel.

Fifty years ago Morton wrote, "*The Cardinal* is neither
propaganda for nor against the Church. Most emphatically
it is not a theological treatise or a handbook to history. It
is a purely fictional tale, a story to be read as a narrative
woven by a watcher of our world, who believes—in spite
of evils fearfully apparent—that faith, hope, and compassion animate men of good will everywhere." If my book
generates a small fraction of the interest in this particular
imagined life as did that great novel, I will be satisfied
beyond my greatest ambition as a writer and a believer.

I wish to acknowledge the assistance and inspiration of the
following people who offered their support, read drafts of
the manuscript at various stages, and helped prepare this
book for publication: Barbara Bara, Paul Block, William E.

Butterworth, Pat Chiarello, Ron Chiarello, Gene Conway, Joseph Cummins, Nelson DeMille, Tom Doherty, John E. Doran, Maureen Mahon Egen, William N. Field and the staff of the Seton Hall University Libraries, Thomas Fleming, Sara Ann Freed, Margaret George, Peter L. Gerety, Thomas G. Guarino, Kate Hartson, John Jakes, Barney Karpfinger, Stephanie Lane, Sterling Lord, Mark Mattheiss, Christopher McCabe, David Nevin, Patrick O'Connor, Barbara O'Neill, Matthew Pawlikawski, Linda Quinton, Daniel Robert, Joseph Sopcich, Charles Spicer, Jacques de Spoelberch, Robert Stanton, Sam Tanenhaus, Brian Thomsen, Bryan Tobin, Maureen Tobin, Patrick Tobin, Robert Vaughan, Ed Volini, and Robert J. Wister.

January 31, 2001
South Orange, New Jersey

It is unusual (to say the least) to offer an appendix to a work of fiction. However, this document—the Apostolic Constitution, which governs the Church during the *Sede Vacante*, the election of the pope, and the immediate aftermath—is the basis for much of the action described in the novel. I have also found it interesting reading in itself, providing insights into the workings of the Roman Catholic Church at the dawn of its third millennium of existence. It is fair to say that without the fact of *Universi Dominici Gregis*, the fiction of *Conclave* would not be possible. This document is reprinted here with the permission of the Libreria Editrice Vatican, the vatican's publication office.

The Apostolic Constitution
Universi Dominici Gregis
On the Vacancy of the Apostolic See and
The Election of the Roman Pontiff

Proclaimed by John Paul II, Supreme Pontiff, Bishop,
Servant of the Servants of God

Introduction

The Shepherd of the Lord's whole flock is the Bishop of the Church of Rome, where the Blessed Apostle Peter, by sovereign disposition of divine Providence, offered to Christ the supreme witness of martyrdom by the shedding of his blood. It is therefore understandable that the lawful apostolic succession in this See, with which "because of its great pre-eminence every Church must agree," has always been the object of particular attention.

Precisely for this reason, down the centuries the Supreme Pontiffs have deemed it their special duty, as well as their specific right, to establish fitting norms to regulate the orderly election of their Successor. Thus, also in more recent times, my Predecessors Saint Pius X, Pius XI, Pius XII, John XXIII, and lastly Paul VI, each with the intention of responding to the needs of the particular historical moment, issued wise and appropriate regulations in order to ensure the suitable preparation and orderly gathering of the electors charged, at the vacancy of the Apostolic See, with the important and weighty duty of electing the Roman Pontiff.

If I too now turn to this matter, it is certainly not because of any lack of esteem for those norms, for which I have great respect and which I intend for the most part to confirm, at least with regard to their substance and the basic principles which inspired them. What leads me to take this step is awareness of the Church's changed situation today and the need to take into consideration the general revision of Canon Law which took place, to the satisfaction of the whole Episcopate, with the publication and promulgation first of the Code of Canon Law and subsequently of the Code of Canons of the Eastern Churches. In conformity with this revision, itself inspired by the Second Vatican Ecumenical Council, I then took up the reform of the Roman Curia in the Apostolic Constitution *Pastor Bonus*. Furthermore, Canon 335 of the Code of Canon Law, restated in Canon 47 of the Code of Canons of the Eastern Churches, makes clear the need to issue and constantly update the specific laws regulating the canonical provision for the Roman See, when for any reason it becomes vacant.

While keeping in mind present-day requirements, I have been careful, in formulating the new discipline, not to depart in substance from the wise and venerable tradition already established.

It is in fact an indisputable principle that the Roman Pontiff has the right to define and adapt to changing times the manner of designating the person called to assume the Petrine succession in the Roman See. This regards, first of all, the body entrusted with providing for the election of the Roman Pontiff: based on a millennial practice sanctioned by specific canonical norms and confirmed by an explicit provision of the current Code of Canon Law (Canon 349), this body is made up of the College of Cardinals of the Holy Roman Church. While it is indeed a doctrine of faith that the power of the Supreme Pontiff derives directly from Christ, whose earthly Vicar he is, it is also certain that this supreme power in the Church is granted to him "by means of lawful election accepted by him, together with episcopal consecration." A most serious duty is thus incumbent upon the body responsible for this election. Consequently the norms which regulate its activity need to be very precise and clear, so that the election itself will take place in a most worthy manner, as befits the office of utmost responsibility which the person elected will have to assume, by divine mandate, at the moment of his assent.

Confirming therefore the norm of the current Code of Canon Law (Canon 349), which reflects the millennial practice of the Church, I once more affirm that the College of electors of the Supreme Pontiff is composed solely of the Cardinals of the Holy Roman Church. In them one finds expressed in a remarkable synthesis the two aspects which characterize the figure and office of the Roman Pontiff: *Ro man*, because identified with the Bishop of the Church in Rome and thus closely linked to the clergy of this City, represented by the Cardinals of the presbyteral and diaconal titles of Rome, and to the Cardinal Bishops of the suburbicarian Sees; *Pontiff of the universal Church*, because called to represent visibly the unseen Pastor who leads his whole flock to the pastures of eternal life. The universality of the Church is clearly expressed in the very composition of the College of Cardinals, whose members come from every continent.

In the present historical circumstances, the universality of the Church is sufficiently expressed by the College of one hundred and twenty electors, made up of Cardinals coming from all parts of the world and from very different cultures. I therefore confirm that this is to be the maximum number of Cardinal electors, while at the same time indicating that it is in no way meant as a sign of less respect that the provision laid down by my predecessor Pope Paul VI has been retained, namely, that those Cardinals who celebrate their eightieth birthday before the day when the Apostolic See becomes vacant do not take part in the election. The reason for this provision is the desire not to add to the weight of such venerable age the further burden of responsibility for choosing the one who will have to lead Christ's flock in ways adapted to the needs of the times. This does not however mean that the Cardinals over eighty years of age cannot take part in the preparatory meetings of the Conclave, in conformity with the norms set forth below. During the vacancy of the Apostolic See, and especially during the election of the Supreme Pontiff, they in particular should lead the People of God assembled in the Patriarchal Basilicas of Rome and in other churches in the Dioceses throughout the world, supporting the work of the electors with fervent prayers and supplications to the Holy Spirit and imploring for them the light needed to make their choice before God alone and with concern only for the "salvation of souls, which in the Church must always be the supreme law."

It has been my wish to give particular attention to the age-old institution of the Conclave, the rules and procedures of which have been established and defined by the solemn ordinances of my Predecessors. A careful historical examination confirms both the appropriateness of this institution, given the circumstances in which it originated and gradually took definitive shape, and its continued usefulness for the orderly, expeditious and proper functioning of the election itself, especially in times of tension and upheaval.

Precisely for this reason, while recognizing that theologians and canonists of all times agree that this institution is not of its nature necessary for the valid election of the Roman Pontiff, I confirm by this Constitution that the Conclave is to continue in its essential structure; at the same time, I have made some modifications in order to adapt its procedures to present-day circumstances. Specifically, I have considered it appropriate to decree that for the whole duration of the election the living-quarters of the Cardinal electors and of those called to assist in the orderly process of the election itself are to be located in suitable places within Vatican City State. Although small, the State is large enough to ensure within its walls, with the help of the appropriate measures indicated below, the seclusion and resulting concentration which an act so vital to the whole Church requires of the electors.

At the same time, in view of the sacredness of the act of election and thus the need for it to be carried out in an appropriate setting where, on the one hand, liturgical actions can be readily combined with juridical formalities, and where, on movements of the Holy Spirit, I decree that the election will continue to take place in the Sistine Chapel, where everything is conducive to an awareness of the presence of God, in whose sight each person will one day be judged.

I further confirm, by my apostolic authority, the duty of maintaining the strictest secrecy with regard to everything that directly or indirectly concerns the election process itself. Here too, though, I have wished to simplify the relative norms, reducing them to their essentials, in order to avoid confusion, doubts and even the eventual problems of conscience on the part of those who have taken part in the election.

Finally, I have deemed it necessary to revise the form of the election itself in the light of the present-day needs of the Church and the usages of modern society. I have thus considered it fitting not to retain election by acclamation *quasi ex inspiratione*, judging that it is no longer an apt means of interpreting the thought of an electoral college so great in number and so diverse in origin. It also appeared necessary to eliminate election *per compromissum*, not only because of the difficulty of the procedure, evident from the unwieldy accumulation of rules issued in the past, but also because by its very nature it tends to lessen the responsibility of the individual electors who, in this case, would not be required to express their choice personally.

After careful reflection I have therefore decided that the only form by which the electors can manifest their vote in the election of the Roman Pontiff is by secret ballot, in accordance with the rules set forth below. This form offers the greatest guarantee of clarity, straightforwardness, simplicity, openness and, above all, an effective and fruitful participation on the part of the Cardinals who, individually and as a group, are called to make up the assembly which elects the Successor of Peter.

With these intentions, I promulgate the present Apostolic Constitution containing the norms which, when the Roman See becomes vacant, are to be strictly followed by the Cardinals whose right and duty it is to elect the Successor of Peter, the visible Head of the whole Church and the Servant of the servants of God.

Part One: The Vacancy of the Apostolic See

Chapter One — The powers of the College of Cardinals during the vacancy of the Apostolic See

　　1. During the vacancy of the Apostolic See, the College of Cardinals has no power or jurisdiction in matters which pertain to the Supreme Pontiff during his lifetime or in the exercise of his office; such matters

are to be reserved completely and exclusively to the future Pope. I therefore declare null and void any act of power or jurisdiction pertaining to the Roman Pontiff during his lifetime or in the exercise of his office which the College of Cardinals might see fit to exercise, beyond the limits expressly permitted in this Constitution.

2. During the vacancy of the Apostolic See, the government of the Church is entrusted to the College of Cardinals solely for the dispatch of ordinary business and of matters which cannot be postponed, and for the preparation of everything necessary for the election of the new Pope. This task must be carried out in the ways and within the limits set down by this Constitution: consequently, those matters are to be absolutely excluded which, whether by law or by practice, come under the power of the Roman Pontiff alone or concern the norms for the election of the new Pope laid down in the present Constitution.

3. I further establish that the College of Cardinals may make no dispositions whatsoever concerning the rights of the Apostolic See and of the Roman Church, much less allow any of these rights to lapse, either directly or indirectly, even though it be to resolve disputes or to prosecute actions perpetrated against these same rights after the death or valid resignation of the Pope. All the Cardinals are obliged to defend these rights.

4. During the vacancy of the Apostolic See, laws issued by the Roman Pontiffs can in no way be corrected or modified, nor can anything be added or subtracted, nor a dispensation be given even from a part of them, especially with regard to the procedures governing the election of the Supreme Pontiff. Indeed, should anything be done or even attempted against this prescription, by my supreme authority I declare it null and void.

5. Should doubts arise concerning the prescriptions contained in this Constitution, or concerning the manner of putting them into effect, I decree that all power

of issuing a judgment in this regard belongs to the College of cardinals, to which I grant the faculty of interpreting doubtful or controverted points. I also establish that should it be necessary to discuss these or other similar questions, except the act of election, it suffices that the majority of the Cardinals present should concur in the same opinion.

6. In the same way, should there be a problem which, in the view of the majority of the assembled Cardinals, cannot be postponed until another time, the College of Cardinals may act according to the majority opinion.

Chapter Two — The Congregations of the Cardinals in preparation for the election of the Supreme Pontiff

7. While the See is vacant, there are two kinds of Congregations of the Cardinals: General Congregations, which include the whole College and are held before the beginning of the election, and *Particular* Congregations. All the Cardinals who are not legitimately impeded must attend the General Congregations, once they have been informed of the vacancy of the Apostolic See. Cardinals who, by virtue of No. 33 of this Constitution, do not enjoy the right of electing the pope are granted the faculty of not attending these General Congregations, should they prefer.

The Particular Congregation is made up of the Cardinal Camerlengo of the Holy Roman Church and three Cardinals, one from each Order, chosen by lot from among the Cardinal electors already present in Rome. The office of these Cardinals, called Assistants, ceases at the conclusion of the third full day, and their place is taken by others, also chosen by lot and having the same term of office, also after the election has begun.

During the time of the election, more important matters are, if necessary, dealt with by the assembly of the Cardinal electors, while ordinary affairs continue to be dealt with by the Particular Congregation of Cardinals. In the General and Particular Congregations, during the vacancy of the Apostolic See, the Cardinals are to wear the usual black cassock with piping and the red sash, with skull-cap, pectoral cross and ring.

8. The Particular Congregations are to deal only with questions of lesser importance which arise on a daily basis or from time to time. But should there arise more serious questions deserving fuller examination, these must be submitted to the General Congregation. Moreover, anything decided, resolved or refused in one Particular Congregation cannot be revoked, altered or granted in another; the right to do this belongs solely to the General Congregation, and by a majority vote.

9. The General Congregations of Cardinals are to be held in the Apostolic Palace in the Vatican or, if circumstances demand it, in another place judged more suitable by the Cardinals. At these Congregations the Dean of the College presides or, should he be absent or lawfully impeded, the Subdean. If one or both of these, in accordance with No. 33 of this Constitution, no longer enjoy the right of electing the Pope, the assembly of the Cardinal electors will be presided over by the senior Cardinal elector, according to the customary order of precedence.

10. Votes in the Congregations of Cardinals, when more important matters are concerned, are not to be expressed by word of mouth but in a way which ensures secrecy.

11. The General Congregations preceding the beginning of the election, which are therefore called "preparatory," are to be held daily, beginning on the day which shall be fixed by the Camerlengo of the Holy Roman Church and the senior Cardinal of each of the three Orders among the electors, and including the days on which the funeral rites for the deceased Pope are celebrated. In this way the Cardinal Camerlengo can hear the opinion of the College and communicate whatever is considered necessary or

appropriate, while the individual Cardinals can express their views on possible problems, ask for explanations in case of doubt and make suggestions.

12. In the first General Congregations provision is to be made for each Cardinal to have available a copy of this Constitution and at the same time to have an opportunity to raise questions about the meaning and the implementation of its norms. The part of the present Constitution regarding the vacancy of the Apostolic See should also be read aloud. At the same time the Cardinals present are to swear an oath to observe the prescriptions contained herein and to maintain secrecy. This oath, which shall also be taken by Cardinals who arrive late and subsequently take part in these Congregations, is to be read aloud by the Cardinal Dean or by whoever else presides over the College by virtue of No. 9 of this Constitution, in the presence of the other Cardinals and according to the following formulas:

We, the Cardinals of the Holy Roman Church, of the Order of Bishops, of Priests and of Deacons, promise, pledge and swear, as a body and individually, to observe exactly and faithfully all the norms contained in the Apostolic Constitution Universi Dominici Gregis *of the Supreme Pontiff John Paul II, and to maintain rigorous secrecy with regard to all matters in any way related to the election of the Roman Pontiff or those which, by their very nature, during the vacancy of the Apostolic See, call for the same secrecy.*

Next, each Cardinal shall add: *And I, N. Cardinal N., so promise, pledge and swear.* And, placing his hand on the Gospels, he will add: *So help me God and these Holy Gospels which I now touch with my hand.*

13. In one of the Congregations immediately following, the Cardinals, on the basis of a prearranged agenda, shall take the more urgent decisions regarding the beginning of the election. In other words:

a) they shall fix the day, hour and manner in

which the body of the deceased Pope shall be brought to the Vatican Basilica in order to be exposed for the homage of the faithful;

b) they shall make all necessary arrangements for the funeral rites of the deceased Pope, to be celebrated for nine consecutive days, determining when they are to begin, in such a way that burial will take place, except for special reasons, between the fourth and sixth day after death;

c) they shall see to it that the Commission, made up of the Cardinal Camerlengo and the Cardinals who had formerly held the offices of Secretary of State and President of the Pontifical Commission for Vatican City State, ensures that the rooms of the *Domus Sanctae Marthae* are made ready for the suitable lodging of the Cardinal electors, that rooms suitable for those persons mentioned in No. 46 of the present Constitution are also made ready, and that all necessary arrangements are made to prepare the Sistine Chapel so that the election process can be carried out in a smooth and orderly manner and with maximum discretion, according to the provisions laid down in this Constitution;

d) they shall entrust to two ecclesiastics known for their sound doctrine, wisdom and moral authority the task of presenting to the Cardinals two well-prepared meditations on the problems facing the Church at the time and on the need for careful discernment in choosing the new Pope; at the same time, without prejudice to the provisions of No. 52 of this Constitution, they shall fix the day and the time when the first of these meditations is to be given;

e) they shall approve—at the proposal of the Administration of the Apostolic See or, within its competence, of the Governatorato of Vatican

City State—expenses incurred from the death
of the Pope until the election of his successor;

f) they shall read any documents left by the deceased Pope for the College of Cardinals;
g) they shall arrange for the destruction of the
Fisherman's Ring and of the lead seal with
which Apostolic Letters are dispatched;
h) they shall make provision for the assignment
of rooms by lot to the Cardinal electors;
i) they shall set the day and hour of the beginning of the voting process.

Chapter Three—Concerning certain offices during the vacancy of the Apostolic See

14. According to the provisions of Article 6 of the
Apostolic Constitution *Pastor Bonus,* at the death of
the Pope all the heads of the Dicasteries of the Roman Curia—the Cardinal Secretary of State and the
Cardinal Prefects, the Archbishop Presidents, together with the members of those Dicasteries—
cease to exercise their office. An exception is made
for the Camerlengo of the Holy Roman Church and
the Major Penitentiary, who continue to exercise
their ordinary functions, submitting to the College
of Cardinals matters that would have had to be referred to the Supreme Pontiff. Likewise, in conformity with the Apostolic Constitution *Vicariae
Potestatis,* the Cardinal Vicar General for the Do-
cese of Rome continues in office during the vacancy
of the Apostolic See, as does the Cardinal Archpriest of the Vatican Basilica and Vicar General for
Vatican City for his jurisdiction.

15. Should the offices of Camerlengo of the Holy
Roman Church or of Major Penitentiary be vacant
at the time of the Pope's death, or should they become vacant before the election of his successor, the
College of Cardinals shall as soon as possible elect
the Cardinal, or Cardinals as the case may be, who
shall hold these offices until the election of the new

Pope. In each of the two cases mentioned, election
takes place by a secret vote of all the Cardinal electors present, with the use of ballots distributed and
collected by the Masters of Ceremonies. The ballots
are then opened in the presence of the Camerlengo
and of the three Cardinal Assistants, if it is a matter
of electing the Major Penitentiary; if it is a matter
of electing the Camerlengo, they are opened in the
presence of the said three Cardinals and of the Secretary of the College of Cardinals. Whoever receives
the greatest number of votes shall be elected and
shall *ipso facto* enjoy all the relevant faculties. In
the case of an equal number of votes, the Cardinal
belonging to the higher Order or, if both are in the
same Order, the one first created a Cardinal, shall
be appointed. Until the Camerlengo is elected, his
functions are carried out by the Dean of the College
or, if he is absent or lawfully impeded, by the Subdean or by the senior Cardinal according to the
usual order of precedence, in conformity with No.
9 of this Constitution, who can without delay take
the decisions that circumstances dictate.

16. If during the vacancy of the Apostolic See the
Vicar General for the Diocese of Rome should die,
the Vicegerent in office at the time shall also exercise the office proper to the Cardinal Vicar in addition to the ordinary vicarious jurisdiction which
he already holds. Should there not be a Vicegerent,
the Auxiliary Bishop who is senior by appointment
will carry out his functions.

17. As soon as he is informed of the death of the
Supreme Pontiff, the Camerlengo of the Holy Roman Church must officially ascertain the Pope's
death, in the presence of the Master of Papal Liturgical Celebrations, of the Cleric Prelates of the Apostolic Camera and of the Secretary and Chancellor
of the same, the latter shall draw up the official
death certificate. The Camerlengo must also place
seals on the Pope's study and bedroom, making provision that the personnel who ordinarily reside in

the private apartment can remain there until after the burial of the Pope, at which time the entire papal apartment will be sealed; he must notify the Cardinal Vicar for Rome of the Pope's death, whereupon the latter shall inform the People of Rome by a special announcement; he shall notify the Cardinal Archpriest of the Vatican Basilica; he shall take possession of the Apostolic Palace in the Vatican and, either in person or through a delegate, of the palaces of the Lateran and of Castel Gandolfo, and exercise custody and administration of the same; he shall determine, after consulting the heads of the three Orders of Cardinals, all matters concerning the Pope's burial, unless during his lifetime the latter had made known his wishes in this regard; and he shall deal, in the name of and with the consent of the College of Cardinals, with all matters that circumstances suggest for safeguarding the rights of the Apostolic See and for its proper administration. During the vacancy of the Apostolic See, the Camerlengo of the Holy Roman Church has the duty of safeguarding and administering the goods and temporal rights of the Holy See, with the help of the three Cardinal Assistants, having sought the views of the College of Cardinals, once only for less important matters, and on each occasion when more serious matters arise.

18. The Cardinal Major Penitentiary and his Officials, during the vacancy of the Apostolic See, can carry out the duties laid down by my Predecessor Pius XI in the Apostolic Constitution *Quae Divinitus* of March 25, 1935, and by myself in the Apostolic Constitution *Pastor Bonus*.

19. The Dean of the College of Cardinals, for his part, as soon as he has been informed of the Pope's death by the Cardinal Camerlengo or the Prefect of the Papal Household, shall inform all the Cardinals and convoke them for the Congregations of the College. He shall also communicate news of the Pope's death to the Diplomatic Corps accredited to

the Holy See and to the Heads of the respective
Nations.

20. During the vacancy of the Apostolic See, the
Substitute of the Secretariat of State, the Secretary
for Relations with States and the Secretaries of the
Dicasteries of the Roman Curia remain in charge of
their respective offices, and are responsible to the
College of Cardinals.

21. In the same way, the office and attendant powers of Papal Representatives do not lapse.

22. The Almoner of His Holiness will also continue
to carry out works of charity in accordance with the
criteria employed during the Pope's lifetime. He
will be dependent upon the College of Cardinals
until the election of the new Pope.

23. During the vacancy of the Apostolic See, all the
civil power of the Supreme Pontiff concerning
the government of Vatican City State belongs to the
College of Cardinals, which however will be unable
to issue decrees except in cases of urgent necessity
and solely for the time in which the Holy See is
vacant. Such decrees will be valid for the future
only if the new Pope confirms them.

Chapter Four—Faculties of the Dicasteries of the Roman
Curia during the vacancy of the Apostolic See

24. During the period of vacancy, the Dicasteries of
the Roman Curia, with the exception of those mentioned in Section No. 26 of this Constitution, have no
faculty in matters which, *Sede plena,* they can only
deal with or carry out *facto verbo cum Sanctissimo* or
ex Audientia Sanctissimi or *vigore spectalium et ex-
traordinariarum facultatum* which the Roman Pontiff is accustomed to grant to the Prefects, presidents
or Secretaries of those Dicasteries.

25. The ordinary faculties proper to each Dicastery
do not, however, cease at the death of the Pope. Nevertheless, I decree that the Dicasteries are only to
make use of these faculties for the granting of favors
of lesser importance, while more serious or contro-

verted matters, if they can be postponed, shall be exclusively reserved to the future Pope. If such matters
admit of no delay (as for example in the case of dis-
pensations which the Supreme Pontiff usually grants
in articulo mortis), they can be entrusted by the College of Cardinals to the Cardinal who was Prefect until the Pope's death, or to the Archbishop who was
then President, and to the other Cardinals of the same
Dicastery, to whose examination the deceased Supreme Pontiff would probably have entrusted them.
In such circumstances, they will be able to decide *per
modum provisionis*, until the election of the Pope,
what they judge to be most fitting and appropriate for
the preservation and defense of ecclesiastical rights
and traditions.

26. The Supreme Tribunal of the Apostolic Signa-
tura and the Tribunal of the Roman Rota, during the
vacancy of the Holy See, continue to deal with cases
in accordance with their proper laws, with due regard for the prescriptions of Article 18, paragraphs
1 and 3 of the Apostolic Constitution *Pastor Bonus*.

Chapter Five — Funeral rites of the Roman Pontiff

27. After the death of the Roman Pontiff, the
Cardinals will celebrate the funeral rites for the re-
pose of his soul for nine consecutive days, in accordance with the *Ordo Exsequiarum Romani
Pontificis*, the norms of which, together with those
of the *Ordo Rituum Conclavis*, they are to observe
faithfully.

28. If burial takes place in the Vatican Basilica, the
relevant official document is drawn up by the Notary of the Chapter of the Basilica or by the Canon
Archivist. Subsequently, a delegate of the Cardinal
Camerlengo and a delegate of the Prefect of the Papal Household shall separately draw up documents
certifying that burial has taken place. The former
shall do so in the presence of the members of the
Apostolic Camera and the latter in the presence of
the Prefect of the Papal Household.

29. If the Roman Pontiff should die outside Rome, it is the task of the College of Cardinals to make all necessary arrangements for the dignified and reverent transfer of the body to the Basilica of Saint Peter's in the Vatican.

30. No one is permitted to use any means whatsoever in order to photograph or film the Supreme Pontiff either on his sickbed or after death, or to record his words for subsequent reproduction. If after the Pope's death anyone should wish to take photographs of him for documentary purposes, he must ask permission from the Cardinal Camerlengo of the Holy Roman Church, who will not however permit the taking of photographs of the Supreme Pontiff except attired in pontifical vestments.

31. After the burial of the Supreme Pontiff and during the election of the new Pope, no part of the private apartment of the Supreme Pontiff is to be lived in.

32. If the deceased Supreme Pontiff has made a will concerning his belongings, bequeathing letters and private documents, and has named an executor thereof, it is the responsibility of the latter to determine and execute, in accordance with the mandate received from the testator, matters concerning the private property and writings of the deceased Pope. The executor will give an account of his activities only to the new Supreme Pontiff.

Part Two: The Election of the Roman Pontiff

Chapter One — The Electors of the Roman Pontiff

33. The right to elect the Roman Pontiff belongs exclusively to the Cardinals of the Holy Roman Church, with the exception of those who have reached their eightieth birthday before the day of the Roman Pontiff's death or the day when the Apostolic See becomes vacant. The maximum number of Cardinal electors must not exceed one hundred

and twenty. The right of active election by any other ecclesiastical dignitary or the intervention of any lay power of whatsoever grade or order is absolutely excluded.

34. If the Apostolic See should become vacant during the celebration of an Ecumenical Council or of a Synod of Bishops being held in Rome or in any other place in the world, the election of the new Pope is to be carried out solely and exclusively by the Cardinal electors indicated in No. 33, and not by the Council or the Synod of Bishops. For this reason I declare null and void acts which would in any way temerariously presume to modify the regulations concerning the election or the college of electors. Moreover, in confirmation of the provisions of Canons 340 and 347 § 2 of the Code of Canon Law and of Canon 53 of the Code of Canons of the Eastern Churches in this regard, a Council or Synod of Bishops, at whatever point they have reached, must be considered immediately suspended *ipso iure*, once notification is received of the vacancy of the Apostolic See. Therefore without any delay all meetings, congregations or sessions must be interrupted, and the preparation of any decrees or canons, together with the promulgation of those already confirmed, must be suspended, under pain of nullity of the same. Neither the Council nor the Synod can continue for any reason, even though it be most serious or worthy of special mention, until the new Pope, canonically elected, orders their resumption or continuation.

35. No Cardinal elector can be excluded from active or passive voice in the election of the Supreme Pontiff, for any reason or pretext, with due regard for the provisions of No. 40 of this Constitution.

36. A Cardinal of the Holy Roman Church who has been created and published before the College of Cardinals thereby has the right to elect the Pope, in accordance with the norm of No. 33 of the present Constitution, even if he has not yet received the red

hat or the ring, or sworn the oath. On the other hand, Cardinals who have been canonically deposed or who with the consent of the Roman Pontiff have renounced the cardinalate do not have this right. Moreover, during the period of vacancy the College of Cardinals cannot readmit or rehabilitate them.

37. I furthermore decree that, from the moment when the Apostolic See is lawfully vacant, the Cardinal electors who are present must wait fifteen full days for those who are absent; the College of Cardinals is also granted the faculty to defer, for serious reasons, the beginning of the election for a few days more. But when a maximum of twenty days have elapsed from the beginning of the vacancy of the See, all the Cardinal electors present are obliged to proceed to the election.

38. All the Cardinal electors, convoked for the election of the new Pope by the Cardinal Dean, or by another Cardinal in his name, are required, in virtue of holy obedience, to obey the announcement of convocation and to proceed to the place designated for this purpose, unless they are hindered by sickness or by some other grave impediment, which however must be recognized as such by the College of Cardinals.

39. However, should any Cardinal electors arrive *re integra*, that is, before the new Pastor of the Church has been elected, they shall be allowed to take part in the election at the stage which it has reached.

40. If a Cardinal with the right to vote should refuse to enter Vatican City in order to take part in the election, or subsequently, once the election has begun, should refuse to remain in order to discharge his office, without manifest reason of illness attested to under oath by doctors and confirmed by the majority of the electors, the other Cardinals shall proceed freely with the election, without waiting for him or readmitting him. If on the other hand a Cardinal elector is constrained to leave Vatican City because of illness, the election can proceed without

asking for his vote; if however he desires to return to the place of the election, once his health is restored or even before, he must be readmitted. Furthermore, if a Cardinal elector leaves Vatican City for some grave reason, acknowledged as such by the majority of the electors, he can return, in order once again to take part in the election.

Chapter Two — The place of the election and those admitted to it by reason of their office

41. The Conclave for the election of the Supreme Pontiff shall take place within the territory of Vatican City, in determined areas and buildings, closed to unauthorized persons in such a way as to ensure suitable accommodation for the Cardinal electors and all those legitimately called to cooperate in the orderly functioning of the election.

42. By the time fixed for the beginning of the election of the Supreme Pontiff, all the Cardinal electors must have been assigned and must have taken up suitable lodging in the *Domus Sanctae Marthae,* recently built in Vatican City. If reasons of health, previously confirmed by the appropriate Congregation of Cardinals, require that a Cardinal elector should have a nurse in attendance, even during the period of the election, arrangements must be made to provide suitable accommodation for the latter.

43. From the beginning of the electoral process until the public announcement that the election of the Supreme Pontiff has taken place, or in any case until the new Pope so disposes, the rooms of the *Domus Sanctae Marthae,* and in particular the Sistine Chapel and the areas reserved for liturgical celebrations are to be closed to unauthorized persons, by the authority of the Cardinal Camerlengo and with the outside assistance of the Substitute of the Secretariat of State, in accordance with the provisions set forth in the following Numbers.

During this period, the entire territory of Vatican City and the ordinary activity of the offices located therein shall be regulated in a way which permits the election of the Supreme Pontiff to be carried out with due privacy and freedom. In particular, provision shall be made to ensure that no one approaches the Cardinal electors while they are being transported from the *Domus Sanctae Marthae* to the Apostolic Vatican Palace.

44. The Cardinal electors, from the beginning of the election until its conclusion and the public announcement of its outcome, are not to communicate—whether by writing, by telephone or by any other means of communication—with persons outside the area where the election is taking place, except in cases of proven and urgent necessity, duly acknowledged by the Particular Congregation mentioned in No. 7. It is also the competence of the Particular Congregation to recognize the necessity and urgency of any communication with their respective offices on the part of the Cardinal Major Penitentiary, the Cardinal Vicar General for the Diocese of Rome and the Cardinal Archpriest of the Vatican Basilica.

45. Anyone not indicated in No. 46 below and who, while legitimately present in Vatican City in accordance with No. 43 of this Constitution, should happen to meet one of the Cardinal electors during the time of the election, is absolutely forbidden to engage in conversation of any sort, by whatever means and for whatever reason, with that Cardinal.

46. In order to meet the personal and official needs connected with the election process, the following individuals must be available and therefore properly lodged in suitable areas within the confines mentioned in No. 43 of this Constitution: the Secretary of the College of Cardinals, who acts as Secretary of the electoral assembly; the Master of Papal Liturgical Celebrations with two Masters of Ceremonies and two Religious attached to the Papal Sacristy; and an ecclesiastic chosen by the Cardinal Dean or by the Cardinal taking his place, in order

to assist him in his duties. There must also be available a number of priests from the regular clergy for hearing confessions in the different languages, and two medical doctors for possible emergencies. Appropriate provisions must also be made beforehand for a suitable number of persons available for the preparing and serving meals and for housekeeping. All the persons indicated here must receive prior approval from the Cardinal Camerlengo and the three Cardinal Assistants.

47. All the persons listed in No. 46 of this Constitution who in any way or at any time should come to learn anything from any source, directly or indirectly, regarding the election process, and in particular regarding the voting which took place in the election itself, are obliged to maintain strict secrecy with all persons extraneous to the College of Cardinal electors: accordingly, before the election begins, they shall take an oath in the form and using the formula indicated in No. 48.

48. At a suitable time before the beginning of the election, the persons indicated in No. 46 of this Constitution, having been duly warned about the meaning and extent of the oath which they are to take, shall, in the presence of the Cardinal Camerlengo or another Cardinal delegated by him, and of two Masters of Ceremonies, swear and sign the oath according to the following formula:

I, N.N., promise and swear that, unless I should receive a special faculty given expressly by the newly elected Pontiff or his successors, I will observe absolute and perpetual secrecy with all who are not part of the College of Cardinal electors concerning all matters directly or indirectly related to the ballots cast and their scrutiny for the election of the Supreme Pontiff.

I likewise promise and swear to refrain from using any audio or video equipment capable of recording anything which takes place during the period of the election within Vatican City, and in particular anything which in any way, directly or indirectly, is related to the process of the election itself. I declare that I take this oath fully aware that an infraction thereof will make me subject to the spiritual and canonical penalties which the future Supreme Pontiff will see fit to adopt, in accordance with Canon 1399 of the Code of Canon Law. So help me God and these Holy Gospels which I touch with my hand.

Chapter Three — The beginning of the election

49. When the funeral rites for the deceased Pope have been celebrated according to the prescribed ritual, and everything necessary for the regular functioning of the election has been prepared, on the appointed day—and thus on the fifteenth day after the death of the Pope or, in conformity with the provisions of No. 37 of the present Constitution, not later than the twentieth—the Cardinal electors shall meet in the Basilica of Saint Peter's in the Vatican, or elsewhere, should circumstances warrant it, in order to take part in a solemn Eucharistic celebration with the Votive Mass *Pro Eligendo Papa.* This celebration should preferably take place at a suitable hour in the morning, so that in the afternoon the prescriptions of the following Numbers of this Constitution can be carried out.

50. From the Pauline Chapel of the Apostolic Palace, where they will assemble at a suitable hour in the afternoon, the Cardinal electors, in choir dress, and invoking the assistance of the Holy Spirit with the chant of the *Veni Creator,* will solemnly process to the Sistine Chapel of the Apostolic Palace, where the election will be held.

51. Retaining the essential elements of the Conclave, but modifying some less important elements which, because of changed circumstances, no longer serve their original purpose, I establish and decree by the present Constitution that the election of the Supreme Pontiff, in conformity with the prescrip-

tions contained in the following Numbers, is to take place exclusively in the Sistine Chapel of the Apostolic Palace in the Vatican. The Sistine Chapel is therefore to remain an absolutely enclosed area until the conclusion of the election, so that total secrecy may be ensured with regard to everything said or done there in any way pertaining, directly or indirectly, to the election of the Supreme Pontiff.

It will therefore be the responsibility of the College of Cardinals, operating under the authority and responsibility of the Camerlengo, assisted by the Particular Congregation mentioned in No. 7 of the present Constitution, and with the outside assistance of the Substitute of the Secretariat of State, to make all prior arrangements for the interior of the Sistine Chapel and adjacent areas to be prepared, so that the orderly election and its privacy be ensured. In a special way, careful and stringent checks must be made, with the help of trustworthy individuals of proven technical ability, in order to ensure that no audiovisual equipment has been secretly installed in these areas for recording and transmission to the outside.

52. When the Cardinal electors have arrived in the Sistine Chapel, in accordance with the provisions of No. 50, and still in the presence of those who took part in the solemn procession, they shall take the oath, reading aloud the formula indicated in No. 53. The Cardinal Dean, or the Cardinal who has precedence by order and seniority in accordance with the provisions of No. 9 of the present Constitution, will read the formula aloud; then each of the Cardinal electors, touching the Holy Gospels, will read and recite the formula, as indicated in the following Number.

When the last of the Cardinal electors has taken the oath, the Master of Papal Liturgical Celebrations will give the order *Extra omnes*, and all those not taking part in the Conclave must leave the Sistine Chapel. The only ones to remain in the Chapel are

the Master of Papal Liturgical Celebrations and the
ecclesiastic previously chosen to preach to the Cardinal electors the second meditation, mentioned in
No. 13 d), concerning the grave duty incumbent on
them and thus on the need to act with right intention
for the good of the Universal Church, *solum Deum
prae oculis habentes.*

53. In conformity with the provisions of No. 52, the
Cardinal Dean or the Cardinal who has precedence
by order and seniority, will read aloud the following
formula of the oath:

*We, the Cardinal electors present in this election
of the Supreme Pontiff promise, pledge and swear,
as individuals and as a group, to observe faithfully
and scrupulously the prescriptions contained in the
Apostolic Constitution of the Supreme Pontiff John
Paul II, Universi Dominici Gregis, published on
February 22, 1996. We likewise promise, pledge
and swear that whichever of us by divine disposition
is elected Roman Pontiff will commit himself faithfully to carrying out the* munus Petrinum *of Pastor
of the Universal Church and will not fail to affirm
and defend strenuously the spiritual and temporal
rights and the liberty of the Holy See. In a particular way, we promise and swear to observe with the
greatest fidelity and with all persons, clerical or lay,
secrecy regarding everything that in any way relates
to the election of the Roman Pontiff and regarding
what occurs in the place of the election, directly or
indirectly related to the results of the voting; we
promise and swear not to break this secret in any
way, either during or after the election of the new
Pontiff, unless explicit authorization is granted by
the same Pontiff; and never to lend support or favor
to any interference, opposition or any other form of
intervention, whereby secular authorities of whatever order and degree or any group of people or
individuals might wish to intervene in the election
of the Roman Pontiff.*

Each of the Cardinal electors, according to the

order of precedence, will then take the oath according to the following formula:

And I, N. Cardinal N., do so promise, pledge and swear. Placing his hand on the Gospels, he will add: *So help me God and these Holy Gospels which I touch with my hand.*

54. When the ecclesiastic who gives the meditation has concluded, he leaves the Sistine Chapel together with the Master of Papal Liturgical Celebrations. The Cardinal electors, after reciting the prayers found in the relative *Ordo,* listen to the Cardinal Dean (or the one taking his place), who begins by asking the College of electors whether the election can begin, or whether there still remain doubts which need to be clarified concerning the norms and procedures laid down in this Constitution. It is not however permitted, even if the electors are unanimously agreed, to modify or replace any of the norms and procedures which are a substantial part of the election process, under penalty of the nullity of the same deliberation. If, in the judgment of the majority of the electors, there is nothing to prevent the election process from beginning, it shall start immediately, in accordance with the procedures indicated in this Constitution.

Chapter Four—Observance of secrecy on all matters concerning the election

55. The Cardinal Camerlengo and the three Cardinal Assistants *pro tempore* are obliged to be especially vigilant in ensuring that there is absolutely no violation of secrecy with regard to the events occurring in the Sistine Chapel, where the voting takes place, and in the adjacent areas, before, as well as during and after the voting. In particular, relying upon the expertise of two trustworthy technicians, they shall make every effort to preserve that secrecy by ensuring that no audiovisual equipment for recording or transmitting has been installed by anyone in the areas mentioned, and particularly in the Sis-

tine Chapel itself, where the acts of the election are carried out. Should any infraction whatsoever of this norm occur and be discovered, those responsible should know that they will be subject to grave penalties according to the judgment of the future Pope.

56. For the whole duration of the election, the Cardinal electors are required to refrain from written correspondence and from all conversations, including those by telephone or radio, with persons who have not been duly admitted to the buildings set aside for their use. Such conversations shall be permitted only for the most grave and urgent reasons, confirmed by the Particular Congregation of Cardinals mentioned in No. 7. It shall therefore be the duty of the Cardinal electors to make necessary arrangements, before the beginning of the election, for the handling of all non-deferrable official or personal business, so that there will be no need for conversations of this sort to take place.

57. The Cardinal electors are likewise to refrain from receiving or sending messages of any kind outside Vatican City; naturally it is prohibited for any person legitimately present in Vatican City to deliver such messages. It is specifically prohibited to the Cardinal electors, for the entire duration of the election, to receive newspapers or periodicals of any sort, to listen to the radio or to watch television.

58. Those who, in accordance with the prescriptions of No. 46 of the present Constitution, carry out any functions associated with the election, and who directly or indirectly could in any way violate secrecy—whether by words or writing, by signs or in any other way—are absolutely obliged to avoid this, lest they incur the penalty of excommunication *latae sententiae* reserved to the Apostolic See.

59. In particular, the Cardinal electors are forbidden to reveal to any other person, directly or indirectly, information about the voting and about matters discussed or decided concerning the election of the Pope in the meetings of Cardinals, both before and

during the time of the election. This obligation of secrecy also applies to the Cardinals who are not electors but who take part in the General Congregations in accordance with No. 7 of the present Constitution.

60. I further order the Cardinal electors, *graviter onerata ipsorum conscientia*, to maintain secrecy concerning these matters also after the election of the new Pope has taken place, and I remind them that it is not licit to break the secret in any way unless a special and explicit permission has been granted by the Pope himself.

61. Finally, in order that the Cardinal electors may be protected from the indiscretion of others and from possible threats to their independence of judgment and freedom of decision, I absolutely forbid the introduction into the place of the election, under whatsoever pretext, or the use, should they have been introduced, of technical instruments of any kind for the recording, reproducing or transmitting of sound, visual images or writing.

Chapter Five — The election procedure

62. Since the forms of election known as *per acclamationem seu inspirationem* and *per compromissum* are abolished, the form of electing the Roman Pontiff shall henceforth be *per scrutinium* alone. I therefore decree that for the valid election of the Roman Pontiff two-thirds of the votes are required, calculated on the basis of the total number of electors present. Should it be impossible to divide the number of Cardinals present into three equal parts, for the validity of the election of the Supreme Pontiff one additional vote is required.

63. The election is to begin immediately after the provisions of No. 54 of the present Constitution have been duly carried out. Should the election begin on the afternoon of the first day, only one ballot is to be held; then, on the following days, if no one was elected on the first ballot, two ballots shall be

held in the morning and two in the afternoon. The
voting is to begin at a time which shall have been
determined earlier, either in the preparatory Congregations or during the election period, but in accordance with the procedures laid down in Nos. 64ff
of the present Constitution.

64. The voting process is carried out in three
phases. The first phase, which can be called the *pre-
scrutiny*, comprises: 1) the preparation and distribution of the ballot papers by the Masters of
Ceremonies, who give at least two or three to each
Cardinal elector; 2) the drawing by lot, from among
all the Cardinal electors, of three Scrutineers, of
three persons charged with collecting the votes of
the sick, called for the sake of brevity *Infirmarii*,
and of three Revisers; this drawing is carried out in
public by the junior Cardinal Deacon, who draws
out nine names, one after another, of those who
shall carry out these tasks; 3) if, in the drawing of
lots for the Scrutineers, *Infirmarii* and Revisers,
there should come out the names of Cardinal electors who because of infirmity or other reasons are
unable to carry out these tasks, the names of others
who are not impeded are to be drawn in their place.
The first three drawn will act as Scrutineers, the
second three as *Infirmarii* and the last three as Revisers.

65. For this phase of the voting process the following norms must be observed: 1) the ballot paper
must be rectangular in shape and must bear in the
upper half, in print if possible, the words *Eligo in
Summum Pontificem*; on the lower half there must
be a space left for writing the name of the person
chosen; thus the ballot is made in such a way that
it can be folded in two; 2) the completion of the
ballot must be done in secret by each Cardinal elector, who will write down legibly, as far as possible
in handwriting that cannot be identified as his, the
name of the person he chooses, taking care not to
write other names as well, since this would make

the ballot null; he will then fold the ballot twice; 3) during the voting, the Cardinal electors are to remain alone in the Sistine Chapel; therefore, immediately after the distribution of the ballots and before the electors begin to write, the Secretary of the College of Cardinals, the Master of Papal Liturgical Celebrations and the Masters of Ceremonies must leave the Chapel. After they have left, the junior Cardinal Deacon shall close the door, opening and closing it again each time this is necessary, as for example when the *Infirmarii* go to collect the votes of the sick and when they return to the Chapel.

66. The second phase, the *scrutiny* proper, comprises: 1) the placing of the ballots in the appropriate receptacle; 2) the mixing and counting of the ballots; 3) the opening of the votes. Each Cardinal elector, in order of precedence, having completed and folded his ballot, holds it up so that it can be seen and carries it to the altar, at which the Scrutineers stand and upon which there is placed a receptacle, covered by a plate, for receiving the ballots. Having reached the altar, the Cardinal elector says aloud the words of the following oath: *I call as my witness Christ the Lord who will be my judge, that my vote is given to the one who before God I think should be elected.* He then places the ballot on the plate, with which he drops it into the receptacle. Having done this, he bows to the altar and returns to his place.

If any of the Cardinal electors present in the Chapel is unable to go to the altar because of infirmity, the last of the Scrutineers goes to him. The infirm elector, having pronounced the above oath, hands the folded ballot to the Scrutineer who carries it in full view to the altar and omitting the oath, places it on the plate, with which he drops it into the receptacle.

67. If there are Cardinal electors who are sick and confined to their rooms, referred to in Nos. 41ff of this Constitution, the three *Infirmarii* go to them

with a box which has an opening in the top through which a folded ballot can be inserted. Before giving the box to the *Infirmarii*, the Scrutineers open it publicly, so that the other electors can see that it is empty; they are then to lock it and place the key on the altar. The *Infirmarii*, taking the locked box and a sufficient number of ballot papers on a small tray, then go, duly accompanied, to the *Domus Sanctae Marthae* to each sick elector, who takes a ballot, writes his vote in secret, folds the ballot and, after taking the above-mentioned oath, puts it through the opening in the box. If any of the electors who are sick is unable to write, one of the three *Infirmarii* or another Cardinal elector chosen by the sick man, having taken an oath before the *Infirmarii* concerning the observance of secrecy, carries out the above procedure. The *Infirmarii* then take the box back into the Chapel, where it shall be opened by the Scrutineers after the Cardinals present have cast their votes. The Scrutineers then count the ballots in the box and, having ascertained that their number corresponds to the number of those who are sick, place them one by one on the plate and then drop them all together into the receptacle. In order not to prolong the voting process unduly, the *Infirmarii* may complete their own ballots and place them in the receptacle immediately after the senior Cardinal, and then go to collect the votes of the sick in the manner indicated above while the other electors are casting their votes.

68. After all the ballots of the Cardinal electors have been placed in the receptacle, the first Scrutineer shakes it several times in order to mix them, and immediately afterwards the last Scrutineer proceeds to count them, picking them out of the urn in full view and placing them in another empty receptacle previously prepared for this purpose. If the number of ballots does not correspond to the number of electors, the ballots must all be burned and a second vote taken at once; if however their number

does correspond to the number of electors, the opening of the ballots then takes place in the following manner.

69. The Scrutineers sit at a table placed in front of the altar. The first of them takes a ballot, unfolds it, notes the name of the person chosen and passes the ballot to the second Scrutineer, who in his turn notes the name of the person chosen and passes the ballot to the third, who reads it out in a loud and clear voice, so that all the electors present can record the vote on a sheet of paper prepared for that purpose. He himself writes down the name read from the ballot. If during the opening of the ballots the Scrutineers should discover two ballots, folded in such a way that they appear to have been completed by one elector, if these ballots bear the same name they are counted as one vote; if however they bear two different names, neither vote will be valid; however, in neither of the two cases is the voting session annulled.

When all the ballots have been opened, the Scrutineers add up the sum of the votes obtained by the different names and write them down on a separate sheet of paper. The last Scrutineer, as he reads out the individual ballots, pierces each one with a needle through the word *Eligo* and places it on a thread, so that the ballots can be more securely preserved. After the names have been read out, the ends of the thread are tied in a knot, and the ballots thus joined together are placed in a receptacle or on one side of the table.

70. There then follows the third and last phase, also known as the *post-scrutiny*, which comprises: 1) the counting of the votes; 2) the checking of the same; 3) the burning of the ballots. The Scrutineers add up all the votes that each individual has received, and if no one has obtained two-thirds of the votes on that ballot, the Pope has not been elected; if however it turns out that someone has obtained two-thirds of the votes, the canonically valid election of

the Roman Pontiff has taken place. In either case, that is, whether the election has occurred or not, the Revisers must proceed to check both the ballots and the notes made by the Scrutineers, in order to make sure that these latter have performed their task exactly and faithfully. Immediately after the checking has taken place, and before the Cardinal electors leave the Sistine Chapel, all the ballots are to be burnt by the Scrutineers, with the assistance of the Secretary of the Conclave and the Masters of Ceremonies who in the meantime have been summoned by the junior Cardinal Deacon. If however a second vote is to take place immediately, the ballots from the first vote will be burned only at the end, together with those from the second vote.

71. In order that secrecy may be better observed, I order each and every Cardinal elector to hand over to the Cardinal Camerlengo or to one of the three Cardinal Assistants any notes which he may have in his possession concerning the results of each ballot. These notes are to be burnt together with the ballots. I further lay down that at the end of the election the Cardinal Camerlengo of the Holy Roman Church shall draw up a document, to be approved also by the three Cardinal Assistants, declaring the result of the voting at each session. This document is to be given to the Pope and will thereafter be kept in a designated archive, enclosed in a sealed envelope, which may be opened by no one unless the Supreme Pontiff gives explicit permission.

72. Confirming the dispositions of my Predecessors, Saint Pius X, Pius XII and Paul VI, I decree that—except for the afternoon of the entrance into the Conclave—both in the morning and in the afternoon, after a ballot which does not result in an election, the Cardinal electors shall proceed immediately to a second one, in which they are to express their vote anew. In this second ballot all the formalities of the previous one are to be observed, with

the difference that the electors are not bound to take a new oath or to choose new Scrutineers, *Infirmarii* and Revisers. Everything done in this regard for the first ballot will be valid for the second one, without the need for any repetition.

73. Everything that has been laid down above concerning the voting procedures must be diligently observed by the Cardinal electors in all the ballots, which are to take place each day, in the morning and in the afternoon, after the celebration of the sacred rites or prayers laid down in the *Ordo Rituum Conclavis*.

74. In the event that the Cardinal electors find it difficult to agree on the person to be elected, after balloting has been carried out for three days in the form described above (in Nos. 62ff) without result, voting is to be suspended for a maximum of one day in order to allow a pause for prayer, informal discussion among the voters, and a brief spiritual exhortation given by the senior Cardinal in the Order of Deacons. Voting is then resumed in the usual manner, and after seven ballots, if the election has not taken place, there is another pause for prayer, discussion and an exhortation given by the senior Cardinal in the Order of Priests. Another series of seven ballots is then held and, if there has still been no election, this is followed by a further pause for prayer, discussion and an exhortation given by the senior Cardinal in the Order of Bishops. Voting is then resumed in the usual manner and, unless the election occurs, it is to continue for seven ballots.

75. If the balloting does not result in an election, even after the provisions of No. 74 have been fulfilled, the Cardinal electors shall be invited by the Camerlengo to express an opinion about the manner of proceeding. The election will then proceed in accordance with what the absolute majority of the electors decides. Nevertheless, there can be no waiving of the requirement that a valid election takes place only by an absolute majority of the votes

or else by voting only on the two names which in the ballot immediately preceding have received the greatest number of votes; also in this second case only an absolute majority is required.

76. Should the election take place in a way other than that prescribed in the present Constitution, or should the conditions laid down here not be observed, the election is for this very reason null and void, without any need for a declaration on the matter; consequently, it confers no right on the one elected.

77. I decree that the dispositions concerning everything that precedes the election of the Roman Pontiff and the carrying out of the election itself must be observed in full, even if the vacancy of the Apostolic See should occur as a result of the resignation of the Supreme Pontiff, in accordance with the provisions of Canon 333 § 2 of the Code of Canon Law and Canon 44 § 2 of the Code of Canons of the Eastern Churches.

Chapter Six—Matters to be observed or avoided in the election of the Roman Pontiff

78. If—God forbid—in the election of the Roman Pontiff the crime of simony were to be perpertrated, I decree and declare that all those guilty thereof shall incur excommunication *latae sententiae*. At the same time I remove the nullity or invalidity of the same simoniacal provision, in order that—as was already established by my Predecessors—the validity of the election of the Roman Pontiff may not for this reason be challenged.

79. Confirming the prescriptions of my Predecessors, I likewise forbid anyone, even if he is a Cardinal, during the Pope's lifetime and without having consulted him, to make plans concerning the election of his successor, or to promise votes, or to make decisions in this regard in private gatherings.

80. In the same way, I wish to confirm the provisions made by my Predecessors for the purpose of

excluding any external interference in the election of the Supreme Pontiff. Therefore, in virtue of holy obedience and under pain of excommunication *latae sententiae*, I again forbid each and every Cardinal elector, present and future, as also the Secretary of the College of Cardinals and all other persons taking part in the preparation and carrying out of everything necessary for the election, to accept under any pretext whatsoever, from any civil authority whatsoever, the task of proposing the *veto* or the so-called *exclusiva*, even under the guise of a simple desire, or to reveal such either to the entire electoral body assembled together or to individual electors, in writing or by word of mouth, either directly and personally or indirectly and through others, both before the election begins and for its duration. I intend this prohibition to include all possible forms of interference, opposition and suggestion whereby secular authorities of whatever order and degree, or any individual or group, might attempt to exercise influence on the election of the Pope.

81. The Cardinal electors shall further abstain from any form of pact, agreement, promise or other commitment of any kind which could oblige them to give or deny their vote to a person or persons. If this were in fact done, even under oath, I decree that such a commitment shall be null and void and that no one shall be bound to observe it; and I hereby impose the penalty of excommunication *latae sententiae* upon those who violate this prohibition. It is not my intention however to forbid, during the period in which the See is vacant, the exchange of views concerning the election.

82. I likewise forbid the Cardinals before the election to enter into any stipulations, committing themselves of common accord to a certain course of action should one of them be elevated to the Pontificate. These promises too, should any in fact be made, even under oath, I also declare null and void.

83. With the same insistence shown by my Prede-

cessors, I earnestly exhort the Cardinal electors not
to allow themselves to be guided, in choosing the
Pope, by friendship or aversion, or to be influenced
by favor or personal relationships towards anyone,
or to be constrained by the interference of persons
in authority or by pressure groups, by the suggestions of the mass media, or by force, fear or the
pursuit of popularity. Rather, having before their
eyes solely the glory of God and the good of the
Church, and having prayed for divine assistance,
they shall give their vote to the person, even outside
the College of Cardinals, who in their judgment is
most suited to govern the universal Church in a
fruitful and beneficial way.

84. During the vacancy of the Apostolic See, and
above all during the time of the election of the Successor of Peter, the Church is united in a very special way with her Pastors and particularly with the
Cardinal electors of the Supreme Pontiff, and she
asks God to grant her a new Pope as a gift of his
goodness and providence. Indeed, following the example of the first Christian community spoken of in
the Acts of the Apostles (cf. 1:14), the universal
Church, spiritually united with Mary, the Mother of
Jesus, should persevere with one heart in prayer;
thus the election of the new Pope will not be something unconnected with the People of God and concerning the College of electors alone, but will be in
a certain sense an act of the whole Church. I
therefore lay down that in all cities and other places,
at least the more important ones, as soon as news
is received of the vacancy of the Apostolic See and,
in particular, of the death of the Pope and following
the celebration of his solemn funeral rites, humble
and persevering prayers are to be offered to the Lord
(cf. Matthew 21:22; Mark 11:24), that he may en-
lighten the electors and make them so like-minded
in their task that a speedy, harmonious and fruitful
election may take place, as the salvation of souls
and the good of the whole People of God demand.

85. In a most earnest and heartfelt way I recommend this prayer to the venerable Cardinals who, by reason of age, no longer enjoy the right to take part in the election of the Supreme Pontiff. By virtue of the singular bond with the Apostolic See which the Cardinalate represents, let them lead the prayer of the People of God, whether gathered in the Partiarchal Basilicas of the city of Rome or in places of worship in other particular Churches, fervently imploring the assistance of Almighty God and the enlightenment of the Holy Spirit for the Cardinal electors, especially at the time of the election itself. They will thereby participate in an effective and real way in the difficult task of providing a Pastor for the universal Church.

86. I also ask the one who is elected not to refuse, for fear of its weight, the office to which he has been called, but to submit humbly to the design of the divine will. God who imposes the burden will sustain him with his hand, so that he will be able to bear it. In conferring the heavy task upon him, God will also help him to accomplish it and, in giving him the dignity, he will grant him the strength not to be overwhelmed by the weight of his office.

Chapter Seven—The acceptance and proclamation of the new Pope and the beginning of his ministry

87. When the election has canonically taken place, the junior Cardinal Deacon summons into the hall of election the Secretary of the College of Cardinals and the Master of Papal Liturgical Celebrations. The Cardinal Dean, or the Cardinal who is first in order and seniority, in the name of the whole College of electors, then asks the consent of the one elected in the following words: *Do you accept your canonical election as Supreme Pontiff?* And, as soon as he has received the consent, he asks him: *By what name do you wish to be called?* Then the Master of Papal Liturgical Celebrations, acting as notary and having as witnesses two Masters of Ceremonies, who are

to be summoned at that moment, draws up a document certifying acceptance by the new Pope and the name taken by him.

88. After his acceptance, the person elected, if he has already received episcopal ordination, is immediately Bishop of the Church of Rome, true Pope and Head of the College of Bishops. He thus acquires and can exercise full and supreme power over the universal Church.

89. When the other formalities provided for in the *Ordo Rituum Conclavis* have been carried out, the Cardinal electors approach the newly elected Pope in the prescribed manner, in order to make an act of homage and obedience. An act of thanksgiving to God is then made, after which the senior Cardinal Deacon announces to the waiting people that the election has taken place and proclaims the name of the new Pope, who immediately thereafter imparts the Apostolic Blessing *Urbi et Orbi* from the balcony of the Vatican Basilica.

90. If the person elected resides outside Vatican City, the norms contained in the *Ordo Rituum Conclavis* are to be observed. If the newly elected Supreme Pontiff is not already a Bishop, his episcopal ordination, referred to in Nos. 88 and 89 of the present Constitution, shall be carried out according to the usage of the Church by the Dean of the College of Cardinals or, in his absence, by the Subdean or, should he too be prevented from doing so, by the senior Cardinal Bishop.

91. The Conclave ends immediately after the new Supreme Pontiff assents to his election, unless he should determine otherwise. From that moment the new Pope can be approached by the Substitute of the Secretariat of State, the Secretary for Relations with States, the Prefect of the Papal Household and by anyone else needing to discuss with him matters of importance at the time.

92. After the solemn ceremony of the inauguration of the Pontificate and within an appropriate time,

the Pope will take possession of the Patriarchal Archbasilica of the Lateran, according to the prescribed ritual.

Promulgation

Wherefore, after mature reflection and following the example of my predecessors, I lay down and prescribe these norms and I order that no one shall presume to contest the present Constitution and anything contained herein for any reason whatsoever. The Constitution is to be completely observed by all, notwithstanding any disposition to the contrary, even if worthy of special mention. It is to be fully and integrally implemented and is to serve as a guide for all to whom it refers.

As determined above, I hereby declare abrogated all Constitutions and Orders issued in this regard by the Roman Pontiffs, and at the same time I declare completely null and void anything done by any person, whatever his authority, knowingly or unknowingly, in any way contrary to this Constitution.

Given in Rome, at Saint Peter's on February 22, the Feast of the Chair of Saint Peter, Apostle, in the year 1996, the eighteenth of my Pontificate.

Turn the page
fo an excerpt from the exciting
sequel to Conclave . . . .

COUNCIL

by Greg Tobin

Now available!
from Tom Doherty Associates

Rome, December 25, 2002

In a city renowned for so many elegant and monumental churches, the Basilica of San Giovanni in Laterano, or St. John Lateran, is sometimes called "the mother of all churches," for its fourth-century provenance, its rich architectural history, and its soaring, spectacular beauty. The facade of solemn, majestic white columns was created by the Florentine Alessandro Galilei in the 1730s; the sanctuary, with its gilded arches and holy frescoes, was erected in 1367 and redesigned in the Baroque style by Borromini in the 17th century, and within its tabernacle are said to be the remains of the heads of the greatest apostles, Peter and Paul, as well as relics such as the sackcloth of John the Baptist, the red robe given to Christ by the Roman executioners, and the cloth Jesus used to wipe the feet of his disciples. The site of the basilica was originally the barracks of the equestrian guard of Constantine—although it is said that in fact he had stolen it from the noble Laterani, the family who held legal title to the property—and that first protector of Christianity eventually donated the property to the pope. For several centuries the Lateran was the administrative headquarters of the Roman Church and the palace of the popes. It is a place of miracles and relics and precious ornaments, including the bronze doors of the central entrance, which came from the ancient senate house of Rome, and one of which is a Holy Door opened only in Jubilee years by the pontiff himself. For some, St. John Lateran is the true heart of Christendom, more sacred even than that relative newcomer, St. Peter's Basilica. And, significantly, it is the pope's own church.

Pope Celestine VI, just five months into his historic pontificate, chose to celebrate mass at noon on Christmas Day in the cathedral of his personal see as Bishop of Rome. Unlike the elaborate midnight liturgy that was broadcast on live television throughout the world, this event attracted a mere two thousand or so of the local Roman faithful, with some several score pilgrims and a handful of reporters and editors who covered the pontiff's every sneeze and eyeblink.

The first American pope, who had been Archbishop of Newark before his surprise election in the second conclave of a tumultuous year, now ending, began his homily by welcoming visitors to the monumental cathedral and greeting the local faithful, whose pastor he was, the third foreigner in a row—that is, non-Italian and (more importantly) non-Roman—delivered to them for their skeptical appraisal. He had found them open and curious, if a bit world-weary and unmoved by the prospect. Perhaps they were little different from any parish in his own home diocese; they always, naturally, sized up the new man. In his white and gold chasuble, designed to accommodate his six-four height, and white silk zucchetto, or skullcap, he stood before the altar, a lavaliere microphone discreetly attached to the neck of his pallium, loosely worn on his shoulders as the symbol of his universal jurisdiction. Even in these sacred vestments whose significance dated back hundreds, even thousands of years, the slender man from North Auburn, New Jersey seemed as contemporary and immediate as any media-created celebrity. The difference was that he quite consciously placed himself in the apostolic line of succession as the 263rd Vicar of Christ and Servant of the Servants of God since St. Peter himself. Sometimes in quiet, private moments that were all too infrequent it nearly overwhelmed him, but he could not and would not put it aside; he lived with the thought of it and the grave responsibility it represented for twenty-four hours each day of his life.

From the moment of his election, Timothy John Mulrennan, a fit sixty-four year old and nearly forty years as a priest, experienced what so very few men ever have: the full weight of the cross of responsibility for Christ's universal Church.

Now, as he looked out over his flock gathered in this magnificent structure, memories of the distant past and hopes for the dimly imagined future collided in his mind, and he forced himself to stand squarely in the present moment. A human life was built of memory and hope; the philosophers may attempt to analyze the existential or phenomenological significance of these manifestations and their origin, but a man simply lived them, built on them, worked and dreamed and suffered—despite rather than because of any school of theology. For this man, there was no turning back, only moving forward, one foot in front of the other . . . with the constant prayer that God's will be revealed and fulfilled. He knew no other way. He spoke the first part of the homily in painstakingly rehearsed Italian.

"My dear brothers and sisters in Christ, as we celebrate the birth of our Savior and His promise of salvation for all mankind, let us open our hearts as never before to the call of the Father, the sacrifice of the Son, and the silent but certain prompting of the Holy Spirit. Let us listen to the cry of the baby who lies in the manger. Such a cry naturally concerns and inspires us. It is the unfamiliar voice of the God of Israel in a very familiar, inescapably human form."

The pope noted that the cardinals and bishops and priests who were concelebrating this mass with him sat to each side of the altar and stared stonily into space or at the floor as he delivered the meticulously prepared text of the homily. His friend and Secretary of State and twice *grande elletore*, great elector in the recent conclaves, Leandro Cardinal Biagi, was not there, nor his personal secretary, Monsignor Philip Calabrese, one of several "refugees" from Newark now serving on the papal staff. These two close advisers were back at the Apostolic Palace in the pontiff's office awaiting his return; they both knew what he was about to announce, in fact they had each had a hand in the draft of the statement.

As recently as two weeks ago, both men had been skeptical and concerned—and had expressed their feelings bluntly to Pope Celestine. He expected nothing less of them, and he had listened to their cautions and reservations.

Calabrese, a former seminary instructor whom Mulrennan had enlisted a few years previously as assistant vicar and director of communications and public affairs for the archdiocese, was a Jersey City native with a laid-back professorial demeanor and a sharp mind for the intricacies of human behavior in the realms of business, politics, the academy and, most importantly, the Church. He had served a few years as a parish priest a dozen years ago, when he had been completing his second master's degree, in Scriptural theology, before embarking upon his doctorate. Amazingly, for such a young man, Calabrese had been able to balance studies and pastoral work, earning high marks in both. The pope valued the clarity of his observations and his writing skills; at forty-two, he also provided a younger and more contemporary point of view that was lacking— to say the least—in the Curia. In contrast to the aristocratic Cardinal Biagi, who had descended from medieval popes and patrons of high art, he sometimes peppered his speech with street language that betrayed his urban roots.

Phil Calabrese stood five-eleven, with a longish mane of silver hair and laughing brown eyes. His face was scarred from childhood acne and lined beyond his years. He spoke with his hands as much as his mouth—which was the subject of some good-natured ethnic ribbing from colleagues. As the pope read his rough first draft of the Christmas homily-announcement, the American monsignor paced the length of the study in the papal quarters, a perfectionist deep in the throes of creation.

"We need to simplify it, Phil," the pontiff had told him, "more for me than anyone else. I don't want to invite criticism for any hidden or double meaning or potential ambiguity. And I have to be convincing in Italian."

"Yes, Holy Father. I'll take another crack at the sonofabitch." Then he caught himself. "Sorry, I didn't mean to say it like—"

"I know what you meant, Father. And you should say what you mean, especially here. You can be certain these walls have heard profanity before."

"Forgive me, Holy Father. I'm still learning. I get excited sometimes . . ."

"This is exciting stuff, for me at least," a tensely smiling Pope Celestine said. "I won't get to hear the *sotto voce* cursing of my holy brothers of the Curia, so I must settle for yours. I suppose there is no way to soften the blow for them." He looked to the Secretary of State.

"Short of a fully-loaded encyclical, this will be the most important statement of your pontificate," Biagi said. "It should reflect your thinking exactly, clearly." The cardinal had sat near the pope, reading each page as Mulrennan passed it to him. "However, do not underestimate the value of ambiguity, when wisely and judiciously applied. I believe the American politicians call that 'wiggle room.' "

"You're right, of course—as always. But don't expect me to do everything you tell me, my friend."

"I know how stubborn you can be, Holy Father. I have a good memory of the conclaves."

"Too good, if you ask me. I hope you don't influence Father Calabrese against me." He turned to the younger priest. "And I cannot caution you enough to be wary of this man—you can see how he ruined my life!"

Calabrese laughed, and Biagi gravely shook his head to deny the accusation. The pope treasured these light moments; they were rare in the highly charged atmosphere of the papal apartments in the Vatican. The pontiff stood by the large-paned window of his private study and peered out at the cold expanse of St. Peter's Square below. It was inaccurate and unfair to consider himself a "prisoner" in this place, but he felt the weight of history and expectations close around him in these thick old walls. He was incredibly grateful to Biagi and Calabrese.

The pope had thanked them and asked them to keep the information to themselves until he had told the rest of the world. He expected that the rest of the world would be as surprised as they had been at first. There had been no rumors, no backroom whispering or second-guessing—because he had kept his intentions *in pectore*, secretly within his own breast. Perhaps the word surprise was an underestimation of the expected response: shock might fit the situation more aptly.

Then, early this morning before he left the Apostolic Palace for the mass, the pontiff had learned of the deaths—the murder and suicide—of the commander of his Swiss Guard and one of the vice-corporals. He received the word in silence and sorrow, went to his chapel for a special prayer for the dead man, then pulled himself together for the day ahead. . . .

"As Christians," Celestine VI continued, "we believe the authentic revelation of the Hebrew Scriptures and the New Testament; we receive the holy tradition passed to us through the apostles and evangelists and the early Church fathers. The Scriptures are the recorded manifestations of the Word of God, and the doctrines of the Church are drawn directly therefrom.

"Think of the wondrous events we celebrate in this holy season: the Savior's birth as a man, the shepherds' vision of the angels' choir, the visitation of the wise men from the East, the miraculous escape from Herod's sword. In later ages, martyrs, saints and holy men and women have been moved to great deeds by the voice of God in their own hearts. And in our day we have the divinely inspired event of the Second Vatican Council as a vivid and immediate example of the stirrings of the Holy Spirit, the divine messenger and truth-teller from the Father, calling us to reexamine and reform the dogmatic and liturgical components of the Body of Christ, His Church in the modern world. In each case, the wailing of the child causes discomfort and an outpouring of love from those who hear and respond. In our imperfection we strive toward a perfection found only in the God-made-man, Jesus Christ, one in being with the Father. He calls us to follow Him, to put down our earthly cares and walk with Him, curing the hurts and diseases of our soul, inspiring us to choose good over evil. He is the Alpha and the Omega of our theology: the cause and the end of every question in the mind of man."

The speaker paused and brought his hands together. He touched the Ring of the Fisherman that he now wore as a sign of his apostolic office, the ring that would be taken from his finger upon his death and broken into tiny pieces with a silver hammer, just as his body would disintegrate into dust within a cold dark tomb. He believed, however, that his own physical mortality and the passing of material things were outweighed on the great Scale of Existence by the revealed knowledge of immortality. He asked himself: What role shall I play—a weak human being who, whether by accident or design, has been assigned a mark upon the stage of the world—in the unfolding drama that is the Church?

The words of a favorite hymn played upon his heart: *Reclothe us in our rightful mind; in purer lives thy service find, in deeper reverence praise . . . O still small voice of calm. In myself, I matter not very much at all, but what I do and how it affects others will be remembered and judged by God and by history.*

"Brethren, on this day of days when we come together to remember that we are children in the loving care of our Father and Mary, the Virgin Mother of Jesus, I wish to make a statement to you, and to our Christian and non-Christian brothers and sisters throughout the world." Mulrennan had made a very deliberate choice from the first day of his pontificate to use the singular personal pronoun rather than the royal and papal "we" when addressing the faithful. Some of the Curia's worst hardliners still had a difficult time with that. "And to the college of bishops, and to our dedicated clergy who serve you humbly and lovingly as earthly vicars of Christ, and to our self-sacrificing religious around the world, I also send this message."

A few of the gathered eminences with whom he shared the altar pricked up their ears at Celestine's words and the change in the tone of his voice. They had learned to expect surprises from this American who seemed from the moment of his election to chafe at the suffocating traditions of the Vatican. Even though he had served for several years in the Church bureaucracy himself, and as much as he respected, even revered the institution of the papacy, this pope had grown increasingly impatient with the diplomatic subtleties and indirect style of communication inherent in every aspect of life and work within the Apostolic Palace.

It had taken every ounce of patience and tact—bolstered by many hours of prayer—for him to contain his temper even as he confronted the frequently passive-aggressive behavior of the Roman Curia and the long-entrenched Vatican apparatus. He now self-consciously shifted to his native English for the balance of the homily.

"At this moment the Vatican press office is distributing a release in sixteen languages that will reflect exactly what I am about to say to you." Pope Celestine VI breathed deeply, felt the increased warmth in his own cheeks and the moisture upon his brow. It was a cold Roman day outside, but sunshot and cloudless. Inside, the basilica was close with incense, candle smoke, and human warmth.

"To you, my spiritual family, I announce a new general or ecumenical council for the Holy Catholic Church, to convene in approximately a year, to be held here, in the Holy See. This proposal will no doubt surprise many of you. You might understandably ask, Why now? It has been 'only' forty years since the last one, but it is self-evidently the time. Why so quickly? I know that there were more than three years of preparation for Vatican II. In the electronic age, however, we require substantially less preparation time—every document can be shared instantly and there need be less travel time for all the bishops before, during and after the council sessions. And the council agenda itself will be focused.

"We are commissioned to be fishers of men, to preach the Gospel to all nations, even unto the ends of the earth. I say we shall go there, to where the people and their priests need us. In the act of convening a council and discussing the crucial issues and problems of our time we shall be fulfilling Christ's commission. Yes, I know there will be some elements of disagreement among the bishops and the laity about this idea. But remember, this is an ancient custom of the Church, to achieve reconciliation with the contemporary world. From the first such council in Nicea 325 to the Vatican Council of living memory to so many of us, there have already been twenty-one councils—and we faithful Christians must benefit greatly from such gathering of today's senior Church leaders. How can it be bad to come together?

"Vatican II has prepared us, a worldwide institution like no other, to face this new millennium head-on, with virtually no important issues that have not been discussed and debated, even if not completely resolved, within the hierarchy, clergy and laity. It is time, then, to take stock, to ask the doctors of the Church to give her a check-up, so to speak. I envision a single session, not years' worth of work and anxiety. Not that it will be easy—but simple. Let us keep in mind the simple, 'small' way of St. Therese, one of my predecessor's favorite saints, and, of course a Doctor of the Church herself.

"I have reflected upon the words of His Holiness, Blessed John XXIII when he first announced to a select group of cardinals his plan. He said, 'We earnestly pray for a good beginning, continuation, and successful outcome of these proposals, which involve hard work directed toward light, improvement, and joy for all Christian peoples, toward a renewed invitation to the faithful of the individual religious groups, for them also to follow us with friendly courtesy in this seeking after unity and grace which so many souls from every part of the earth eagerly desire.' "

The pontiff watched one of the Curial cardinals more keenly than the rest: Bernard Tyrone, the prefect of the Congregation for the Doctrine of the Faith. The Irishman remained expressionless but stiffened noticeably as the pope spoke the words that would electrify the Church at large. This one will oppose me with as much strength and skill as he can muster, Mulrennan thought. Yet, he is a sincere and worthy opponent—a man I respect, a man of God. Pope Celestine had left his predecessor's choices for the Curia in place, including the fiercely orthodox theologian who was both beloved and reviled, in roughly equal measure, throughout the Church.

The prelates' faces remained unmoving, noncommital, uncertain. The pope turned again to the congregation.

"To the lay brothers and sisters, to the press representatives, and to members of other faiths who have come to this Liturgy of the Eucharist on such a special day, I invite you to participate fully in the council with your prayers and observations, be they supportive or critical—God does not ignore any well-intentioned human utterance. Even so, I cannot necessarily say the same of myself or the bishops of the Church." Much of the audience laughed, in part politely, in part with recognition of the truth of Celestine's remark. "I can only assure you of my commitment to the discovery and pursuit of the very best course of action. Again quoting Blessed Pope John, one of his favorite maxims was: 'See everything. Disregard much. Correct a little.' I believe we are called upon to correct a little of what we see is wrong, both within and outside the body of the Church, and to do this work in a spirit of lightness and joy, as an example to the world."

Mulrennan smiled and bowed his head for a moment, the white silken zucchetto a bright contrast to his steel-silver hair, which he kept cut severely short, a habit from his long-ago days of military service. He prayed silently with and for the congregation for the space of a few heartbeats, then returned to stand at his throne beside the altar to recite the creed, the statement of belief that always punctuated this phase of the mass. Later, as he sat during the presentation of the gifts, he watched the senior men discreetly whispering and gesticulating among themselves, communicating in gestures and with few words the way priests do.

The pontiff managed to focus on the sacred liturgy of the mass for the next forty minutes or so that it took to conclude the celebration. As he served the host to a number of the people he looked into their faces, listened to their responses of "Amen" to his presentation of the thin white wafer: "The Body of Christ." What did he see there, what did he hear, what did he sense in their inflections and body language? It was impossible, beyond his mortal abilities to know. . . .

The remnants of incense invaded his nostrils and made his nose itch. Mulrennan, Pope Celestine, ended this Christmas mass with his blessing in Italian, English, Polish, French, Korean, Vietnamese and Spanish. He processed deliberately with his entourage down the central aisle of the basilica; he carried the tall crosier in his left hand, pausing to touch the outstretched hands of the people and to offer his blessing in abbreviated motions with his right.

He enjoyed these moments of contact with people, however brief and glancing, and made a mental note to request that more of the traditional larger, public audiences be scheduled, despite the very legitimate security concerns of those charged with protecting the person of the pope. No doubt, the first successful assassination of a pope in seven hundred years had shaken them severely. He felt them closing in around him as he was escorted to the limousine that would take him home. He hadn't even the time to change his vestments—he would do that when he reached his private quarters for a "post mortem" with his advisers. No doubt, they awaited him impatiently.

Perhaps, he thought, I should engage a private security consultant, as Biagi had advised—more to ease others' minds than my own. He, in fact, cared little about his personal safety. That consideration had died a quick death five months ago.

Mulrennan vividly, viscerally recalled the moment of his election: the feeling, the tears, the doubt, the decision, the simple words that had sealed his fate forever, "I accept." *Accepto.* The Holy Spirit had filled the dry and empty vessel of his being in that instant and had never since left him empty of grace. Try as he might to share what he had been given, it came back to him in abundance. *Your will be done,* he prayed silently, as the black papal limousine whispered savagely across Rome behind a screaming police escort. *Not mine . . .*